THE DARK PALACE

THE DARK PALACE

A SILAS QUINN MYSTERY

R.N. Morris

CRÈME de la CRIME

This first world edition published 2014
in Great Britain and the USA by
Crème de la Crime, an imprint of
SEVERN HOUSE PUBLISHERS LTD of
19 Cedar Road, Sutton, Surrey, England, SM2 5DA

British Library Cataloguing in Publication Data

Morris, Roger, 1960
  The dark palace. – (A Silas Quinn mystery; 3)
  1. Quinn, Silas (Fictitious character)–Fiction.
  2. Assault and battery–England–London–Fiction.
  3. London (England)–History–1800-1950–Fiction.
  4. Motion picture industry–Fiction. 5. Detective and
  mystery stories.
  I. Title II. Series
  823.9'2-dc23

ISBN-13: 978-1-78029-059-1
ISBN-13: 978-1-78029-544-2

All Severn House titles are printed on acid-free paper.

Severn House Publishers support the Forest Stewardship Council™ [FSC™],
the leading international forest certification organisation. All our titles that
are printed on FSC certified paper carry the FSC logo.

Typeset by Palimpsest Book Production Ltd.,
Falkirk, Stirlingshire, Scotland.
Printed and bound in Great Britain by
TJ International, Padstow, Cornwall.

ACKNOWLEDGEMENTS

My thanks to Andrew Martin and Piers Connor for their help with certain details of the London Underground of the period, and to Britta Osthaus for help checking the German. Any mistakes in either case are entirely mine.

Thanks also to everyone at Severn House, especially Kate Lyall Grant and Sara Porter, my copy-editor, Claire Ritchie, and proofreader, Emma Grundy Haigh, and to my agent, Christopher Sinclair Stevenson.

Love constitutes a great human interest, of course. Money has an appeal as strong or sometimes even stronger. Then there is death, horrid enough one might think, yet capable like the rest of being turned for the occasion into an unwilling pay box attendant.

The Handbook of Kinematography
Colin N. Bennett, F.C.S., and collaborators
(London: *Kinematograph Weekly*, 1911).

PART ONE
Love

ONE

The darkness liberated him. He moved through it like a fish through the depths. It was his element.

He was clad in black, a loose black hood over his head. He felt the cloth of the hood against his face. As if the darkness had formed itself into a soft membrane and drifted on to him.

He smiled beneath the hood. A smile that no one would ever see.

There was no darkness like the darkness in this place. It was leavened by a silver cast of moonlight from the high windows. But it was what he knew about this darkness that distinguished it. His knowledge of what it contained.

And he was part of it now. He was at one with it. More than that, he was about to make off with its secrets, the source of its unique potency.

He had a right to smile. He had earned it.

He picked his way through a lattice of shadows, his arms held out as if to initiate an embrace. He had trained himself to move without reliance on sight. It was a perverse skill for one who lived by the visual to develop, but it served him well at moments like this. And there always would be moments like this. He had counted the steps earlier in the week, when the assistant he had bribed and flattered and cajoled had led him to the room where treasures he wanted would be stored.

The door was a looming presence, a sentinel.

His black-gloved hand flicked out to test the handle. Locked, as he knew it would be. He tensed a muscle in his hidden smile. He knew how little municipal workers were paid. It had not taken much to buy the privilege of handling the keys for long enough to make an imprint. Naturally, he had been ready with a perfectly innocent explanation. And the promise of fame and riches had been enough to quell any doubts the man might have had.

That was all it had taken: to locate the vanity of a weak, overlooked man and exploit it. Every man had his vanity, which was only the same as saying every man had his price.

The key resisted. He kept the pressure firm and constant, careful not to force it.

Click!

He looked behind him anxiously, a redundant gesture. He knew there was no other living soul in the place at this time of night.

And now, as he stepped into the room, he had the sense that the darkness here had been waiting for him. There seemed to be an eagerness contained in it.

Of course, he was enough of a psychologist to know that these were his own feelings he was projecting on to it. But that was the thing about the darkness, the beauty of it. It was a fantastic receptacle of projections.

He shivered. The room was cold, icily cold. But it was more than that. It was as if something had come out of the darkness and gripped him.

For a moment, it seemed that he might lose his nerve.

But then he remembered why he was doing this. And how far he had come, all he had been through, to get to this point. He reminded himself, too, of what would be the consequences of this act. Of everything that he stood to gain.

He felt his hidden smile return.

A fine layer of moonlight lay over everything, like a midnight frost. He could just about make out the grid of drawer-fronts that filled one wall of the room.

The first one he chose was empty. Wisps of refrigerated vapour teased him. The next several he tried were the same. He had not reckoned on this; that he might make his raid on a night when the darkness had nothing to offer him.

He opened and shut drawers with mounting panic, like a mad organist working the stops of a giant organ. The silence was shattered by the metallic squeaking and slamming.

Finally he came to a drawer that resisted his first effort to open it. It took both hands and the weight of his shoulders to ease it open. It gave a screech of protest as it shifted on its mechanism. The released vapour rushed upwards as if desperate to make its escape.

In the moonlight, the sheet that concealed the drawer's contents appeared like a flow of mercury. He studied the mounds inside the drawer, the contours of the body beneath.

His hand shook as he lifted the sheet.

TWO

Peregrine Alexander Launcelot Dunwich, Baron Dunwich of Medmenham, held open a copy of that morning's *Times*. He lifted the pages of the broadsheet to block out the sunlight from the window, then settled back in the winged armchair to study the markets.

Momentarily blinded by the direct glare of the sun, he perceived the shadowed paper as a charcoal negative of itself. It took his eye a moment to adapt, a moment of blankness.

His mind, as it often did, resorted to a lascivious magic lantern show of remembered pleasures: a breast, a nipple, thighs parting, the exquisite curvature of the mons pubis topped with those plush scented curls, beneath which . . . *the entrance to paradise!* The phantom images provoked the physical responses associated with them. His lungs seemed to expand, as if filled with a volatile, intoxicating gas. His heart quickened. His mouth flooded with saliva at the thought of licking that questing nipple. His fingertips tingled as he imagined them delving into the gleaming moist cleft. He felt the pressure of a rigid erection tent his trousers and shook down the newspaper to hide his embarrassment.

He did what any man in his position would do. He cleared his throat. And slyly glanced about to check that there was no servant there to witness his priapism.

But why should he be ashamed of himself? He delighted in his virility. It amazed him to think that after all the cavortings of the previous night, he still had it in him to deliver a vigorous cockstand. It was a pity that Emily, or Amanda, or whatever the whore's name had been, was not there to relieve him of it.

He tried to focus on the market prices, to no avail. The rounded numerals brought to mind luscious female rotundity, while those consisting of straight lines reminded him of his own stiffened rod. Even if he said it himself, he had to be the most satyric man he knew. A veritable pagan. A goat of a man.

But it was a devil of a job to concentrate. If he carried on at this rate, it was going to be hard going at the ministry this morning. Unless he resorted to the practice of his youth and took himself in hand in the lavatory of his club. It was simply a question of hygiene, nothing shameful about it at all. A man couldn't be expected to keep his mind on his work if he had a heavy load of spunk to discharge. And with all the rumblings from Germany, not to mention the troubles in Ireland, he was going to need a clear head today and in the days ahead.

That was why he had taken to associating with ladies of the night in the first place. He had sought out prostitutes because he believed that his inability to concentrate was putting his country at risk. Damn it all, it was his patriotic duty to frequent brothels. Of course, there were risks involved. The thought of contracting a vile disease horrified him. He knew too that he was laying himself open to the threat of blackmail. It wasn't just money-grabbing whores that he had to worry about. A man in his position was especially vulnerable. If the enemies of the Empire had an inkling of his nocturnal activities, there was no doubt they would attempt to use it for their own nefarious purposes.

And of course, it would hurt Virginia awfully if she ever found out.

He could hear her now.

Oh, Perry, how could you!

This was the damned awkward thing about having to be in London while one's wife remained in the country. One was driven to such measures. Having said that, he had to admit that even when they were living in the same house, they seldom slept in the same room, let alone the same bed. Virginia had made clear almost from the outset her distaste for all things *animal*, as she termed it. Certainly there was no question of it after the boy had come along. He was curiously grateful to her. He felt it relieved him of the obligation of trying.

But she was no fool. A damned sensible woman, in fact. He wouldn't have married her if she hadn't been. And so, she had to know that he looked elsewhere for his gratification.

At first he had meant it to be a single, solitary indulgence. Something that he could explain in retrospect, if it ever came out, as a lapse. One visit to one prostitute to get him through a particularly difficult patch. At the time, it was not simply the satisfaction of his physical urges that he had craved. Even more shaming was the terrible loneliness that came upon him in the middle of the night.

The feeling that everything that made him what he was had been scraped out of him, leaving him empty, bereft, a weeping wreck in the darkest hours. Inexplicable, in the cold light of day. That he had been so weak as to hunger for the warmth of another human being. Humiliating.

Once it had occurred to him as a possible solution, he had been unable to get the idea of it out of his mind.

He had been confident that one discreet visit was all it would take to get the whole sordid fascination out of his system. His self-loathing and disgust would be such that he would never want to repeat the experience.

Strangely – if he was honest with himself – it was the self-loathing and the disgust that drew him back. The knowledge that he was sinking as low as a man could, debasing himself, as well as betraying everything he held dear. Putting himself, his good name, his family, his reputation, his honour – not to mention his country's security – in jeopardy. It was part of the attraction, part of the excitement.

And so he indulged again. He was careful to spread himself thinly, to frequent different brothels and ask for different prostitutes, so as not to give any one woman power over him. But his appetites were such that before long he found himself going back to the same women. He became well known in that world. Naturally, he used an assumed name. But sooner or later there was bound to be someone who recognized him, if not as an individual, then at least as a type. The type that could be blackmailed.

The simple truth was the more he used prostitutes the more he needed them.

He began to wonder if this was the only true thing that could be said about him. Everything else – his family, his lineage, his position, his upbringing, his club, his role within the government – none of that meant anything. None of that was real. Or true. None of that was *him*.

All that he was, his core, his truth, was the hot ache throbbing beneath his trousers.

It felt a little wet in there. A small amount of pre-ejaculate had leaked out from the tip of his penis. It would not take many strokes to have the whole joyous spend shoot hotly out.

That was his truth: that moment of immense release. And there were times when he didn't care who knew it. When he almost longed to be discovered naked in a moment of high engorgement and its messy aftermath. When he wanted the world to see him for who he really was.

Dangerous thoughts. Dangerous thoughts for a senior official in the Admiralty, with access to state secrets.

He looked up just in time to see one of the club's servants enter the breakfast room. He arranged his newspaper carefully, but felt his erection wither anyhow.

The man placed a silver tray of breakfast things on the table by his chair. Coffee and a soft-boiled egg, with toasted bread soldiers.

Lord Dunwich noticed a small square package neatly wrapped in brown paper on the tray. 'Thank you, Etherington. I say, what's this?'

'It was delivered for you this morning, My Lord.'

'Was it, indeed?' Lord Dunwich studied the address. The script was formal, calligraphic. It was not a hand he recognized. 'Green ink? Who uses green ink?'

'I cannot say, My Lord. Shall I pour the coffee, My Lord?'

'Please do, Etherington, there's a good fellow.' Lord Dunwich frowned down at the package. The colour of the ink unnerved him. He noticed too that there was no postage attached. He was beginning to have a decidedly uneasy feeling about this package. Perhaps the moment he had so long dreaded had at last arrived. And yet it seemed the wrong size and shape to contain incriminating photographs. Besides, he would have known if anyone had ever taken photographs of him *in flagrante delicto*. He would have seen the flash gun discharge. 'I say, Etherington. Did you see who delivered it?'

'I did not, My Lord. I could ask Mr Cork, if you wish. He took delivery of it, I believe.' The servant replaced the china coffee pot on the tray with delicate precision.

'No need. All will be revealed when I open it, I'm sure. Thank you, Etherington.' Lord Dunwich made his voice sound cheerier than he felt.

The servant bowed. 'Will there be anything else, My Lord?'

'No, thank you. That will be all, Etherington.'

Lord Dunwich waited until the man was out of the room, then cast sidelong looks at his neighbours in the breakfast room. All the other members were thoroughly engrossed in their morning newspapers. No one appeared to pay him any heed, at any rate.

The package was heavier than he expected it to be. He held it to his ear and shook it. There was an audible rattle. He felt the contents shift minutely within the tight constraint of the box. It was a single object, he reckoned. Solid, hard, possibly spherical. Not photographs, then. That was cause for some relief.

Lord Dunwich took out his pipe knife and opened the blade. The sun flared in the unsheathed steel. The string on the package popped as he cut it. He pulled the brown paper away, revealing a white cardboard box, a cube of approximately two inches along each side.

No card enclosed. And nothing written on the box.

Lord Dunwich could not imagine anything more sinister than this plain, white box.

The hand holding it began to shake, once again rattling whatever was inside. The only way to quell his fear, he realized, was to confront it. He lifted the lid.

A gleaming white eye, its iris a circle of blue, grey and brown flecks, stared up at him.

With a cry that startled the other occupants of the breakfast room, he threw the box away from him. The eye bounced and rolled along the carpet, before coming to a stop.

The beautiful, fascinating iris was fixed in his direction.

THREE

Quinn opened his eyes, tearing himself away from the darkness, as if from urgent business. The day was already established. The April sunshine intruded into every corner of his room, an unwanted busybody. No wonder spring was always associated with cuckoos.

He pulled aside his bedding and sent one foot out to test the reality of the floor.

He pulled his green candlewick dressing gown together over striped flannel pyjamas and tied the cord protectively, before venturing out of his room. He was never anything less than aware of the proprieties. At least here at the lodging house. Some might say he was less scrupulous in his professional life.

As he descended the stairs, he rubbed his Adam's apple, half-remembering the dream he had just woken from. Something to do with his time in Colney Hatch asylum. He had been lying down in

a darkened room, recounting a sordid dream to an unseen doctor.
But he could not remember any details of that dream within a dream.

He reached the landing below and paused. His heartbeat hardened
into a muscled pounding. One of the doors had been left slightly ajar.
One of the doors!

He realized immediately how disingenuous – how downright
deceitful – was his initial reluctance to acknowledge which door.
Or rather, *whose* door.

It was the door to Miss Ibbott's room.

He stood and tensed, straining to listen. Was she in there? Or
had she gone down to the bathroom herself, beating him to it?
Perhaps he could justify his standing there outside her door on the
grounds that he was merely trying to settle that one, perfectly
reasonable question.

It certainly could not justify what he did next, not even to himself.

He moved closer to her door, lifting and placing his slippered
feet with deliberate stealth. He put his ear to the inch-wide gap.

His heart, his pummelling heart, must give him away! Its tocsin
clamour surely filled the house. Certainly it made it hard for him
to ascertain whether she was in her room or elsewhere.

But if she was in her room, why would she leave the door ajar? At
this time of day, she would no doubt be engaged in her toilet, perhaps
combing her hair before her mirror. Or perhaps she was still in bed,
rousing herself drowsily from whatever dreams girls like her experienced. Not wholly innocent dreams, he speculated. But perfectly natural
ones. Dreams, perhaps, coloured by cruelty and spite.

Whatever she was about, it would be of an intimate nature. She
would brook no intrusion. And yet this door-ajar business, did it
not have about it something of the aspect of an invitation? Or if not
that, an expectation?

The question was, an invitation to whom?

Not Quinn, that was for sure. A man more than twice her age.
Leaving aside all his other disadvantages.

More likely it was either Appleby or Timberley, the two young
male lodgers who made it their life's work – or perhaps their sport
– to vie for her fickle affections. Who was in the ascendancy at the
moment, he wondered.

Quinn had recently observed in Timberley signs of stress and
upset – tears, in short. Quinn could think of nothing guaranteed to
make a man less attractive to a woman than emotional weakness.

And so, he speculated that the door was left ajar for Appleby. Was this to be the moment he would finally snatch the coveted prize? A kiss from Miss Ibbott? And all before breakfast.

But was she even in there? The more he thought about it the less sense it made. Would they risk a liaison at this time of the day, when lodgers such as himself were trudging up and down the stairs? There had to be some other explanation. Either she had left the door open by accident. Or she had indeed slipped out of her room. If the latter were the case, she could return at any moment and catch him there in what could only be described as a compromising position. Not only that, by such carelessness she was laying herself open to the risk of burglary. Or, if she was in the room, to the risk of assault.

He knew better than she did what men were capable of. Any man; all men. The criminals he hunted down all lodged somewhere. The fact that she was the landlady's daughter was no protection.

He now realized that it was his duty as a policeman to settle the question of her whereabouts once and for all.

'Mr Quinn?'

Quinn pulled the door to hurriedly and spun away from it. He held his head bowed, eyes averted from Miss Dillard's. For it was Miss Dillard, coming up the stairs to return to her own room, who now challenged him, her voice edged with confusion and fear.

No, he could not bring himself to look into those eyes. Not now. Not after this.

'I was just . . . I . . . I couldn't help noticing that Miss Ibbott had left her door open. I thought it wise to close it for her.'

'I see.' But her voice was reproachful, as well as hurt. And no, he still wouldn't look at her. He refused to face the same reproach, the same hurt, in her eyes.

'One cannot be too careful. Even in a respectable house such as this.'

'Of course.'

And then Quinn remembered that he maintained the fiction that none of his fellow lodgers knew the nature of his work. 'Well, no, not that. But . . . you never know. Mr Appleby and Mr Timberley.'

'What about them?' There was genuine alarm in her voice now, panic almost.

Quinn realized that he had made a tactical mistake. 'Nothing! I say nothing against them. I know of nothing against them. Fine fellows, they are, I'm sure. We can all agree on that. But young.

Youth, you see. Mischief and youth. You cannot rule it out. Young
men such as them . . . not them, no . . . quite explicitly not them.
But young men such as them might see her open door as . . .'

'As what?'

He could not say *an invitation*; that would seem to put Miss
Ibbott at fault. 'A provocation,' he settled for.

Miss Dillard let out a little shriek. It was an unfortunate word to
choose.

'You must understand,' protested Quinn. 'I know of nothing
specific against them. Nothing at all, in fact. But you cannot blame
me for taking precautions.'

At that moment, the controversial door opened and Miss Ibbott
herself peered out. From what he saw of her shoulders, Quinn
conjectured that she was in a state of *deshabille*.

'What do you want? What's going on? Did you shut my door?'

'Ah, good morning to you, Miss Ibbott. Yes, indeed, as I was
explaining to Miss Dillard, I did indeed shut your door. A mere
precaution, you understand. For your own safety. One can never be
too careful. Did you, in fact, realize that it was open, I wonder?'

'Betsy must have left it like that when she fetched me my hot
water.'

'Ah, there you are! Mystery solved! Betsy left it open. Careless
girl. But good-natured. A careless but good-natured girl, I think we
can all agree on that. Or perhaps not, as regards carelessness, at
least. Not careless, no. Too harsh. Just overworked perhaps? No,
that won't do, implying as it does criticism of your good mother,
the irreproachable Mrs Ibbott. I will not hear the word overworked
used in this house. Worked to just the right, proper and above all
proportionate extent of her capabilities and . . . and duties. As your
maid. As maid to us all. An onerous but worthy calling, no doubt.
So, what are we to make of the door being left ajar? A simple
mistake, it turns out, which I, in my foolish, fond – one might even
say innocent . . . In my solicitude, at any rate . . . closed. On your
behalf. For you. But no harm done, I'm glad to say.'

Miss Ibbott offered no comment on Quinn's outburst, unless
shutting the door in his face is to be considered a comment.

He could not look at Miss Dillard. He wondered if the consola-
tion of her pewter-grey eyes was denied him forever now, their
startling beauty an unreliable memory he struggled to conjure.

FOUR

The lights in the carriage flickered in time with the clatter and sway of the Tube train, the darkness reasserting its presence.

Quinn had entered its realm voluntarily, lowering himself into it in a shuddering cage. Today he was shunning the daylight. Dipping his face away from its intrusive glare. Something to do with the awkward episode on the landing, no doubt. He had wanted the ground to open up and swallow him. Taking the Tube was a practicable alternative.

Under normal circumstances, Quinn rarely took the Tube. But at least on the Tube he didn't have to meet anyone's eye. Most of his fellow travellers hid themselves away behind their newspapers. If they did not, they stared fixedly at a chosen point. A spot on the carriage wall. An arbitrary word in an advertisement. A cigarette stub caught between the wooden slats of the floor. Occasionally they might look away to catch the eye of one of the pale ghosts riding the darkness outside, mournful, perplexed, perpetually excluded. In that moment they understood: how incomprehensible we are to our own reflections. To ourselves.

Quinn could not say when he had first been aware of the man looking at him. But his sense was that the whole reason the man was there was to look at him. There was a purpose to his staring. Being a policeman, Quinn might have said it was *premeditated*.

The fellow must have followed him on to the platform and into the train carriage. That meant that he must have been waiting outside the lodging house for Quinn to leave that morning.

Yes, he had registered something out of the corner of his eye, or at least in hindsight he believed he had. A blur of movement configured by intent. Resolving itself into a human form shadowing him. Footsteps moving in time with his own.

He had thought nothing of it. Or very little. He had registered the sensation and dismissed it. No, not quite dismissed it. He *was* a policeman, after all. Over the years he had put away more than his fair share of villains, and dispatched another quota to face a higher justice. The former would have grudges of their own against him, which they would nurture and fatten as they served out their sentences (if they had not paid the ultimate price); many of the latter would have left behind associates who might be presumed to have sworn oaths of vengeance on their behalf.

It was a plain fact that there were people in the world who were out for Quinn's blood.

He accepted this, but the thing was not to become obsessed by it. No doubt the day would come when he would find himself face to face with a man who would calmly aim a revolver between his eyes and fire. In the meantime, he couldn't go around jumping at shadows.

And so, he had registered the sensation of being followed and pushed it to the back of his mind. It was most likely a coincidence. Someone else on their way to Brompton Road Tube Station, whose footsteps would naturally follow Quinn's.

It occurred to him that this sensation of being followed was simply a fact of modern life. This is how it feels to live in a crowded metropolis at the beginning of the twentieth century, he realized. To notice it, to become preoccupied with it, disturbed by it, was perhaps the sign of a man at odds with his existence. There was danger in that. The danger of alienation, and madness. Quinn knew enough about that to recognize the signs. It was something he in particular needed to be on his guard against.

On the platform, he had felt sufficiently invisible to put the sensation from his mind. The brown and green tiles seemed to suck the life out of the feeble electric lights. It was a space that fell away at its soft dark edges. He had instinctively sought out a place on the periphery, slipping away into the welcoming gloom.

A tide of bobbing bowler hats had closed behind him. He had found a spot at the end of the platform, peering expectantly into the black abyss of the tunnel. He was in fact at the closest point to that abyss that it was possible for him to be without falling into it. A spot of light appeared, signalling the approach of the next train. Almost simultaneously came the first stirring of the air. And then the distant rattle that grew into a scream. The light expanded as it hurtled towards him.

He had entered the train by the gate at the rear of the last car. And – or so he thought – he had been the only one to do so. Was it possible that he had missed the entrance of this other man, who had somehow slipped on after Quinn but before the gateman closed the gate and rang his bell?

Or was it all in his head? Was this sensation of being looked at of a piece with the sensation of being followed?

Quinn turned his head. The man was seated on the opposite side of the car, just to Quinn's right. And he was staring fixedly at Quinn. There could be no mistaking it.

The blinking of the carriage lights grew more insistent. The intervals of blackness increased in duration. Then all at once, the lights died completely, all along the length of the train.

There was a collective groan and a rustle of protest from the newspaper readers. But a moment later, the groan became a cry of anger tinged with alarm as the train came to a screeching, grinding halt.

It was strange how calm Quinn felt. After all, if the man was going to kill him, now was his opportunity. In fact, Quinn felt that he would be disappointed if there was not some attempt made on his life.

The darkness cloaked the movement of his hand. And hid the sleek steel object that weighted it with death. He held the gun out straight in front of him, then turned it slightly to his right. If the man got up to attack him, he would walk straight into the barrel. At which point, Quinn would squeeze the trigger.

There was risk involved in this strategy. The man might not mean him any harm. He might simply be an odd cove. Also, someone else might get hurt. The innocent bystander so beloved of newspapers, although Quinn doubted the existence of anyone who was wholly innocent.

Nevertheless.

He imagined the screams and panic that would ensue once the lights came back on and he was discovered holding a revolver out in front of him. That was bad enough. It would be worse still if the gun had been discharged and some harmless old buffer lay stretched out on the floor, blood pooling around him. He had seen enough violently slaughtered men to know it was not a good way to start the day.

Quinn returned the gun to its holster. There was a leather tightening around his chest. His heart beat harder, glad to have it back.

The brief outing of fatal metal had gone unwitnessed in the darkness. And no one saw now which of their number gave out a burst of sharp, nervous laughter. No one could mistake it for the sound of amusement. It was the sound of a man on the edge of losing control. A dangerous hilarity.

But this had gone on long enough, seemed to be the consensus in the compartment. Voices cried out, '*What the devil . . .?*' They disapproved of the loss of power. They were affronted by that laughter. The door to the carriage opened and a yellow beam projected from the gateman's electric torch. As the beam licked wanly at their faces, Quinn saw that the man opposite was still looking at him. The direction of his gaze had not changed one iota. In the brief play of light across the man's features, Quinn formed an impression of his age and character. He was not a young man. No. He was more or less the age Quinn's father would have been, had he lived. Had he not taken his own life, that is to say. There was something set and determined about the face. As if it was held in the grip of a great and unchanging emotion. The torch beam moved on. The face sank back into darkness, but Quinn was haunted by it. A deep, perpetual frown was cut into the forehead. The lips were pressed together in a grim, tense clench. The emotion he had seen on the man's face was unspeakably bitter. And for some reason it was directed at him.

Quinn had the sense that if he shot the man now in the darkness, he would be doing him a great service.

Steadfastly ignoring all enquiries, the gateman walked the length of the carriage and pulled down the window to communicate with the gateman in the next carriage. It was decided that he would do the same, so that a chain of communication could be established with the driver.

Quinn had the sense that the darkness was enjoying itself now. And that the game it was playing was with him personally. Only he and the darkness knew the nature of that face. Only he and the darkness knew about Quinn's careless gun-wielding.

And only the darkness knew where both these secrets might lead.

As unexpectedly as they had gone out, the lights flickered back into life. Newspapers were snapped back up in front of faces. Eyes flitted to find the points they had focused on before.

It almost seemed as if the darkness had brought them together. Some level of communal feeling had been allowed by it. Now that light was restored, every man fled back into himself, as if from an unseemly spectacle.

Quinn refused to look at the man. He stared at the dim reflection of his own face in the window opposite. It was blurred and hollow, almost featureless. The idea of a ghostly outrider came back to him. *We are haunted by ourselves*, he thought. *And also sealed off from ourselves.*

If we cannot understand ourselves, what hope do we have of understanding one another?

The gateman in the next carriage returned to pass on a message to their own gateman. Whatever the news was he seemed little inclined to share it with the passengers, and carried on a gloomy exchange with his colleague.

One of the pushier examples of the City type demanded to know what was going on.

The gateman turned to him with a sour, almost insubordinate eye. Weighing up his options, which for a moment seemed to sit between personal insult and social revolution, the gateman at last remembered the uniform he was wearing and touched the peak of his cap in deference. He sniffed noisily, deeply, as if the shifting of snot in his nose would imbue his words with more authority. 'We're being held at a signal.'

From another quarter came the question, 'Why did the lights go out?' To which he merely replied, 'They're back on now, in't they?'

How easy it was for him to say that, thought Quinn. He had not nearly killed a man in the darkness.

To forestall any further interrogation, the gateman took himself back out on to his platform.

At last, the train lurched back into motion. Before long it was pulling into the next station. After the darkness of the tunnel, even the subdued platform lights appeared dazzling. Quinn rose to his feet. It was not his stop. But he could not bear the thought of sitting in the same carriage as that face for a moment longer.

FIVE

Quinn switched carriages at Knightsbridge. At Piccadilly Circus, he took the Bakerloo Railway south. He was not aware of anyone following him.

When he emerged into the daylight at Charing Cross Embankment station, the sensation of being followed returned.

Quinn paused at the entrance to the station. The man emerged from the lift after the one Quinn had taken. If he was following

Quinn, he was doing so in a manner that was both haphazard and conspicuous. It was far more likely that there was nothing to it.

Quinn waited for the man to pass him. If the man betrayed no sign of emotion or interest as he did so, and went purposefully on his way, it would show that Quinn had been mistaken. He would be able to dismiss the stranger's earlier fixed stare as mere eccentricity. Perhaps the man had stared at Quinn as he might stare into space. The bitterness of his expression was entirely unconnected to Quinn. And how did he know, really, that it was bitterness that was written in those features? He could not look inside the man's heart. Perhaps that was simply the expression his face assumed when in repose.

But as the man reached the threshold of the Tube station, he turned decisively towards Quinn. His face was lit up in the cold glare of the sun. That same bitter expression was in place, as if it had been sculpted into his features. There was no mistaking it. This was a deliberate provocation. Quinn felt the heat rise in his face. *Who was this man? What did he want with him?*

He noticed the man was wearing brown leather gloves. For some reason the detail struck him as sinister. It was not a particularly cold day. To his policeman's mind, the only reason a man might don gloves on a day like today was to commit a crime.

He watched the man cross the Embankment and then lost sight of him behind a London plane tree. The only possible conclusion was that he was hiding – waiting for Quinn to make a move before following him.

Quinn conjured up an image of the man's face and mentally ran through the archive of his memories to see if he could find a match. He could only think that the man had some connection to one of his old cases. His age would suggest a case from the distant past. The bitterness was consistent with long years wasting away behind bars.

Quinn tried to deduce his way to the man's identity. He had obviously not received a capital sentence, which meant he was not a murderer. Some lesser but still serious crime. Manslaughter, perhaps. The gloves, perhaps, were worn from habit: the habit of the professional housebreaker. And yet the peculiar ravage of his face suggested a ruined reputation. Was he, perhaps, the perpetrator of serial frauds? Something snagged, an emotional memory that went back further than Quinn had expected, to a time before he had become a policeman. But he could not translate it into a precise recollection.

What he ought to do was confront the man. But all at once a

strong sense of repugnance came over him. Whatever it was that had carved that expression on to the man's face, it was not something Quinn wanted to get to the bottom of.

He set off down the Embankment towards New Scotland Yard, his gaze fixed steadfastly ahead of him.

Sunlight flooded the cramped attic room. Quinn squinted and turned his face away from the dazzling square in the window. The wall opposite was blank. The photographs and sketches from the previous case had already been taken down.

He took off his bowler and hung it on the coat stand. There was no sign of DCI Coddington's Ulster.

Detective Sergeant Macadam looked up from the journal he was reading. 'Morning, sir.' Quinn detected a boyish excitement in his sergeant's fidgeting. It seemed likely that Macadam was in the grip of a new enthusiasm.

'Good morning, Macadam. Is himself about?'

'Who, sir?'

'Coddington.'

'I've not seen him yet, sir. At least not in the department. I think I did catch sight of him on one of the lower floors earlier.'

'So . . . he is in the building?'

'I believe so, sir. Unless I was mistaken. However, his herringbone Ulster is very distinctive.'

'*His* herringbone Ulster?'

Macadam frowned, presumably at Quinn's peculiarly pointed tone.

'I was the first Scotland Yard detective to wear a herringbone Ulster, Macadam. Coddington copied me.'

'If you say so, sir.'

'I'm not wearing it today, of course. No need for it on a day like today.'

'You can never tell at this time of the year though, sir, can you? Granted, it's fine now.' Macadam looked out of the window dubiously, as if he suspected the weather of malicious designs. 'But it could change like that, sir. It's the sort of thing you have to bear in mind if you wish to make a kinematograph.'

Quinn thought it best to make no comment on this cryptic pronouncement. He sat down at his desk and sorted through the correspondence that was waiting for him. One envelope drew his attention. It was addressed to 'Quick-Fire Quinn of the Yard'. The

form of address provoked a feeling of sour dismay in Quinn. He
was tempted to throw the letter away without opening it. But from
the envelope, it did not look like the work of a crank. The address
was typewritten, on business stationery. The symbol of an eye
was embossed on the back, beneath which was printed: VISIONARY
PRODUCTIONS.

Inside was a card:

You are cordially invited to the world premiere of
THE EYES OF THE BEHOLDER
The latest moving picture drama from VISIONARY
PRODUCTIONS, of Cecil Court
With scenes of unprecedented MYSTERY, SENSATION,
HORROR & EMOTION
Astonishing visual presentation
Featuring MADEMOISELLE ELOISE, the international
star of the silver screen,
in the role of
THE LOVED ONE
Written and directed by the renowned maestro
KONRAD WAECHTER
The world premiere of THE EYES OF THE BEHOLDER
will be screened at
PORRICK'S PICTURE PALACE, Leicester Square
On Friday, April the 17th, 1914, at 7 p.m.
Before an audience of specially invited celebrities

Handwritten in the top-left corner in green ink were the words:
Quick-Fire Quinn and guest.

So. This was what it had come to. He was a celebrity. He supposed
he had *The Daily Clarion* to thank for that. He wouldn't go, of
course. It was beneath his dignity. And if Sir Edward ever found
out, there would be hell to pay. The Special Crimes Department
was meant to keep its head down, a creature of the shadows. Sir
Edward Henry, Commissioner of the Metropolitan Police Force who
had created the department, was far from happy with the notoriety
Quinn had already attracted.

Quinn put the invitation to one side and shuffled the rest of his
mail. As it happened, there was a memorandum from Sir Edward's
office. The brief typewritten note exercised a peculiar hold. He

thought of the person who had typed it. He was tempted to sniff it to see if he could discern a trace of her scent.

'You're probably asking yourself, why on earth should I wish to do that?'

Quinn was startled by Macadam's voice. He looked across to see his sergeant brandishing the journal he had been reading.

'But have you considered that the kinematograph could be a valuable aid to policing?'

A cheery whistling on the landing inhibited Macadam. He hurriedly put the journal down as Sergeant Inchball stooped into the room.

'Mornin', guv'nor. Whatcha got there, Mac?' Inchball didn't miss a trick. He leaned over and read the title. 'The *Kinematograph Enthusiast's Weekly*? What the bloody 'ell you readin' that for? You thinkin' of leavin' us and goin' into the moving picture business?'

'Of course not. I'm looking into it to see if we could incorporate it into our investigative techniques.'

'What the . . .? I've 'eard it all now!'

'Think of the evidence-gathering possibilities. We already use photographic cameras. A kinematograph is merely taking that technology one step further. Imagine if we could record a kinematograph of a criminal in the very act of committing a crime.'

'Don' make me laugh! What villain's gonna consent to have himself filmed?'

'I am talking about secret filming, of course. It could be used in a surveillance operation.'

'Secret filmin'? 'Ave you lost your bleedin' mind? 'Ave you ever been on a bleedin' surveillance op?'

'Yes, of course I have.'

'Day or night?'

'Both.'

'Ever see anything naughty?'

'Once or twice.'

'And was that during the day or during the night?'

Macadam hesitated before answering, his head dipped in embarrassment. 'Night-time, mostly.'

''Ow you gonna film in the dark? Won't those big bleedin' lights they use give the game away? And besides, why you filmin' this geezer when you could be nicking 'im?' Inchball appealed to Quinn. ''Ave you 'eard this, guv?'

Quinn nodded distractedly and rose to his feet, in the process cracking his head on the sloping ceiling. He rubbed the back of his head. 'Sir Edward has asked to see me.'

Inchball exchanged an ominous glance with Macadam.

'I shall be back forthwith.'

The two sergeants looked far from certain, united at least in their concern for their superior.

He stood watching her from the other side of the room, reluctant to make his presence known. If she knew he was there she would lose the heedless, charming ease with which she held herself as she worked at the typewriter. She would become angry and angular and awkward. It was true that she seemed a little harassed as he watched her, but beautifully so. Innocently so. And the thing of which she was innocent, he realized, was him. He was the thing that spoilt her.

How would she feel if she knew he was watching her? Angry, of course. She would say he had no right to spy on her. He could well imagine the look of implacable reproach she would turn on him.

He would never forget her stinging words, or the force with which she had insisted upon them: 'I can't ever, *ever* love you!'

But in those words, in the utter denial of hope that they represented, hope had paradoxically been born. Until that moment he had never imagined that she could contemplate such a circumstance, even if only to dismiss it as an impossibility.

It was ridiculous, of course. A man like him, brutal and contaminated, a man whose business it was to delve into the darkest, vilest recesses of the soul, to dip his fingers into the filth of human psychology. A man besmeared in gore, who knew himself to be capable of far worse a crime than any committed by the villains he hunted down . . .

He was aware of figures moving between them, intermittently blocking her from his view. Clerks and secretaries, the civilian staff of the Metropolitan Police Force. Perhaps occasionally one of these busy people would stop and glance inquisitively at him, before following the direction of his stare and then, taking it all in, move on, perhaps with a sly smile of understanding.

At last she looked up and saw him. The colour rushed to her cheeks. Her eyes stood out in indignation.

He hastened to her desk.

'Sir Edward asked to see me.'

'What were you doing?' Her tone was sharp and suspicious.

'I wasn't doing anything. Sir Edward asked to see me,' he repeated pointlessly. 'I wondered if he was free. His door is closed, I see.'

'You were looking at his door? Is that it?' Scepticism was etched in the curve of one eyebrow.

'Y-yes.' Quinn flashed a glance towards the door, as if to prove it. 'Who is in with him? Is it . . . DCI Coddington?'

'I am not obliged to tell you.'

'But I will see them. When they come out.'

'It is not DCI Coddington.'

'But DCI Coddington *has* been to see him?'

'If Sir Edward wishes you to know the answer to that question, then I am confident he will divulge it himself.'

Quinn nodded. 'I wasn't . . .' He had intended to say, 'I wasn't spying on you.' But, of course, the denial was a lie. 'I wasn't sure you had seen me.' That was true, but meaningless.

She frowned in distaste, recoiling slightly from his suddenly intimate tone.

'You looked so . . . busy.' Not the word he had wanted to say. 'I didn't want to disturb you. I was hesitating because I thought my intrusion would be unwelcome.'

'As you have pointed out, you have an appointment with Sir Edward. Therefore you have an excuse, I suppose.'

The door to Sir Edward's office opened. So surprised was Quinn to see the tall, frock-coated gentleman who came out that he could not help saying his name: 'Sir Michael Esslyn!'

Esslyn paused and contrived to look down the length of his patrician nose at Quinn.

Quinn held out his hand. 'It's Quinn. Detective Inspector Silas Quinn.'

Esslyn frowned as though the name meant nothing to him. He ignored the proffered hand.

'I interviewed you in the course of a recent investigation. The case of the exsanguinated renters.'

Esslyn's frown deepened. At last he shook his head, as if he was shaking off the memory of an unpleasant dream. He brushed past Quinn without a word, though his step quickened eloquently.

Quinn glanced at Miss Latterly. 'He cannot have forgotten. It was only . . .' But Quinn had no sense of how long ago it had been. A matter of days, or a lifetime. He could not say.

Miss Latterly had resumed her typing with the heavy,

overdetermined energy that she always used when she knew she was being observed.

Quinn presumed he might go in now.

Sir Edward Henry, Commissioner of the Metropolitan Police, had his head bowed over a file. Quinn recognized it as that he had just submitted on the House of Blackley murders.

'Please be seated, Quinn.' Sir Edward did not look up until he had finished reading Quinn's report. Of course, Quinn understood that this was for effect. Sir Edward would have already acquainted himself with the contents of the file. 'He's gone.'

'Sir?'

'Coddington. You needn't worry about him any more. I've had him transferred back to . . . wherever it was he came from.'

'South Kensington, sir.'

'If you say so.' Sir Edward winced suddenly. The old wound troubling him, no doubt.

'Thank you, sir.'

'What? Eh? Oh . . . Don't thank me. The man was a bloody idiot.'

Quinn was taken aback by the force of Sir Edward's language. It was more the commissioner's style to indulge in a bland biblical homily than a profanity when moved.

For some reason, Quinn decided to supply the shortfall. 'Judge not lest ye be judged.'

'Are you suggesting that I'm a bloody idiot too, Quinn?'

'It's from the Bible, sir.'

'Is it, by Jove?'

'Yes, sir.'

'Well, I wouldn't blame you, if you did. I put him in charge, after all.'

'I know you had your reasons, sir.'

Quinn kept his satisfaction under restraint. Victories were only ever temporary. Vindication, a provisional state. If it wasn't Coddington, it would be someone else. There was always someone, or something, set against him, or to set himself against. 'Was that Sir Michael Esslyn I saw leave your office, sir?'

'What? Eh?'

'Sir Michael Esslyn, sir. I saw him outside. The strange thing was he pretended not to know me.'

'Know you? Why should he know you?'

'He was involved in the renters case, sir, if you remember.'

'That doesn't mean he *knows* you.'

'I interviewed him, sir. Several times.'

'Dear God, Quinn. You presume to think that that entails a man like Sir Michael Esslyn's *knowing* you? There is a vast, yawning gulf between you and him. A chasm of immeasurable expanse. If he appears to look at you from the other side of it, you must under-stand that what he is seeing is a tiny speck. I had not thought it would be necessary to explain such things to you, Quinn.'

'I understand, sir.'

'Of course, he is a horrid man. I do not approve of him. I suspect him of being a Satanist.'

'I see, sir.'

'Or at the very least, a pagan. But he is very important in the Home Office. He has the ear of the Home Secretary, you know.'

'Yes, sir. I remember your mentioning it once before. May I take it, sir, that I have command of Special Crimes restored to me?'

'I'm not putting anyone else in over you, if that's what you mean.'

'I have been thinking, sir. While Coddington was in charge, the rank of the commanding officer of the Special Crimes Department was Chief Inspector.'

'What of it, Quinn?'

'My own rank is Inspector, sir. I wonder if there isn't an anomaly here.'

'You've got the department back, Quinn. Don't push it.'

'Thank you, sir. And the Home Secretary? Can I count on his confidence?'

'The Home Secretary is minded to let you continue. For the time being, at least.'

'Do we have a new case, sir? Is that why Sir Michael was here?'

'What my business was with Sir Michael Esslyn is none of *your* business, Quinn.'

'I'm sorry, sir.'

'There is no specific new case, Quinn. Though you and your men are to be given what I might call a watching brief.'

'With regard to what, sir?'

'I take it you read the newspapers?'

'I try to be selective, sir, in those I look at.'

'Tired of seeing yourself depicted as some kind of penny dreadful villain, eh?'

'I rather think I am generally seen as the hero, not the villain, sir. Either way, my brush with the gutter press has taught me not to believe everything I read in the papers.'

'You are wise not to. You may be aware that some of the papers have been trying to whip up anti-German sentiments for years now. In the past, we might have taken the threat of the Kaiser invading our shores with a pinch of salt. Well, now it seems that the Admiralty is taking it seriously. Spy fever is nothing new, of course. But something has changed.'

'What has this to do with Special Crimes, sir?'

'"You too, be patient." James, chapter five, verse eight.'

A wash of well-being came over Quinn. Hearing Sir Edward quote the Bible, it seemed that the proper order of things had been restored. The world was back in balance.

'Our masters wish you to keep an eye on German nationals.'

'All German nationals, sir?'

'That would be asking rather a lot, even of you and your redoubtable men, Quinn. The brief is to be alert for anything that seems suspicious, in connection with any German nationals who come to your attention.'

'It seems a rather loose brief, if you will forgive me for saying so, Sir Edward.'

'Nonsense. Go out there. Keep your eyes open. Ferret around. If necessary, infiltrate yourselves into the circles in which these individuals move.'

'Are we to assume German identities?'

'Do you speak German, Quinn?'

'No, sir.'

'Do any of your men?'

'Not that I am aware, sir.'

'Then I advise against that particular course of action.' Another twinge of pain racked Sir Edward's frame. Quinn recognized it as a sign that Sir Edward wished to draw the interview to a close. The commissioner gave a terse concluding nod, but was stayed by something he saw in Quinn's expression. 'You look perplexed, Quinn.'

'It is merely that I am not sure how to go about this.'

'I'm sure you'll think of something. "Be not dismayed." Isaiah, chapter forty-one, verse ten. Or we might quote Jeremiah, chapter one, verse seventeen. You know that one, of course, Quinn?'

'I . . . I seem to have temporarily forgotten it.'

'"Thou therefore gird up thy loins, and arise."'

Quinn suddenly found Sir Edward's fondness for biblical quotes less endearing than he had a moment earlier.

Sir Edward closed the file on his desk and pushed it towards Quinn. 'A sordid little case, that one. Too many people dead, as usual, Quinn.'

'I cannot be . . .'

'Don't worry. I wasn't blaming you. Not this time. We cannot always be held responsible if people insist on going around killing one another. But at least we can close the file on it now. Although there was one curious epilogue to the case that you may be interested to hear about. It signifies nothing, I am sure.'

Quinn sat up sharply in his seat. 'What has happened?'

'Oh, it appears that the West Middlesex mortuary was broken into last night. One of the bodies was tampered with. By a strange coincidence, it happens to have been the body of the second victim in your House of Blackley case. Edna Corbett. Some ghoulish prankster, I'm sure. Of no significance, as I say.'

'What do you mean by *tampered with*?'

'A body part was removed.'

'Which body part?'

'Oh, for goodness' sake, Quinn! If I had known you were going to react like this, I should never have told you.'

'Was it an internal organ, sir?'

'I really don't want to sit here while you engage in gruesome speculation. So I will tell you. It was one of the eyes.'

'Should I look into it, sir?'

'Look into the missing eye? I don't see how you can, Quinn. No, put it from your mind. That case is over. Germans. That's the thing. Keep *your* eye out for Germans.' Sir Edward's renewed grimace had about it the air of finality. Quinn felt himself dismissed.

SIX

There was no place Inti liked better than this. The soft red glow from the safety light was his whole world. Nothing existed beyond its quivering sphere. All pain and confusion were banished to the darkness beyond. There were no memories here. Only the sense of miracles forming in the chemically pungent darkness.

Each time he entered the darkroom, he was reborn.

He watched his uncle Diaz work with practised speed. Diaz was a wizard. In truth, Diaz was many things. But when it came to coaxing out the secrets he had trapped in the light-sensitive layer of emulsion on his strips of film, he was a wizard. It went without saying that Inti loved his uncle, with a fierce, unwavering love forged under a relentless sun, and in a heartless landscape. The natural bonds were strengthened by his awareness of all that Diaz had done for him. But the feelings he felt when he watched Diaz operate in the darkroom came close to awe.

Diaz always did his own processing and printing. He had taught Inti that it was an essential part of the kinematographic cameraman's art. Everything depended on the interaction between chemicals and time. Each part of that precarious marriage had to be carefully controlled. Minute adjustments could be made to produce particular effects; it was up to the cameraman, Diaz insisted, to make these decisions. They could not be surrendered to anyone else.

The formulation of the developer was one of Diaz's own devising. The exact proportions of active ingredients to water had evolved over years of trial and error, together with the temperatures at which they were mixed and subsequently maintained in the glazed earthenware trough.

These were trade secrets which Diaz refused to impart to any of his friends, let alone a rival. But it was a sign of the bond that existed between uncle and nephew that he had passed his precious formulae on to Inti. Nothing was written down. Fully conscious of the privilege that had been bestowed on him, Inti had memorized the relative weights of metol, hydroquinone, soda sulphite, soda carbonate and potassium metabisulphite that had to be mixed to every thirty litres of water.

Inti had also been initiated into the mysteries of the stopwatch. Today, as always, it was his job to keep his eye on the dashing second hand and call out the minutes to his uncle.

First, though, Diaz opened the box of steel pins. In the darkroom's sombre glow, they looked like fine shards dipped in blood. Diaz drew out two and pinned them to the lapel of his lab coat. Now he opened the take-up box that was lying on the work bench and teased out the end of the exposed film.

Sometimes Inti felt his uncle would have been able to perform the operation blindfold. Certainly the necessity to do everything in that parsimonious half-light was no handicap to him. He must have had magical eyes in the tips of his fingers. From somewhere, a pair of scissors had appeared in one of his hands, their blades burnished with a ruby fire. He moved with an impressive combination of speed and precision to cut off two lengths of the exposed film, each of about fifteen centimetres. The hands shuffled in the darkness, returning the scissors to their appointed place out of sight, closing the front of the take-up box, and – with a nod to Inti for him to begin the timing – plunging the two lengths of film into the bath of developer. It was all executed in one fluid motion.

Everything took place in silence, apart from the occasional liquid plinking as Diaz gently stirred the development fluid. There was no need for instructions to be passed between them. They had worked together like this many times.

When it came to other matters, it was not that they had nothing to say to one another, but rather that there were no words for the things that needed to be said.

They limited themselves to banal exchanges. And never spoke of what was dearest and most troubling to them.

Only once had his uncle referred to such matters. Diaz had perhaps caught something in his nephew's expression. He had placed his hand on his nephew's shoulder and said quietly and simply: 'We shall make them see, Inti. One day we shall make them see.'

Then he had nodded once and removed his hand from Inti's shoulder.

For such men, in such circumstances, it is good to have an absorbing task that requires intense concentration and can be carried out in near darkness.

But it was strangely appropriate, this silence of theirs. A mute conjuring of silent, flickering ghosts from out of the coiled void.

Inti watched the hurtling of the second hand, knowing that the moment was approaching when he would have to break the silence.

'*Cinco.*'

The announcement served as a marker. It gave them the measure of infinity.

Sometimes, as now, while they waited for the tiny images to form in the test strips, other images came unbidden to Inti. These were not memories. The darkroom was where he came to escape the past.

A past he barely understood, but which held him in its grip none-theless. No, these were images of a future in which he found release. He saw the promise of his uncle's words fulfilled. He saw the moment when, at last, the world was made to see.

'*Diez.*'

This was the crucial marker. He always added, with a note of firm, but good-humoured command, his uncle's name: 'Diaz.'

And Diaz always smiled the same indulgent smile as he lifted out the first of the strips of film to rinse it in the running water of the washing bath, before transferring it to the final bath, containing fixer.

It didn't matter to Inti what the film depicted. If he was honest, he wondered why his uncle squandered his talents working for that disgusting Austrian. For Diaz, the perfection of his craft was all that mattered. Inti understood this. The beauty that Diaz was able to create, the masterful interplay of dark and light, the bold compositions, the instinctive understanding and faultless control of movement and depth . . . these were all things that existed independently of Waechter's tawdry melodramas. And they were all the things for which Diaz was responsible. They were also, incidentally, the elements for which Waechter, as the director, received the most lavish praise.

It all came down to light and dark and time and chemicals. These comprised his uncle's stock in trade. And no one understood them better than Diaz. Was it possible to hope that Inti too would one day reach a similar level of familiarity?

In the meantime, he had better keep his mind on the task in hand.

'*Quince minutos.*' He didn't know why, at fifteen, he always felt the need to make explicit exactly what it was that he was counting out.

Diaz took the developed strip out of the fixer and pegged it to the darkness. The line that traversed the darkroom was hardly visible, just a single silken thread cast out by a bloodthirsty spider.

Diaz turned to Inti, as he always did at this point in the proceed-ings. The muted, coloured light fogged the circular lenses of his spectacles. Diaz's gaze was unwavering; watchful, but not appraising; accepting, a little solicitous, but respectful. Inti was well aware of the high regard in which his uncle held him. It weighed heavily on him at times. He was not sure that he was capable of living up to it.

There was something, too, in the nature of an invitation embodied in his uncle's facing him. Inti sensed the openness there. It was as if his uncle was saying to him, '*You know, if there ever is anything you want to say to me, you may say it to me any time.*' Or, at its simplest, '*I am here for you.*'

But the only answer Inti ever gave to this invitation was, '*Veinte.*'

Diaz pegged up the second test strip. Brilliant white light swamped the room, chasing out the lambent gloom.

The sudden glare struck Inti as harsh and unwelcome. There was no comfort in it, nowhere to hide. It was almost as if the pain came looking for him.

Inti could see that each strip was now divided into six or seven frames. He was eager to have a closer look at the frames, but it was his uncle's prerogative to examine the test strips first. Diaz opened up a folding brass eyeglass and held the first of the strips up to the light. When he was satisfied, he passed it on to Inti without comment.

Inti already had his own magnifying glass at the ready.

Barely visible against a grey field of tone, a dark spherical object was repeated in each frame. A smaller, lighter-toned disc was just emerging from the centre of the sphere.

'What do you think?' said Diaz.

Inti shrugged without committing himself. He held out his hand for the second test strip.

The same repeated image, but this time the contrast between the now black sphere and paler background was clearer. The lighter-toned detail in the centre of the sphere was bleached to white, and lacked any internal detail.

Inti gave the strips back to his uncle. 'First one not enough. Second one too much.'

'What about the exposure? Is the exposure correct?'

'Of course.'

'How do you know?'

'Because you shot it, Uncle.'

Diaz smiled and cuffed his nephew affectionately. He waved one of the strips. 'This one is not much under. Thirteen minutes should do it. No, say thirteen and a half minutes. Do you agree, Inti?'

Inti nodded unhesitatingly. Diaz laid the test strips on the winding bench next to the pin-frame and consulted a notebook. This was his shooting record. In it he had written down the length of the shots to be processed and the lighting conditions for each one. In fact, today it had been a simple shoot. One sequence. A stationary object for a detail that Waechter wanted to insert at the last minute into the film they had believed was finished. The lighting had been constant throughout. That meant the film could be processed in one piece, instead of having to be divided up into separate scenes, each needing its own tests and separate times in the development bath.

Inti had been there at the shoot, working as Diaz's assistant, turning the camera crank whenever Diaz needed his hands free to pull the focus or move the camera on its tripod. But there had been little that was technically demanding today. They had simply shot the prop from a number of different angles and distances so that Waechter would have a choice when he came to editing.

The light in the darkroom was switched back to safety. Diaz lifted out the complete reel of film and folded over the end, securing it with one of the pins from his lapel. He fastened this loop of film over one of the central pins on the pin-frame. He nodded for Inti to begin winding.

And now Inti was the spider, spinning a web of celluloid. When he had spun out the entire length of film, Diaz plucked the other pin from his lapel and created a second loop at this end to fasten the film securely on to the frame.

Diaz immersed the frame in the bath of developer. Inti began the stopwatch.

As he watched the second hand in its frantic dash to nowhere, he pictured the images forming in the bath of chemicals.

A single unblinking eye placed on a table top, endlessly repeated.

SEVEN

Thick clouds squatted over the city, shutting out the infinite and stifling hope. The sun was nowhere to be seen. They had to settle for a dim, filtered pallor and call it daylight.

It seemed that spring had ventured out but quickly lost heart and thrown in the towel. An existential chill filled the vacancy. Quinn donned the herringbone Ulster once again and hunkered down in it as if he never intended to come out. Even when it wasn't raining, you felt that it soon would be. The day was something hostile on the other side of a fragile pane.

Now that the usurper Coddington had been banished, Quinn felt a need to reassert his right to the trademark garment. He wore it not so much to stay warm and dry, rather to confirm his identity, and even to proclaim his triumph. *I am the man who wears the herringbone Ulster*, he seemed to be saying.

Inchball took to the assigned task – of monitoring suspicious German nationals – with a peculiar ugly relish that seemed to match the weather. As soon as Quinn had briefed his sergeants, Inchball announced that there was a German barber's off the Strand that he had had his suspicions about for some time. Quinn attempted to divert his sergeant from what seemed to be an irrational fixation with this particular barber by instructing him to draw up a list of all German businesses, associations and institutions in London. He had some idea that the exercise might enable Inchball to put his suspicions in context, and lead him to an understanding of their arbitrariness. Sifting through various volumes of Kelly's London Directory and Post Office directories certainly served to reinforce Inchball's xenophobia. But the focus of it was still directed almost exclusively against the hapless barber.

'All these bleedin' Germans 'ave to get their 'air cut somewhere, don' they? Stands to reason. I'll bet you anythin' they all go to this feller off the Strand. Dortmunder. That's 'is name. Fritz Dortmunder. I mean. Summink like that. I ask you. If that ain't the name of a German, I don't know what is.'

'I don't doubt Herr Dortmunder is German, Inchball,' said Quinn. 'The question is, is he a spy?'

'He's more than that! He's a bleedin' spy master. See, all the other spies come to 'im to get their 'air cut, don' they! I'm certain of it. It's the perfect cover. People comin' and goin' all the time without drawin' suspicion. Chattin' away in that lingo of theirs. Who knows what they're talkin' about? Coastal defences in Kent? The Royal Navy's new submarine design? Inland lines of communication? Could be anythin'. We don't know. That's the point. Why don' you let me go there, guv? I'll find out what he's up to.'

'And how do you propose to do that, Inchball?'

'I shall masquerade . . . as a gentleman in need of a haircut.'

'And then?'

'Well . . . and then we shall see.'

'I don't quite understand, Inchball.'

'We shall see what we shall see, guv. I know how to keep my eyes open, don't you worry.'

'For what in particular will you be on the look-out?'

'What would you say, guv, if a man who was *not* in need of a haircut – nor indeed a shave! – went into a barber's, sat down in a barber's chair, and consented to have a sheet thrown over him and a pair of scissors taken to his neck? This a man, mind, who is in need of neither haircut *nor* shave. What would you say to that, guv?'

Quinn kept his counsel as to what he would say to that.

'You would say it was suspicious, guv. And you'd be right. You could even go so far as to say it was mighty suspicious.'

'How do you know that is what you will see?'

'I already seen it! Yes! With my own bleedin' eyes! And shall I tell you where I saw it? At Fritz bleedin' Dortmunder's. That's where.'

Quinn was not entirely sure that he believed Inchball's tale but in the end he approved the initiative. It would at least keep his sergeant busy for a while. And besides, it was true that Inchball needed a haircut.

Macadam's enthusiasm for kinematography showed no signs of abating. By the middle of Tuesday, Quinn had had enough. He snatched up the copy of the *Kinematograph Enthusiast's Weekly* from which Macadam was fond of reading aloud. The chosen extracts usually propounded the benefits of this or that camera. On the back page, there was an advertisement for the Moy and Bastie Kineto, the latest model to catch the sergeant's eye. 'Very well, Macadam. Put in a procurement application for one of those and we'll see where it gets you. It will have to go up to the top, you know. I can't approve such expenditure myself.'

'But you will sign the form?'

A flicker of his eyelids was all the assent Quinn was prepared to give. It was enough for Macadam, whose face lit up with such simple gratitude that Quinn almost felt guilty. He did not expect the application to be successful, and had no intention of going out of his way to support it. And yet, to see a grown man buoyed up with the innocent pleasure of a thirteen-year-old boy promised a toy yacht provoked a kind of nostalgic sympathy.

An unexpected shadow passed over Macadam's face, his head dipped in sudden reticence. 'With respect, sir, for all the undoubted virtues of the Kineto camera, and it *is* a very good camera; you certainly cannot be faulted in your discernment for choosing it . . . However, for all its virtues, I am not entirely certain that it is the model I would recommend for the department, sir. I have no wish to impugn your judgement . . .'

Quinn cut him off. 'Macadam.'

Sergeant Macadam's eyes widened in hopeless, innocent uncertainty.

'I don't care about the damned camera.' Quinn dropped the journal back on Macadam's desk.

'No, sir. I see, sir.'

'What I mean to say is I shall leave it up to you.'

'In that case, sir . . .' Macadam leafed rapidly through the pages of the *Kinematograph Enthusiast's Weekly* as if he feared it would be snatched from his hands again. 'May I draw your attention to Messrs Butcher and Sons Empire Camera Number Two? It boasts many of the advantages of the Kineto camera which you selected . . .'

'I *didn't* select it, Macadam.'

'The Empire Two can hold its own against the Kineto – that is what I'm saying, sir. And yet, it retails at a significantly – a *significantly* – lower price. What is more, from everything that I have read, this saving is achieved not through any sacrifice of quality, whether in the standard of engineering, manufacture, or the durability of parts. On none of those heads does the Empire Two give ground to the Kineto. Indeed, there are those who would argue that in one or two respects – I don't wish to overstate the case, sir – in one or two respects only, it has the upper hand.'

'Very well, the Empire Two it is, Macadam.'

'Although . . . you may be wondering why I am not recommending the Empire Number *One* Camera, also manufactured by Messrs Butcher and Sons.'

'I would expect that, Macadam. If they produce the Empire Number Two, I should expect them also to produce the Empire Number One.'

Macadam was momentarily thrown by Quinn's observation. 'Qu-quite right, sir.'

'Just complete the procurement form with the details of the camera you recommend and your reasons. I shall sign it and it will go up to Sir Edward.'

'We shall need a projector too, sir. That goes without saying. As well as film stock and, uhm, there will need to be budgetary provision for processing. I am not sure the photographic lab here at the Yard will be up to it, sir. I could undertake to set up a darkroom myself, of course. It would require further expenditure initially, but . . .'

'You are a policeman, Macadam. Not a lab technician. We shall have the films processed elsewhere.'

'I agree, sir.' Macadam gave an eager nod of obedience. 'How long do you think it will take, sir, before we have the camera?'

'I make no promises, Macadam. It is up to you to make the application as compelling as possible.'

'Sir Edward is a great believer in innovation. I am confident he will see the benefits to the department. Indeed, I wouldn't be surprised if he extended the use of kinematography across the whole of the Met.'

'We shall have to see.'

'At any rate, the sooner we have the camera the better. There is no time like the present, after all. It would be invaluable in the present investigation of the German barber. I could, for instance, set up a concealed camera outside the barbershop and film everyone who comes and goes.'

'Let us get the camera first,' said Quinn. 'And then we will decide what to do with it.'

To Quinn's relief, further discussion was cut off by the arrival of the post boy with the latest bundle of internal mail. There was a note from Sir Edward:

> *Quinn,*
> *Have arranged for you to talk to a chap at the Admiralty for background and guidance. Present yourself to Lord Dunwich, at the Admiralty Extension, 1500 hours today.*

Quinn consulted his pocket watch. He had ten minutes to spare.

EIGHT

Lord Dunwich peered over the screen that separated his desk from the civil servants in his department. He couldn't shake off the feeling that he was being watched. Even here, inside the Admiralty.

He knew that it was absurd, to think like this. But receiving that preposterous object at the club had shaken him.

He sat down at his desk again, opened the drawer where the object was confined, still in its box. He stared at the box for several minutes, as if gazing at it could help him understand it. Then he closed the drawer. He took the further precaution of locking it and pocketing the key.

Thankfully, that day in the club, he had not called for help or drawn any attention to the object itself. There had been that initial involuntary cry, which had brought one or two disapproving glances from over the tops of newspapers. But he had kept his wits about him enough to clear his throat loudly and mutter something about a kipper bone.

The august members had gone back to their papers. And, rearranging his armchair so that he was shielded from further view, he had lowered himself down on to his hands and knees and confronted the object.

He had stared at it for a long time, wondering whether it really could be what it appeared to be.

And it had stared back at him.

He had been reluctant to touch it. The very idea repulsed him. But he knew he had to get rid of it somehow. And so he took a fountain pen from the writing table and prodded the object with that. It did not respond in the way he might have expected an enucleated eye to respond. It was hard, for one thing. The pen made a tapping sound against it and caused the thing to roll.

Is this what happens to eyes when they are removed from their sockets? he wondered. *They toughen up?*

Also, it was too perfect. Too perfectly spherical, and the surface utterly unblemished. Surely a real eye would have lost its shape a little? Become wrinkled, pitted or deflated. And he might have expected the lustre to have faded from it. And where were the tendrils of nerves trailing from the back of it, the loose attachments of gristle and fibre, the specks of gore? The flaws in the surface?

It was immaculate. Gleaming. Polished.

Then he thought back to the way it had bounced and rolled across the floor.

No, it wasn't what he had first thought it to be. It was not an eye, certainly not a human eye. Not even a pig's eye, or an ox's eye.

It was a billiard ball. A white billiard ball, with a blue iris painted on to it.

After the first half-laugh of incredulity and relief, he had to admit he had felt a little disappointed. Cheated, almost. And then, slightly ashamed. He had been taken in. He was the butt of a ridiculous prank. The visceral horror he had felt had been duped out of him, a wasted emotion.

If it was a practical joke, what was the point of it? What *was* the joke? He simply didn't get it. And he couldn't for the life of him think of anyone who might have perpetrated it. His set didn't really go in for this sort of thing. The odd bit of mild ribbing at his expense, perhaps, but nothing as elaborate, or grotesque, as this. It was a question of taste, as well as style. Admittedly in his youth, at Oxford, he had taken part in the usual high jinks and horseplay. But the truth was these days everyone he knew (that is to say, everyone he was prepared to acknowledge knowing) was just too lazy to go to all this trouble.

If it wasn't a joke, he was forced to conclude that it was something more sinister. A warning, perhaps. Or a threat.

You are being watched, it seemed to say. *We have our eye on you!*

'*We*', yes. For he was sure that a grouping rather than an individual was behind this.

As he had peered down at the object on the floor of his club reading room, he had had the sense that he was being watched right then, that the eye (which was not really an eye) was capable of seeing him. And through the eye, *they* somehow knew everything there was to know about him. They were watching him there and then. They had been watching him the night before. They had been watching him for weeks, months even. They had witnessed all cavortings and couplings. And now, in sending him this fake eye, they were merely signalling their readiness to make use of everything they had seen. This was the first move in a blackmailing operation, he felt sure.

A chill passed through him. What if they wanted more than money from him? What if they wanted control, or access? What if they were not just some grubby opportunists out for their own profit? What if they were agents of a foreign power?

He imagined the darkness enclosing the loathsome object as it lay dormant in the drawer of his desk. In his mind, it had become the thing that it was meant to represent. It had become an eye. No, it was more than an eye. It was a sentient thing. It could see, but it could also think. It was self-aware. It had intent. It was malign. And it hated the darkness into which he had plunged it. It would bide its time, feasting hungrily on the thin slivers of light that leaked through the cracks in the box. Storing up its hatred. Plotting its revenge.

He knew that the darkness to which he had now consigned it could not contain it forever.

NINE

A wan light seeped thinly through the packed clouds above Whitehall. But straightaway it seemed to retract, as if cowed by the grandiose buildings of government.

Quinn held his head self-consciously high as he strode across Horse Guards Parade. Once or twice he had to blink away the memory of Miss Dillard's reproachful expression. Her eyes, dewy with disappointment, had become the eyes of his conscience.

Blink!

He had to get on with the job. Duty demanded it. And right now the job consisted solely in striding purposefully across the empty parade ground. That was all that was asked of him for the moment, and on balance he felt himself equal to the task.

The thing was if he did not get on with the job, if he did not continue striding – in other words, if he gave in to the mute reproach of those eyes . . . No, it did not bear thinking about. That way, madness lay.

Blink!

He allowed the rhythmic crunch of gravel beneath his shoes to signal his determination. It was time to bring some purpose to the investigation. He would have it out with this Admiralty fellow, no matter that he was a lord of the realm. They needed specific information about a real danger; names and photographs of suspect individuals, addresses to be monitored. Details of a concrete plot against which they could pit themselves.

Otherwise his men were just aimlessly prowling.

Ahead of him, the Admiralty Extension was a concrete enough presence. Its very existence was testimony to the dangers the country faced. It had been built with one purpose only, to prepare for war. And even while it was being built, it had grown in scale from its original conception, spawning additional corridors and offices as its sense of imminent threat increased. At the same time, it had something of the air of a fairytale palace. The baroque frontage, in red brick and white stone, created a fussy pink effect that put Quinn in mind of sleeping princesses, rather than grey, frock-coated men on a constant war-footing.

*   *   *

He was shown into a high-ceilinged room that for all its daunting scale still managed to seem gloomy. The walls were covered in dark oak panelling worked into elaborate mouldings. The heavy brown field was relieved in places by monumental oil paintings of sea battles in the age of sail. The colours were muted and sombre. The action, static and timeless. Sea foam frozen in a wall of spray. Sharp tongues of rigid fire, sculptures of smoke cast around silent cannons. Immense charts and maps mounted on boards and stuck with coloured pins were propped up around the room, in a surprisingly haphazard way, giving an air of improvisation and confusion. The blinds were drawn over the windows, presumably to keep out prying eyes.

The room was shared by a number of officials, seated in silence at massive desks. From the solemnity of their expressions, they gave the impression of conducting the most momentous and onerous of tasks. There could be no doubt, they were engaged in nothing less than steering the Empire. One or two looked up as Quinn came in. All those who did, frowned.

Quinn was led to a desk in the far corner of the room, partitioned by a Japanese lacquered screen. The civil servant who escorted him rapped on the screen to attract the attention of the thin, rather anxious-looking man with receding hair and greying temples behind the desk. The man looked up and regarded Quinn through half-moon spectacles, which he pushed up his nose as he lifted his head. His expression was mild, not without kindness.

'Inspector Quinn to see you, sir,' said the civil servant. He bowed and retreated into the room.

'Ah, yes, please do sit down, Inspector.' Lord Dunwich's voice was deep and richly toned. His expression relaxed somewhat as he spoke, as if he too found the sound he emitted reassuring. He closed the folder he had been studying, revealing the official stamp of CLASSIFIED on the front of it. He smiled encouragingly at Quinn. There was something undeniably sympathetic about the man. He was not entirely successful at suppressing the weighty matters that troubled him, and yet he clearly took pains to put others at their ease. 'I understand from Sir Edward that your department is now engaged in counter-espionage work? And that you require some further guidance as to how to conduct your operations?'

'This is all rather new to us, your lordship.'

'Please . . . you may simply call me "sir". I don't stand on my dignity here.'

Quinn nodded in gratitude. 'I do not have a large department, sir. I am naturally concerned about squandering what little resources I have at my disposal. Sir Edward seemed to suggest that it was simply a matter of looking out for suspicious foreigners. But I am at a loss to know what we are to do should we find any.'

'Have you not read *Spies of the Kaiser*, Inspector?' Quinn could not be sure, but he thought that Lord Dunwich's expression was wry, not to say mischievous.

'That is a work of fiction, is it not, sir?'

'Is it? Is it really, Inspector? Or is it a polemic?' Lord Dunwich paused for a moment to give the question due consideration. 'I think there was a time when that book, and others of its ilk, were dismissed as nonsense. But I have to tell you that they are taken increasingly seriously within the Admiralty.'

'And so . . .?'

Lord Dunwich was fingering the classified folder on his desk, as if impatient to get back to it. He looked up at Quinn in some confusion.

'Would it be permissible to ask for more specific instructions, sir?'

'Instructions? It's not a question of instructions, I'm afraid. One either has a talent for this kind of work, or one does not. One has to keep one's eyes and ears open. If I were you, I would start small. Focus on one specific target.'

'But how do we identify this target?'

'We're looking for German spies, Inspector.'

'I know that, sir.'

'What do you think a German spy looks like?'

'I have no idea, sir.'

'Exactly.'

'I'm afraid I don't understand, sir.'

'Put aside your preconceptions – your prejudices. You think you're looking for men in alpine hats with funny little moustaches and thick accents? No. The consummate German spy will not even appear to be a German. He will be the least likely spy you can imagine.'

'Someone like you, perhaps, sir?'

Lord Dunwich's eyes expanded in astonishment. His expression then dissolved into hilarity. 'I say, Inspector, that's rather droll! Priceless!'

'One of my men wishes to investigate a German barber's shop off the Strand. He believes that he has witnessed suspicious activity there.'

Lord Dunwich shook his head discouragingly. 'No, no. A classic mistake. That's far too obvious. You must do better than that, I'm afraid.'

Quinn wondered at the speed with which Lord Dunwich dismissed Inchball's initiative.

'You need to develop your instincts beyond the superficial.'

It was interesting advice. Quinn's instincts were suddenly telling him that he could not entirely trust this man. In fact, he was now more strongly inclined to back Inchball's investigation than he had before.

At any rate, he sensed that he would learn nothing more from continuing the interview. He nodded and rose from his seat. But before he could leave, Lord Dunwich cleared his throat. His voice when he spoke was hesitant and broken. 'Inspector, what do you know about . . . green ink?'

'Green ink?'

'What does it say about a man if he uses green ink? It is not a colour of ink you see often, is it?'

Quinn frowned. He had seen something written in green ink himself recently. The coincidence struck him as sinister. 'Blue, blue-black and black are more common. But one does occasionally come across it. It may suggest an Irish connection.'

'Interesting. Thank you, Inspector. Please keep me informed of how your investigation proceeds. You may write to me here.'

'Of course.'

'I will have to get someone to show you out, I'm afraid.' Lord Dunwich picked up a small brass bell which gave an effete tinkle. He then half-rose and offered Quinn his hand, although without looking him in the eye, Quinn noticed. It seemed that whatever was troubling his lordship deterred him from meeting the challenge of another man's gaze.

TEN

The darkness was hot and damp and scented. He feared it at the same time as he surrendered to it. How stupid he had been, to walk into the enemy's lair, to place himself utterly at the enemy's mercy.

He suspected the towels were infiltrated with some kind of

narcotic drug. His face felt as though it was melting. The feeling of warmth and physical dissolution began to spread out. He had to keep his wits about him.

How could he have been so careless? Allowing this man, this patent German, to stand over him with a cut-throat razor in his hand. How had it come to this?

Inchball knew this end of the Strand well, from his days in the Vice Squad. Holywell Street was now demolished; the dealers in rare prints, specialist booksellers and suppliers of French goods were long gone. For years it had been the centre of the city's pornography trade. In some of the upstairs 'Show Rooms' an even more dubious trade had been conducted. Inchball had a nostalgic sense of the street, just out of sight, always around the next corner, like a street you might look for in a dream but never find. He sensed too the ghosts of all the generations of men who had congregated there, crowding round the window displays and street wares, blocking the traffic and chesting each other out of the way in their tense eagerness to get to the front.

Happy days, he might have said. You only had to reach out to feel a collar. The punters were so distracted by their appetites that they never saw you coming.

A few echoing footsteps away from the ghost of Holywell Street, the alley in which Dortmunder's barber shop was located had survived the swing of the wrecking ball. Inchball half-suspected that this was because the demolition team had not been able to find it, not because it didn't deserve to be torn down. It was as dirty, dark, crooked and claustrophobic a passageway as any you might find in a medieval town. Once you passed through the whitewashed arch that separated it from the Strand, you entered into a squalid underworld begrimed with black soot, the pavement littered with dank scraps, and broken by great standing puddles into which it was unwise to venture, for fear that they might be bottomless sinkholes. Children dressed in little more than rags clustered in the rotten doorways. Too exhausted to beg, they eyed every intruder with sullen, lifeless suspicion.

It was the shop's location that had first attracted Inchball's attention. Some of the clientele he had noticed frequenting the shop could safely be classified as 'toffs'. Foreigners, admittedly, but toffs all the same. Why on earth should such men choose this shabby little barber shop in a god-forsaken blind alley? Unless they had some nefarious purpose in going there.

Whatever the guv'nor might say about his plan, there was method to his madness.

The shop front protruded in a bulbous bay, with an old-fashioned leaded window. The sign above it advertised: FRITZ Dortmunder, BARBER.

Another sign, over the door, read: HAIR CUTTING, SHAVING, SHAMPOOING, SINGEING.

The shop was tiny. If you entered it hoping for relief from the narrowness of the alley, you would be disappointed. However, it was certainly spruce inside. The floor was freshly swept. Every surface was spotless. Gleaming implements were arranged in impeccable order. Mirrors glinted. The metallic components of the adjustable chairs shone as if they had just been polished. The air was scented with talc, hair oil and incense, no doubt burning to disguise the inescapable smell of damp and sewer gas.

There were two chairs in the shop. Yet in all the years he had been casually keeping an eye on this place, he had only ever seen one barber working in there, the man he presumed to be Dortmunder. The surplus chair added to the cramped atmosphere. The shop seemed full even before a single customer entered.

Dortmunder was seated in one of the chairs reading a newspaper when Inchball entered. It was an English newspaper, the *Clarion*. Inchball couldn't decide whether this was more or less suspicious than if he had found him reading a German newspaper.

Dortmunder folded the paper away and sprang to his feet, dusting the cracked leather seat of the chair with a cloth. He then bowed to Inchball and gave what might have been a slight click of the heels. 'Please be seated, good sir.' He gestured to the chair he had just vacated. 'I was keeping it warm for you!' The man betrayed barely a hint of an accent; it was more that there was something uncertain and alien about the cadence of his speech. This in itself was deeply suspicious.

The man's obsequious joviality did nothing to reassure Inchball. He had read enough spy literature to know that this was precisely the tactic these individuals adopted to put their victims at ease.

Physically, Dortmunder was a dapper little man, dressed in an immaculate apron and wearing silver wire-rimmed glasses. It was perhaps as well that he was no bigger than he was, otherwise he would not have fitted in his shop. His hair was dark and cut in a severe short back and sides, which Inchball thought of as being particularly Germanic. The extraordinary crispness of the cut at first inspired confidence, but then led Inchball to speculate on the question of who barbers got to cut their own hair, or whether they somehow contrived to do it themselves. He half-remembered a riddle, something to do with choosing between the only two barbers in a village. One had an excellent haircut, the other had a terrible one. Of course, the answer was you chose the man with the bad haircut. Which meant that Dortmunder's own hair was no recommendation at all. It was simply some kind of trick.

'You speak very good English,' Inchball commented as he lowered himself gingerly on to the seat. Inchball was enough of a detective to disguise the suspicion in the question. He made it sound like a compliment.

Dortmunder shook out a dark blue sheet and threw around Inchball, fastening at the back of his neck. 'Of course. My parents brought me to this country when I was a boy. It has been my home all these years. Now, sir, what can I do for you?'

'Just a trim.'

'Very good, sir. And after that, perhaps, hot towels and a shave? It is a speciality of the house.'

'I don't think so. Not today.'

Dortmunder started on the haircut, wielding the scissors with convincing dexterity. If he was not a professional barber, he had pretended to be one for long enough to more than pass muster. 'But today, there is no charge. I think it is your first time in my shop, is it not?'

Inchball nodded. The scissor blades snapped eagerly over his head, sending tiny dark sparks flying.

'Yes. Very well, as it is your first time here. And I am not busy. I will give you the full treatment for no extra charge. If you like it, you will come back. And next time, it will not be free. Perhaps you will become a regular customer. But is it really your first time here?'

Dortmunder pinched tufts of hair between outstretched fingers and made a cut of surgical precision. Inchball watched him in the mirror. The German's technique matched that of any other barber he had visited. He worked carefully but swiftly, gently tilting Inchball's head with his fingertips each time he needed to adjust his angle of attack. There was something mesmerising about the deftness of his touch. Inchball seemed to fall into a light trance. It was some time before he answered the question that had been left hanging: 'Yes, that's right.'

'Your face seems familiar, somehow. I have a good memory for faces. I study them in the mirror, you see.' And at this point the two men exchanged a look in which each seemed to challenge the other to frankness. And if the meaning of Inchball's look was *Are you really a barber?* then equally, the meaning of Dortmunder's was *Can you really be a customer?* But of course, neither man gave voice to whatever suspicions they might have been harbouring, except obliquely, perhaps with an edge of mischievous sarcasm, Dortmunder said, 'Are you a star of the moving pictures? I do like to go to the kinematograph shows. Perhaps I have seen you in one of the films? Playing a detective perhaps?'

'No. I'm not in films.'

'But I have seen your face, upon my life. Are you sure you have not been to my shop before?'

'I have walked past a couple times. And looked in.'

'And now you have plucked up your courage to come in. So, you are entitled to hot towels and a shave at no extra charge. What do you say to that?'

'I don't really . . .'

'Good, it is settled! Now, please, good sir. You will sit back and relax and allow me to perform the services for which I am justly famous. And if you like what I will have done, you may tell your friends, no?'

So it was that Inchball came to sink back into the barber's chair and consented to have his face covered in what he had every reason to believe were narcotic-infused hot towels.

Immersed in a fragrant, seductive darkness, he found that it was not such a bad place to be after all. Dortmunder was massaging the crown of his head and speaking to him in a low, constant murmur.

'It is good, no? The steam from the towels, it opens up your pores and relaxes your skin. Close your eyes, please. You may go to sleep if you wish. You are in my safe hands.'

The gentle teasing pressure on his scalp was an elusive, strangely ambiguous pleasure, at times not a pleasure at all, but never, quite, unpleasant. It made him think of birds alighting. As soon as he thought of this, the sensation ceased. He found that he instantly missed it.

Let's not get bleedin' carried away, he said to himself.

At least he was still conscious, which led him to conclude that the towels were not drugged as he had feared.

But what was that smell, the scent of the darkness? If only he could identify it he would know what he was up against.

The smell brought back bad memories. It wasn't so long since Inchball had been drugged and trussed in a house in Camden, a house that stank of pomegranates, of all things, by a man even more repulsive than the German. Then, he had panicked and wet himself. Embarrassing, when Macadam and the guv'nor found him. Still they had been decent enough not to mention it.

The stench of those pomegranates would never leave him. He smelled it in his sleep, as it infiltrated his dreams with its cloying perfume. One thing he could say for certain was that the smell he was inhaling now was not of pomegranates.

It might just be that the fiend had used a milder drug than Inchball had imagined, one capable of inducing a feeling of well-being and wooziness, without knocking him out. One that would make him susceptible to suggestion, and might even cause him to lower his defences.

Just let the bastard try something!

He was determined not to allow himself to be tied up this time. And whatever happened, he would not wet himself.

By the sound of it, the man was stropping a razor, somewhere to Inchball's right. So, the moment was approaching. The moment when a German spy would place a razor against his throat.

Inchball heard the shop door open, a reprieve.

There were voices. Dortmunder's and another man's. Both speaking German.

Inchball lifted his right hand and pulled a flap of towelling away from his eye. He swivelled slightly in the chair and looked out towards the door. Dortmunder had his back to him. Over his shoulder he could see, on the threshold of the shop, a large man with an absolutely bald head, his face clean-shaven apart from a well-groomed handlebar moustache. Dortmunder and the other man were engaged in a low, intense discussion. Suddenly, the man must have noticed Inchball's eye peeping out at him. He nodded to Dortmunder, who turned to look at Inchball.

'I will be with you in a very short moment, good sir. Please, relax, enjoy the soothing vapours of the towels.' Dortmunder stretched out a hand – the shop was so small he could reach Inchball from where he was standing – and replaced the damp cloth over his eye. In the last moment before darkness returned, Quinn noticed that Dortmunder was holding a large envelope in his other hand. He wasn't able to make out the address, which looked foreign to his eye. One thing he did notice was that it was written in green ink.

In his scented darkness, Inchball strained to pick up a word that he could understand or that might be useful to him. A name. The name of a coastal town, perhaps. Or something that sounded like an English battleship. All that he was able to make out was Dortmunder clicking his heels in apparent military subordination and hissing, '*Sehr gut*, Herr Hartmann.'

Inchball heard the door close. The sound of razor against strop resumed. The other man – Herr Hartmann, it seemed – was gone. And whoever Hartmann was, it was clear that he was Dortmunder's superior.

Dortmunder removed the towels, his face beaming with ersatz bonhomie. If he had been rattled by Inchball's seeing Hartmann, and overhearing their conversation, he was determined not to show it. As Inchball knew from experience, that forced cheerfulness was the clearest indicator of guilt.

Well, the guv'nor would eat his words now. This had been far from a wasted trip. He had witnessed the handing over of suspicious documents and he had a glimpse of the man who really did seem to be the spy master of Dortmunder's cell.

And if the scent of the rich, warm foam that was being worked into his cheek was anything to go by, he was about to have a very good shave indeed.

ELEVEN

The camera arrived the following Monday. Quinn had to admit he was amazed. In the normal run of things, procurements took longer than this.

Macadam, of course, was beside himself with pleasure as he unpacked the camera. To Quinn's eye, the Empire Number Two was a rather unprepossessing object: a plain-looking oblong box made of some indeterminate wood with a number of metal fittings. 'Ooh, there's some weight in that.' There was a note of personal pride in Macadam's voice as he hefted it, as if he had played some part in making the camera so heavy. 'That's the quality of the manufacturing for you.' He proceeded to demonstrate at some length the numerous virtues of the camera, opening and closing its various compartments, pointing out the precision of the engineering, looking through the eye piece, turning the crank, adjusting whatever knobs would allow themselves to be adjusted.

Quinn caught Inchball's eye at the height of its exasperated roll.

'You see, sir, focusing is done from the front *and* the back. The lens is a Zeiss Tessar, with a focal ratio of F6.3, which should serve us well in the conditions under which we shall be using it.'

'What did you say?' Inchball sat up sharply. His tone was dark and laden with suspicion. His brows contracted in a watchful frown. This was a man alert to every danger the nation faced.

'F6.3. It's commonly known as the f-number, although I prefer to call it the focal ratio.'

'No, before that. The lens. Wha' did you call it?'

'A Zeiss Tessar.'

'German, is it?'

'Well, the lens is, yes. The Germans manufacture excellent optical equipment. Zeiss lenses in particular are considered to be the very best available. Rather more expensive than other lenses, but considering the importance of the work we will be undertaking, I felt that it was worth it.'

'I don't trust it.'

'What?' Macadam flashed a look of appeal towards Quinn, which Quinn did his best not to notice.

'Get rid of it,' insisted Inchball.

'You are joking!'

'It's unpatriotic. We should have an English lens on there. Besides, what if it's a dud?'

'What on earth are you talking about? How could it possibly be a dud? Zeiss lenses are the best in the world.'

'The Germans, righ', they're plannin' to invade us, righ'? So . . . no, hear me out . . . there's all sorts of things we get from Germany. These lenses is jus' one example. But wha' they do, righ', is deliberately send over 'ere a load of substandard merchandise. A load of crap, basically. Not jus' these lenses. Everythin'. Bicycles, motor cars – I dunno. You name it. Tyres.'

'Tyres?'

'Yeah, tyres. That would be your main one, that. So . . . righ' . . . when the moment of truth comes, and we need to use any of this stuff we've bough' from them, it all breaks down. All the tyres go flat. Nothin' works – nothin' we got from Germany. So while we're all distracted tryin' 'a fix it all – that's when they strike. Get us at our weakest. It's all part of their plan.'

'Zeiss. Lenses. Are. *The* best. In *the* world!' insisted Macadam with slow, deliberate emphasis. He could no longer keep his appeal to Quinn mute: 'Sir?'

Quinn let out a sigh. 'I do not believe that an application for additional equipment will meet with success. We have been fortunate to get what we have. We must make the best of it.'

'With respect, sir, I hardly think that using a Zeiss lens is *making the best of it.*'

Quinn pinched the bridge of his nose. 'Macadam, you have your camera. You have your lens.'

'Bleedin' German lens,' muttered Inchball.

Quinn stood up decisively, although he did remember to bow his head at the last minute. 'Perhaps we can now give some thought as to how we are going to employ this equipment in our current operation?'

They were now committed to keeping the barber shop under surveillance, as far as the limited resources of the department allowed. Quinn had to accept that Inchball's first instinct had been tested and proved sound. His description of the man who had come to the door – 'He was as bald as a bleedin' coot, I'm tellin' yer!' – somehow clinched it. So too had the detail of the green writing on the envelope. When Inchball had told him about this, he had immediately thought back to his interview with Lord Dunwich. *'What does it say about a man if he uses green ink?'*

Quinn tried to remember where he had seen green ink. He searched through the old correspondence on his desk until he found the card from the film production company. There it was in the top left-hand corner: *Quick-Fire Quinn and guest.*

He had meant to throw it away, having no intention to accept its invitation:

> *You are cordially invited to the world premiere of*
> THE EYES OF THE BEHOLDER

The main reason he discounted the possibility of going, or so he told himself, was his annoyance at being addressed as *Quick-Fire*

Quinn. But he had found the addition of 'and guest' after his name troubling in a different way. Whom would he invite? Of course, he fantasized about taking Miss Latterly. But what he was really frightened of was that in a moment of weakness he would ask Miss Dillard.

But now, the mention of green ink by Lord Dunwich and the green ink on the package handed over in the barbershop . . . was there some connection between the film company, the barber's and Lord Dunwich's spies?

He scanned down the type: *Written and directed by the renowned maestro KONRAD WAECHTER.*

The name sounded German. Perhaps there was something here after all.

He knew that Lord Dunwich was holding something back. His sort always did. But surely it didn't follow that his lordship was in league with foreign spies? Perhaps the question about green ink had been prompted by a completely unrelated matter. Had Lord Dunwich received an invitation to the premiere too?

He made a mental note of the date of the event before returning the card to its place in his pile of correspondence.

Could it be that the spy operation was a red herring, designed to divert the department from something even more nefarious? Quinn had noted a hunted quality to Lord Dunwich's eyes, a way they had of simultaneously seeking out and shying away from any questioning gaze. Those were not innocent eyes. They were eyes that longed to reveal the secrets that burdened them. It was a quality he recognized. He saw it every time he looked in the mirror.

Whatever was the truth, Quinn felt a bridling of resentment. It would not be the first time he had been sent into the field without being afforded the courtesy of full disclosure.

He experienced a momentary flash of Miss Dillard's eyes. He had to admit, he did not always tell his men everything that he knew, and sometimes his reasons for withholding information were obscure even to himself.

'Inchball, you are the one who is most familiar with what's going on at the German's.'

'Yes, guv. I've been keepin' me beady eye on the place ever since I visited it last week.'

'I trust you were not observed? Dortmunder knows you now.'

'I've been very careful, guv. I've taken steps to . . . err . . . blend in, you might say. Even my own mother wun' recognize me.'

Quinn's involuntary grimace betrayed his unwillingness to know any more about the details of Inchball's disguise. 'What is the layout of the street? Would it be possible to set up Macadam with his camera so that he could record the comings and goings?'

'We could get a vehicle in there from Maiden Lane, guv. If we had a van, we could put Macadam in the back, drill a hole through the side and Fritz is your uncle.'

'What about that, Macadam? Would you be able to film success-fully through a hole in the side of a van?'

'It should be possible, sir. As soon as we get the film, I could run a test.'

'You mean they haven't sent you no film? Bleedin' typical.'

'I'm sure the film will turn up in due course, as will the other items I requested, such as the tripod. Oh, and the projector, of course. We will need that to see what we have filmed. In the mean-time . . .' Macadam opened up the side of the camera, revealing a series of spools and cogs and other mechanisms. There was a set of printed instructions stuck to the inside of the hinged cover. 'I daresay I can be usefully employed in familiarizing myself with every aspect of the machine's operation.'

Inchball snorted derisively. 'While you're playing with your new toy, I shall get on with some real policing.'

'What do you have in mind, Inchball?'

'With your permission, guv, I intend to go back to the barber's. I have been allowing my whiskers to grow for the last few days expressly for that purpose.' Inchball drew the fingertips of both hands down across either side of his face.

'And what do you hope to achieve?'

'Well, what if I was to let it be known that I'm a copper? What do you think Herr Dortmunder would say to that?'

'Go on.'

'So, I'm a copper, righ'. I can get in an' out of certain highly secure premises, the sort where state secrets are kept. I have keys that can open doors. I even know the combination to some government safes.'

'What kind of a copper are you?' challenged Macadam, warming to the subterfuge.

'I'm the sort what guards the Admiralty, or some of the high-ups in it, say.'

'Interesting,' said Quinn.

'And what if I also let it be known that I am not a happy copper? That I am, in fact, a thoroughly disgruntled copper, 'arbourin' a grievance against them very high-ups I is supposed to be lookin' arfter? What if all that – and what if I was also to let slip certain warm words of admiration for the Bismarckian state? What if I were to let slip that there were days when I wished England could be more like Germany? What do you think our friend Fritz Dortmunder would say to all that, guv?'

'It's a dangerous game, Inchball. If these men are all that we suspect them to be, then you could be placing yourself in extreme danger.'

Inchball shrugged.

'By all means go back there for another shave. It will be a good thing if you establish a rapport with this fellow by becoming a regular customer. But don't, for now, mention anything about being a policeman. Let's keep that up our sleeve. If we proceed too quickly, he may smell a rat.'

'May I say I admire the Bismarckian state, guv?'

'For now, confine yourself to complimenting him on his barbering skills.'

'Ah, subtle. Very subtle.'

'It may be enough to hook him at this stage.'

Quinn cast his gaze towards the window. It signalled either his release of Inchball, or his own desire to escape the confines of that room and soar into the pale bleak glimmering sky beyond.

TWELVE

Furled in the darkness, that was how it felt. Macadam was furled, like the film inside his precious camera. Both man and film poised, ready to spring into action.

But the operation was more difficult than he had envisaged. He could not look directly through the camera lens, and using the viewfinder was out of the question because of their concealed location. To get round this, back at the garage, he had drilled two holes in the side of the van. One for the camera to film from. Another, alongside the first, for them to look through. But essentially, he had to rely on guesswork when it came to positioning the camera. He was more or less filming blind.

Naturally, he kept his apprehensions to himself. He was reluctant to give Inchball any ammunition for his constant barrage of mockery. Neither did he want to worry the guv'nor unduly. He would make this thing work. He would justify the guv'nor's faith in him.

He gripped the crank handle lightly, testing the sprung tension in its resistance. He murmured soothingly to the machine, as if it were an animal that he was about to unleash. At other times, in the potent darkness in the back of the van, he imagined that the camera was an extension of his own being. He almost believed it.

And yes, there was something peculiar about this darkness. It was a darkness born out of bloodshed. A darkness with a vile and sordid history. The vehicle had been impounded because of its involvement in a previous case. It was the means by which that queer-killer had distributed the exsanguinated corpses of renters around London.

He put his eye to the peephole, so that his vision could escape for a moment from these grim associations. But the prospect that greeted him was scarcely more cheery. *Bereft*, that was the word that came to mind. Bereft of light, and hope. Among the dark, soot-blackened buildings, most with boarded-up windows, the German barbershop was a curious anomaly. It was not surprising that it had caught Inchball's eye. Admittedly it was at the end of the alley nearest the Strand, just in from the arched passageway that communicated with that thoroughfare. The passageway itself was reasonably well-maintained; it appeared to have received its last coat of whitewash within living memory. The shop could be seen as part of that world, looking out on to the Strand, turning a blind eye to the dilapidation and despair that lay two paces along.

Macadam's faith in human progress was momentarily shaken. The existence of these houses at the beginning of the twentieth century outraged him. *How could people live like this?* His outrage settled into an easy disgust.

For reasons of his own, he was more troubled by the effect the alley seemed to have on light. It sucked it up. It was not an excessively bright day to begin with. But what light there was drained away into the porous fabric of that starved and stricken turning. There was a very real possibility that the operation would end in failure.

To make matters worse, he had only been given a single two-hundred-foot-long roll of film to play with, some of which he had already used in the tests he had conducted the previous day. He had not yet been able to see any of the results of the tests, in the first place because the film had not come back from the processor's, and secondly because there was still no projector to view it on. He couldn't be sure that he was pointing the camera in exactly the right direction. He was far from certain that there was enough light to effect a successful exposure. There was the very real possibility that he would run all the film he had through the camera without capturing a single decent image.

As yet he had not once given the handle a turn. There had simply been no movement worth recording. A mange-ridden dog had cocked its leg and relieved itself in a doorway. In the same doorway, soon afterwards, a pile of rags had stirred and shifted, revealing itself to be a human being, now presumably one soaked in dog urine.

How could people live like this?

Behind him, crouched against the other side of the van, Inchball sighed and stretched. Macadam felt the van rock on its suspension. 'Steady!' hissed Macadam between his teeth.

'Well!' came Inchball's barely voiced justification.

'*Sshh!*'

Suddenly there was movement outside. Macadam's hand tensed on the handle, but still he held back from cranking it. A diminutive figure had peeled itself away from another doorway and stepped out into the gloom. A child, a grubby-faced girl, lifted her head slowly, as if it was immeasurably heavy, and looked around. Her expression was resentful and at the same time confused, as if she did not understand how she came to be here. She eyed the van suspiciously. Formerly, it had been a baker's van, and the advertising was still painted on the outside. A look of cunning settled over the girl's features. She glanced furtively up and down the alley, before pulling her shawl over her head.

Then she stepped out and approached the van, causing Macadam to lose sight of her as she went to the back. The rear door handle began to rattle and pivot.

Macadam turned in Inchball's direction and held his finger tensely over his lips. In the darkness, he could not make out Inchball's expression, but he could sense his partner's stiffening.

Naturally, Macadam had taken the precaution of securing the door. But the little would-be thief was persistent. Soon, more children emerged from different doorways and joined her. A lively and surprisingly foul-mouthed discussion broke out.

'Ge' a fuckin' brick and smash the fuckin' window,' one piping voice suggested. The rear door had a window that had been blacked out and painted over.

'My ol' man's got a fuckin' crowbar. We can fuckin' crack it open.'

'Wha' the fuckin' 'ell is it?'

'It's a fuckin' baker's van, innit?'

''Ow you know that?'

'I can fuckin' read, carn I?'

'Who taugh' you 'a fuckin' read? You fuckin' cun'.'

The van began to rock. The handle on the rear door rattled even more violently than before. Macadam closed his eyes and shook his head, willing the awful creatures to go away. This was a circumstance he had not foreseen. His face tightened into a grimace of despair.

He felt one of Inchball's fingers prod him in the side. He could make out the other man's dim silhouette. His arms seemed to be raised in a questioning gesture. Macadam shrugged his response.

Their options were limited. They could sit still and hope that the brats lost interest and went away. Or they could make their presence known and hope to drive them away.

The rocking motion of the van accelerated. For a moment, it seemed possible that the gang might be capable of upturning it.

Macadam risked putting his eye to the peephole again. A small boy with an enraged expression – as if he were personally affronted by the van's refusal to open up and deliver its bounty – was prowling along its side. Suddenly, he stopped in his steps and glared up directly into Macadam's eye.

There was no doubt about it. He had been seen.

''Ere, you,' said the boy to one of his companions, an older, lankier version of himself. 'Gi' us a fuckin' piggy back.'

'You wha'?'

'You fuckin' 'eard me. You wan' some of that fuckin' bread, don' ya?'

The other boy scowled but did as he was directed. Despite his smaller stature, the first boy seemed to exercise some authority over the group. Macadam thought he recognized his voice as that of the child who could read.

Now the boy's angry face was level with the peephole. He leaned in and put his own eye to the hole, so that he was eyeball to eyeball with Macadam. Then he leaned away and, before Macadam realized what was happening, stuck his forefinger through the hole straight into Macadam's eye.

Macadam cried out, and recoiled from the attack, falling back into Inchball, whose reaction was characteristically profane. The boy started to laugh. His laughter was an ugly, jagged sound, every bit as angry as his expression.

'Wha' is it? Wha' the fuck is it?' demanded one of his fellows.

'There's some dirty geezer in here. Some dirty fuckin' peepin' Tom.'

Macadam groaned.

Someone banged on the side of the van. Presumably the boy. Immediately, the rest of the gang joined in.

Uncharacteristically, Macadam cursed under his breath. It felt as though they were trapped inside a kettle drum.

All at once, the drumming stopped.

An accented man's voice addressed them. 'What is going on, you children?'

'A German!' whispered Inchball. He pushed Macadam out of the way to peer out of the peephole.

'There's some fuckin' geezer in there.'

'I see. Here. Money for you all. Now leave. I will sort this. You children go and play now.'

Whatever largesse the German had bestowed was met with approval. 'Ta, mister. You're alrigh', you are! A proper gent.'

The children's unruly hilarity scattered. The alley fell suddenly quiet. Macadam could hear the German's footsteps as he paced round the van. And then, without a further word, the footsteps went away.

THIRTEEN

Only one vertical wall extended to the full height of the department. Usually, in the middle of an investigation, it was covered in photographs of victims, maps, crime-scene diagrams, as well as lists of suspects' names, together with photographs if available, and any other relevant notes. It was blank now, dully reflecting the wan sunlight from the window opposite, and reflecting also their lack of a case.

Since the fiasco in the van, it had naturally been difficult to continue

the surveillance of the barbershop. Inchball had gone through his reper-
toire of disguises, before settling on the identity of a vagrant and taking
up residence in a doorway opposite the shop. He had fallen into a turf
war with the other tramp in the street, but had succeeded in seeing the
fellow off thanks to his superior physical strength and sobriety. He had
only had to tap the man once to knock him to the ground. A blow from
which he did not immediately get up. For one sickening moment,
Inchball thought he had killed the man. Not that he would regret his
passing, simply that it would be another inconvenient distraction. What
on earth would he do with the body? Fortunately, Inchball's brusque
encouragements – 'Come on, ya bastard! On ya feet, ya louse!' –
coupled with a mild toeing, succeeded in rousing him.

As well as taking over the tramp's patch, he also inherited the
attentions of the pissing dog, who seemed to exist solely to add
misery to the lives of the abject.

But the main problem with this disguise was that, while it enabled
Inchball to linger unobtrusively in the alleyway, it was all too
conspicuous elsewhere. It made it impossible for him to follow
anyone who came out of the shop and down on to the Strand.

Quinn was especially keen to track down the man they called
Hartmann, who appeared to be Dortmunder's most frequent visitor,
despite being – as Inchball continued to point out – 'as bald as a
bleedin' coot', and in no obvious need of a shave. Inchball was
convinced that it had been Hartmann who had paid off the urchins.

Macadam had sunk into a slough of despond over his failure to
record anything significant on the kinematographic camera, and the
subsequent abandonment of that particular method of investigation.

Even the arrival of the projector – a Gaumont Chrono – did little
to rouse him from his depression. He withdrew into the task of familiarizing himself with its operation and morosely informed Quinn that
there was a discrepancy between the voltage of the power supply at
the Yard and that required by the machine. The explanation went over
Quinn's head, but what he understood was that another piece of
equipment had to be bought: a rheostat. This entailed the submission
of a second formal request to the Procurement Department. There
was no guarantee they would approve it. In fact, it was likely they
would take the view that they had already spent enough on Special
Crime's new toy. Quinn felt sure they would refuse the application,
even though the equipment they had already purchased was useless
without this new piece of kit, and therefore the money they had spent

so far, wasted. At any rate, there would be a delay.

The setback seemed to act as a spur to Macadam. He remembered that he had a pal who was something of a dab hand at all things electrical. The pal was able to lend them a suitable rheostat of his own, which he set up in the department so that Macadam could operate the projector, and spark the electrical arc lamp that provided the illumination.

And so Macadam was able to show them the test footage he had got back from the processors.

They did what they could to turn the department into a kind of picture palace, draping Quinn's trademark herringbone Ulster over the window to block out the light. It was only a partial success.

However, as the film began to ratchet through the escapement, Quinn felt the same anticipatory excitement – the sense that he was about to witness wonders and magic – that he always experienced when he went to a moving picture show. But as the seeping blurs of grey, white and black began to swoop across the glowing patch of wall, his excitement turned to bemusement. It was hard to tell exactly what he was seeing. Part of the frame was cut off in a block of heavy shade. The rest appeared to be out of focus.

The show was over in a matter of minutes, seconds even. There was an equal interval of deep, contemplative silence. Inchball broke it with a slow, sarcastic hand-clap.

'There are one or two adjustments to be made,' admitted Macadam as he removed Quinn's Ulster from the window. It was a relief to get the light back. 'I think I know what I have to do. The camera was not in the best position within the van. The lens was partially obscured. And I need to adjust the focus. I evidently made a mistake in calculating the depth of field. It's all to be expected. Next time . . . next time, we'll get it right.'

Quinn felt sorry for his sergeant and so mooted the possibility of setting up the camera in one of the boarded-up houses opposite. However, it turned out that the buildings were far from derelict. The occupants guarded their thresholds with all the jealous pride of suburban householders, but with a more suspicious and leaner glower. There could be no question of prevailing upon their public spiritedness or patriotism. Money might have bought access to a viewpoint, but the venality that allowed that also made them unreliable conspirators. They were just as likely to betray them to the Germans in return for a few bob.

And so Quinn had shifted the focus of the operation away from the shop on to the mysterious Hartmann himself.

He and Macadam took up positions on the Strand, on either side of the arch that led to the alley. Neither of them had seen Hartmann, but Inchball had repeated his incredulous description of the man so often that they felt sure they would recognize him. Should they see a large, bald, mustachioed man enter the passageway, Macadam would follow him in at a discreet distance and seek confirmation from Inchball, who would be in position on the other side.

Macadam's spirits had rallied decisively when Quinn had held out the prospect of setting up the camera at whatever location they followed Hartmann to.

For Quinn, maintaining his concentration and enthusiasm proved harder. He continued to be visited by the image of Miss Dillard's reproachful eyes. For example, once when he was looking into a ladies' outfitters, he noticed that every one of the plaster dummies seemed to possess eyes of the same pewter grey, eyes that were not just *like* Miss Dillard's; they *were* Miss Dillard's. And every pair of those eyes was turned on him. If it was a sign that his conscience was troubling him, he could not think why. Or at least, why now, more than any other time. He had not spoken to her since the incident on the landing, over a week ago now. In fact, he had avoided all contact with any of his fellow lodgers. And so he had committed no new blunders. Her eyes had nothing fresh to hold against him, unless it was the very fact of his isolation that was the source of her reproach.

The weather continued to be changeable. Brief bursts of sunlight were quickly forgotten in the pervading damp gloom. The constant flow of traffic around them worked in their favour, creating an ever-changing population on the street. No one else was there for long enough to remark on the two men who never seemed to go anywhere. (Quinn took the precaution of flashing his warrant card at the local bobby, in order to forestall any unwanted enquiries from that quarter.)

They took it in turns to break, either to grab a hurried pie or a chop in a cheap restaurant on the Strand, or to take a leak in the public convenience in Fleet Street. The rest of the time they pretended interest in shop windows into which they barely glanced, Macadam because he had one eye on the entrance to the alley, Quinn because . . . well, it was enough to say his mind was usually elsewhere.

Herr Hartmann did not return to the shop. Dortmunder appeared to live over his shop, alone. When he pulled down the shutters in the evening, a light came on upstairs. As far as they could observe, he went out only to buy provisions from nearby shops. Not only did Hartmann not show, but there were no visitors to the shop at all, at least during the hours that they watched it. Apart from Inchball, who on Thursday afternoon put aside his disguise to return for another shave, Dortmunder did not have a single customer for three days. The incident with the van had clearly spooked Hartmann. Whatever operation he was running from the shop, it appeared to have been shut down. Their surveillance was effectively stalled.

And so, at the end of a fruitless, unrewarding week, Quinn called his officers in.

It was Friday morning. He stared at the wall, willing something to appear on its blank surface, a photograph, a diagram, anything that might give them a lead.

'We have to look at this from a different angle,' he said at last. As if to prove the point he turned his back on the wall and sat down at his desk. As it was, neither of his sergeants contradicted him.

Quinn looked down at the card lying on his desk.

You are cordially invited to the world premiere of
THE EYES OF THE BEHOLDER

'The German community in London would naturally be interested in any cultural event which is connected to their country of birth. This film, for example. I would hazard a guess that Konrad Waechter, the man responsible for it, is a compatriot of theirs. Perhaps he is known to them.'

'I should say so!' Macadam sat up with sudden energy. 'I have read about Waechter in the *Kinematograph Enthusiast's Weekly*. His last film was very popular, I believe, and the new one is set to cause even more of a sensation. By Jove, sir! You have been invited to the premiere!'

Quinn's gaze went to the end of the text on the card:

On Friday, April 17th 1914, at 7 p.m.
Before an audience of specially invited celebrities

'The seventeenth. That is today. Perhaps I *will* go, after all. I will take Inchball with me so that he may look out for Hartmann. And Dortmunder too, for that matter.'

Macadam was crestfallen. Quinn couldn't bear to see the

enthusiasm knocked out of his sergeant. If Macadam was to be morose, then there was no hope at all.

'Macadam, you may come along too, of course. We will get you in somehow. Now, you said you have read about this fellow, Waechter. May I see the article?'

Macadam's expression lit up. With an eager bustle, he retrieved his collection of *Kinematograph Enthusiast's Weeklies* from a drawer in his desk. A few moments of happy thumbing later, he spread out the article in question in front of Quinn. There was a photograph of a young man whose most distinguishing feature was the black patch over one eye. Though dressed in a vaguely bohemian fashion, his bearing seemed somewhat stiff and formal, his expression stern. This was in marked contrast with the rather foolish grin of the man whose hand he was photographed shaking. The second man was dressed ostentatiously in a flamboyant overcoat with astrakhan cuffs and collars. The caption read: *Renowned Austrian director Konrad Waechter agrees two-week exclusive with Mr Porrick of Porrick's Palaces for his new masterpiece,* The Eyes of the Beholder.

'So he is not German?' said Quinn.

'Same thing, ain't it?' put in Inchball, peering over his shoulder to see the photograph. 'They're all bloody foreigners.'

'Why does he wear the eye patch, do you know?' wondered Quinn.

'It is rumoured that he lost his eye in a duel,' said Macadam. 'According to that story, he can't go back to his native Austria on account of charges relating to the duel. He killed his opponent.'

Quinn felt the kick of a familiar excitement chivvy his heart. 'He killed a man?' He stared for a moment longer at the photograph, suddenly very interested in Konrad Waechter.

FOURTEEN

'Do you have it?' The words crackled urgently in the darkness.

Solly 'Max' Maxwell ignored the question, and kept his back turned to the questioner. He was bent over the glowing rods, intent on his task. He had to admit he took pleasure in keeping the great man waiting. Porrick may have been the boss, but it didn't hurt to remind him where the power really lay in their relationship. Whatever Porrick was, he was nothing without Max.

Max brought the darkness to life. He made it pulse and flicker. He even gave it its voice, a soft, rhythmic ticking that was so close to silence that it was easy to miss it. The pianist's jarring tinkle drowned it out. So too did the coarse laughter that broke out at intervals from the audience. A single gasp of wonder or horror was too much for its nervous stutter. But he was closest to that voice. He heard its endless mechanical whisper even when others did not. At times it seemed the darkness spoke to him alone.

It was a painstaking task. His back ached with the effort of it, crouched over the illuminant, keeping his eye on the arc light, always ready to turn the handles and draw the imperceptibly diminishing rods together. It required skill and precision, to strike the rods and then draw them apart to the perfect distance for the spark to leap and burn the carbon. It required application, to maintain the optimum gap. It required concentration, to stay watchful for the ever-present threat of conflagration.

'Max?'

The urgency in Porrick's voice was echoed by a high-pitched yelp. This was something new. Despite his determination to keep his boss waiting, Max could hold out no longer. He risked a quick backward glance to discover the source of the animal sound. A small, wiry-haired dog stirred restlessly in Porrick's arms.

'What the hell is that?'

'What? Oh . . . this is Scudder.'

At the mention of his name, the dog gave another highly strung yelp and redoubled its efforts to free itself from Porrick's restraining hold.

'Why have you brought a dog into my box? A Yorkshire terrier at that!'

'Don't you like Yorkies?'

'I hate them. They're so . . . nervy. The operator's box is no place for an animal like that. For any animal! Have you any idea what would happen if it ran amok and knocked the machine over?'

The nitrate film stock was the most flammable material imaginable. It was as if this was the price that had to be paid for the revelations it effected – some kind of secret compact between the film and the darkness. And Max knew better than anyone what could happen if you allowed your vigilance to slip. He'd seen his mate Ted's charred body after they'd dragged it out of the basement of Porrick's Palace, Islington. The flames had been so hot and fierce they had lifted the paving stones outside.

Surely Porrick would have had no desire to repeat that experience? But it seemed that Porrick was incapable of learning from his mistakes. He truly had a genius for irresponsibility.

'Are you insane?'

'I wanted to show him to Waechter.'

'Waechter?'

'Have you seen him? He was supposed to be delivering the final print for tonight.'

'He's not here. He hasn't been. I don't have the print.'

'You don't have it?'

'That's what I said, isn't it?'

'You shouldn't talk to me like that. You ought to remember . . .'

'What?'

'Your position. You ought to show me more respect. I could . . .'

'You could fire me?'

'Yes.'

'Go on then.'

'Well, I just want you to show me more respect. That's all.'

'If that's all . . . I have a job to do here. If you will be so kind as to bugger off and leave me alone, *Mister* Porrick, *sir*. And take your nasty little dog with you.'

Max was bent over the rods again, as if his own words had spurred him back to vigilance. He heard the door shut as Porrick left him to his asbestos-lined brick box.

His whole body ached with the strain of watching the fierce white glow that he kindled just inches from the running film. He thought of a caveman nurturing the precious spark of fire. Like the audience in the kinema gathering in front of the glowing screen, the members of the tribe would huddle around the source of warmth and light, as the fire-bearer span tales to ease their fears. He thought of the honour in which such a man would be held. He would be seen as a magician or a priest; he might even be considered the tribal chief, Max reflected ruefully.

They ran films on a continuous programme at Porrick's Palaces, which put a strain on Max's back all right. Audience members came and went as they wished. It made sense when all the films they showed were single-reel shorts. But nowadays the trend was for longer films, with advertised starting times. And if there was any technical problem that delayed the start of the main feature, it was Max who got it in the neck.

For all this, for the long hours, the back ache, the physical danger, for all his skill and expertise, his facility at operating the projector, his calm and expert handling of the film, his knowledge of the mysteries of electricity (who else there understood how the rheostat worked – or even what it was?) he was paid sixty shillings a week. True, it was more than any other member of the staff, but it was nothing when you compared it to Porrick's box office takings. And it was a long way short of the respect that the prehistoric fire-bearer had received.

One thing he would say for Porrick: he had not skimped on the machinery. The operating box was equipped with two Brockliss Motiographs, each adapted to run off electric motors. The initial expense of installing the motors might be thought surprising for a man like Porrick. But it paid off in the long term as it meant that the box could be manned by a single operator: Max. This was fine by Max. He didn't need any company other than the darkness. He resented every intruder.

The Brockliss Motiograph was an imposing, double-headed machine. The twin light boxes allowed for seamless dissolving transitions between reels. It was almost like having four projectors in there. Even more important was the efficiency of the shutter mechanism, which retained thirty or forty per cent more light than other kinematographic machines on the market. When you coupled this with an electric light source (as Porrick had) and fitted a Dallmeyer projection lens (as Porrick had) the intensity and quality of the image projected was second to none.

Of course, all this was simply sound business sense on Porrick's part. The Leicester Square Picture Palace was his showcase theatre, in the heart of the West End. It was essential that the picture-going experience he offered matched – or surpassed – that provided by his rivals. Gone were the days when you could get away with a flickering display of dim shapes viewed through a shifting fog.

Whatever he laid out in projection equipment would be recouped in takings.

But Max knew all about Porrick's reputation. The rumours of fraud. The spell as a patent medicine salesman. Hair restorer, he had heard. *Good God, how did you get from hair restorer to picture palaces!* There was even a rumour that he had left America under a cloud and could never return. But you didn't have to just listen to the rumours. The manslaughter charge was a matter of public record, even if he had got off. Well, a man like Porrick *would* get off, wouldn't he? It stood to reason. He'd got to the witnesses, so it went. Max wouldn't put it past him.

On paper, everything about Porrick was flashy and fake. You could only expect a man like that to cut corners. But he hadn't. You could see it in the uniforms of the attendants. They were as crisp and smart as any you would find on a railway guard. The tip-up seating was provided by Lazarus and Company, and the plush burgundy upholstery was regularly repaired. That time some idiot had taken a knife to the seat backs? Porrick hadn't just settled for the gashes to be sewn up; he'd had the whole row reupholstered.

He had spared no expense. Max had to give him that. Even splashed out on a Tyler vaporizer to refresh the air with disinfectant.

But most importantly, you could see the level of investment out there on the screen.

The condenser of the Brockliss Motiograph threw the trapped light forward, gathering up the tiny shadow-dances in the gate, shooting them through the projection lens and out over the heads of the audience. Motes spun in the beam, dizzied and dazzled by its passage through them. And where the beam touched the far wall, silent, shimmering beings sprang into life, luminous spirits conjured out of the darkness.

Why, though? Why had a fraudster and snake-oil salesman gone to all this expense? There were cheaper machines than the Motiograph. And he needn't have paid extra to fit a Dallmeyer projection lens. He could have simply painted the screen on the wall with whitewash, instead of using the patented Whitisto screen paint at 7/6d a gallon.

There could only be one explanation. And you could hear the answer in the urgent impatience of his enquiry about the missing print, and see it in his eyes, in the jealous, coveting gleam that shone as he handled the cans of film when they came in. Magnus Porrick had got the bug. He had fallen in love with moving pictures. No doubt he had been drawn into the business with the intention of turning a quick profit. Riding the fad until it ran out of steam, at which time he would move on to some other way of duping the public – and investors – out of their cash. But something unexpected had happened. He had taken the trouble to look up at the screen. And what he had seen had transfixed, and then trans-formed him.

There was a quiet knock at the door. *Won't they leave him alone!* At least this time, the intruder had had the courtesy to knock, and was waiting for Max to admit him.

'Yes?'

He heard the door open. 'Herr Maxvell?'

Max turned to see the half-silhouetted form of Konrad Waechter in the doorway; his upright, almost military bearing was unmistak-able. As always, he was dressed in a cream silk shirt with a mandarin collar, jodhpurs and riding boots. And, of course, the black patch was in place over one eye. The right eye, he could see. Was it always the right? He doubted it. He was sure Waechter wore the patch for effect and liked to alternate the eye he wore it over, presumably because it amused him to do so.

Waechter was clutching a small film can to his chest. Max was a little surprised at the size of the singular can. 'Is that it?'

Waechter frowned.

'The print for this evening's screening?'

'This?' Waechter tapped the can. '*Nein.* Diaz is bringing the film. He vill be here presently. I have just now left him in Cecil Court making the final touchings. I have come only to tell you not to *vah*-rry. You vill have the film presently.' Waechter's accent was heavy, almost incomprehensible at times.

'I wasn't worried. Don't make no difference to me, one way or the other. I get paid whether there's a film to show or not. And besides, I'd just rerun today's programme.'

Waechter's eye bulged in alarm at this prospect.

'Nah.' Max turned to check on the rods of the arc lamp. 'It's Porrick you need to worry about. He was looking for you, by the way. He had some dog with him. Wanted to show it to you.'

'A *daw-g-g*?'

'That's right. Horrible little blighter.'

'Vy does he vant to show me a *daw-g-g*?'

'Why does Porrick do anything? He must think there's money in it.'

'*Mah-ney*? But how could there be *mah-ney* in a *daw-g-g*?'

Max shrugged. 'Ain't you seen *Rescued By Rover*? A very popular title, that is. Everybody knows Porrick has ambitions to go into the motion picture production business. He's been in his element, hobnobbing with all you motion picture types. And it makes sense, don't it? If he can make the films *and* show the films . . .'

'But vy does he vant to show the *daw-g-g* to *me*?'

'Look, I don't know. You'd better talk to him yourself. But the way I see it, he's gonna need someone to direct these films, ain't he?'

'No! No! I do not make films with *daw-g-gs*! *Ich bin ein Künstler!*'

Max put his finger to his lips. 'Sshh! There's no need for language like that. They'll hear you out there.'

'But I am an artist! You understand?'

Max glanced uneasily at the film counter. It was getting near the end of the current reel. There was a possibility that he had left it too late and there would be a gap in the programme.

'Listen, I've got work to do here. So, if you don't mind . . .' He put his eye level with the arc light in the second projector, turning the screws to close the gap in the rods in preparation for striking.

'Ah, there you are, Waechter!' It was the very worst moment for Porrick to return with his yapping dog. The loathsome animal must have run between Waechter's legs. It skittered into the operating box and ran in and out of the iron stands of the projectors. It looked to Max like nothing so much as a wig pulled along on a wire.

'Get that animal out of here!' cried Max, trying to fend it away from the delicate, combustible machinery.

Fortunately, for some reason, the dog became suddenly very interested in Konrad Waechter, jumping up at him and snapping excitedly.

'You've met Scudder, I see!' said Porrick, cheerfully. 'Down, Scudder, down . . . good boy!'

Waechter's eye glared imposingly. Evidently fearing that the dog's purpose was to rob him of his precious film can, he held it up over his head.

Max saw that the film counter on the Motiograph that was in operation was getting dangerously close to the end. The reel was about to run out any moment. And with all the interruptions, he hadn't got round to setting up another film on the second projector.

Waechter's hand holding the film can dropped a little. It seemed as though he was handing it to Max.

In his confusion and panic, Max reached out to take the can. 'Do you want me to play that? What is it, a preview?'

Waechter's reaction was as fast as it was shocking. He swung his hand out wildly, catching Max on the side of the head with the edge of the can. The blow was sharp and painful, as well as unexpected. It threw Max off balance. Luckily he didn't fall on to either of the Motiographs. Instead, he crashed into the winding table, causing empty spools to fly up and scatter.

The voice of the darkness changed subtly. The mechanical stutter ceased. A high, free-wheeling whine took its place. The film passing through the projector had now run out. The motor whirred without resistance. There was a rhythmic click as the full spool raced round inside the covered take-up.

Cries of derision could be heard from the auditorium as the screen went blank.

Waechter clutched the can to his chest protectively. 'It is not for you. Do you understand?'

The director darted from the operating box, the unwanted dog yap-yapping eagerly after him.

'You'd better get the next film on, quick,' said Porrick, dashing out after his latest investment.

FIFTEEN

The days were longer now. There was an expansive feeling to the evenings, as if they were being spun out of a weightless, elastic material. A net to keep the night at bay forever. Quinn was reminded of a springtime long ago.

The trees in the centre of Leicester Square bore white glimmering fruit, light bulbs strung on wires through the branches. The restaurants and theatres around the outside blazed with a gaudy allure: pushy, self-confident, alive with a shallow glitter.

Electricity still had the power to take his breath away, as well as the power to turn night to day. It created a world in which there was nowhere to hide. As a policeman, Quinn might have been expected to welcome this. But Quinn's peculiarities of temperament were such that often he found himself in sympathy with those who sought out the shadows.

The luminaries milling in the square seemed to crackle and buzz, as if an electric charge was passing through them. Or perhaps they generated their own energy. The men were, for the most part, in evening dress – top-hatted and tailed; the women, furred and bejewelled. Quinn had come straight from the Yard in his Ulster. Eyes were turned on him with something that he took for mockery. He was pointed out, his name – or rather his nickname – confidentially imparted behind the backs of hands.

It was all intensely embarrassing, though Macadam and Inchball seemed to be enjoying themselves well enough.

'We should have dressed,' muttered Quinn.

'With respect an' all that, guv, that's a load of eyewash, an' you know it. They would 'ave been disappointed if you 'adn't come as you are.'

'But people are laughing at us.'

'They ain't *larfin'* . . . not as such. Seems to me, guv, more like they're . . . *delighted*! They wanted Quick-Fire Quinn, an' they got Quick-Fire Quinn.'

'You're not making this any easier, Inchball.'

'I wonder who's paying for all this electricity?' said Macadam, gazing up at the luminous spots on the trees with a look of mingled incredulity and admiration. 'It must cost a tidy fortune to keep this lot burning. It's not as if it has gone dark yet, is it? And had it done so, the lights in the trees would hardly afford the most effective illumination.' Macadam shook his head in disapproval. 'They are merely for decoration!' The realization struck him with the force of a scandal.

'Get *out* of it!' scoffed Inchball. 'You love it. 'Ere, Mac, what did Mrs Macadam say to your comin' to the picture palace without her?'

Macadam appeared shame-faced. 'I . . . err . . . thought it best not to tell her the precise nature of our operation.'

'I betcha din'!'

'You fellows would be well-advised to remember that we are indeed here on an operation,' put in Quinn. 'Inchball, keep your eyes open. If you see that Hartmann fellow, or the barber, Dortmunder, don't let them out of your sight.'

'What if Dortmunder sees me, guv? He'll recognize me and give the game away. I don't reckon Hartmann will know me, seeing as 'ow I was all wrapped up in a towel when 'e came in.'

'Feign surprise. You're entitled to be here in a public place, I think. There need not be anything suspicious in it.'

'Do I express my admiration for the Bismarckian system yet, sir?'

'No, but it would be a good opportunity to express your admiration for German motion pictures.'

Quinn drew himself up and looked around. The half-inquisitive, half-mocking gazes had settled down, the novelty of his presence there having apparently worn off.

It is strange to find people you are not looking for, in a context you do not expect to find them. So disconcerting was it for Quinn to see Miss Ibbott in the crowd that he did not acknowledge her.

Mr Timberley saw him first and pointed him out to Mr Appleby and Miss Ibbott with a kind of shy, evasive grin. The two men waved cheerily, though a sour expression settled over Miss Ibbott and her hands remained firmly by her sides. It was Mr Appleby who pushed his way through the crowd to speak to Quinn (taking some risk, Quinn thought, leaving Miss Ibbott alone with his rival).

'I say, Mr Quinn! Fancy seeing you here!'

'Good evening to you, Mr Appleby.'

'Are you here on a mission?'

'Good heavens! Whatever gave you that idea?'

'That was not a denial. I therefore deduce that you *are* here on a mission!'

'I most certainly do deny it. I am here to see the moving picture presentation at Porrick's Palace.'

'The premiere? Do you have a ticket?'

'I do.'

'Lucky blighter. I wish I had a couple of tickets. You can't get them for love nor money, now, I believe.'

'Are there not three in your party?'

'What of it?'

'You said you wanted a couple of tickets. I am wondering whom of your companions you would abandon.'

'Need you ask? I say, has Miss Ibbott ever said anything to you . . . you know, about myself or Timberley? About where her preference might lie?'

'You will hardly be surprised to learn that I am not in Miss Ibbott's confidence.'

'What about Miss Dillard? Perhaps Miss Ibbott said something to her and she confided it to you?'

'I am no more in Miss Dillard's confidence than Miss Ibbott's.' Quinn had a vision of Miss Dillard's grey eyes, looking searchingly, sadly, into his. As if to say, *And whose fault is that?*

'At any rate, it is pleasant to promenade the square, rubbing shoulders with famous celebrities such as yourself.' Appleby made this comment without any real enthusiasm. He looked morosely over to where Timberley had succeeded in provoking uncontrolled – and unladylike – guffaws from Miss Ibbott. The young man nodded decisively. 'Enjoy the show, Mr Quinn.' He pushed his way back to rejoin his companions, his face resolutely set.

A fresh charge of energy passed through the crowd. There were cheers and applause. Flash powder explosions signalled the presence of the press.

As far as Quinn could gather, it was all in honour of a small group who had just come out of the entrance to Porrick's Palace. The three policemen found themselves unconsciously pulled along with the crowd towards this group, until they were just a few feet away from them. There was a strange and impressive intensity to the physical presence of these individuals. They were no larger than ordinary mortals, and there was nothing abnormal about the surfaces of their beings – that's to say, they did not glisten or pulsate, and were not fashioned from burnished steel. But there was no denying that they exercised an inordinate hold over the gathering.

Leading them out, with a high-stepping, almost prancing gait, was a tall, fair-haired man wearing an eye patch. Quinn recognized Waechter from his photograph. He reached a point in front of the theatre and held himself excessively upright, almost bending over backwards in his desire to reach the perpendicular. There was something defiant about this stance, his chest pushed aggressively forwards. It was as if he believed that people expected him to be cowed and defensive, and he was determined to prove them wrong.

Waechter held out his right arm towards a woman so petite she might almost be described as a midget. And yet she was compellingly attractive. Her physical beauty, as well as Waechter's strange air of authority, had been part of what had drawn them towards the group. This was magnetism, Quinn realized. He believed she was the first truly gorgeous woman he had ever seen. His heart quickened at her proximity. The evening sun seemed to lavish its last rays on her alone, glinting in the golden bed of hair in which her pretty pillbox hat was settled, twinkling in her cornflower-blue eyes, burnishing her perfect cheeks with a gentle glow. As if this moment, and her loveliness, was the whole focus of its existence.

Her smile was serene but, more than that, it was generous. You felt, when it was directed towards you, that a blessing had been bestowed. And yet, there was no element of condescension in it. It made you believe that you were worthy of it. That you had some share in it. It was as much your smile as hers.

'Who is she?' asked Quinn.

'Don't you know?' said Macadam.

'An actress?' Quinn knew as he asked the question that she could be nothing else.

'She's more than an actress, sir. She's a star. She's Eloise.'

'She has beautiful eyes,' observed Quinn.

His two sergeants nodded in agreement, but said nothing.

'She is . . . French?' asked Quinn.

'Yes.'

Quinn thought back to his last case. He had believed the girls working as professional mannequins at Blackley's department store to be attractive. Certainly they were youthful and bold and female enough to thoroughly discomfit him. But not one of them, he saw now, could hold a candle to this Eloise. Except perhaps the girl whose death had sparked that last investigation. He could not say for sure, however, because by the time he got to see her, she was beyond such considerations. Ironically, she had been French too, the only one of Blackley's fashion mannequins who really was.

He wondered whether Eloise would turn out to be genuinely French. This was a business based on illusion and pretence. It was possible that no one was who they seemed to be.

The thought brought him back to the reason they were there. 'All right, you men. Time to find our Germans, if they're here.'

But neither sergeant could take his eyes off the actress.

There was some mute buffoonery with a stout man whose deep-set eyes gave his face a mournful but slightly seedy cast. The crowd responded with far more hilarity than the dumb show warranted. Quinn understood that their laughter was not for the mournful comedian. It was for her, Eloise, to reciprocate the generosity of her smile. She brought out the best in them.

Quinn studied the rapt expressions of some of those watching. Mouths open, hanging on every gesture: for there were no words, as if the actors really were mutes, and it was for that reason that all the films they appeared in were silent. But, of course, what they were doing was playfully showing their commitment to their chosen medium. They were bringing the voiceless world of the film out into the lively bustling clamour of Leicester Square. And in so doing, they were beginning the enchantment.

As Quinn scanned the faces, he had a premonition that he would see someone else that he recognized. A moment later, he caught sight of Lord Dunwich, standing to one side of the group of film people.

It was an electrifying discovery.

Quinn tracked Dunwich's gaze back towards the troupe of performers. In among them, he spotted a couple who seemed strangely awkward and ill at ease considering they were presumably actors. They stood slightly back from the play-acting, distancing themselves from it. Their expressions of hilarity were disengaged and forced. Perhaps they were simply bad actors, amateurs essentially, who had been roped in to take on walk-on parts as servants or bystanders. Or perhaps they were the sort of people who had more ambition than talent, and had been drawn into the motion picture business because they thought it would be an easy way to make their fortune. Whatever the reason, they seemed to be connected, in their shared contempt for the activity in which they were engaged.

The girl – a brunette in her twenties – was pretty enough, but of course she suffered in comparison to Eloise. There was something affecting about her face, a kind of frailty, but he realized that it was just as likely to make you despise her as love her. It seemed put on. A delicate, gossamer mask covering a hard-faced egotism. He couldn't quite believe in her, and certainly didn't trust her.

As for the man, if Quinn had been forced to make a snap judgement of his character based on this first impression, he would have said *lazy* and *selfish*. He might even have gone further than that. There was a ruthless quality to his undoubted good looks, something cruel as well as calculating. It was clear that he approved of his own handsomeness, and valued it considerably, but only for what it brought him, for the doors – and purses – it opened.

If he was not a gigolo, then he was a pimp. And that was not to exclude many other unsavoury things that he might also be.

Of course, Quinn accepted that he might well be doing them both a great injustice. And really they were nothing to him, and he should not have let himself become distracted by them. Except . . . except that he detected that they were somehow interested in Lord Dunwich. He had noticed subtle glances pass between them, indicative of some dark purpose regarding his lordship. He did not think it boded well for Lord Dunwich that they had him in their sights.

But really, he was not here to babysit the man from the Admiralty. 'Get on with it, you two. If Hartmann is here, I want to know.'

Quinn watched Macadam and Inchball milling through the crowd. Despite the differences in their characters, evident in their distinctive gaits, it had to be said that Quinn had never seen two men who were more obviously policemen. If the crowd had not been so intent on the brilliant creatures who were cavorting in front of Porrick's Palace, his sergeants would not have escaped its wary attention.

Quinn turned back to the group of film people. Eloise, of course, drew his gaze. But he found that the man with the eye patch, Waechter, also interested him. The mere knowledge that he had taken a life once suggested that he could do so again. Whether one called it manslaughter or murder, it was the ultimate crime. A man capable of that could reasonably be considered capable of anything.

Waechter directed a few urgent – possibly angry – words towards a man holding a Yorkshire terrier. Quinn was momentarily distracted by the dog, so he did not immediately recognize Porrick. But the fellow's overcoat gave him away. A third man was drawn into the discussion, a dark-complexioned individual, of excessively short stature, and with the look of an indigenous South American. He nodded eagerly as if to reassure the others of something. The dog joined in with a few bad-tempered yaps of his own for good measure.

The exchange had no impact on the actors, who maintained their good-natured rapport with each other and the audience. At least this was the case with Eloise and the stout comedian with the mournful expression. The other couple he had picked out, the ones who had taken an interest in Lord Dunwich, followed the discussion with greedy eyes, as if they suspected that there was profit to be made from whatever might fall out from it.

But the altercation petered out. The reassurances of the South American played a part. So too did the intervention of a large, imperious-looking woman with a spreading bosom who spoke sharply and decisively to the man with the dog.

Quinn looked back to where Lord Dunwich was, and was surprised to see him in conversation with another man he recognized, Harry Lennox, the Irish proprietor of the *Clarion*. He supposed it shouldn't really surprise him that Lennox was here. If he himself had been considered enough of a celebrity to be invited, then the publisher of one of the most widely read newspapers in the country would surely have merited an invitation. But he found it troubling all the same. It was not so long ago that he had been investigating the case in which Lennox had been indirectly involved. He had no wish to be seen by Lennox, or more specifically by his daughter Jane, whom he now noticed was there with her father. She was dressed in an eye-catching gown that seemed to be made entirely of black sequins and black-dyed ostrich feathers attached directly to her skin. Presumably she was in mourning. But she could not mourn discreetly, of course. Being who she was, the spoilt and savage child of a millionaire, she had to mourn fashionably.

The group of film people began to wave and make their way back inside Porrick's Palace. But just as they were doing so, an ugly scene broke out.

A man with his back to Quinn began shouting and gesturing angrily.

Waechter, who was herding his company away, turned for a moment to look at the shouting man. He frowned as he tried to take in what the man was saying. Presumably there was some difficulty with the language. Quinn couldn't be sure, but he thought he made out the word 'Parasites!' followed by something which could have been: 'Without me, you're nothing!'

Waechter dismissed the heckler with an impatient shake of his head and a dark look towards Porrick. The latter took this as a cue to step forward and confront the shouting man. There was something about his manner, a weary brusqueness, that suggested to Quinn that this was not their first encounter.

The crowd had greeted the outburst with nervous hilarity, neutralizing any danger through ridicule. Quinn, however, was gripped by the same ominous sensation that had come over him earlier, the sense that this incident too had something to do with him personally; that dark events were moving towards some kind of climax.

Waechter hurried his actors inside, to be followed in by Porrick and his wife, together with Lord Dunwich, and Harry and Jane Lennox, who presumably were in some way connected with the party of film people. A wider entourage followed behind them.

At the removal of the film people, the man stopped shouting and turned disconsolately away, pushing against the tide of the crowd, who were now forming a queue to be admitted.

As soon as he turned, and Quinn got a clear view of his face, the premonitory feelings that Quinn had experienced earlier were fulfilled. It was the man he had seen in the Tube train compartment.

Quinn observed that the man was wearing the same leather gloves as before. Had he subconsciously noted the gloves already? That would explain the curious dream-like sense of inevitability he had experienced when he saw the man's face.

Quinn felt a strange conflict of emotions. He wanted to detain and challenge the man. But some fierce and almost threatening glint he had caught in the other's eye deterred him. It seemed that he held in his gaze a secret, inexplicably pertinent to Quinn, and which it would not profit Quinn at all to discover.

The man knew that he had been seen. He held Quinn's gaze for long enough to suggest that this did not unduly concern him, that he almost welcomed it. At last he turned and pushed his way through the square. Any thought Quinn might have had of following him was forgotten by the excited return of Macadam and Inchball.

''E's here, guv! We seen 'im, ain't we, Mac!'

For a moment, Quinn thought Inchball was referring to the same man. He frowned in confusion.

''Artmann, guv! 'E was with them film people. Went in with them. Looks like 'e knows Waechter! You was righ', guv!'

Quinn nodded calmly. 'Very well. Inchball, you watch the front. Macadam, go round to the back. There must be a rear exit. I want a man in place to tail him whichever way he comes out. And whatever you do, don't let him know that he's being followed. I shall go inside to watch the film. If Hartmann does have some connection with Waechter, as it now seems likely, then it would be as well for us to familiarize ourselves with what kind of a man Herr Waechter is. This film of his would be a good place to start.'

He looked up at the trees in the centre of the square. The lights in the branches seemed brighter now. But that was merely a function of the darkness thickening around them.

SIXTEEN

A s the lights went out inside the auditorium, bubbles of excitement seemed to float in the darkness. Voices rose to an urgent clamour. It was as if each member of the audience was rushing to get out the single most important thing they would ever say, which had for some reason occurred to them at this inappropriate moment. Then, everyone ran out of words at the same time. Silence hung momentarily above them. Quinn thought he heard a short hiss, like liquid being squirted from a number of atomizers. The air was suddenly pleasantly scented. He felt himself relax. He sensed an easing in the expectant tension all around him.

The band began to play. Because this was a gala occasion, the management of the theatre had evidently supplemented the usual pianist with some string players and a percussionist. The violins came in with a highly charged romantic overture. The darkness seemed to throb and quiver, as if a spasm of emotion had passed through it. Then all at once it burst into shimmering life.

A pair of enormous eyelids opened slowly. Two equally enormous eyes stared out at him. At *him*, at him alone. That was certainly what Quinn felt. Every other man in the auditorium must have felt the same.

For these were the eyes of a woman. And their gaze was one of desire. What man would not wish to think himself the subject of that gaze?

He knew immediately that they were the eyes of the woman he had seen outside the theatre. Eloise. They held the same magnetic power. But something had changed about them, and not just their scale. In the flesh, her eyes had been warm and engaging. They had possessed a human empathy that reached out to whomever they settled upon. Their gaze was inclusive and generous.

Enlarged and isolated from the rest of her features, the eyes became self-possessed and steely. Yes, they desired the unseen object they gazed upon. But this desire was something fierce, dangerous, frightening. It was a desire in which there would be no room for compromise. The gaze of those gigantic eyes demanded everything. And promised nothing in return. It was a gaze that threatened to possess its object, like a demonic force. A gaze that would take you over and make you forget yourself. It would transform you into something you had never imagined you could be. It would never let you go.

The small, sympathetic, very human personality that had charmed the crowd outside the theatre was nowhere to be seen.

The eyes blinked. The viewpoint receded slightly, to show the whole of the face. And now some of that humanity came back into the eyes. The fierceness of the gaze was given a context, and seemed more comprehensible. What defined the gaze, he understood now, was despair. There was a frailty in her expression that the eyes alone had not communicated, a potent combination of vulnerability and defiance.

A hand came sharply into shot, slapping her across the left cheek. The percussionist threw out a perfectly timed snare-shot.

The audience gasped.

The camera closed in again on her eyes. They flared with indignation and then softened into something more recriminatory, regretful even. The music corresponded to these modulations.

At no time was there fear in those eyes.

Then, at last, the camera angle shifted to show the man who was both the recipient of her gaze and her assailant.

Quinn recognized the mournful-faced actor who had been with Eloise outside. But he too had been transformed by the alchemical processes of kinematography. In front of the theatre, he had appeared to be simply a more intense example of humanity, but the same in type as those around him. Somewhat livelier in the fluidity of his expressions, but possessing a self-deprecating jokiness that was comparable to Eloise's blatant generosity of spirit. His face was fascinating, compelling even. But he did not appear to be a different category of being all together.

Paradoxically, devoid of colour and reduced in its dimensions, his image became something far more than the man it represented. Dressed in a white dress uniform, he became the embodiment of every dark and difficult male emotion. (The music from the band rather overstated this, striking up a heavy, melodramatic motif.)

One sensed every aspect of his potential – for love, for violence, for rage, for self-annihilation and forgiveness. And one understood immediately the meaning of that slap, which was not the same as to condone it.

No, Quinn could never forgive that slap. Whatever befell the character in the unfolding drama – and Quinn was certain there would be many and terrible consequences – he had brought it all upon himself with that single act of violence.

But Quinn knew the blow was borne out of impotence. He knew that the cavalry officer was in thrall to her. That the only way to free himself from her was to destroy her.

He himself had felt everything that was expressed in that brooding presence.

And so the film began with a rift between the lovers. In the scenes that followed, set in a city Quinn took to be Vienna, the soldier threw himself into what was clearly meant to be a life of debauchery, indicated by the presence of dancing girls, seedy gambling parties and drunken brawls. It didn't surprise Quinn to see the brunette he had noticed outside among the troupe of semi-naked dancers. The man he had associated with her cropped up too, as a card sharp. He was given a scene in which he upturned a table and threw a punch, only to be horse-whipped by the officer.

Meanwhile, Eloise – or rather, the character she was playing – took to the stage and pursued a career in the dramatic arts. And it seemed she was a great success. Garlands were hurled at her feet. She was shown in her dressing room after a performance as Cleopatra, surrounded by the gifts and cards of admirers.

Quinn's expectation was that her former lover would come to see her in this part, and a resolution effected. But this possibility was not fulfilled. She was visited and wooed by an aristocratic-looking man, who turned out to be the Count of Somewhere or Other. Quinn wondered if it was significant that the man wore a monocle, which he removed to gaze upon Eloise? He did not remember seeing this actor outside. Presumably the cast was mostly foreign, and not all of them had been able to travel for the London premiere.

The storyline reverted to Eloise's former lover, whose descent into ruin and disgrace had evidently progressed. A title screen informed the audience that he had lost his fortune and been forced to resign his commission from the army. When the camera caught up with him, he was living the life of a penniless drunkard in a cheap boarding house. There was a scene in which his rapacious landlord – a crudely depicted Jew – came after him for the rent. An argument at the top of a steep flight of stairs resulted in the impoverished drunk pushing the Jew downstairs. The percussionist had fun matching his drum beats to the actor's tumble. The strings came in piercing and high, a wash of melodrama. The Jew was dead.

The disgraced cavalry officer fled the boarding house in panic, having first helped himself to the coins in the dead man's pockets, and the bank notes from his safe.

As he trudged the banks of a river, which Quinn presumed to be the Danube, a gigantic pair of eyes appeared in the night sky, looking down on him. They were the accusing eyes of his erstwhile lover. Quinn could not help thinking of the way he had been similarly haunted by Miss Dillard's eyes, after the unfortunate incident outside Miss Ibbott's room.

To escape this relentless recrimination, he took refuge in a beer cellar and bawdy house. But the eyes pursued him, and were cleverly superimposed over the eyes of every woman he encountered. Even the prostitute who led him up to a squalid bedroom. She lay back on the bed and looked up at him with Eloise's eyes – in fact, she had become Eloise. There was only one thing he could do. Quinn understood instinctively. In fact, he felt his own hands tightening as the murderer's caress turned into a stranglehold. The woman writhed and died in his hands, and in another clever camera effect, Eloise melted back into the coarse-faced, dull-eyed prostitute.

The band whipped themselves into a frenzy as the killer made his escape.

And then the shocking revelation: the camera returned to a close up of the prostitute's face; both her eyes had been removed.

There were screams from the audience. Even Quinn felt his heart quicken in shock. The cello and double bass hacked a jagged, tuneless seam of notes out of the black abyss.

The music then became abruptly celebratory. Something about it suggested the tolling of church bells.

It seemed to be snowing. And then the snow was revealed as confetti.

Eloise was coming out of a church, newly married to the Count of Somewhere or Other. Her eyes were hidden behind a bridal veil.

A shadowy figure attached itself to the edge of the crowd of well-wishers. Quinn immediately recognized the former cavalry officer, though his appearance had undergone another transformation. He was heavily bearded and wearing dark-lensed spectacles, as well as a homburg and cape. But Quinn's training enabled him to look beyond the surface details. He could tell by the physique and gait that it was the same man. Besides, the band gave the game away by playing the killer's theme.

The couple climbed into an open carriage. The camera picked out the sinister onlooker among those celebrating their departure. The bride's former lover had moved into broad daylight now, so it was possible to see that he was dressed in well-tailored clothes that gave the impression of affluence; certainly he no longer cut the disreputable figure of a drunkard. The money he had stolen from the Jew had evidently enabled him to set himself up. Ironically, the full beard gave him a distinctly Jewish appearance and he looked strikingly similar to the man he had murdered. For the first time Quinn wondered if the landlord and the cavalry officer had both somehow been played by the same actor. He supposed it must have been possible.

The carriage pulled away with a lurch. The camera watched it into the distance. The sense of peril was suspended momentarily as a brief, cheery scherzo played. But the sequence closed with a reprise of the killer's face. The scherzo fell apart into a low, inarticulate rumbling of dread.

The film caught up with the newly-weds in a train compartment. The groom was reading a newspaper. An inter-title flashed the headline to the audience: POLICE IN DARK OVER GRUESOME MURDERS. VICTIMS' EYES REMOVED.

Sensing his bride's interest in the morbid article, he hurriedly folded the paper away and began to make love to her, with kisses on her hands, wrists and neck. Her eyelids fluttered in delight. The audience was once again treated to a close-up of her magnetic eyes.

A ticket collector entered the compartment. Quinn recognized him immediately as the cavalry officer, although his beard was now trimmed into an imperial. Some nagging rationality questioned how he came to be here, dressed in a ticket collector's uniform, but Quinn realized that he had to accept the logic of the motion picture. Things only had to be shown to be made possible. The literal consequence of events, one thing happening after another, was more persuasive than any notion of cause and effect. Nothing caused anything. It simply led to it.

He was watching a dream, he realized. And if he accepted it as that, then whatever happened in the darkness made sense.

For example, there was no point in asking, *How was it possible that Eloise did not recognize the man she had once loved?* By the conventions of the kinematic picture play, it was enough for a character to put on a false beard for him to become utterly unrecognizable.

Of course, the real point, as Quinn instinctively grasped, was not that Eloise had once loved the cavalry officer, but that she still loved him. That she would always love him, no matter what he did. That was evident in the first frames of the film, those which showed her eyes in extreme close-up. It was also, by the logic of melodrama, the reason why her lover had had no choice but to strike her and precipitate their separation.

All of this made absolute sense to Quinn.

And it was not so surprising, really, that she didn't recognize him. It wasn't just that he had put on false whiskers. He had put himself into an entirely different class. He had donned the uniform of a working man. Of course she wouldn't recognize him. She barely looked at him. He had become invisible to her.

Naturally he knew who she was and so stared at her with a dangerous fixity that was underlined by a reprise of his theme from the band.

She only noticed the ticket collector – with a vaguely troubled frown – when he refused to move on, long after he had examined their tickets. It took an interjection from her husband to prompt him to leave them in peace.

By the time the police found the real ticket inspector in the mail carriage, stripped to his underclothes, trussed up and gagged, his imposter had long since jumped from the moving train.

The couple honeymooned in Venice. Inevitably there was a scene on a gondola, and even more inevitably, the extravagantly mustachioed gondolier turned out to be none other than the former cavalry officer. If there were titters at the implausibility of this, Quinn did not hear them. It occurred to Quinn that, by virtue of the murders he had committed, the character had acquired a kind of mythical status, becoming almost a supernatural being, like a Hindu avatar. Or perhaps these scenes were merely the mirror images of those in which the murderer was haunted by the eyes of his beloved? That is to say, the former cavalry officer was not really there, it was simply that Eloise's character saw him wherever she looked.

When the couple dined in a restaurant, the waiter bringing them their food was the former cavalry officer. He stood over them, curling his lip, as they fed each other ice cream from tall glasses with long spoons. The friendly priest who pointed out the mosaics in St Mark's Basilica – Quinn knew him immediately. The flower vendor in the Piazza di San Marco, the Carabiniere lurking on the Rialto Bridge, the attendant who showed them to their box at the theatre, the tenor on the stage, the dancer in the beaked *Medico della Peste* mask who led the masquerade through the midnight alleyways, the night porter who greeted them on their return to their hotel . . . they were all him. Of that Quinn had no doubt.

So it was clear that the psychological explanation was the one that the film was forcing on the audience. Although she was on honeymoon with the Count of Somewhere or Other, Eloise's character could not get the image of her former lover out of her mind. But just when Quinn persuaded himself to be satisfied with this explanation, he remembered the trussed-up guard on the express train.

On the surface, Eloise remained untroubled by these visions, if indeed she was conscious of them. She dined and danced and visited the sights with her bridegroom. On her lips was always the happy smile of a new bride. But her eyes were a different matter. There was no doubt now that her eyes had a haunted quality to them.

The director again chose to present an extended close-up of those eyes, just as he had done at the beginning of the film. As before, the camera's viewpoint moved back to show her whole face. In contrast to the earlier sequence, a hand – her husband's, presumably – came into the frame, this time though to caress her cheek with a loving touch. Tellingly, Eloise flinched away.

A dramatic flurry of high, discordant intervals from the band underlined the significance of this gesture. Her husband's expression was wounded. To repair the damage, she grasped his hand and held it to her cheek, her eyes closed longingly. She was wishing herself into love for this man. But Quinn knew that the truth was concealed behind those eyelids. Her eyes still desired the disgraced cavalry officer. This was clear the next time she opened them and the director once again treated the audience to an extreme, overwhelming close-up. Eyes were not meant to be seen so large, nor looked into for so long. Quinn became aware of how long she had held them open without blinking. He began to feel tense and uncomfortable. It was inhuman, almost cruel, to force him to continue looking into those eyes.

The eyes themselves, once objects of beauty, became objects of terror. It was not just the melodramatic music that suggested this idea.

There was horror in their gaze, a dawning realization of the tragedy and abasement that lay ahead. A despair so complete that it took away hope from all who gazed into them.

By another of his clever camera tricks, the director revealed that the isolated eyes were looking down from a cracked plaster ceiling at the former cavalry officer, who was stretched out on the grubby mattress of an iron-framed bed. A metallic object glinted in his hands. Quinn recognized it as one of the long spoons with which the couple had eaten ice cream. And so, once again, he had to reassess his interpretation of what he was seeing. Was he to take it that the cavalry officer really had been the waiter in the restaurant, and therefore all the other manifestations?

The next scene showed the couple asleep in a hotel suite. The large window was open on a night dominated by an enormous full moon. Eloise stirred and woke as a shadowy figure appeared silhouetted against the moon, climbing in through the window.

She did not cry out. She knew it was him. The man she had seen wherever she looked. He had come for her.

She rose from the bed; they looked into each other's eyes. And then threw themselves at each other.

As they kissed, the Count of Somewhere or Other woke. He leapt from the bed with a cry, which the band did its best to convey music- ally. A struggle ensued between the count and the former cavalry officer. But the latter had come armed. A close-up showed a stiletto blade sinking into the count's soft flank. He fell to the floor.

The lovers confronted one another. Once again, Eloise's eyes held and conveyed the entire meaning of the moment. The horror that had been nascent in them before bloomed into a deep revulsion. The former cavalry officer had to see that all was lost. Quinn certainly understood this.

She hated him. There was only hatred in those eyes now.

The next sequence showed the cavalry officer stealing away from the couple's suite. The band rumbled ominously and then fell silent as the camera returned to the bedroom.

There were now two bodies on the floor. The director went in for his favourite close-up. But where Eloise's eyes should have been there were two black chasms.

Quinn couldn't say whether he was one of those who shrieked. But he certainly felt himself bodily leave his seat.

Of course, he had seen worse in reality. But there was something about having such horrors depicted in art that he found more shocking than to discover them in the course of his professional life. Their representation signified some kind of acknowledgement. It opened a door.

If it was only policemen and police surgeons – and the occasional accidental witness – who were obliged to confront such crimes, they could be contained and prevented from contaminating the wider society. It was part of his job to take these things on himself. It was his responsibility. He thought of Sir Edward's secretary, Miss Latterly. Her horrified reaction to the little he had inadvertently let slip about his work was perfectly proper. This was how the public ought to view such things.

This wallowing in horror and violence, this fascination with grue- some and macabre spectacle, it was unwholesome. It was obscene. More than that, it was dangerous. Who knew where it would lead?

But the film wasn't over yet. Quinn could not imagine what else, what new horrors, the makers could have in store for the audience. But he sensed the eager anticipation in those around him.

The murderer returned to his lair. It was not clear where this was, whether in Venice, or Vienna. It didn't matter. It was a psychological place. It existed both as an idea in the murderer's head, and – now that it had been filmed – as an external reality. It was inside all their heads now.

He was hunched over something, a bundle in a knotted handkerchief, through which dark stains had seeped. The shape of the bundle, the suggestion of a double rotundity, left little doubt to its contents.

The film showed the killer decant the eyes into a jar, which he topped up with a clear liquid before sealing. By chance, the dead eyes were looking out, suspended midway in the preserving fluid. He held up the jar so that the eyes were level with his own. He then addressed a bitter soliloquy to them, the gist of which was represented on a series of inter-titles. In short, he blamed the eyes for all the misfortunes that had befallen him. They had haunted him, given him no peace, driven him to murder. And worse. It was to rid himself of the spectre of those eyes that he had been forced to remove the eyes from the women he had killed. Women in whose faces he had seen her eyes.

The camera then showed a close-up of the killer placing the jar on a shelf, the eyes still looking out into the room, and towards the audience. A wider shot revealed it was not the only such jar on that shelf. And that that was not the only shelf. In fact, the wall was lined with jar after jar, each containing a pair of eyes looking out.

In the final frames of the film, as the killer moved out of shot, all the eyes in the jars swivelled to watch him go. The violins produced a suitably chilling glissando. The audience went wild, delighted and terrified in equal degree.

SEVENTEEN

The lights came up.

The audience was wrenched away from another man's shimmering dreams back into their own duller, if more solid, realities. But though the glow of the projector had died on the screen, its silver cast lingered in their minds. The glamour as well as the horror of what they had just witnessed enlivened them. They sprang to their feet and filed out of the auditorium in a state of heightened excitement, almost shouting their pleasure, laughing nervously at the memory of their earlier disturbed emotions. The horror they had felt had now abated. It was safe to make a joke of it.

Their own attempts at lustre, the sheen on the top hats of the men and the cosmetic gloss of the women's lips, struck Quinn as tawdry and counterfeit. An attempt to stave off the great unspeakable truth: their own mortality. The sour odours of too many bodies enclosed in a confined space were beginning to cut through. Whatever it was that had been sprayed over their heads, perfume or disinfectant, it was losing its efficacy.

In contrast, the weightless entities spun out of the criss-crossing of light and darkness – Eloise and the mournful-eyed actor who played the cavalry officer – embraced the great unspeakable and in so doing transformed and transcended it. It was a kind of alchemy.

Like every other mortal lumbering to his feet, Quinn felt the leaden tug of returning anxieties. For the first time since the lights had gone down, he remembered why he was there.

The audience was streaming out through two exits. He had them both covered, so he should not have been overly concerned. But he had just seen a film in which a man managed to pass himself off as a series of different individuals. Admittedly, that was fiction. But still it mooted a possibility. If Hartmann changed his appearance in some way, it might be enough for him to get past Macadam at least, who had only had one brief look at him.

No, it was preposterous. Hartmann had no reason to believe himself under observation. He was there at a social occasion, and from what Inchball had said, he was mixing with the film people. If there was a celebration afterwards, there was every chance that he would be part of it. He would be leaving through the front entrance, in the full glare of the newspaper photographers' flash guns.

Quinn began to relax as he drifted with the crowd. He allowed himself to take in his surroundings. The interior was done out like someone's idea of the tea salon of a fashionable hotel, with potted palms trees, reproduction statues on pedestals, and burgundy drapes and plush on the walls. Moulded details, no doubt bulk purchased at an architectural wholesalers, were stuck on to add decorative interest. None of it bore up to close examination, but Porrick's customers did not go there to look at the walls.

As Quinn came out on to Leicester Square, he caught Inchball's eye but kept his distance.

Inchball was an experienced officer. He contrived to acknowledge

Quinn's presence without signalling any obvious connection between them. To a casual observer, they might have appeared as two strangers warily sizing one another up before going their separate ways. But such was the excitement after the picture show that it was unlikely that anyone would have registered the two men at all.

The crowd was still voluble, communicating largely in shouts. No doubt this was due in large part to the emotional agitation caused by the film. But perhaps, also, it was a reaction to their enforced silence of the last hour or so.

As a police officer, Quinn could not help considering the dangers of the new medium from the standpoint of public order. Its capacity to incite as well as excite was evident all around him.

Even more worrying for Quinn, given his unique insight into a certain kind of criminal mind, he believed the graphic depiction of violent crime provided an example that some individuals might wish to emulate. It opened a door in more ways than one. The general public was exposed to horrors that would cause them needless anxieties. Whereas the admittedly much smaller but nonetheless significant constituency of the depraved would take from it a licence.

Perhaps it was because his mind was alert to these potential risks that Quinn was so quick to sense a different category of agitation impinge on the mood of the crowd. He became aware of one man shouting, not in pleasurable enthusiasm, but in what seemed like genuine panic. Terror, even. Turning to the source of the noise, he saw the man running towards them at full pelt.

'Police! Quick! For God's sake, someone fetch a doctor! There has been an horrific crime committed!'

EIGHTEEN

Quinn gave a brief, commanding nod to Inchball for him to remain at his post, and went with the fellow.

He was led at a half-run – 'Please, hurry!' – out of Leicester Square, across Charing Cross Road and into a dimly lit alleyway, one of the two passages through to St Martin's Lane. Quinn glanced at the street sign, which told him it was Cecil Court.

There were voices ahead of him, and a horrible, high-pitched wailing. It was the sound of shredded flesh. The cries of a tortured animal. Although there was something in it that enabled him to identify its source as human, and probably female.

Quinn made out a huddle of crouching men. A light went on in one of the shop windows, which was filled with kinematographic cameras and lighting equipment. It seemed that some of these lights had been activated, and their beams directed towards the scene unfolding in front of the premises. Whether this was to aid the actions of the men in the alley, or to provide illumination for filming, Quinn could not be sure.

His escort cried out for them to be let through. The handful of men rose and parted as one, turning towards Quinn as though they had been waiting for him. There was a peculiar solemnity to their movements that seemed almost choreographed. Perhaps in these circumstances some instinct takes over, and affects all men in the same way. It seemed that everyone knew what to do.

A young woman lay on the ground, writhing and gasping for air so that she could keep up her savage keening. She held both hands to her right eye. Blood seeped out through her fingers and was smeared across her face. Her hair appeared to be matted with it too and there were bloodstains on the pavement.

Drawn by an irresistible urge to know what lay behind her hands, Quinn swept forward and stooped over her. The lights from the shop window were directed unflinchingly on her face. Quinn gazed on her gaping lips as a lover might on his beloved. He reached out a hand and gently touched hers. The shrillness of her screams intensified.

'Please, it's all right. I'll not hurt you. I'm a policeman. I'm here to help.'

The woman seemed not to understand him. Certainly she showed no sign of being reassured by his words. The one eye that was visible bulged with renewed fear.

'What happened here?' Quinn addressed his words to the men at his back. But when he turned, he saw that they had all gone. No doubt it was the word *policeman* that had seen them off.

The only one who remained was the man who had raised the alarm.

'She needs a doctor,' said Quinn.

He heard the clatter of a horse-drawn cab pulling up. A moment later, as if responding to a cue, a tall clean-shaven gentleman in evening dress presented himself. The man was probably in his late thirties. He walked with the brisk upright confidence born of authority. 'I am a doctor.' His accent was foreign, but its precise origin was unidentifiable, at least to Quinn.

Quinn moved to one side and allowed the doctor to attend to the injured woman.

Perhaps sensing his professional authority, she allowed her hands to be teased slowly from her face.

There, where her right eye should have been, there was a rusting circle of gore around a black chasm that not even the lights from the kinematographic supply shop could illuminate.

Quinn stared for a long time into that hole. Its darkness was like nothing that he had ever seen, or wanted to see again. It seemed to go on forever, to extend far beyond the dimensions of the young woman's eye socket, further even than the extent of her head.

'I must staunch the bleeding,' said the doctor. He removed a handkerchief from his pocket and placed it over the empty eye socket. The woman whimpered at his touch but allowed it.

The doctor turned to Quinn. 'I have a cab waiting. I can take her to the nearest hospital.'

'She has been attacked. I am a police detective. I will need to take a statement from her.'

'First we need to get her to a hospital. We must stabilize her condition. She is in severe shock, of course. You will get nothing out of her now. She will need sedation and medication for the pain. When she has had a chance to rest, you will be able to talk to her.'

Quinn ignored the doctor's opinion, which he had not solicited. 'Who did this to you?'

The woman became agitated, turning her head rapidly from side to side in fearful denial.

The doctor placed a hand behind her head to protect her from the effects of her own agitation. 'I must protest!'

The victim's teeth locked together, as if in spasm. A stifled gargling sounded in her throat. Quinn leaned forward, edging the doctor out of the way. He lowered his head to place his ear close to her mouth.

'You would do better to help me get her into my cab! Our first duty is to preserve her life. Then, there will be time to go after the perpetrator.'

But Quinn was insistent. 'Did you see him? The man who did this to you?'

A strangled stuttering eked itself out between her clenched teeth. 'T-t-t-t-d-d-d . . .'

'Yes?' Quinn nodded encouragement.

He sensed her body tense. She seemed to be gathering her powers for a supreme effort.

'My dear! You must not exert yourself.' The doctor cast a disapproving scowl at Quinn. In an undertone he hissed: 'Stop this now! You are putting her life at risk!'

'You saw the man! You saw him!' It was no longer a question, but an urgent insistence.

The woman raised herself in the doctor's arms. '*Tayyy-vvvvl!*'

'What did she say?' Quinn turned to the doctor.

'I don't know. I didn't hear.' But there was something suspect about his demurral.

She repeated the sound, more quietly, but also more calmly. 'Tayvl.'

'Table? Is she saying something about a table?' wondered Quinn.

'No, I don't think so. I think . . .'

'Is it German? Is she German? Are *you* German?'

'I am not German. My name is Casaubon. I am French.'

'But you understand what she is saying?'

'I know that she is not speaking German.'

'Tell me, what language is she speaking?'

'I believe it may be Yiddish. Tayvl is the Yiddish word for—'

But the woman herself cut in: 'Day-vil! The day-vil did this!'

Quinn was aware of a stir behind him, footsteps running, a flash of light. He looked around and saw Bittlestone of the *Clarion* with his photographer. 'Sensational!'

Sergeant Macadam was on their heels.

Quinn turned back to the woman in time to see her one remaining eye swivel and judder as it lost focus before closing. She fell back limply.

'We must get her to a hospital!'

Quinn stood up and turned on the journalist angrily. 'You will not publish that photograph. You will not release any details of this crime, not without my authorization. Do you understand?'

The photographer scuttled away under the force of Quinn's ire, though Bittlestone stood his ground: 'You cannot stifle a free press, Inspector.'

Quinn relented a little. 'There may be an aspect of national security here. Even *your* proprietor must have some sensitivity to that. I must consult with my superiors. I suggest you do the same. In the meantime, you can make yourself useful. Help Doctor

Casaubon.' He turned to the man who had led him there. 'You too.'

Bittlestone and the other man took a step closer to the wounded woman but, for the moment at least, would go no further than that. It was as if they had walked into an invisible fence. A vacant inertia came over them both. They showed no sign of horror, but rather watched her writhing with fascinated frowns. They seemed to have become disassociated from the moment.

'Macadam, you and I will search the area for evidence.'

'What are we looking for exactly, sir?'

Quinn angled his head sharply. He looked down at the woman. Dr Casaubon still held the folded handkerchief in place over her wound. Quinn felt a strong urge to ask to see the empty socket again, and was trying to work out a way he might justify such a request on the grounds of the investigation.

The woman's groans increased in volume and frequency. Casaubon glanced up uneasily. 'I fear the worst if we do not get her to a hospital soon. She has suffered a tremendous shock. The effect on her nervous system, not to mention her heart, we cannot conjecture. She is only a woman, after all.'

'Help him,' Quinn ordered Bittlestone and the other man. They sprang forward and crouched down to hold her under her armpits. Quinn watched as they struggled to lift the lifeless woman to her feet, the doctor still trying to cover the wound with his handkerchief, which had somehow managed to retain its pristine, white crispness.

'Won't you help us?' demanded Bittlestone.

'I have work to do.' Quinn narrowed his eyes as if it pained him to say this. But really he did not see why it should take more than three men to get the young woman into the hansom. She was of slight build, and the walk to the cab on Charing Cross Road was only about fifteen yards.

At that moment, the lights in the shop window went out, plunging the narrow passage into semi-darkness. 'Damnation. Get them to switch the lights back on, will you, Macadam. And talk to all the businesses along here to see if there were any witnesses to the attack. Someone must have seen something.'

As always, Macadam was quick to obey.

The woman had partially revived and was able to take faltering steps with the help of the three men attending to her. Quinn noticed that one of her hands was tightly clenched. The other one splayed tensely, as if to push against her assailant.

'One moment. I *will* help you.' Quinn took the clenched hand in one of his, while stroking her knuckles soothingly. Her single eye looked into his face uncomprehendingly. He felt her fist tighten in his hand.

They walked her slowly towards the cab. Quinn had his back to the direction of travel, keeping his gaze fixed on her eye. As they neared the Charing Cross Road end of the alley, he cast a glance back over his shoulder, just at the moment a boisterous crowd was rounding the corner. At their head was Porrick, still carrying the Yorkshire terrier. The dog was perched in his arms, its head cocked in an angle of entitlement, the gleam of latent aggression in its nasty little black eyes. As soon as it saw Quinn, it started yapping.

The rest of the party was made up of the other film people and their entourage. Waechter appeared to be in jubilant mood; he had his arms around his two principal actors and was singing in German at the top of his lungs. All seemed to be affected by nervous stimulation of some kind. They might not have been blotto – yet – but they had the air of those who were determined to become so, and as quickly as possible.

They appeared intent on revelry. Quinn could only assume that they had not heard about the attack.

He had less than a second to take all this in. For in less than a second Porrick had collided with him, pushing him into the woman he was guiding. She let out a sharp scream, more of surprise than pain. He felt her grip relax. Something passed from her hand to his.

In the commotion, the dog jumped out of its master's arms and ran off, with a blast of high-pitched yelps that sounded like the canine equivalent of bad language. 'Scudder! Scudder!' cried Porrick. 'Heel! Heel now! Come on, boy.'

Quinn glanced quickly into his hand. A piece of card lay crumpled and balled in his palm, damp and flaky with sweat. He looked up to see Waechter considering the wounded woman with a look that was, for the time being, impossible to interpret. It seemed to hint at some kind of affinity – a recognition of kindred bonds. But perhaps there was more to it than that.

Some instinct made Quinn watch the dog. The animal ignored all commands, but did at least stop barking. He was sniffing the air with the serious concentration of a concert pianist about to perform, having apparently picked up a scent. After a moment, he trotted away purposefully, oblivious to what was expected of him, aware only of the scent, and his own need to get to the bottom of it.

Just then the lights in the shop came back on. The dog's pace quickened, he gave one happy yelp and then pounced on something. He turned proudly, his head high to show what he had caught.

Held between his jaws, pointed out at them, was a single human eye. There were screams. A woman fainted. Someone else was sick.

Quinn rushed towards the dog. 'Come on now. Drop it. There's a good boy!'

But the dog just curdled a snarl in the back of his throat.

Quinn appealed to the owner. 'You – Mr Porrick, isn't it?'

'Yes?'

'Can you get him to surrender it?'

'I don't know . . . I . . . He is a very wilful creature.'

'You must have some control over him!'

'He likes his treats.' Porrick held out a dog biscuit. 'Come on, Scud. Drop it now. There's a good Scudder boy.'

The dog cocked his head from one side to the other as he made his calculations. He evidently realized that the man very much wanted the interesting object he had in his mouth. More than he himself wanted a dog treat. And for that reason, he decided to hold on to the object. This was power beyond his size. He was not going to give it up easily.

Quinn drew his revolver and pointed it at the dog. 'If he will not give up the eye, I will be forced to put him down.' There were cries of horror. 'I am a policeman,' he added, somewhat superfluously.

Porrick pleaded with his dog. 'Come on, old chap. Give it up, give it up now.'

Quinn released the safety catch on his gun.

'You can't! You can't do that!' cried Porrick. He desperately scattered a handful of dog treats on the ground in front of Scudder. 'Look boy! Delicious treats!'

It took the intervention of a third party to induce the dog to comply. Eloise startled them all by bending down and inserting a finger behind the eye, which was held at the front of the animal's jaws. The finger induced the gag reflex, releasing the eye. She deftly seized the dog and handed it back to Porrick, leaving Quinn to retrieve the valuable piece of evidence, which he wrapped in his handkerchief.

When he turned back to face the Charing Cross Road end of the alley, he noticed that the waiting hansom was no longer there. The woman whose eye he was holding had gone, together with the mysterious Dr Casaubon and the man who had first raised the alarm.

PART TWO
Money

NINETEEN

'Must you insist on carryin' that *blarsted* thing around with you?' The question was asked by the lady with the spreading bosom. Porrick's wife, Edna, it turned out. Her manner was naturally imperious, though her accent betrayed her origins. She had the look of a woman who believed that everyone else in the world was there to facilitate her comfort and convenience. It would not be long before she started giving him orders. She could not be an easy woman to be married to, he speculated. Uppity, was the word that came to mind.

They were in the offices of Visionary Pictures, the premises next to the kinematographic equipment shop. They had been admitted by a bald man with a drooping handlebar moustache, who had turned up shortly after the main group of film people. Soon after his arrival on the scene, Quinn spotted Inchball walk past the end of Cecil Court. His sergeant gave the most minimal of signals in the direction of the newcomer.

So, as he suspected, this was Hartmann.

Hartmann spoke impeccable English and seemed to be on good terms with everyone, particularly Lord Dunwich, who was also attached to the party.

Quinn gave no answer to Edna Porrick's question, except to pocket the eye. He had got everything he was going to get from the feel of it in his hand. And yet, he could not quite give up all claim to the potent relic. His hand stayed in his pocket with it, feeling its springy rotundity through the fabric of his handkerchief.

As soon as he got in, Hartmann went round switching on all the electric lights. He seemed to be acting under some kind of compulsion.

Some of the lights were contained behind frosted-glass panels which lined the stairs down to the basement. An ethereal milky-white glow enticed the eye downward, as if inviting subterranean thoughts. It was of a piece with the office's self-consciously modern style. Quinn noticed that the only two colours used anywhere were black and white. For example, the place was furnished with slightly uncomfortable-looking lounge chairs, perched on black wooden legs, upholstered in black and white zebra-striped fabric.

The walls were decorated with framed posters of the company's various productions, including one for the film they had just seen. Beneath the title, a pair of isolated eyes looked out from a black background. The eyes were wide open, as if in terror, the enlarged whites gleaming starkly.

Quinn squeezed the eye in his pocket. It was almost as if it had become a talisman. And he hoped to absorb some of its power through touch.

He looked around at the crowd crammed into the office. The mood struck him as sullen, as if they resented the attack on the girl, not because of the injury perpetrated on the victim, but because it had curtailed their festivities. Glasses of champagne had already been poured and laid out on tables in readiness for their arrival. But there was a reluctance to be the first to take a drink. Quinn had the sense that they wanted him out of the way so that they could get on with their party.

The first thing to do was to establish the girl's identity. He peeled open the crumpled card. As he had suspected, it was an invitation to the premiere. But there was no name written on it, whether in green ink or any other.

Quinn climbed on to one of the zebra-print chairs. There was a scandalized gasp. 'Ladies and gentlemen. I am Detective Inspector Quinn. I believe many of you saw the girl who was attacked tonight. I have reason to believe that she attended this evening's screening. Can any of you tell me who she is?'

All that his enquiry prompted was a bemused and faintly outraged rumbling, with much head-shaking. It seemed that his ploy to gain their attention by elevating himself had served only to arouse their indignation. After the attack on the young woman, this was insult added to her injury. Also, his behaviour seemed to give them licence to begin drinking, as if that transgression opened the door to others. There was a sudden crush at the champagne tables, a rise in the general hubbub, an unseemly sense of release.

Quinn jumped down. He was approached immediately by Lord Dunwich. 'Good heavens, Quinn! Was that strictly necessary? These chairs are genuine Viennese Jugendstil. Have you any idea how much they cost?'

'And have *you* any idea who that man is?' Quinn kept his voice down as he nodded towards Hartmann.

'Yes. I know full well who he is.'

'He is German.'

'I know that.'

'I thought you wanted us to investigate Germans.'

'Not all Germans are spies, Quinn.'

'We believe *he* is. Indeed, we believe he is the head of a spy network.'

'Nonsense. Oskar Hartmann is a businessman. In fact, he is a business associate of mine. I have invested in several of his companies, including Visionary Productions. We do have some friends in Germany, you know, Quinn. And we must foster and strengthen those links that do exist. It is not too late to avert the thing that we all fear. War can be avoided if we can forge an alliance of well-intentioned men on both sides.'

'You might avoid war if you contrive to deliver England over to the Germans without a fight.'

'What are you suggesting?'

'That man, Hartmann, was seen at Dortmunder's barbershop . . .'

'I expressly instructed you not to investigate the barbershop.'

'Yes, and now I am wondering why.'

'You impertinent fool!'

'Hartmann was witnessed by one of my officers handing over secret materials to the barber.'

'What secret materials?'

'We do not know the precise nature of the materials in question.'

'Then how do you know they are secret?'

'The lettering on the envelope was written in green ink.' Some instinct persuaded Quinn that this was the one detail that would make Lord Dunwich take his suspicions seriously. Even so, the reaction was far in excess of what he had expected. Lord Dunwich's eyes widened in fear. The colour went from his face.

'What is it?' Quinn's voice became an urgent whisper. 'There is something you are not telling me, I know it.'

'Nothing. I . . . what happened to that girl has set my nerves on edge . . .' Lord Dunwich's gaze flitted wildly. His aggressive superiority had abandoned him. He was afraid.

'I cannot do my job if you're not completely frank with me.'

'You don't know what you ask.'

'Did something happen, Lord Dunwich?'

'I was sent something. A package. The address was written in green ink. That's all.'

'What was it?'

'Now is not the time, Quinn. It has nothing to do with Herr Hartmann, I am sure. It was just someone's idea of a joke.'

'What were you sent?'

'Just . . . a billiard ball.'

'Why would anyone send you a billiard ball?'

'I don't know. There was no explanation. No name. Just a billiard ball. It had been painted to look like an eye, that was all.'

Quinn's hand tightened on the eye concealed in the darkness of his pocket. 'A rather significant detail, don't you think? Do you have any idea who sent it?'

'No . . . I can't imagine.'

'Do you still have it? And the packaging it came in? The writing in green ink?'

'Yes. I have kept it. It's locked in a drawer at the Admiralty. For some reason I didn't like the idea of throwing it away.'

'Will you kindly have it sent round to me at the Special Crimes Department at your soonest convenience. Were you intending to go into the Admiralty tomorrow, for example?'

'Yes. We're frightfully busy at the moment. Between you and me, Quinn, the country is not far from a war footing. If things deteriorate much further, you will see us move to Total War as soon as May.'

Quinn nodded grimly. 'That makes it all the more urgent that I see this . . . object.'

'Do you really think it could be important?'

'You are a minister in a department that plays a vital role in our country's defence. You may well be a target for our enemies. I would not be surprised to discover that this bizarre package has some sinister significance. The green ink is very telling, I believe.' He lifted the handkerchief with its gruesome contents out of his pocket and looked down at it. 'What colour was the eye you were sent?'

'Blue, I seem to remember.'

Quinn realized that he had not registered the colour of the eye in his hand. He knew that he had looked into the iris, as he had into the iris of the eye that remained in place. But he could not remember the colour of her eyes. It became suddenly important for him to check this detail. He folded back the flap of the handkerchief and turned the object it contained. It was already beginning to shrivel and the white of the sclera was turning a dull grey. The iris, he saw, was brown.

'Good God, man! Do you have to?'

Quinn regarded Lord Dunwich with an expression of mild, absent-minded curiosity. He frowned and folded the handkerchief back over, restoring the eye to his pocket.

'And then there's the fact that you were sent a package containing an eye – or something that was made to look like an eye. That links it with what has happened tonight. Although the colours of the eyes are different. At any rate, what has happened tonight is connected with your friend Hartmann. It happened outside his company, following the showing of a motion picture made by his company. And Hartmann is linked with another package addressed in green ink – the one that my sergeant saw at the barbershop.' Quinn glanced over to Hartmann, who was now in earnest conversation, sotto voce, with Waechter. 'What do you know about the fellow he's talking to? The one with the eye patch?'

'Waechter? I know that many believe him to be a genius.'

'He killed a man, I believe.'

'It was in a duel, Inspector. And it did happen in Austria.'

'Does that make it acceptable?'

'It makes it no concern of mine.'

'He cannot go back to Austria, I hear.'

'I believe that is the case.'

'Perhaps he is looking for a powerful ally to intercede on his behalf? To facilitate his return to his homeland? If he were to prove himself in the service of this ally, things might go better for him at home?'

'Interesting. At the time of his duel he was an officer in the Landwehr. But he was dishonourably discharged.'

'For duelling? But isn't that all to do with honour?'

'I don't think it was anything to do with his duel. There were rumours . . . of a scandal.'

'What kind of a scandal?'

'Not here, Quinn. My God, what do you take me for? I have said too much already. What you have to understand about Konrad Waechter is that he is first and foremost an artist. No, I don't see it. I just don't see what role he could possibly play in issues of national security.'

'He knows how to handle a camera. It could be used for recording sensitive material. Naval defences, for example.'

'Have your officers seen Waechter at the barber's?'

'No. Only Hartmann.'

'What else has this misguided operation of yours uncovered?'

'You will excuse me if I don't answer that. Not now. Here.' With a curt nod, Quinn crossed to Waechter and Hartmann. The two men broke off from a conspiratorial conference and regarded him for a moment warily.

Hartmann was the first to recover his composure. 'This is a terrible business, Inspector . . . Quinn, is it?' The only hint of an accent he betrayed was the slight weight he gave to some of his consonants. That was all that distinguished him from a native speaker.

'That's right, Herr Hartmann.'

'You already know who I am? Should I be worried?'

'Not unless you have a guilty conscience.'

'Don't we all have something on our conscience?'

Quinn was in no mood for such drollery. 'Do you know a man called Dortmunder? A compatriot of yours, I believe.'

Waechter interrupted, with a click of his heels and a bow. Unlike Hartmann, his accent was thick, his words almost incomprehensible. 'Please, you vill *airk-scuse* me?'

'No, Herr Waechter,' said Quinn. 'I have some questions for you too. So please, stay where you are. Now, Herr Hartmann, you were about to tell me about Dortmunder.'

'I know the man. Of course. He is something of a celebrity within the German community here in London. Does he have something to do with what has happened tonight?'

'You will forgive me, but you do not strike me as a man who is much in need of a barber's services.'

'I appreciate a good shave as much as the next man. But really, do you believe Dortmunder to be behind the outrageous attack on that poor woman?'

'You were seen handing Dortmunder a package.'

'I say, Inspector, have you been spying on me?'

'We have been watching Dortmunder's place. I think you know that.'

'I did drop off a script. The other day.'

'A script?'

'Yes. Herr Dortmunder has been trying for some time to break into motion picture scenario writing. Like many who go to the picture palaces, he imagines that it will be a way to easy money. Unfortunately it is not as easy as many people believe. However, I will say one thing for Dortmunder. He is persistent. Over the years, he must have asked me to look at literally hundreds of scripts. He will not be discouraged.'

'And you return the scripts to him personally, yourself? Have you not thought of using the Royal Mail? I am sure you have junior staff who can take care of such things.'

'As you said, he is a compatriot of mine. Besides, he shows promise. He has not come up with anything I can use yet, but perhaps one day he might.'

Quinn turned to Waechter. 'Do you know the woman who was attacked tonight? She had in her hand an invitation to the premiere.'

'Many people were invited. I do not know all of them.'

'There must be a list?'

Waechter shrugged impatiently. Such things did not concern him. 'Hartmann?'

'Yes, of course. I will see that it is sent to you, Inspector. Where may I send it?'

'New Scotland Yard. For the attention of DI Quinn.'

'What you must understand, Inspector, is that sometimes people pass on their invitations. We cannot say ultimately into whose hands an invitation will fall. Was there no name on the invitation in her possession?' Hartmann's tone struck Quinn as false, mocking almost. As if he already knew the answer to the question. 'I do hope the young lady recovers from the shock of the assault. I wish to send her some flowers. Do you know which hospital she has been taken to?'

Quinn sighed. 'Naturally she will have been taken to the nearest hospital, which from here is the Middlesex.'

'Please inform me of the details when you know for certain.'

'Do you have any *kvestions* for me?' Waechter spoke in a curt, aggressive growl. He had the habit of giving extra emphasis to the words he had most difficulty in pronouncing, as if his struggles with the language were the source of his anger.

Quinn looked into the Austrian's face and found that he was fascinated by the thought of what lay behind the man's eye patch. The memory of the small abyss he had stared into earlier that evening was still fresh and compelling. A brief, absurd fantasy flashed into his mind, of his lifting Waechter's eye patch to refresh his contact with the darkness within. 'Your film . . . I saw your film . . . I was one of the invited guests . . .'

Waechter bowed in expectation of praise.

'There are certain similarities between the theme of your film and the crime that was committed tonight.'

'I am *ein Künstler*! You know? An artist. *Ja*? Every artist is also – how do you say – *ein Profet*?'

'Prophet. It is the same word,' put in Hartmann.

'*Ja*, zere is prophet in every artist.'

'And *profit* too,' observed Quinn, immediately regretting his attempt at a quip. 'You hope to make a lot of money from this film, no doubt.'

'Are you looking for investment opportunities, Inspector?' asked Hartmann suavely. 'It is true, if one succeeds in meeting the public's desires, one may be fortunate in achieving a healthy return. However, the risks are considerable. Even when one has a genius such as Herr Waechter on hand, and a star like Eloise, it is still possible to fall flat on one's face. To catch a cold, I think is the expression. Nothing is guaranteed. The more cautious investor would be well advised to look elsewhere.'

'I am not looking to invest. A policeman's salary does not run to gambling on the stock market.' Quinn was aware that his tone was becoming puritanical. He found that he did not approve of these people at all. And he was determined not to be in their thrall. Their thin, continental glamour would cut no ice with him. 'Do you think it is ethical to profit from such depictions of violence and horror? Especially as – as now seems likely – some madman has been encouraged by watching your lurid drama to emulate the crimes you portray.'

There was an exchange between Waechter and Hartmann in German, while the latter translated for the former.

Hartmann nodded as he listened to a question from his director. There was an eagerness and energy in Waechter's voice, a gleam in his one good eye. Hartmann turned to Quinn. 'Is that the theory you are pursuing?'

'I am considering submitting a legal application to have the film withdrawn from public exhibition.' In fact, the thought had only just occurred to Quinn.

There was an outraged exchange between Waechter and Hartmann. Hatred glared from Waechter's eye towards Quinn. He could well believe that this man was capable of killing.

It was up to Hartmann to argue their case. 'We cannot be blamed for the acts of this horrible person who is not known to us, and who, as you say, is clearly insane.'

'The one thing I cannot risk is a repetition of this crime.'

Waechter drew himself up to intimidate. 'The public vill not allow it! You vill have *ein* revolution on your hands if you forbid the people from seeing my film.'

Quinn was so startled by the self-aggrandizing statement that he did not for the moment know what to say. He turned to Hartmann. 'You will have that list of guests with me tomorrow morning. There will be no need to deliver it in person.'

Quinn had made up his mind to leave, but his way to the door was cut off by the party from the *Clarion*: Harry Lennox, the Irish proprietor, and his daughter, Jane, together with the paper's star reporter, Bittlestone.

Out of the corner of his eye he saw Lord Dunwich engaged in an intimate tête à tête with the brunette who had played the part of a dancer in the film, the fake ingénue Quinn had noticed earlier. He looked around for the man whom he associated with her. If he was connected with the woman, he was paying her no attention now, and was in deep conversation with Porrick (whose dog was thankfully nowhere to be seen) and another man, as yet unknown to Quinn.

With the intake of alcohol, the sombre mood had turned into something fiercer. A kind of savage excitement had taken over. Quinn recognized the peculiar gleam that enlivened every eye. This was how it affected some people. To have had a brush with the destructive forces in the universe, and to have escaped.

'I 'ope you find him.'

Quinn looked down towards the source of the sentiment, which had been expressed in a warm, softly accented female voice. He felt her words throb in his solar plexus. Two large eyes – eyes he recognized, eyes that seemed so familiar they might have belonged to some part of his soul – stared up at him. Eloise stared up at him.

He was struck by the wonder of her presence next to him; by the improbability of it: that the one woman desired by all the men in the room was talking to him. And to him alone. He looked around incredulously, as if he suspected she was about to be snatched away from him.

'I admired what you did tonight.'

'Ah, I did nothing.'

'You showed remarkable presence of mind. How did you know what to do?'

'My father, he had a troupe of performing dogs. It is how I commence in the business.' Like Hartmann, she spoke good English, though her accent was stronger. She dropped the occasional H and showed a betraying uncertainty over the odd vowel sound, or even word. Inevitably, for Quinn, it added to the charm of her speech.

'I see. You were not disgusted by . . . by the object you were forced to handle?'

'Did you not see the film?'

'Yes, but surely those were not real eyes?'

'And I pretend to myself that it is not a real eye in the mouth of the dog. I think to myself it is a prop, no?'

'None of the men stepped forward.'

'Men can be such babies. But I pity them.'

Quinn noticed that Eloise was the only other person apart from himself who did not have a drink.

'Do you believe there will be a war, Inspector?'

The question took him by surprise. 'The German state is certainly preparing for something. Why do you ask?'

'It frightens me.'

'I believe there are those on all sides who are determined to prevent it.'

'I hope they will succeed. For the sake of the men. In war, it is always the men who are sent off to be killed. What horrors they must see.' He might have said that a glow of sympathy seemed to come from her eyes. But what really happened was merely that she looked at him as if she truly wanted to see him. 'What horrors you must have seen. Worse than tonight, is it not so?'

It seemed to be an invitation for him to tell her about his work. But he remembered how such confidences had back-fired on him in the past, repelling the woman whom he had subconsciously sought to impress. But Eloise was not Miss Latterly. For one thing, she had sought him out, and initiated the conversation; Sir Edward's secretary only tolerated his presence because she was obliged to.

She had made her position abundantly clear to him: *I can't ever love you!*

He knew full well what had forced her to make this unhappy declaration. The very horrors that Eloise was asking to be told about now.

Would it drive her away too? Or would it bring about some kind of miraculous understanding between them?

No, miraculous was not the word. Inconceivable. Absurd. He was ridiculous. To think of any kind of understanding between himself and this goddess . . . He was an absurd man indeed. The moment a beautiful woman took an interest in him, he lost his head, not to mention his heart.

'It's the nature of the job.'

And really, now that he thought about it, there was something suspect about all this. Something he could not quite believe in. Why had she come over to speak to him? At just that moment, so soon after he had spoken to Waechter and Hartmann? She was an actress, not a goddess.

They had sent her over. She was meant to charm him into withdrawing his threat to have the film banned.

Everything fell into place.

'I see what's going on here.'

'I beg your pardon?'

'I'll tell you, I've seen some horrible things in the course of my duties, it's true. But the most horrible thing I've ever seen was that film I was forced to sit through tonight. You film people . . . you have no idea . . . no idea what you are dealing with. No idea of the forces you are unleashing. If you want to know who is responsible for the attack tonight, just look around you. No, better than that, look in the mirror. You people make me sick.'

He found that his aversion for the whole lot of them was greater than any concerns he had about running the gauntlet of the *Clarion* crowd. In the event, he brushed past Jane Lennox without provoking a flicker of recognition from her. If she drew more self-consciously on her cigarette in his wake, he did not see it.

TWENTY

Magnus Porrick held up his hand to cut Kirkwood short. He didn't like the sound of his accountant's voice at the best of times. If only the fellow were a character in a movie, whose words were conveyed silently by letters on a card. That would at least impose the virtue of brevity on him. But Porrick had the feeling that Kirkwood would be one of those characters who were shown delivering long speeches, the contents of which were never conveyed, or somehow reduced to a single word. The blighter never had anything interesting to say. Besides, Porrick didn't like the unhealthy interest Novak was taking in his business affairs. That slimy Yank always had his nose in other people's business. He should concentrate more on his own, then he might be a half-decent actor. As it was, he was an awful hack. Porrick couldn't see why Waechter always had him in his films. He would have to have a word with him about that, if they were to go into production together. No, he didn't like Novak. He didn't like Novak one bit. Especially as he had a habit of dropping 'the Big Apple' into the conversation in a knowing way, as if he believed he had some hold over a fellow just because he had once been in New York.

'Has he gone?'

Kirkwood blinked behind his wire-framed glasses. His expression put Porrick in mind of an indignant rabbit. 'Who?'

'The policeman.'

A devious smile came over Novak's lips. 'Yes, I saw him leave. He was talking to the charming Eloise and then he did a bunk.'

Porrick clapped his hands together and looked around for the head of Visionary Productions. 'Hartmann, old chap. Can't we do something about the lights? We can't have a decent rag with all these lights blazing, you know.'

'My dear Porrick, under the circumstances, I wonder whether—'

'Damn the circumstances. We have a premiere to celebrate. Besides, what happened tonight could be very good for the box office. Don't you agree, Kirkwood?'

'Let's hope so. Porrick's Palaces could certainly do with an upturn in revenue. Urgently.'

The lights began to go out, one by one. There was a small cheer of approval. The only illumination that Hartmann left on were the panels leading down to the basement.

Porrick smiled. 'That's more like it. Put the gramophone on, why don't you. Let's make this a real party.'

'Do you not 'ave any pity for the poor girl who lose her eye, Monsieur Porrick?'

High horns strained and blared in the semi-darkness, giving way to shimmering strings. Then Al Jolson's rich baritone came in singing *You made me love you, I didn't want to do it, I didn't want to do it.*

Porrick turned to Eloise, a dim figure now in the dark press. He raised his voice to be heard over the recording. 'Of course, I'm very sorry for her, my dear. But us being miserable won't put that eye back in her head now, will it? Come on now, let's be more cheery. You're not a bun strangler, are you?'

Eloise frowned in incomprehension.

'A teetotaller!'

'*Non*, I am not that.'

'Well then, allow me to get you a drink so we can toast your triumphant performance. You are a sensation, my dear! A veritable sensation. You make the film – and you will make all our fortunes, I'm sure of it.'

Hartmann's doom-laden voice cut in. 'Perhaps it's too soon to celebrate, Porrick. If that policeman gets his way, Waechter's master-piece will be withdrawn from public exhibition.'

'What? He can't do that! I have a two-week exclusive! I'm relying on this dear lady's eyes to fill my Palaces for the next two weeks. I have nothing else to show if I can't show that!'

Porrick sensed the rabbit twitch of his accountant's nose, scenting disaster. 'The business can't sustain a loss of revenue on that scale. Coming on top of everything else, this could spell the end.'

Porrick shook his head. 'You ought to be glad you don't have Kirkwood as your accountant, Hartmann. He's a proper Cassandra.'

'I will remind you that Cassandra always prophesied the truth. It wasn't her fault if no one ever believed her.'

'I say, there's a film scenario idea in that! Waechter, why don't we make a film about Cassandra? We could give her Scudder as a lap dog. Eloise could play Cassandra. She's never believed but her faithful lapdog proves that she was telling the truth. Somehow. You'll make it work.'

There was no comment from the Austrian director on Porrick's impromptu outline.

'I am not sure, given the difficulties you face already, that you should still be considering a move into production, Mr Porrick.'

'Nonsense, Kirkwood. Fortune favours the brave, and all that. With Eloise and Scudder together in a film – no, let's think big! In a series of films – what's stopping us? We can't fail, I tell you!'

'I should tell you I had a letter from the City regulators this morning, Mr Porrick. They are intending to instigate an investigation. They are claiming certain irregularities concerning the raising of funds. They say that you are over-capitalized. That the dividends you have paid have not been earned. That the whole business is a sham, in other words.'

Novak gave a low whistle. Then his odious cackle cut through over Al Jolson's emotional pleading: *Gimme gimme gimme what I cry for. You've got the kind of kisses that I die for.* 'I don't know much about finance, Porrick, but it sounds to me like you're in a bit of a pickle, old chum.' The American put on a phony English accent that made his words even more unwelcome.

Edna loomed up, an immense, inescapable silhouette of doom. 'Porrick? What are they talking about?'

'Nothing, my dear. Pay them no heed. It's just Novak trying to be funny.'

Kirkwood bristled. 'But *I* wasn't trying to be funny.'

'I'm sure you weren't.'

'I will never forgive you if we lose the house, Porrick.'

'There's no danger of that, my dear.'

'On the contrary, there is every danger of that, Mr Porrick.' As well as having no sense of humour, Kirkwood was unable to tell a lie.

'Enough of this . . . pessimism. I'll sort the finances out tomorrow. Tonight, however, I fully intend to get blind drunk on Hartmann's champagne!'

'Typical!' concluded Edna. 'Well, you needn't think I'm going to stay around watching that unedifying spectacle.'

'Edna, don't go, love! The party's just getting going!'

Al Jolson was at that moment coming to the end of his emotional confession with an emphatic, rousing *Ritardando. You . . . know . . . you . . . made me . . . love yoooooouuuu.*

'You can come with me now, Porrick. Or don' bother comin' home at all.'

'Edna!'

But it was too late.

'Hell hath no fury like a woman whose husband is about to be declared bankrupt.' Porrick could hear the sly grin in Novak's observation.

'Mrs Porrick has been my staff and my support – my rock – over the years. I am sure she will not abandon me now.'

'She sure looks like she's abandoning you, Porrick, old chum.'

'She'll see things differently in the morning.'

'And if you lose the house?'

'I'm not going to lose the house! Am I, Kirkwood?'

'Taking into consideration the very latest box office from all your theatres, and allowing for a highly optimistic forecast regarding the expected box office from your exclusive deal with Visionary Productions – taking all that into account, I do not see any prospect of your being able to turn around your fortunes. My honest opinion is that you will not only lose your Mayfair property; there is every chance that you can look forward to a short spell of being detained at His Majesty's Pleasure. I'm afraid the City regulators take a dim view of fraud, Mr Porrick.'

'You're my bloody accountant, Kirkwood! Can't you do anything?'

'I am professionally bound to cooperate with the investigators in any way I can.'

'Marvellous. First my wife deserts me, then my accountant.'

'Haven't seen that dog of yours recently, either,' quipped Novak.

In the darkness, they had kissed. Indeed, it was as if the darkness had grown lips and his mouth had latched on to them.

And all the while Will Oakland sang about the curse of an aching heart.

There were other things the darkness had grown too. Soft, yielding, female things. And it had become scented with a hot, intoxicating breath that left him hollowed out and weightless, as if he had been filled with helium.

All this was to say, she had permitted him a certain licence. His hands had strayed, first tentatively, and then with more confidence when no resistance had been met.

His hollowed out, weightless heart hammered at the wickedness of it. This was a progression from the prostitutes he usually favoured. She was an actress, a dancer. And more to the point, another man's wife.

He found the thought of it simply exhilarating; deliciously wicked. Especially considering that her husband was there in the same room, and had even seemed to connive in his wife's blatant infidelity. There had been the barest, most minimal of nods. A granting of consent, if not approval. A strange fellow, that Novak. He seemed to take as much delight from their liaison as Dunwich himself did.

They were a racy set, all right, these film people. No wonder his heart was pounding.

And besides, the sound of Will Oakland's high, vibrating counter-tenor voice disturbed him. It sounded harsh and accusatory to his ear. A bleat rather than a lament. As if the voice itself was the curse that had been visited upon the singer. If there was a warning in the lyrics, the sound repelled him so much that he could not hear it. He preferred to focus his senses on the darkness.

The darkness had a name. Dolores. And a voice. A voice that rode on hot, scented breath and filled his tingling ear with sensation. A voice that touched him like a gentle stroke of passion on the inside of his flesh. A voice that had fingers that stirred and stiffened his cock.

He gasped at the sharpness of his lust. And groaned at the frustration of it. He wanted her now. He would not wait to have her. The darkness would yield completely to him, or he would go mad.

'No . . . not here. Not yet,' the darkness murmured. And in that 'not yet' was a promise of fulfilment that would sustain him.

Dunwich could relax now, though there was no relenting in the fierce ache in his trousers. He was sure now where the evening would end. The particular hotel had yet to be decided. Or perhaps they would go to one of the restaurants he knew that were discreetly furnished with private rooms.

The details didn't matter. What was important was that he knew now how it would end. She had said, 'Not yet.'

The lyrics of Oakland's song grew darker and darker. The singer was the victim of a vicious woman who had somehow dragged him down – to Hell, it seemed. There was no wit or charm to the litany of accusations. It was a bitter, self-pitying complaint warbled out by a freakishly high voice.

The darkness withdrew its lips. 'I have to talk to Novak.'

'Novak?'

'My husband.'

While she was gone, he sensed someone looking at him. The indirect glow from the illuminated panels picked out a diminutive form, standing on its own against the wall. It was one of those midget wogs. The one with long hair, the boy. Dunwich shuddered. There was something peculiar about that child.

Hartmann had said the older wog was a brilliant cameraman. Waechter insisted on having him in his crew. The boy was his nephew, apparently. They were Chilean, Hartmann said. Native Indians. Dunwich accepted that Hartmann knew his business. And it was nothing to do with him really. But he didn't like the way the wog boy was looking at him and it was a rum do having the help here at the party. These film people had a queer way of going about things, that was for sure.

He didn't like the Chilean connection either. He had mentioned it to Hartmann, but the German had shrugged it off. He said he could vouch for Diaz, and Diaz could vouch for his nephew, and that was good enough for Hartmann.

Well, it wasn't good enough for Dunwich. Not since the business with the billiard ball.

She was back beside him in the darkness. Her voice went straight for his aching phallus. 'Let's go.'

'Where to?'

'We can go back to my flat.'

'But what about . . . Novak?'

'He has other plans.'

'If you don't mind me saying, you have a strange marriage.'

'Why should it worry you?' The darkness soothed away his fears with a gentle pressure at the place he needed it most. 'Novak doesn't care what I do.'

He groaned. 'But do you like me a little bit, Dolores?' He knew that he had revealed his weakness in the question. And he knew in the callous tinkling of her laughter that she would do everything she could to exploit it.

The sound of Will Oakland's voice grated more than ever. His song of shattered dreams was the last thing Dunwich wanted to hear.

The gramophone played on. Harry Macdonough was singing now, 'When Irish Eyes Are Smiling'.

Whenever Bittlestone heard this song, he could only think of his proprietor, Harry Lennox, whose Irish eyes never smiled. They occasionally narrowed in a look of low cunning; satisfaction at a rival's misfortune, for example, or the besting of a supplier in a deal, or any advancement in the irresistible career of Harry Lennox.

No doubt Lennox considered himself a principled man. He was, after all, the proprietor of a principled newspaper. And there was the rub. His principles were largely commercially motivated, which is to say he was ruthless in private and righteous on paper. The one exception was the question of Home Rule, in which he not only held a conviction but also allowed his newspaper to be used as a mouthpiece for it. But the line he held was the same as that of the government of the day (and of all intelligent men, Lennox would no doubt add). It was unlikely to threaten his commercial concerns.

Bittlestone found it unsettling to be in this social situation with his employer. He was wary; nervous of putting a foot wrong. He decided the best course of action was not to say anything unless he was directly addressed. Meanwhile, he had ample opportunity to study the interesting people around him. The most interesting of whom was Konrad Waechter.

He recognized the telltale signs in Waechter: the familiar lightness and precision, the secret vigilance he might even say, with which such men – men of his own kind – carried themselves. And Waechter betrayed himself too by his fluttering eyelids as he presented his cheeks to be very nearly kissed by Jane Lennox. 'Vell, dah-link, did you like my film?'

Bittlestone smiled to himself. Yes, Waechter was most definitely one of the brotherhood.

Jane Lennox blew out a long funnel of opium-scented smoke. 'I loved it, darling. You're such a clever old thing.'

'You understood vot I voz sayink *mit der* film?'

'Of course, darling. You were saying how horribly frightful it is to have one's eyes plucked out.' Jane Lennox gave a brittle, broken laugh. Bittlestone detected the welling of suppressed hysteria.

Waechter must have sensed it too. He became suddenly solemn. 'I voz werry sorry to hear about your fiancé.'

'Let's not talk about it now, sweetie.'

Harry Lennox shifted his weight from one foot to the other. He was evidently struggling with some dilemma, sensitive to his daughter's reluctance to dwell on the past, but nevertheless eager to get something off his chest. In the end his dominant nature prevailed. He was a man who spoke his mind, or he was nothing. 'Did you see him? Here! Quinn?'

'Don't mention that man to me, Daddy.'

'He has a lot to answer for, that's for sure. Bittlestone, do you not agree?'

'Oh, I do, Mr Lennox. I most certainly do.' If in doubt, agree.

'And will the *Clarion* be the paper to hold him to account?'

'Of that you can rest assured, sir.'

'What's our angle on this eye attack business? Have you filed your story yet?'

Lennox's eyes were piercing and expectant. This was a sensational story. The *Clarion* had been first on the scene. If they could not capitalize on it, they did not deserve to be newspapermen. 'I was just about to, sir. I thought I might garner a few quotes from the film people first. Herr Hartmann has kindly allowed me to use the company's telephone to call through the story when I'm ready.'

'Do you have a headline for me?'

'I was thinking of . . .' Bittlestone hesitated. In point of fact, he had not given a thought to the headline. Inspiration came to him suddenly: '*Eyeless in Cecil Court.* There is a strange irony about it, given that this alleyway happens to be the centre of the English film industry.' Bittlestone broke off anxiously. It might have been too 'clever' for Lennox, too intellectual. Literary, even.

'Can't you give me something snappier?'

Jane Lennox's head assumed an angle that infuriated Bittlestone. It seemed to express the conviction of her father's infallibility – more than that, of his genius. She certainly took her father's interference as a cue for her own critiquing of his work. She blew out more smoke and subjected him to a look of slow, bovine scrutiny. 'She's not *eyeless*,' she said, at last. 'She still has one eye left. *Eyeless* would be if she had lost them both.'

'She has *one . . . eye . . . less*,' insisted Bittlestone with slow, deliberate emphasis. His irritation was heightened by the suspicion that she might have a point.

Jane Lennox shrugged. It didn't matter to her in the slightest. In fact, it bored her. Her face spasmed into a grimace of a smile for Waechter's benefit.

Lennox was on the attack again. 'Who's the girl? That's the question. For crying out loud, Bittlestone! What are you doing here, when you should be out tracking her down? You could be the first to get her story!'

'But even the police don't know who she is.'

'Don't you worry about the *po*-lice! Find out which hospital she was taken to. Get to see her, man. Get her story.'

'I rather thought she might need some time to recuperate from her experience. Besides, the hospital won't let me see her at this hour, I'm sure.'

'Do you have no gumption, man? To be sure, when I was a cub reporter such lily-livered, weasel-minded equivocations never got in my way!'

His daughter confirmed this with a terse nod, as if she had been there to witness her father's early reporting triumphs.

Bittlestone produced his notebook and pencil. 'Very well, if that is what you wish me to do. However, if you have no objection, sir, I think it wise first to file an intermediate account based on what we know already. That way, we will have something in the morning edition. While I'm here, I will take some statements. Herr Waechter, how do you feel about this bizarre attack happening so soon after the showing of your film? Given the fact that, according to the police, she attended the screening.'

'My film is proven to be *ein Werk* of prophecy.'

'There, Bittlestone, you have your film people quote. Now find the girl. *Cherchez la femme!* That's the thing!'

Jane Lennox blinked her eyelids rapidly before turning on Bittlestone a look of focused contempt.

TWENTY-ONE

Max stood in the light. He was not going to hide away. He was not going to join the others in the darkness. Let them indulge in their wanton acts of revelry, cloaked by the shadows, hiding their faces from him. Well they might.

Only let them see him. Let them see his stern outrage. And be shamed by him.

But you could not shame these people. Did they have no human feelings? Were they incapable of sympathy, or respect?

Did they have no conscience? He would stand at the top of the stairs, his body haloed by the glowing white panels that led down to the basement; he would stand like an avenging angel. He would stand as their conscience.

Of course, Porrick was the worst of them. His crass reaction to the attack on the girl was typical of the man. All he cared about was the effect it would have on his box office. He had been delighted when he thought that the sensational news might serve to publicize the film. But outraged when his chance to profit from it was under threat.

Max had noticed two others who stood apart from the unseemly festivities. The small blackavised man from South America, and the equally swarthy long-haired youth who was almost always in his company. They watched the proceedings impassively. It was difficult to say what they made of it all. But when he had caught the eye of one or other of them, he thought he had seen sorrow there, pity even. It was as if they were saddened rather than outraged by the antics of the shallow, self-obsessed creatures around them.

When the man – Diaz, he thought he had heard him called – walked by, Max took the opportunity to vent his feelings. 'It was the same when my pal got killed. Ted. Ted Lapidus. Perhaps you have heard about it? You being in the business and all. It was in the newspapers at the time. A terrible blazing conflagration. It was a wonder that more weren't killed. Porrick was the same then. He didn't give a jot about Ted, or his widow. Or his three little ones. All he cared about was his precious Porrick's Palace. And the box office. I still remember now what he said when he heard about the fire. "How soon can we start showing pictures again?" A man had died then! Because of him. Make no mistake. It was all Porrick's fault, though he got off. A man like Porrick will always get off.'

Diaz looked steadily into Max's eyes. He at least was not afraid to meet his gaze. 'It is better not to dwell on the wrongs of the past. This is what I say to Inti.'

'Inti?'

Diaz indicated the youth, who was staring at a couple whose love-making had progressed almost beyond public decency. His interest in them seemed to be rather unwholesome, but it was perhaps to be expected given his age. 'My nephew. But it is easy for me to say. I have not suffered as Inti has suffered.'

'How has he suffered?'

Diaz squinted. His shoulders heaved. 'One day I tell the story of

his sufferings. I tell it to the world. That is my dream. I work for
Señor Waechter making his . . . fantastical dramas. But all the time
I save money. One day I make my own film. It will tell the truth
to the world. It will tell the story of what happen to Inti and his
people. That is my dream. One day you come to see my film. One
day you understand.'

'I will do better than that, my friend. I will show it. I will operate
the machine that projects it. And I will consider it an honour.'

Diaz looked back towards his nephew, his expression glazed with
sadness. Max followed his gaze. At just that moment the couple
Inti was watching pulled apart. Max recognized the woman as the
tart from the film. She was married to some Yank, who was also
an actor, and also there. Max felt sick to his core. The situation
epitomized everything that was wrong with these people.

The woman led the man out. Max would have said she led him
by the hand. But it was clearly some other part of his anatomy that
he was following.

Inti passed his uncle, hurrying in the wake of the couple. Diaz
put a hand out to detain him and spoke some firm but gentle words
in a language Max did not recognize. Inti shook his head and pulled
away sharply from his uncle's grip. His words exploded angrily in
his uncle's face. And then he was gone.

Diaz met Max's questioning gaze with a look of mild self-
reproach. 'He is good boy, really. But young.'

'Ah yes. What is a youth? Impetuous fire.'

Diaz frowned. 'I must go after him. This I promise my brother.'

'Of course.'

It seemed like the party was breaking up. A moment later, Porrick
himself was carried out, more than a little worse for wear. He was
leaning on the shoulder of the Yank. They were belting out the
words to one of the songs that had been playing earlier.

I want some love that's true . . . yes I do . . . indeed I do . . .
you know I do . . .

As he drew level with Max, Porrick turned to his projectionist.
The milky glow from the stairs gave the kinema showman a ghostly
aura. A look of sudden seriousness seemed to descend upon Porrick's
face, and for one mad moment Max thought he was about to make
some admission of responsibility, or expression of contrition. But
all he did was give his hoarse, drunken rendition of the next line:
'Gimme gimme gimme what I cry for . . .'

His companion joined in: 'You know you got the kind of kisses that I'd die for!'

Of course, the two drunks fell about at that. They were like some two-headed braying beast, staggering on hobbled legs. In that moment, Max hated them both. His hatred for the Yank was a passing thing. But the hatred he had for Porrick was of a different kind. It pre-existed the moment, and would continue long after it. Its roots went deep into his heart. And like a cancer, as it strangled his heart, it changed the sinews of that muscle into its own poisonous material. The hatred would kill him, unless he found a way to expunge it from his being.

TWENTY-TWO

At first Porrick had little sense of where he was or whither he was being led. Only, always, deeper into the London night. The air crackled with a fierce laughter. Faces came out of the darkness to leer at him. Rowdy men and blowzy women.

But gradually, the cool night air, and the imposed break from consuming alcohol, began to have a sobering effect.

The thoughts that he had sought to escape, first in getting drunk, and then in fleeing the party, began to make their presence felt again. He felt as if his body was about to liquefy into a pool of fetid matter. So, this was how it felt to be staring financial ruin in the face.

All that kept him upright was the support of a man he detested. And this was how it felt to be friendless.

But no. He would show them. He would show them all. He was not beaten yet.

Edna's vocal disapproval of his behaviour came close to a public humiliation. Black bitter thoughts curdled in the dark. He would teach her a lesson. He had hidden reserves she knew nothing about. He would leave her high and dry; cut her off without a penny. Hurt her where she would feel it most. And he needn't worry. He was Magnus Porrick, for heaven's sake! Hadn't Magnus Porrick been in a tight corner before? And always come out fighting?

No, he wasn't beaten yet. The film would be a great success.

And even if it wasn't – even if that fool of a policeman had his way – there was still the other business with Hartmann. That was a stroke of genius. He had to hand it to Hartmann, he was pretty deep when it came to financial matters. It had been the luckiest day of his life when he fell in with the German.

When all was said and done, there was no reason to be despondent. It was too early to write off Magnus Porrick. And if Edna did cut and run – well, then, good riddance to her, that's what he said. 'Good riddance to her!' he even cried out, giving voice to his thoughts.

'What's that?' said Novak.

'Edna. She's a damn bitch!'

'Language, Porrick! That's not the language of a gentleman! You wouldn't let another man speak that way about your wife, so y'ought not do it yourself.'

The momentary up-turn in Porrick's mood was suddenly dispelled. A soggy, faintly nauseous depression settled on him. How had he got himself saddled with this detestable fellow? He tried to pull away from Novak's arm around his neck, but the Yank clung on to him, as if refusing to let him out of his clutches.

'You stick with me, Porrick! I'll look after you. I know a place we can go. Girls there will help you forget about Edna. Do whatever you say and never answer back. *Whatever you say!* You understand me, Porrick?'

'Where's your wife? Didn't I see her leave with Lord Whassis-name?'

Novak waved a hand dismissively.

'You don't mind?'

'We're all grown-ups, ain't we? Marriage is all very well, but monogamy . . . She don't expect it of me and I don't expect it of her.'

Porrick shook his head dubiously.

'You're telling me you've never been unfaithful to Edna?' cried Novak incredulously.

'There have been . . . occasions. But I would never dream of telling her about them.'

'That's double standards, Porrick. Dolores and me, we believe in being honest with each other. We're partners, see. In life's great . . . you know . . .' Novak's hand described spirals in the night air. To compensate for his inability to conjure up the *mot juste*, he began whistling. The blasted Al Jolson song again.

Porrick's mood sank further. The tune brought back to mind
the business with Max Maxwell. That had left an unpleasant taste
in his mouth all right. Porrick knew very well the grounds of
Maxwell's resentment. But hadn't the court exonerated him?
Charges had been brought and he had been acquitted. From a
strictly legal point of view, Porrick was in the clear. As far as the
Old Bailey was concerned, that fellow's death all those years ago
was not on his conscience. So what right did Maxwell have to
look at him like that?

The thing was the fellow was dead and it was a terrible, unfortunate accident. But there was nothing he could do about it now.
And no amount of soul-baring and hair-shirt-wearing was going to
bring him back.

So why did he still wake in a cold sweat from dreams of crackling
flames and choking smoke?

Once, waking in the grey dawn, with the din of the morning
chorus chiding him, he had seen Ted Lapidus's charred body lying
across the foot of his bed. The image had quickly resolved itself
into the crumpled sheets kicked down to the bottom of the bed. But
that first vision had printed itself indelibly on to his memory. It was
with him always, now. A dim shadow lurking behind more pressing
preoccupations: the need to keep the punters coming in, to raise
cash, to ward off the City regulators, to get the new production with
Waechter under way, at all costs to keep the celluloid frames flying
through the gate of his projection machines . . . But no matter how
many distractions he sought, no matter how many other flickering
images he layered over it, it was always there. The dark inert shape
of a man's flame-blackened body.

The thing was . . . the only thing was . . . A drink. He needed
another drink. 'How much further, Novak?'

'Not far now, Porrick, old chap.'

One of the things Porrick hated about the Yank was his phony
way of affecting an English accent.

'I just want to make a quick stop at our little pied à terre.'

And now he was indulging in phony French. 'You have a pied
à terre?'

'We do. We find it awfully convenient.'

'And where is your country seat?'

'Haw haw! Very funny, Porrick. You got me there, all right!
Country seat . . . I like it. All right, you got me. This ain't so much

a pied à terre as a bolt hole. We all need a place to lie doggo from time to time.'

'Who do you need to hide from, Novak?'

'You got me wrong, Porrick, old bean. But sometimes you need a place to do some thinking . . . You unnerstand? You might find yourself in a tight situation one day. I'd be more than happy to put the place at your disposal.'

Porrick was beginning to have more of a sense of his surroundings. He realized that they had just turned into Dean Street. The window of an Italian restaurant drew his interest. The diners inside appeared happy in the candle glow. A warm smell of food seeped from the open door, where a waiter stood enticing passersby with a wide smile and a constant stream of patter. He offered a rose to every woman that passed.

'I say, Novak, what about a bite to eat?'

'Of course, yes. But first . . . it's just here, old chap. Come up for a moment and have a snifter. I just need to pick up some money, then I'll stand you some dinner.'

They came to a door a few paces on from the restaurant.

Novak grinned sheepishly as he put his key in the lock. 'I say, you're not going to be a prude, are you, old chap? If you're going to be a prude, we won't have any fun at all.'

The narrow stairwell smelled of every variety of fungal rot. Porrick stumbled in the dark. He heard a sharp hiss from Novak, shushing him urgently. It struck him as odd that the Yank should be so considerate of his neighbours. But he did not have time to draw any definite conclusions as to why it should be.

It struck him as odd, too, that the door had been left open, as if there was someone already inside the flat, someone who was expecting them.

TWENTY-THREE

As soon as the lights went on, and the heaving naked male arse was revealed in the blazing glare of electricity, Porrick understood everything.

The arse carried on pumping for a moment. It was an ugly,

dispiriting sight. A stark, pale obscenity moving with brutal energy in the shabbiest rented room imaginable.

Novak's startled oath – 'What the devil?' – was enough to bring Lord Dunwich (Porrick remembered his name as soon as he saw his face) to his feet, his sorry aristocratic member bobbing disconsolately, before drooping and shrinking rapidly. His lordship grabbed a cushion and held it in front of him.

The woman, Novak's wife of course, pulled her skirt down and sat up in the bed. Her expression might have puzzled an observer who didn't fully grasp the situation. A mixture of annoyance and boredom. She all but rolled her eyes at her husband.

She retrieved a cigarette from the bedside table and lit it. Soon, she was wholly preoccupied by the pleasures of smoking.

'Now, it's not what it seems!' pleaded Lord Dunwich. Porrick had to laugh at that. Despite his loathing for Novak and his wife, he had little sympathy for Dunwich.

'On the contrary, Lord Dunwich, it's crystal clear what's going on here,' said Novak.

'I didn't know . . .'

'You didn't know she was my wife?'

Porrick noticed a flicker of a smile on Dolores Novak's face. Lord Dunwich had his back to the woman, so he missed this hint of collusion between husband and wife.

Novak showed no sign of registering his wife's amusement. 'Please, Lord Dunwich, don't insult me. Don't add a lie to the offence you've already committed.'

'No, no. I wasn't going to say that. I knew. I admit I knew. It's just that I didn't think you minded, you see.'

'Not mind? Why would you think I wouldn't mind? Because you're an aristocrat? You forget, I'm an American. We don't acknowledge *droit du seigneur* in America.'

Mrs Novak tossed her hair appreciatively.

'I honestly thought you film people were more lax about these things. I thought you and Dolores had an understanding. Look . . . may I put my trousers back on? I feel that I'm at something of a disadvantage.'

'You shoulda oughta thoughta that before you took 'em off!'

His wife's tongue licked out, as if to taste the acrid flavour of her husband's histrionic ire.

Porrick had had enough of this. 'Let him put his trousers on,

Novak. I for one am not very comfortable with him undressed like
that. In fact, I think I should step outside.'

'Now look what you done! You've upset my friend, Mr Porrick!'
Porrick felt his lip curl at Novak's bogus protests. He resented being
dragged into the sordid affair.

'Actually, come to think about it . . . it's probably time for me
to go home.'

'You stay where you are, Porrick. I want you to bear witness to
this man's . . . depravity!'

Dolores Novak lifted her head self-righteously, as if she were the
innocent party.

'Steady on, Novak. You're rather overdoing it, you know. After
all, didn't you say to me . . .'

Novak cut him off with hasty indignation. 'Overdoing it? Would
you say that if you caught some bounder in flagrante delicto with
Mrs Porrick?'

Porrick was momentarily distracted by the unlikelihood of this
possibility.

'My dear fellow.' The smooth, soothing confidence in Lord
Dunwich's voice was the sound of a man mentally reaching for his
wallet. 'I'm most dreadfully sorry about this whole unfortunate
misunderstanding. I quite, *quite* understand your being in a funk
about it.' It was also the voice of a man used to paying for his
pleasures – not to mention buying his way out of trouble.

'I ought to whip you like a dog.' Novak turned his stagy ire on
his wife. 'And as for you, you she-devil . . .'

Her eyes widened theatrically. She snarled back at him. She was
evidently enjoying herself greatly.

'Now listen here, you mustn't take it out on Mrs Novak. Do what
you must to me, but please, leave Dolores out of it.'

'I'm an American!' declared Novak proudly. 'You can't tell me
what to do!'

'I wouldn't dream of telling you what to do. But perhaps we can
find some way to . . . effect a suitable form of restitution.'

It had all been engineered with the utmost skill, Porrick had to
give the Yank that. But it was despicable all the same. He'd been
responsible for a few windy schemes himself over the years. But
nothing as blackguardly as this. He was in two minds whether or
not to blow the gaff. He did not care to look too closely into what
prevented him. He discounted a dim presentiment that the situation

might turn out to be to his advantage. If that did turn out to be the case, he could at least excuse himself by arguing that he had done nothing to bring it about. He was not actively complicit in Novak's blackmail scheme. (Oh, it was pretty clear to him that this was something Novak and his wife had cooked up between them.) And as far as he was concerned, Lord Dunwich had brought it on himself.

Porrick had to admit that Novak had chosen his third-party witness well. Of course, he needed someone else there, because otherwise Lord Dunwich would have been able to say that it was just one man's word against another's. And the aristocrat's word would always be preferred over a seedy Yank with Serbian antecedents. But his choice of Porrick – a man he knew to be in financial difficulties and to have few moral scruples – revealed Novak's instinctive talent for exploiting human weaknesses. Porrick smiled ruefully.

Novak seemed to sense which direction Porrick's thoughts had taken. 'All I can say is I'm sorry you had to see this, Porrick.'

'As am I,' said Lord Dunwich.

Porrick was suddenly aware that he had sobered up entirely. His head was marvellously clear as he began to calculate the best way to play this.

'Perhaps it's better if you do go home. And leave his lordship and me to sort this out between ourselves. Man to man.'

Porrick pursed his lips, then nodded. 'Yes. I've seen enough here.'

If he understood a man like Novak at all, he was sure he would use his advantage to touch Lord Dunwich for more than one compensatory contribution. He would become a veritable leech. So, for now, the best thing was to let Novak do his worst. The time would come when his intervention – for either party, or even for both – would reap the maximum dividends.

And now he understood at last why he had conceived such an instinctive antipathy towards Novak. The man reminded him too much of himself.

'I'll go then,' he said. 'But for God's sake let him put his trousers back on.'

The gleaming, raw gratitude in Lord Dunwich's eyes both touched and shamed him. As soon as he saw it he knew that he had the peer in his grip. And he knew too that he would not balk from exploiting that power to the full.

Against his better judgement, he glanced one last time at the woman on the bed. She was brushing specks of ash from her skirt.

An arch of odious complacency was described in one eyebrow. She knew, as did her husband, that he would play his part exactly as they had predicted. They knew they could count on Porrick to do the base thing, if that was what his interests required.

He fled the shabby rented room in haste, as if he were fleeing the worst part of his own nature.

TWENTY-FOUR

George Bittlestone's step slowed as he approached the entrance to the Middlesex Hospital on Mortimer Street.

It was all very well for Lennox. He claimed to be a newspaper man – and all right, he had a sound instinct for the angle that would sell. That was because he was a businessman first, and a newspaperman second. Put a notebook in his hand and send him out on the streets in the night looking for a story, and he wouldn't have a clue where to start.

After all, you couldn't very well just walk through the front door and march up to the admittance desk and demand to see the girl who had had her eye gouged out.

If she was there, every member of the staff would know about it. Equally, they would do everything in their power to keep you away from her.

He carried on walking past the hospital, the railings of the hospital's courtyard to his right. The courtyard was quiet and badly illuminated: a shadowed expanse on the other side of which the hospital lights twinkled and glowed, beacons to the infirm.

Of course! That was it! The one sure way to gain admittance to where she was.

He saw ahead of him the lights of a public house. If his memory served him right, it was The George, a popular haunt of the musical and literary sets of Fitzrovia. There was a chance he might bump into someone he knew, which would be inconvenient, but not disastrous. He didn't see any way of achieving his goal without calling in. For one thing, he needed a fair dosing of Dutch courage for what he had in mind.

The George was heaving. He could only imagine that the

performance had just finished at the nearby Queen's Hall and the place was packed with concert-goers and musicians. He believed he could discern a musical lilt to the laughter, an exuberant delight that he felt was in keeping with an evening of symphonic appreciation.

When he eventually got served, he ordered a large whisky from the barmaid. She was a young chit of a girl, dead on her feet, with dark smudges of exhaustion under her eyes. He held the glass up to the light. It was clean enough to the naked eye, and no doubt the alcohol would prove beneficial on that score. He downed the contents in one gulp and pushed through the crowd, sheltering his empty glass against his chest like a fairground prize.

He took the glass outside.

Very well. The easy part was done. He had formed the intention. He had acquired the means. Now he had to carry it through.

He held the glass up to his face and ran the rim of it along his forehead.

Yes, somewhere there. Above his eyes.

But not the forehead. No.

He was going for immediate spectacle, rather than permanent disfigurement. No story was worth that.

He dashed the glass against the wall. The distinctive brittle explosion of sound interrupted the flow of joviality inside the pub. There were noises of mock solicitude and then laughter. The smashing of a glass was a trivial catastrophe after all.

In the glow from the pub windows, Bittlestone could see the jagged edge of the broken glass in his hand. He felt suddenly nauseous. A familiar, safe, useful object – a vessel for containing liquid – had been transformed into a dangerous weapon.

He stood and swayed on his feet. Either the alcohol was beginning to kick in, or he was about to faint. He knew that he would have to act quickly, and decisively, or not at all.

He felt with a finger around his eye, probing the loose skin beneath the bony ridge of his forehead.

Yes, there. Dangerous. But convincing.

He raised the glass and touched one point – the longest, most savage-looking – delicately to the place he had just explored. If he pushed it upwards he would avoid the eye. He would not need to go deep to produce the effect he wanted.

He felt the tip of the point bite his skin. His hand shook. The whole of his arm ached from the tension of holding that glass against his face.

The door of the pub creaked and sprang open. Bittlestone moved his hand away from his face and waited for the group which had emerged to make its way down Great Portland Street.

There was no more time for hesitation. That departure no doubt presaged a more general exodus.

It was now or never.

He brought the glass up briskly. Every vein in his body pulsed as his heart pounded and pumped the blood into and away from itself, in a fierce, vital roar of protest. As his hand went up, he felt a soaring exhilaration fill him. This was the most alive he had ever been. Even when he allowed himself to be pierced by lovers, he did not experience this intensity of being.

The moment the point broke through his skin was one of exquisite pleasure. His hand was no longer shaking. And so he was able to control the depth and angle of the intrusion.

He moved the glass slightly to one side, increasing the first shallow nip to a gash of – he judged – a quarter of an inch in extent.

He felt the hot liquid begin to trickle over his eye and down his face. He pulled the glass sharply out and let it drop, smashing to pieces on the pavement.

He held out a hand to fend off the wall. For some reason, the left hand side of his body went icy cold for a moment. His legs felt as if the bones had been removed from them and replaced with particularly elastic springs.

There were more people coming out of the pub. He turned his back on them. And began to grope his way back towards the dark quadrangle of the Middlesex Hospital.

TWENTY-FIVE

The following day, Saturday, the weather was dreary again. Quinn woke from a dissatisfying dream which was understandably coloured by the events of the previous night. Something troubling, a residue of horror lingered. He drew back the edge of his curtain to escape it, confronting the meagre gleam of the day.

He could hear raised voices coming from outside his door; high, anxious cries of female agitation. It was this altercation that had woken him.

He could make out Mrs Ibbott's voice, though not what she was saying. The other voice, well, it was a while since he had heard that other voice. It was not recognizable as belonging to any of the other residents in the lodging house, but it did.

Quinn felt a dreadful sinking feeling as he put on his dressing gown and went out on to the landing.

He found Mrs Ibbott on the landing below, outside Miss Dillard's room. There was a ferocious, oath-littered stream of invective coming from the other side of the door.

'She's drunk,' said Mrs Ibbott bluntly.

'But . . .'

'Yes, I know. It's not even eight o'clock yet. I do believe she has been drinking through the night.'

'Is there anything I can do?'

'Mr Quinn, I am not a hard-hearted woman. I hope that I am not.'

'Of course not, Mrs Ibbott.'

'I have made allowances over the years. Considerable allowances. You would not know.'

'Oh, but I do know, Mrs Ibbott.'

'Well, I don't mean to bring *that* up, but yes, there were months, when – because of her weakness – she had insufficient money for both rent and food, and I . . . I . . .'

'You made allowances.'

'I could not see a lady lodger of mine starve to death in my own house. Neither could I see her turned out on to the street to die in a gutter somewhere.'

'It speaks volumes for your humanity, Mrs Ibbott.'

'Mr Quinn, I ask you . . . do you hear . . . do you hear what she calls me?'

'I do. I'm very much afraid I do. Would you like me to . . . would you like me to see if she will speak to me?'

'Oh, Mr Quinn, I am not sure that is a good idea. You know, do you not, that Miss Dillard is rather . . . soft on you?'

'I . . . I didn't . . .'

'Oh, come now, Mr Quinn. Surely you realized?'

Quinn felt himself blush. Thankfully, he noticed that it had gone quiet inside Miss Dillard's room, so was able to change the subject. 'Perhaps she's gone to sleep?'

But it was not entirely silent within. A small regular throb of weeping came to them.

Quinn rapped gently on the door. 'Miss Dillard? May I come in? It is I, Mr Quinn. Silas.'

Mrs Ibbott shook her head dubiously. 'She will not want to see you, Mr Quinn,' she whispered. 'She will not want to see you like this.'

But as if solely to contradict Mrs Ibbott, the door to Miss Dillard's room began to open.

Quinn had never been in any of the other residents' rooms before. What shocked him most about Miss Dillard's room was how small it was. The dimensions of his room seemed palatial in comparison. But, of course, he was a lodger who always paid his rent on time, and could afford the greater rent required for a larger room. He was a working man, in fact, a solidly respectable officer of the law. He may have fallen from the social class of his parents, but in so doing he had become his own man. He wasn't dependent on the crumbs of a tiny private income, from a pitiful inheritance divided by God knows how many sisters.

His eye darted around the gloom-soaked room like a buzzing fly looking for an escape point. The curtains were open, but the window was so small and grimy that the light barely penetrated it. It looked as if it had never been opened. The air was cloying. Sour and sickly sweet at the same time. At first he thought it was the smell of gin. But he began to suspect it was the smell of gin-drenched vomit. *Where was that?* he wondered. *What had she done with it?* He found the question vaguely preoccupying.

But, God, it was untidy in there. The vomit could have been anywhere. It was probably in a pot under the bed. She might have had just enough presence of mind to push it out of sight. It amazed him how much chaos could be packed into a tiny space. This was a corner of the universe that had let itself go. The single bed was a mess of grubby sheets and bedding, rucked up to expose the stained mattress beneath. The floor was littered with clothes, and – embarrassingly for Quinn – underclothes, some of which were exhibiting evidence of soiling. He had to look away quickly, pretend he hadn't seen, and resist the temptation to look again.

He looked instead into her eyes, which were pink and moist from crying. The beautiful pewter grey of her irises eluded him. She would not meet his gaze. It was her turn to be ashamed now. She hid her face in her hands, and then, as if that wasn't concealment enough, turned her back on him.

'Miss Dillard . . .'

She groaned.

'Are you all right, Miss Dillard?'

'Leave me alone.'

'*You* let me in, Miss Dillard.'

'It's all a terrible mess.'

'It's nothing that can't be . . . sorted out.'

'I don't have any money. I don't have any money to pay her. She's going to turn me out on the street.'

'No. Mrs Ibbott would never do that.'

'But I don't have any money, I tell you! What else can she do?'

'Perhaps your sisters . . .?'

'My sisters!'

Quinn tented his fingers on either side of his nose and breathed in deeply. The sound was amplified by the vibration of his nostrils against his fingers. It caused Miss Dillard to turn round. Her eyes solicitously sought out his. 'Are you all right, Mr Quinn?'

'Me? Why, yes, of course.'

'You sound as though you have a cold.'

'I am perfectly well, I assure you.'

Miss Dillard gave a weak smile. It was almost as if his answer consoled her for whatever else was wrong in her life. She sank down on to the bed and then lifted her legs, turned over and in less than a minute was snoring loudly.

Quinn let himself out.

Mrs Ibbott greeted him with an inquisitive arching of her brows.

'She's sleeping now.'

'That's something, I suppose. At least I will be spared her abuse.'

'Mrs Ibbott . . .'

'Yes, Mr Quinn?'

'If it is a question of her rent . . .'

'What are you saying, Mr Quinn?'

'If it is a question of her rent, and whatever other expenditure, you may come to me for it. Until Miss Dillard is feeling quite well again.'

'But, Mr Quinn, I cannot permit you to do that. I do not believe that Miss Dillard would want you to do that. Charity is not the solution.'

'Miss Dillard will never know.'

'But what if she asks?'

'She will not ask. If you cease to trouble her for her rent, she will not – I think – trouble you.'

'I cannot have someone else's generosity ascribed to me.'

'Then say it is her sisters' doing.'

'She will not believe that.'

'Then say . . . then say it is a secret benefactor. But do not mention my name.'

'But is this not simply indulging her in her weakness?'

'We shall take steps to help her, shall we not? I feel that it is her sense of hardship and financial misery that prompt her to seek recourse in the bottle. If we alleviate that, then perhaps . . .'

'I fear it is not that, Mr Quinn. I fear it is something else entirely.'

Quinn frowned in confusion.

Mrs Ibbott shook her head impatiently. 'Ah, for a police detective, you are awful dense. But then you're a man, are you not?'

TWENTY-SIX

Harry Lennox breakfasted on kippers, washed down with coffee. He liked to start the day with a strong taste in his mouth. It was his habit also to take his breakfast in the conservatory, surrounded by potted palms and sweating panes. It did him good to feel the sun on his bald patch as he bent over his copy of the *Daily Clarion*. And on a day like today he was at least protected from the chill that the season seemed unable to shake off.

His conservatory was an elaborate wrought-iron-and-glass affair. Its design suggested a distant pavilion in some eastern outpost of the Empire. It was a fantasy that Lennox enjoyed. In his mind it was not the British Empire, of course, but the Empire of Harry Lennox. He saw himself as a pioneer, pushing forward the boundaries of his influence and success. Hacking through a forest of *terra incognita*. He dreamt of a global newspaper empire, with a Lennox title in every major English-speaking city in the world. It might have seemed a ludicrous ambition to some. But he had achieved it in London, which was to all intents a foreign capital to him. At times, a hostile capital, even. He had had his fair share of anti-Catholic – and anti-Irish – prejudice to overcome, especially in the early days. But if Harry Lennox had a talent for anything, he had a talent for making the right friends. There were few people who would call him a jumped-up Mick nowadays. At least not to his face.

Somehow breakfasting in the conservatory reinforced his myth of self-creation. The conservatory looked out not just on to the well-tended garden of a well-to-do house at the foot of Primrose Hill, but on to the *future*. And Harry Lennox's future was going to be every bit as spectacular as his past had been so far.

Lennox began his newspaper career as a boy on the streets of Cork, selling the *Echo*. Inspired by the example of Thomas Crosbie, he charmed his way into a job as a cub reporter, at the age of fifteen. But right from the start his sights were set beyond the city of Cork, beyond the shores of Ireland even. What Crosbie had achieved in Cork, by the age of forty-five, Lennox was determined to emulate in London, by an even younger age. In fact, he would be thirty-seven when he founded the *Clarion*. It was an exceptional, breathtaking ascendancy.

Charm is a valuable asset for a newspaper reporter to have, especially when it is combined with ruthless ambition, and an entire lack of moral scruple, which is only another way of saying 'clarity of purpose'.

His first job in London was with the *Thunderer*, which gave him the serious reporting chops he needed to get on in the business. From there he moved to the fledgling *Daily Mail*, and within a year had risen to be its Society Editor. His talent for making friends was put to professional use. It was at that time that he met Hartmann, and through him was introduced to the Jewish financiers who would, five years later, back his own plans for a new title. He realized that it was unlikely that he would ever achieve the editorship of one of the established papers, so he had decided to bypass that stage of Crosbie's career, and go straight to proprietorship.

The first edition of the *Clarion* carried Bittlestone's earliest filed story, the one he had called in from Cecil Court. There was a vivid account of the girl's discovery, a lurid retelling of the incident with the dog, a rather dismissive reference to Quinn, and the quotation from Waechter. He had to say Bittlestone made rather a hash of the film people angle. It was all too symbolic and artistic. This was not symbolism; it was a bloody brutal act. If the film people were involved, it was a scandal because they were famous and rich and beautiful and glamorous, not because they created images for the rest of us to look at.

And no mention of Bittlestone tracking the girl down and getting her story, he saw. He would have to call into the office first thing and find out what was going on there. For Bittlestone's sake, he hoped that he had come up with something in time for the later editions.

The door to the conservatory opened. A silver tray bearing the morning's post appeared on the table in front of him. He did not look up. He did not smile. He did not thank the maid who placed it there. It was as if his famous charm was a scarce resource that he had to preserve for when he really needed it.

He folded away the newspaper and turned his attention to the correspondence. One envelope drew his attention. He frequently received begging letters from the Old Country, essentially feckless Irishmen touching him for money, and basing their appeals purely on their compatriotism. As if he ought to give a penny to every Irishman in the world! Some of the letters dressed themselves up as investment opportunities (*encl.: incomprehensible plans for half-baked schemes*); others were chain letters in which semi-mystical means to success were promised, we all know the kind of thing – *send ten pounds to this address and good luck will surely follow*; others again were barely disguised extortion rackets, with thinly veiled threats and invariably shocking spelling: *yor dorter is a bewty wuld be a sham if ennythin hapent to her now.*

Lennox's response to them all was to ignore them.

With its green-inked address, this had the look of being another of the same. Green for Ireland, presumably. He was in half a mind to throw it in the wastepaper bin without opening it. But he wasn't a newsman for nothing. The old curiosity always got the better of him.

The envelope was small, the size of a personal letter. It did not feel as though there was any enclosure, so no plans for a harebrained invention in this one. In fact, he could not be sure that the envelope contained anything. He looked for the post mark, but couldn't find one. It seemed that it had been delivered by hand, presumably just after or before the postman had called.

He tore the envelope open distractedly and took out a single playing card, the Jack of Hearts, a one-eyed Jack. But where the eye should have been, a small hole had been pierced.

There was nothing written on the card, face or reverse. He looked inside the envelope, but found no cover note.

The conservatory suddenly seemed a dark and inhospitable place, as if a shadow had settled over it. A shiver seemed to lurk in the air, waiting to take possession of him. And yet there had been no change in the external quality of the light, no drop in the temperature. It was simply that, for some unaccountable reason, he had experienced real and physical dread.

TWENTY-SEVEN

He found a medical supply shop open on Wigmore Street, where he purchased a pair of spectacles with darkened lenses. It was not that his eyes' sensitivity to light had increased since his self-inflicted wound. Just that if he was going to return to the office he wanted to forestall for as long as possible any questions regarding the stitches over his eye.

With the swelling and dressing in his injured eye, he was half-blind anyhow. Such was the prevalent gloom of the morning that once he put the glasses on he could hardly see a thing. Even so, it was a relief to be hidden behind the blessed darkness of the celluloid-coated disks.

He groped his way out of the shop and headed south to Oxford Street. At one point he was even helped across the road by a solicitous gent. He was used to giving himself over to the hands of strangers, but not under these circumstances.

On Oxford Street, he stumbled into a Lyons tea house and made his way to a table in the gloom-encompassed rear. After a moment or two, the waitress came up to take his order: tea and a crumpet.

As he waited for his morning sustenance to arrive, he tried to get his story straight.

Of course, it would have been a different matter if his stunt had come up trumps, if he had found the girl and got a story out of her. But he had drawn a blank on both fronts.

It had all seemed so simple in the picture palace of his imagination. Without his having to say a word, the nurses would rush him to the very same ward where she was being held. The affinity of their wounds would make sure of that. And even if that did not happen, someone would be bound to comment on the startling coincidence of their admitting two patients with eye injuries on the very same night. He could get into easy conversation with said someone, and tease out of them where the girl was now.

In the event, the first nurse who saw him had smelled the whisky on his breath and assumed that he had sustained his injury as the result of a drunken brawl. And so he was given a wad of cotton wool to hold to his eye and kept waiting for three hours.

A second nurse stitched his eye, without any attempt to anaesthetize the area. When he cried out in pain, she commented that she should have thought all the whisky he had drunk would have numbed the pain.

He did not see the girl in the ward, and no one who spoke to him made mention of her. When he tried to ask in a casual manner whether they saw many eye injuries, his enquiries were met with sullen silence. And when he resorted to telling the nurse who stitched him what he had witnessed in Cecil Court, it was clear she regarded him as the worst kind of lunatic.

And so, at last, he had been discharged. He had wandered the streets until he found the medical supply shop.

His tea and crumpet arrived. He let the sugar flow freely from the jar. And asked the waitress for jam.

He felt a childish need for sweet and comforting consumption.

Only one conclusion could be drawn. The doctor had taken her to UCH, despite the fact that the Middlesex was closer to the scene of the attack.

Once he had finished his tea, he would head there. This time he would walk up to the front desk, present his credentials and ask for them to confirm the admittance of a female patient suffering from a vicious wound which had resulted in the enucleation of her eye. Sometimes, the most straightforward approach was the best.

That was something a man like Lennox would never understand.

TWENTY-EIGHT

The clanging siren ripped into the morning's torpor. The morning answered with a pale indignant glare, but was essentially powerless to resist.

Quinn stepped to one side as the St John's ambulance sped into the courtyard of the Middlesex Hospital. He followed the gleaming white vehicle with his gaze. A bowler-hatted man in black was standing at the entrance to the hospital, just where the ambulance came to a screeching, grinding halt. But he ignored the vehicle's dramatic arrival and instead stared fixedly in Quinn's direction. Quinn immediately recognized the deep-furrowed frown. It was the man he had first seen in the Tube carriage, the man with the unspeakably bitter face. The same man who had reappeared last night in Leicester Square to berate first Waechter and then Porrick.

On that occasion, Quinn had avoided confronting the man. He wondered now if that had turned out to be a fatal error. The persistent recurrence of this bitter-faced revenant was forcing upon Quinn the very real possibility that he was the girl's attacker. Quinn tried to unravel the complex psychological contortions that would make this hypothesis plausible. The attack was an attempt to injure Waechter and Porrick, against whom he seemed to have some kind of grudge. Possibly, even, it was an attack on the entire film production, distribution and exhibition industries. From what he had heard of the man's tirade, his grudge was fairly widespread. He seemed to think the film industry owed him something. It was not unfeasible that he would set upon a course of action to injure its interests.

But why had he shown himself to Quinn before the attack? Perhaps he did not intend for Quinn to see him. Perhaps, having been ignored by the film industry, he now believed himself to be invisible to the world. He had been watching Quinn, because he believed that it would be Quinn who would be called upon to investigate whatever crimes he was intending to commit.

The man stood rooted to the spot, still staring at Quinn. If he were the girl's attacker, it might make sense that he had come here

to find out news of her condition. But wouldn't he make some
attempt to evade capture, instead of standing there in the open?

Quinn waved and shouted, as he trotted across the courtyard.
'Wait! I want to speak to you a moment.'

The man made no move to get away, nor did he acknowledge
Quinn's hail. However, there was something awkward – an unnat-
ural constraint – to his posture. His body was held at an angle,
and he kept one hand determinedly behind his back. Looking
down at the other hand, Quinn noticed that for once it was not
gloved.

'Who are you? What do you want with me?'

For an answer, the man looked deep into Quinn's eyes. Quinn
found his gaze both troubling and compelling. He recognized that
secret quality that marked not just a capability, but also a willing-
ness, to do anything. It was a capacity that was released when an
individual went beyond despair. He had seen it in many murderers.
He had seen it in himself.

Neither the man nor Quinn blinked, as if they had gone too far
for that.

'I knew your father,' he said at last.

Quinn's heart took up where the ambulance's siren had left off.

'How is that possible?'

'I know what happened to him. I know why . . . why he took
his own life.'

'No!'

'Do you not wish to know?'

'What has this to do with what happened last night? A girl was
viciously attacked last night after the premiere of a new motion
picture. I saw you there. You argued with the maker of that film.
You came here to see her . . .'

'How do you know that?'

'Why else would you be here?'

'Your logic is faulty. However, it is true that I made some enquiries
at the desk. They know me here. I was able to ask questions without
arousing suspicion. She was not admitted.'

'Do you know her name?'

'No. But I think they would have remarked upon the nature of
her injury sufficiently to identify her. No one with an enucleated
eye was admitted last night.'

'Why do you care? What has this got to do with you?'

'I believe Waechter did it. I have reason to believe he is a Satanist. This may be connected to some kind of perverted ritual.'

'Who are you?'

'My name is Hugh Grant-Sissons. I knew your father.'

'Yes, you said. Are you a doctor? Is that why they know you?'

'No. I am an inventor. I worked with your father on some ideas for a new apparatus that could have transformed medical science. Unfortunately, nothing came of it. Various unfortunate circumstances, including your father's death, cut our enterprise short. Do you not find it strange that there is no record of her admittance?' To Quinn, the abrupt change of tack seemed indicative of a dislocated mind.

'She must have been taken to a different hospital.'

'That will be a simple matter for you and your officers to confirm.'

'Are you still following me?'

'How could I be following you when I was here before you?'

'What if you were the one who attacked her?'

The furrow in Grant-Sissons's brow seemed to ripple and deepen, as if the invisible hatchet that had caused it had landed a second, firmer blow. 'Why would I do that?'

'Revenge.'

'To the best of my knowledge, that poor girl has never done anything to me. Indeed, I have no idea who she is.'

'That's not what I mean. You know what I mean. This is an attack on Waechter.'

Grant-Sissons took some time to consider this. At length, he decided on his answer. 'On the contrary. It will do no harm to the success of his film whatsoever. In fact, if my understanding of the baseness of human nature is correct, it will serve to promote considerable public interest in Herr Waechter and his odious films. As that is the last thing I want, I think you must agree that I am the last person who would carry out this attack.'

'Why do you hate Waechter so much?'

'Oh, I don't hate him any more than I hate them all. Every single person who has profited from my invention – for which I never received a penny, may I say. My ideas were stolen from me by Edison. I have devoted my life since to exposing this injustice and reclaiming what is mine by rights.'

'So do you picket every screening of every film?'

'Not every. I cannot be everywhere. But there are other reasons

for objecting to Waechter. He is a degenerate pervert. He cannot go
back to Austria because he is wanted there for buggery.'

Quinn suppressed a smile. 'I thought it was for duelling?'

'That is a pretext. And as for that creature Porrick – in many
ways he is even worse. He caused a man's death, you know.'

'Really?' As always, Quinn's interest in a person was piqued by
an association with death.

'Yes. He had a workman solder a tin trunk shut.'

'How did that cause his death?'

'The trunk contained film stock, which as you know is made
from highly flammable cellulose nitrate. One spark was enough to
send the whole thing up in flames. The poor fellow was working
in a tiny basement room, the way out blocked by more film stock,
all of which caught fire. He didn't stand a chance.'

'How do you know all this?'

'I make it my business. This industry was spawned from my
invention. Creatures like Porrick would be nothing without me.
Naturally, I follow news of their doings closely.'

'What exactly was it you invented?'

'I invented the mechanism that allows the staggered passage of
a roll of sensitized film through a metal gate, at the same time as
activating a synchronized shutter, so that a rapid series of photographs may be taken – and by the same mechanism, projected. In
layman's terms, I invented the motion picture camera and projector.
I have here a copy of a letter I sent to Thomas Edison in 1889,
together with the reply, which proves that they received it even
though they claimed that the plans I enclosed were impracticable.
So impracticable that, in the following year, they produced a machine
which is in all essentials identical to mine!'

The hand that was not hidden behind his back delved into the
inside of his jacket. After a moment of struggling, Grant-Sissons
waved a set of greasy, well-thumbed papers in front of Quinn's
nose.

Quinn couldn't help raising an objection. 'Why did you send him
your plans? Wasn't he . . . a rival?'

Grant-Sissons withdrew the documents, without giving Quinn a
chance to read them, and one-handedly replaced them with as much
difficulty as he had taken them out. 'Some ideas are greater than
petty rivalry. I was hoping for his financial support. I thought he
would recognize me as a fellow inventor. I thought he would realize

the potential of my ideas and fund my business. Oh, he saw the potential all right.'

'Forgive me for saying so, Mr Grant-Sissons, but it seems to me that you were a little naive.'

Grant-Sissons seemed to take offence at this. And a moment later proved that he did at least have the instinct for revenge. 'Shall I tell you why your father took his own life?' There was a sadistic edge to his voice.

Quinn had been on the verge of taking the man in as a suspect. But he was deterred by the prospect of discovering at last the information that had for so long tormented him. Furthermore, he had to accept that without the girl, there was little to charge anyone with. 'I am in the middle of conducting an investigation.'

'It won't take a moment.'

'Tell me where I can find you. When I am ready, I will come to you.'

Again, his one visible hand probed his coat, on the other side this time, his left hand bending back into the left breast. It was evidently too difficult for him to achieve this manipulation. His right hand involuntarily came round to help. Quinn saw that it was bandaged. With both hands, Grant-Sissons was able to fish out a card. He withdrew the bandaged hand from sight immediately. 'This is my workshop. I am often there. When I am not . . . elsewhere.'

Quinn declined the offered card. 'What happened to your hand?'

'It is an old injury. In fact, a skin condition for which I must seek regular treatment. I have just had it dressed at the hospital. So you see, I did not come here with the intention of looking for your girl. It is simply a coincidence that I happened to be here.'

Quinn endeavoured to communicate his deep mistrust of coincidences through some complex fluctuations of his brows. At last he deigned to take the card. It bore an address in Clerkenwell: *3, St John's Passage.*

'I *will* be in touch.' Quinn heard the reassuring insistence in his own voice, as if it were more important to Grant-Sissons to tell him what he knew than to Quinn to hear it.

'You cannot bear it, can you? You cannot bear the truth.'

'I must find the girl,' said Quinn. But even to his own ears it sounded like an excuse.

TWENTY-NINE

S cudder was trapped inside the darkness. He couldn't move at all. The darkness struck him against the snout whenever he tried to spring out of it. And when he scratched his paw against the darkness, it was hard. Not like the darkness through which he was used to scampering, navigating with his twitching nose across the trade routes of scents. In this darkness, his feet tapped and scraped without him getting anywhere. And the only scent was that of his own fear.

All he could do was open his jaws and let the fear and the rage snap and whine in the tensioned sinews of his throat.

He turned and twisted in the tiny black corner of darkness. There had to be a way out. There was always a way out. If you pushed with your snout or scratched with your paw, whatever was in front of you would eventually yield.

But there was no yielding in this darkness. This darkness held him in its jaws. This darkness held his howls too, and the smell of his fear. And the smell of his fear made him more afraid.

There were moments when the darkness rattled and seemed about to fall apart. But then the darkness boomed terrifyingly. He cowered down and back, away from the heavy pounding on the top of the darkness.

All he could do was scratch and snarl and whine. But the darkness was not touched by anything he did. The darkness held him.

The darkness filled and echoed with his whining. His whining wrapped itself around him. His whining pierced his ears. His hairs stood up and a shiver took hold of him. His shiver set the darkness rattling.

Then the deafening *boom-boom-boom* sent him cowering into the corner of the hard darkness.

THIRTY

'So . . . what do we know?' Quinn straightened tentatively. He was standing in the highest part of the attic-room headquarters of the Special Crimes Department. He knew that he should have been able to reach his full height here without cracking his head, but, even so, a habit of caution cramped his movements.

Inchball yawned and blinked. His eyes were red with exhaustion. Even the soft reflected glow from the blank wall that faced the skylight seemed to be too much for him. He held his hands in front of his face, rubbed vigorously into his aching sockets, then glared, a bewildered, ravaged wreck of a man. 'We know where Hartmann lives. I followed him after that shindig to an address in Forest 'Ill.'

'Forest Hill?'

'Yeah, Forest bloody 'Ill. I will need you to sign off the taxi fare, guv. Four shillings and sixpence.'

'Of course.'

'I waited outside the 'ouse all bleedin' nigh' and then followed him back into town this morning. Fortunately, he took the train and I was not obliged to splash out on another bleedin' taxi. I would have been in a pickle otherwise, I can tell you. I can also tell you that he did *not* return to Cecil Court. He took the train to London Bridge, and from there he proceeded on foot – my poor achin' legs! – across the river to an address in the City. On St Swithin's Lane, to be precise. You want the number, do ya?' Inchball sighed monumentally. He then tried each of his pockets in turn until at last he found his notebook. His bemused expression seemed to suggest that he had been unaware of the very existence of that particular pocket until that moment. He leafed through the pages. 'A 'undred and nineteen, St Swithin's Lane. A number of businesses is located at this address.' Inchball read from his notebook. 'Palgrave 'Oldings. Jacobs and Jacobson, Solicitors.' Inchball paused as if he was going to make a comment but thought better of it and continued reading the list. 'Imperial Trading Consortium. London Nitrate Company. The Colonial Financing Corporation. The

Panamanian Investment Syndicate – parenthesis London, close parenthesis. The England and Continental Finance Bank. That's it.'

'And which of these offices did he enter?'

Inchball rolled his eyes at Quinn's question. 'Do me a favour, guv! Ain't it enough I got all this for you? I 'ad 'a be careful, you know. Din' want him to see me. I couldn' afford to go breathin' down 'is neck or nuffin'. By the time I got through the front door, 'e was nowhere to be seen.'

'Of course, Inchball. I understand. This is excellent.'

'The way I see it, he either went into one of the offices on the ground floor, which would be the Panamanian Investment Syndicate – parenthesis London, close parenthesis – or the England and Continental Finance Bank. Or, 'e went into the office what was on the second floor, that is to say, the London Nitrate Company.'

'How do you figure that out?' asked Macadam.

'I 'eard the lift come to a halt above. I took the stairs and found it on the second floor. Where this London Nitrate Company is.'

'It is more likely that he had business with the Finance Bank on the ground floor,' suggested Quinn. 'I imagine that the Panamanian Investment Syndicate . . .'

'Parenthesis London, close parenthesis,' added Inchball.

'I would imagine that they are concerned largely in raising investments for Panama specifically, and perhaps for Central and South America more widely. It is possible that Hartmann has business interests there. But if his film production business is legitimate, as it seems to be – he has after all produced at least one film that I saw with my own eyes – then he will need to raise finance from time to time.'

'We can't assume that any of these set-ups is legitimate, guv,' objected Inchball. 'Any one of 'em could be a cover for his nefarious activities.'

Quinn remembered his conversation with Lord Dunwich the night before. The peer had been at pains to impress upon Quinn Hartmann's bona fides. He had also let slip that he had business interests in common with the German. It was likely these interests went back a long way. Perhaps some of these interests were tied up in one of the companies on St Swithin's Lane.

Quinn sensed his sergeants watching him expectantly, like pupils awaiting instructions from their teacher. They would have to wait. There was a tangle here and Quinn set himself to tease it apart.

Dunwich had tried to steer them away from the barbershop. Perhaps this was out of loyalty to his friend Hartmann, whom he perhaps knew to be connected to Dortmunder. Dunwich's robust defence of Hartmann last night could be put down to a self-protective reflex. If Dunwich was in hock to Hartmann, or his associates, that made him vulnerable, not to say suspect. He would naturally wish to divert attention away from an object that had the potential to blow up in his own face. Not only that, the connection meant that Dunwich would be a tool that the German could employ when he needed to. Quinn had a sense of Herr Hartmann as a very patient individual indeed. He suddenly remembered the sinister package that Lord Dunwich had been sent. 'Did anything come for me from Lord Dunwich?'

Macadam shook his head. Inchball had actually dozed off.

'Oh, there was one thing came for you.' Macadam handed over an envelope. Quinn noticed immediately that his name and the address were written in green ink.

Quinn took out a mimeograph of about two hundred names arranged in several columns on a single sheet of paper. Some of the names were marked with a green *x*.

Also enclosed was a brief note on stationery headed 'Visionary Productions', handwritten and signed in the same green ink by Hartmann.

> *My Dear Inspector Quinn,*
> *Please find enclosed the list of guests invited to last evening's gala screening of 'The Eyes of the Beholder'. I have marked the names of those who also attended the party afterwards, approximately 50 in number. I sincerely hope that this is of some use to you in your endeavours to apprehend the vicious attacker of that poor girl.*
> *Your servant,*
> *Oskar Hartmann*

Quinn glanced down the columns of names, until he found his own. Then he handed the sheet back to Macadam.

'I want you to go through that and check the names against the files.'

'Each and every name, sir?'

'You may overlook mine.'

'And may I ask, sir? Are we to switch our surveillance operation to this new address of Inchball's? Perhaps deploy the kinematographic camera again? It would have to be in a different van, sir, as Hartmann has seen the baker's. If we could catch Dortmunder on film coming to this address it would clinch it. What possible business could a German barber have with one of these companies?'

Quinn nodded thoughtfully, without committing himself. 'An interesting idea. First, however, I would like you to do some background checks on the companies. See if you can find out the names of the directors. Then you can cross-check them with the list of names from Hartmann. Oh, and did you have a chance to follow up on the girl for me?'

'The telephone is just one of the many boons of modern technology that have revolutionized police work. Instead of wearing out my boots tramping the streets, I was able to make my enquiries without leaving my desk.' There was a tone to Macadam's voice that suggested the thought: *You really ought to try it one day, sir!* 'No girl was admitted to any London hospital last night with injuries consistent with the removal of an eye.'

'And this Doctor Casaubon?'

'There is a Doctor Augustus Casaubon listed in Kelly's Directory on Harley Street. Number seventeen.'

'Does his surgery possess a telephone?'

'It does. But no one is answering it this morning. I will keep trying, of course.'

'In this case, perhaps it might be worth our while to apply a little boot leather to the task. I shall go there myself. Inchball . . .'

'Nguh?'

'I have a very important task for you.'

Inchball blinked and winced as he struggled to sit up in his chair.

'Go home and get some sleep.'

THIRTY-ONE

Magnus Porrick stirred in the darkness, turning his back on fitful, flickering dreams. The four tip-up auditorium seats he was stretched out across shook and groaned in protest.

He had not slept well. His back began to ache almost as soon as he lay down. It was now locked in a muscle clench of pain. And he was cold. God, it was cold in the Palace at night, after the massed bodies of successive audiences had finally vacated the rows. Once he had started shivering, he could not stop. And every shiver sent a fresh jolt of pain shooting through his limbs.

No, he had not gone home. He had thought it best to give Edna a little time to calm down. She would come round eventually, he felt sure. He had needed time too. Time to sober up.

The plush of the seat dug into his face, stubble against stubble. He kept his eyes closed tightly though he was awake, as if dreading what the day might offer to his sight. The image of that aristocratic erection was a chastening example. Some things, once seen, are hard to eradicate from the memory, however much we might wish it. Some sights change everything.

Movement was painful. It was as if the darkness was a vice that gripped him tightly. It was fruitless to struggle. The vice held him facing the memory of last night.

Granted, it was all very sordid and unpleasant. There was nothing he could do about that. It was a question of business now. And there are all sorts of unpleasant businesses that men steel themselves to undertake. (Undertaking being one of them. Was the undertaker squeamish about manhandling the dead? Porrick doubted it.) A lesser man might give in to the natural instinct to put it all behind him. But he could not afford to take that view. The darkness would not let him take that view. He was a businessman. A businessman was obliged to look for the commercial opportunity in any given situation, and exploit it.

Business consisted of the relationships between men. That was why the handshake was so important. Last night, something had changed in the relationship between Magnus Porrick and Lord Dunwich. Both men knew it. Why, Lord Dunwich would have been amazed if he had not taken advantage of it.

But he need not be in any hurry. Indeed, it was preferable to wait for Lord Dunwich to come to him. And when that happened, the first thing to do would be to reassure his lordship of his goodwill. He must insist that he had known nothing about the Novaks' grubby plan to entrap him; he was a pawn in their game. And if Lord Dunwich doubted it was a plan, he would reluctantly disabuse him. At which point he would offer to intercede with the Novaks. He could put himself forward as a man of influence in the motion picture business. It wouldn't be overstating it too much to say that he could see to it that neither of them ever made another film. Certainly, if his plans with Waechter came to fruition, he could ensure that they never appeared in another of the Austrian's films.

And so, without doing anything very much, he would manufacture that most valuable of commodities: the gratitude of a rich and powerful man.

Porrick kept his eyes closed, as if he was afraid to let reality intrude on his daydreams. And yet, what was there to worry about? It all seemed watertight. And whatever happened, he would be in the clear. He himself had done nothing wrong. What he was proposing was not blackmail. It was more a question of leverage.

Something, however, nagged at the edge of his consciousness, a vague awareness that there was something he had forgotten.

Of course, this would all take time. Things had to be allowed to unfold at their own pace. You couldn't force it. And in the meantime, if Kirkwood's warnings had any substance, his chain of Porrick's Palaces could come tumbling down around him.

No, no, it'd be all right. He'd show them all. He'd turn it round. He had a plan. And he didn't just mean the business with Lord Dunwich. He had another plan . . .

But there was so much to keep in mind. Everything contingent on everything else.

The other plan, the business with Waechter. Yes, that was the thing. The production company. He'd turn it round with the production company. That would be a great success, he'd show them. He had a secret weapon. He had . . .

And at that point he sat up and opened his eyes. The released seats sprang into the upright position. The auditorium was in utter darkness still. Porrick had no way of knowing what time it was, but the lights would not be put on until it was time to admit the matinee audience at eleven. The heavy drapes at the entrance prevented any light from the foyer from seeping in.

'Scudder?'

How could he have been so stupid? So drunk! Scudder was not just a dog, he was a valuable business asset. He might even put it more forcibly than that: Scudder was his ticket to future prosperity. And he had just abandoned him, as if he was a worthless street mutt! Would Hartmann have treated his star, Eloise, with equal carelessness?

Porrick rose to his feet. The remaining tip-up snapped shut. He

groped his way to the end of the row and felt for the wall ahead of
him. When he had that, he turned to the right and made his way along
the wall towards what he knew was the rear of the auditorium.

At last the solidity of the wall gave way to the swing of drapery.
He burst through into the dim half-light of the foyer before opening.

It took a while for Porrick's eyes to adjust, for him to realize
that the silhouette coming towards him was Max Maxwell.

'Have you seen Scudder?'

'Scudder?'

'My dog. The Yorkie.'

Maxwell scrutinized Porrick's face closely, as if he were struggling to remember ever having seen him with a dog. 'No. I haven't
seen him since last night.'

'What do you mean by that?'

Maxwell held up a rolled newspaper that he was carrying. He
used it to point at Porrick, almost accusingly. 'You had him at the
party with you last night, did you not?'

'Yes, but you meant something, I'm sure.'

Maxwell dropped the hand holding the newspaper. 'Did you not
take him home with you?'

'No . . . I . . . I did not, as it happens. I lost sight of him during
last night's . . . celebrations.'

'That was very careless of you.'

'I imagine he found a corner somewhere, where he curled up and
went to sleep. Now he will be hungry, poor chap.'

'That's probably it. Try Hartmann's place in Cecil Court. That
was where I last saw him.'

There was something in Maxwell's eye that Porrick didn't like.
An open hostility, brimming with impertinence. He had long
suspected Maxwell's hostility towards him, his hatred even. He
knew that the man who had died in the fire in Islington had been
a friend of his. It was reasonable that he would harbour a grudge.
As an employee, Maxwell had kept his feelings close to his chest,
until now. Porrick sensed that something had changed in their
relationship.

'Yes. I'll do that. Thank you.'

Maxwell again lifted the newspaper. 'Have you seen it?'

'What?'

'It's all over the front page of the *Clarion*. It mentions Porrick's
Palace. And there's a quote from Waechter.'

Porrick took the tubed paper and unfurled it.

Maxwell grinned sarcastically. 'Was it right, I wonder, to have *celebrations* after this?' Maxwell's emphasis of the word that Porrick had just used was pointed. 'Mind you, it will be good for the box office, I dare say. Unless they shut us down.'

'You'd better hope that doesn't happen, Max. Or you'll be out of a job. I shall order prints of all Waechter's previous films. Perhaps the time has come for a Waechter retrospective. I fear that this incident may indeed have excited a morbid interest in his work among the public.'

'Which you of course will do your best to pander to!'

'You know what pays your wage as well as I do, Max. If we don't get them through the door and on the seats, then you and me both will be in the workhouse.'

Max held out his hand for his newspaper. As he took it back, a brief, mechanical smile spasmed across his mouth. 'I hope you find your *dog*.' But his voice was an emotionless sing-song.

THIRTY-TWO

As Quinn walked across Cavendish Square, the sun broke through a crack in the marbled clouds and ignited the shuddering foliage with a frail, green, luminescent pallor.

Quinn half-expected to see Grant-Sissons lit up in the unexpected flare, hiding ineffectually behind one of the London plane trees. He imagined the strange, bitter man beckoning him over. This time he would walk right up to him and hear him out as he divulged the secret of his father's death. He wondered at his reluctance earlier. Why, after so many years of longing to know the answer to that mystery, he had turned and run from the first real opportunity of a breakthrough. He told himself that he was not ready to hear what Grant-Sissons had to say. It had come too much out of the blue. He had not been able to prepare himself. When he was ready, he would seek the man out and demand to be told what he knew.

Quinn's heart seemed to fold and flutter. He had the taste of something bitter and empty in his mouth. The taste of regret, of a missed opportunity.

He had to accept that his fear of what Grant-Sissons might say had got in the way of his conduct of the investigation. One minute the man was a suspect in the attack on the girl. The next, Quinn was refusing to bring him in.

But he had enough acquaintance with violent death to know that whatever was behind it, it was never anything good. He did not doubt that the same would hold true with his father's death.

When he was younger, he believed that his father had been murdered. This was the truth that he would one day prove. But Grant-Sissons had spoken categorically of suicide. Although he had consciously given up the consoling myth of his father's innocence in his own death, it was clear that he retained some barely registered hope that the hero of his youth would not turn out to be a self-murderer.

The air temperature dropped perceptibly. The clouds huddled into a sudden mass. From nowhere, a shower of hail clattered over the pavement. Quinn hastened his step. The hailstones pelted his face in an icy assault.

The shower was over as suddenly as it had begun. The clouds began to scatter. The sun fingered its way through, the mottles of blue spreading until the sky was almost completely clear. It was like the lights going up at the end of a stage show. The weather seemed to be bowing for applause at the startling trick it had just pulled off, fishing for an encore.

Quinn's spurt of energy carried him across Wigmore Street and into Harley Street, propelling him up the three steps to Dr Casaubon's door.

The brass plaque revealed a little more than Macadam's enquiries had been able to turn up: *Augustus Casaubon, MD, FMPA*.

From his own dealings with the medical profession Quinn was familiar with the last set of initials. He knew very well to what specialism they referred. Augustus Casaubon was a Fellow of the Medico-Psychiatric Association. He was a psychiatrist.

Quinn rang the bell and, when it wasn't answered after several minutes, tried the door. He was surprised to discover it wasn't locked. Presumably Dr Casaubon's surgery was open now, and the door was left open for patients. Quinn dispelled the notion that Casaubon was waiting for him.

The door led on to a marble-tiled hallway. Gilt lettering and a pointing hand symbol on a small wooden sign indicated the reception.

There was no one there. Quinn hit the bell push. When that produced no response, he leaned over the reception counter and called out into the cave of medical records behind it. 'Hello?'

At last, a stooped, elderly man with silver hair and a neatly trimmed imperial beard appeared tentatively from a door at the rear of the practice office. 'You must bear with me. I'm all on my own today.' The man's accent was genteel Edinburgh. 'My nurse is ill. And the secretary, well, we had to let her go. Between you and me, she was an absolute disaster. Take the appointments book. I have no idea what she's done with it. Would you credit it? How on earth are we meant to run a practice without an appointments book? I hope to God she hasn't taken it with her. Out of spite, you know. People do the most extraordinary things out of spite. It's hardly rational, but, well . . . I'm used to dealing in the irrational. Very well, you'll just have to come straight in. I shall see people today on a first-come, first-served basis.'

'Who are you?'

'Doctor Casaubon, of course.'

That may be the case, thought Quinn. But you are not the Dr Casaubon I'm looking for. He was about to say something to that effect, when the elderly Dr Casaubon cut in. 'Go back out the way you came, then turn right. Take the first door on the right. I'll be waiting for you.'

'But . . . I . . . I am a police officer. A detective. I'm here on an investigation.'

'Yes, of course you are. I understand. A detective.' Dr Casaubon chuckled. 'We'll have a good long chat about it. We'll sort out the paperwork afterwards.'

No, Dr Casaubon, I really am a police detective, thought Quinn. But for some reason, he said nothing.

THIRTY-THREE

D r Casaubon directed Quinn to recline on a leather-upholstered chaise longue while he drew the drapes, cloaking the tribal masks and fertility symbols that adorned his surgery in discreet semi-darkness. The doctor had a persuasive manner that was hard to resist. But although Quinn took a seat, he refused to put up his feet. That would be a retrograde step, he felt.

'So, how long have you been a policeman?' The question came to him from out of the darkness. Its tone managed to be both sardonic and indulgent.

Quinn sensed Dr Casaubon moving to position himself behind him. Yes, they always sat behind you, so that you couldn't see them as they observed you.

'I really am a policeman, you know. I can show you my warrant card.'

'That won't be necessary.'

'You seem to be under the misapprehension that I am one of your patients. I don't want to waste your time, Doctor. I am not . . . That is to say . . . I am not . . .'

'What are you not?'

'I am not . . .'

'Why can't you complete the sentence, I wonder? Could it be because you wish to say, *I am not ill*. But your mind, your unconscious mind, will not permit you to state this blatant lie. When were you first aware of this desire to be a policeman?' Dr Casaubon's intonation made it clear that, in his mind, having a desire to be a policeman was not the same thing as being a policeman.

'I *am* a policeman. My name is Silas Quinn. I am Detective Inspector Silas Quinn of the Special Crimes Department.'

'The Special Crimes Department?' The psychiatrist's tone became openly sceptical. 'I haven't heard of *that one*.'

'I don't wish to take up any more of your time. If you have seen the papers this morning, you may know that there was a vicious attack on a young woman in central London last night.'

Dr Casaubon's pen scratched the darkness. 'It was in the *papers*, was it?' Quinn had experience in interpreting psychiatrists' intonations. He understood the doctor clearly enough. He was insinuating that Quinn was a fantasist who had taken the basis of his fantasy from a newspaper account.

'One of her eyes was forcibly removed from her head.'

'The newspaper said that, did it?'

'The woman in question was taken from the scene – it was assumed to hospital – by a man who claimed to be a doctor. Indeed, he gave his name – *to me* – as Doctor Casaubon. That is why I have come to see you today.'

'You believe I was the doctor who took her away?'

'No, it was not you. It was someone else. I apologize for wasting your time.' But Quinn made no move to get up from the chaise longue.

'Rest a while. Before you press on with your investigation.'

'I don't have time.' Quinn swung his legs up and lay back on the chaise longue.

'There is always time to tend to the needs of the soul.'

'It was after my father died,' said Quinn suddenly. He was aware of feeling slightly surprised that he had blurted out this confidence. It had been the last thing he had wanted to divulge. He was puzzled as to how the doctor had managed to induce him to confess it, merely by urging Quinn to tend to the needs of his soul. Perhaps that was a technique he could apply when interrogating suspects.

'Your father's death affected you badly?'

'The inquest verdict was death by misadventure. But there were rumours that he took his own life. That was certainly what my mother believed.'

'And you did not?'

'Not then.'

'And now?'

'There's a man, who claims he knows the truth about my father's death. I . . . I ran away from him, from finding out the truth. I had always thought of myself as a seeker of the truth. And yet, when presented with the opportunity to find out the one thing that I most desired to know, I . . . ran away.'

'If you don't know the truth, you can make it be whatever you want it to be.'

'They write about me in the newspapers.'

Quinn heard the doctor's pen scratch excitedly in the dark.

'They have begun to call me Quick-Fire Quinn.'

'How does that make you feel?'

'I don't like it.' But Quinn wondered if this were true, even as he said it.

'There is no truth in it?'

'No . . . well, it is true that some of the suspects I have hunted over the years have . . . died at my hands. But it has been necessary. These are invariably dangerous men. I have a duty to protect the public, and my men.'

'And yourself.'

'Is that so wrong?'

'Not wrong at all. You do what you have to do.'

'But today, I thought . . . on the way here to see you . . . the thought occurred to me . . . What if I kill them for the same reason that I ran from this man? Because I don't want to know the truth. I am afraid of the truth! After all these years in the force!'

There was a long pause. Eventually Dr Casaubon coughed, as though in some embarrassment. 'You really are a policeman, aren't you?'

'Of course.'

'I believe I can help you. If you wish to be helped.'

'I don't need that kind of help.'

'And yet you came here today.'

'As part of my investigation.'

'Of course. That's how the unconscious works. It always provides a plausible specious reason – a rational explanation – alongside the true reason.'

'What are you saying? I had no idea what kind of doctor you were before I came here. And I had no control over what name that man last night would give. My unconscious has played no part in bringing me here.'

'I wasn't talking about *your* unconscious especially. The world has an unconscious, you know. You may call it God, if you wish. Although sometimes it seems more like the Devil. In point of fact, it is both. In psychoanalysis, opposing forces are reconciled. The polarity of good on the one hand and evil on the other becomes resolved into a unity in which both good and evil coexist. For instance, it was undoubtedly an evil that this poor girl was attacked. And yet some good has come of it. It has led you here to me, and perhaps to your psychic salvation.'

'It's just a coincidence.'

Dr Casaubon chuckled, as if the notion of a coincidence was the most ridiculous thing he had ever heard. 'The unconscious is cunning. It always allows us that explanation too. It is consistent with the polarity I have touched upon. It presents us with the path to our own healing, but at the same time provides us with the excuses for not taking it.'

'With respect, Doctor, this all sounds like mumbo-jumbo.'

'Yes. That is how you feel about it now. I expect you will change your mind. At any rate, you have found me once. You may find me again.'

In the shadowed gloom of the doctor's surgery, Quinn was momentarily disorientated. There was some quality in Casaubon's voice that took him back to an earlier time in his life, to a place he had long believed he had left behind for good: the Colney Hatch Asylum. Indeed, so intense was the sensation that he wondered if he had ever left there.

THIRTY-FOUR

Quinn noticed the gleam of a familiar excitement in Macadam's eye as soon as he stepped back into the department.

'There's been a development, sir. They've found her. A girl with one eye missing. We're to go to an address in Soho. Shall I fetch the Ford?'

'How . . . how is she?'

'She's dead, sir. It's a body they've found.'

Of course, he had known right from the start that that was what Macadam would say. He knew it as soon as he saw that gleam in his eye.

PART THREE
Death

THIRTY-FIVE

Quinn was aware of a ticklish apprehension, a sense of inevitability and dread. He had the feeling that they were moving under a cloud of spreading blackness, towards something very black indeed. And yet the day was bright enough. The blackness was of entirely psychological origin.

His encounter with the second Dr Casaubon had unnerved him. And the fact that the girl had now apparently turned up dead depressed him. It was another death that could be lain at his door. He had permitted the man who had called himself Dr Casaubon to take her away. Impressed by the man's natural air of confidence and authority, and the superficial evidence he gave of medical knowledge, he had failed to ask for any credentials. But had instead surrendered a vulnerable, wounded girl to a complete stranger.

And now it seemed possible, if not likely, that this man was her attacker come to finish off what he started. If he had been wearing a mask at the time of the attack – a devil's mask perhaps, in keeping with the woman's insistence that she had been attacked by the devil – she would not have recognized him. Even more chillingly, perhaps he was a second predatory individual. One more violent than the original attacker, one drawn to the acts of horror that others had initiated, but prepared to take them to their ultimate conclusion. Prepared, in other words, to kill, whereas the first attacker had only maimed.

Macadam drove them north to Dean Street. A couple of uniforms on the street signalled the door they were looking for. Inside, Quinn's psychological darkness was almost equalled by the gloom of the narrow stairway. Male voices, and the clumping of boots on boards, drew them up to the first-floor landing.

A door was open on to a small rented room. It was even darker in there than on the landing, as the curtains were still drawn from the night before. Hard to see what was what, especially as a wall of burly backs filled the threshold, screening the scene of crime from Quinn's view.

Macadam took umbrage at this cluster of detectives from the

local Great Marlborough Street nick. 'What's all this? Come on, out of the way, out of the way! Don't you lot know anything about forensics? You can't go clodhopping all over the place like this.'

The wall of backs parted. Several bewildered, bewhiskered faces turned at once to confront their admonisher. Initial aggression turned to chastened deference when they saw Quinn.

Macadam confirmed their suspicions. 'That's right. Special Crimes. It's our case now. You men better make way.'

There was a moment while the locals filed out. In fact, there had only been three men in there, but the room was small, and the men were big.

The air was dead and stifling, filled with the odours of the night before. Alcohol and cigarette smoke were the strongest, but there were also more obscure and somehow more potent smells. Quinn was able to identify blood, the metallic tang of a body leeching out its life fluids. In the tenebrous gloom, it seemed as though her face had been painted black. But the darkness was especially thick around the left eye, or rather where the left eye had been. He realized it was blood that caked her face, not make-up. There was blood on her throat too, and a glistening disruption of flesh on one side.

Of course, he knew straight away. 'This is not her. It's not the girl who was attacked in Cecil Court.'

'Are you sure, sir?'

'You saw her, did you not, Macadam?'

'That I did, sir. But it was dark.'

'For one thing, it was the other eye. But this girl – this is someone else. This girl is an actress, of sorts. She was in the film, last night. And she was at the premiere. And I believe at the party afterwards.' Quinn turned back towards the three policemen who were waiting out on the landing. 'Do you have a name for her?'

One of the men stepped forward with a barely perceptible dip of the head, a gesture in the direction of a bow. His face was sunken-cheeked, its grey pallor tinged by bristles like iron filings. At the sides, the bristles burgeoned into mutton-chop whiskers. 'The room was rented by a couple by the name of Novak. A neighbour has identified her as the wife. Dolores Novak.'

'And her husband? Do you know where he is?'

'Done a bunk, we reckon.'

Quinn nodded. This was consistent with the impression he had formed of the fellow from watching him the night before. 'Have you circulated a description to the ports? The chances are he will try to get abroad.'

'We thought of that, guv. He's a foreigner, see.'

'And has the medical examiner seen her yet?'

'He has, guv.'

'Did he have anything of interest to say?'

'Cause of death as you'd expect, guv. Loss of blood caused by her wounds.'

'Wounds?'

'She had her throat cut as well as her eye taken out. He seemed to think it was a botched job. The entry point of the blade ought to have missed her carotid artery, according to the doctor. But somehow it found it.'

'So there was a lot of blood?' Quinn's question might have seemed redundant, fuelled by simple ghoulishness.

'You could say that, guv. It was that, coupled with the excessive shock to the heart what did for her. Whoever did this, left her to die.'

'And her husband, if he was here, did nothing to help her either, it seems. Even if he is not the man who took her eye out.'

'Neighbours attest to some rum comings and goings in the night, guv. Seems there may have been some other individuals here. No one saw anyone, of course. A question of raised voices.'

'An altercation?'

'There may have been. A level of intoxication was attested to. Some kind of party. If you take my meaning.'

Quinn at last identified one of the other lingering smells. 'Did the medical examiner offer any opinion about whether there had been recent sexual activity?'

'He did. And there had. Someone had shot their bolt inside her. It may or may not have been her husband. Them other individuals were thought to be men.'

Quinn gave voice to his thoughts: 'Was she an actress or a prostitute?' He scanned the room, as if he would find the answer nailed to the wall. 'Or a little of both, perhaps?' He remembered the interest the couple had seemed to be taking in Lord Dunwich. 'Macadam, you stay here and look the crime scene over. You might also see if you can get anything else out of the neighbours.'

'What am I looking for in particular, sir?'

'Any evidence of her visitors would be helpful. If someone left in a hurry, there is a chance they might have left something behind.'

Macadam's ruthless eye was already taking in the room. From his bearing, it was clear that he would consider it a matter of pride to come up with something.

Before he left, Quinn allowed himself one last glance at that centre of darkness in her face. In the dim obscurity of the curtained room it was hard to know what he could see and what he was imagining. The impossible depths of blackness that he had seen in the other cavity came back to him. In truth, they had never been far away. Last night, he had told himself that he never wanted to see that blackness again. Now he realized that was another of his self-deceptions. There was nothing he wanted more than to stare into it. It was with some effort of will that he tore himself away.

THIRTY-SIX

As he turned from the open expanse of Charing Cross Road into the sun-starved alleyway of Cecil Court, Quinn felt a physical chill descend. The events of the previous night came back to him, as if the ghosts of all those involved were now in place. The huddle of men around the screaming girl. Her body racked with uncontrollable shudders. The man who stepped from the carriage and took over with the assumed authority of a doctor. The arrival of the party from Leicester Square. The nasty yapping dog with the eye between its teeth.

The scene replayed itself in his mind. It took on the quality of a kinematograph projection, flickering, grainy, juddering and monochrome. In fact, it was like several films projected simultaneously, and repeatedly. At first, the layered multiplicity of images confused him. It was hard to see through the ever-shifting fog of movement.

But then his perceiving mind got used to the patterns of repetition in the presentation that his subconscious mind was trying to force on him. One detail cut through. The iris of the eye he had held in his hand.

This was the only part of the mental diorama to have colour.

But his mind must have been playing tricks on him. It presented the eye to him as blue. And yet he remembered – not as a visual memory, but as a factual memory – the moment when he had first consciously registered the colour of her eyes.

He had been talking to Lord Dunwich. He had opened the handkerchief in which the eye was wrapped and looked down to see a brown eye looking back at him.

This was why, as Macadam would no doubt remind him, it was so important to gather firm evidence, and subject it to meticulous scientific scrutiny. Memory was unreliable. His own mind could not even agree with itself as to the colour of her eyes. Fortunately, he had retrieved the enucleated eye and sent it for analysis by a pathologist. All that he lacked was the girl from whom it had been taken.

He was admitted by Magnus Porrick, who was apparently on his way out, and highly distraught. He stared wildly into Quinn's face as they crossed paths on the threshold.

Something about that look persuaded Quinn that he ought to detain Porrick. 'One moment, sir. I would like to talk to you. There has been a serious development in the case. Please, if you will step back inside.'

'But I have to find him!'

'Who?' For a moment Quinn thought Porrick was referring to the missing Novak.

'Scudder.'

Quinn was not sure what Porrick had said: a name, an oath, a command, or possibly he had not said anything at all. He had merely emitted a meaningless involuntary sound, like a sneeze. 'I beg your pardon?'

'My dog, Scudder. He's gone missing.'

'That was the animal who found the girl's eye?'

'What?' Porrick's distress was such that he was evidently finding it hard to concentrate.

'Last night. Just here, outside. You must remember?'

'Oh, yes . . . yes.' Porrick suddenly looked at Quinn with staring, accusatory eyes. 'You were the man who was going to shoot him! What have you done with him?'

'I have done nothing with him, I assure you.'

'You're a policeman, aren't you? You have to help me find him.'

'I'm afraid I have rather more pressing duties. However, I am sure your dog will turn up. Or if not, it has probably met with some fatal road accident. A dog like that can have little road sense, and from what I saw, you had no control over it last night. Either way, it is not a matter for me.'

'Do you think Scudder could be dead?'

'I really don't know. Mr Porrick, will you come back inside with me? I have some questions.' Quinn was about to impress upon Porrick the seriousness of the situation, given Dolores Novak's death. However, another thought occurred to him. 'We may be able to throw some light on the whereabouts of your dog.'

Porrick's gaze became pathetically fixed on Quinn. Docile and trusting, he allowed himself to be turned back.

The offices of the Visionary Production Company had the stale, dead air of the morning after. The gloom of Cecil Court permeated the interior, depressive and grey, like a hangover waiting to be claimed. Empty champagne bottles littered the floor and furniture. Cigarette stubs had not always found their way into ashtrays. The white of the decor seemed dingy and weak, unable to hold its own against the negative power of the black. The black sucked the energy out of everything.

Konrad Waechter was sitting at a desk, tapping away at a typewriter. He barely looked up when Quinn and Porrick came into the room. Quinn gestured for Porrick to sit down, but his own attention was now drawn by the director. In particular, he found that he was fascinated by the patch over Waechter's eye; or more accurately, by speculations as to what lay behind it. 'Mr Waechter?'

Waechter grunted but did not look up.

'I would like to speak to you too. Something has happened. I am afraid it is my duty to tell you both of a very great tragedy that has occurred.'

It seemed Quinn had said enough to get the man's attention. Though judging by his questioning frown, he did not fully understand the detective's words. He had clearly been impressed by his tone, however.

'Last night, as you know, a woman was attacked just outside these offices. We have reasons to believe that she attended the screening of your moving picture film at this gentleman's picture palace in Leicester Square.'

'Picture Palace is another chain. Mine are Porrick's Palaces.'

'It has now come to light that a second woman was attacked last night. Dolores Novak.'

Quinn paused to observe the effect of the name on the two men.

Magnus Porrick leaned slightly – almost imperceptibly – backwards, as if recoiling from a blow. The speed of the reaction suggested that Porrick's shock was genuine. If anything, it seemed that Porrick was trying to minimize it, although he could not control the colour draining from his face. Maybe Porrick had not known that Dolores Novak was dead. But he did know something – something that he was at pains to keep to himself.

Waechter seemed to draw energy from the news. His visible eye widened, as if the entrance to his inner self was opening up, so that he could drink in all the horror of this sensational revelation.

Quinn reminded himself that he was dealing here with film people. Waechter no doubt came from a theatrical background. If he had not been an actor himself, he had certainly spent a lot of time in the company of actors. He understood the techniques they used and was probably adept in them himself.

He wondered whether behind the patch was an eye that Waechter could not control, that on the contrary would always betray his true feelings. And that was the reason it had to be kept hidden away.

'There are similarities between the two assaults. Both victims were subject to the removal of one eye.'

Waechter thumped the desk excitedly and let out a stream of German.

'I'm sorry. I didn't understand that. What did you say?'

'I do not believe . . . Vot you say is not *possible*!'

'Why do you say that?'

Waechter merely shook his head.

Porrick at last was prompted to ask the question. 'And how is she? Mrs Novak?'

'She's dead.'

'No!'

Again Waechter gave vent to his thoughts in his native language.

'I am naturally interested to recreate Mrs Novak's movements after the party last night. Did either of you gentlemen see her leave?'

'It is hard to say,' said Waechter.

Porrick concentrated on avoiding Quinn's scrutiny.

'Hard to say? I don't see why it should be particularly hard to say. If you saw her leave, you simply say yes. If you did not, then you say no.'

'There were many peoples here. Many peoples coming and going . . .'

'You did not see her leave?'

'I am not sure.'

'And what of you, Mr Porrick?'

Porrick shook his head.

'Neither of you gentlemen saw her leave?'

The two men did nothing to confirm or deny this proposition.

'What about her husband, Mr Novak? We are anxious to locate him.'

'Porrick left with Novak,' said Waechter quickly.

'I see. Mr Porrick, is this true?'

'I don't . . . I was very drunk. I can't remember much about last night.'

'But did you leave with Mr Novak?'

'I suppose I might have done.'

'And was Mrs Novak with you?'

'No.'

'You don't remember much about last night, but you can say that with certainty?'

'I remember now,' said Waechter. 'He is right. Dolores was not with them. Dolores left earlier.'

'Alone?' Quinn had a strong sense what the answer would be.

'*Nein.*'

Waechter and Porrick exchanged a look that was so conspiratorial it was almost comic.

'Did she leave with a man who was not her husband?' prompted Quinn. 'Are you trying to protect the reputation of this gentleman? I understand the instinct that motivates this behaviour. However, it will be better for the gentleman concerned if we are able to talk to him at the soonest possible opportunity in order to eliminate him from our enquiries.'

'She left *mit* Lord *Dunsch.*'

'Lord *Dunwich*?' insisted Quinn pedantically, as if there could have been two lords at the party with such similar names.

'*Ja*, Lord *Dunsch.*'

'Mr Porrick, where did you go with Mr Novak after you left the party?'

'I'm afraid to say I was very drunk. It is all rather hazy. All I know for sure is that I slept in the auditorium of the Leicester Square Palace.'

'Why did you not go home?'

'I had had a row with my wife.'

'This is true,' confirmed Waechter, as if everything hinged upon the settling of this point.

'You did not see Lord Dunwich with Mrs Novak after you left here?'

'What kind of a question is that?'

'It is a perfectly reasonable question, and one by which I hope to establish the truth of what happened to Mrs Novak.'

'It was all a bit of a blur. All I can say with any certainty is that I was exceedingly drunk.'

'Mr Waechter, you must accept now that the parallels between what has happened and the incidents portrayed in your film are striking.'

'My film is a poem. A poem expresses a truth. A truth of the soul. I cannot be held responsible for the actions of a *madman*. He has twisted the truth of my poem. It is not my doing.'

'Dolores Novak had a part in your film, did she not? What was your impression of her? Did you enjoy working with her?'

'Dolores cannot act. But I do not ask her to act. I ask her to *dahhnsse*.' Waechter rippled his arms in a balletic swaying motion. 'It is vot der men come to see, *ja*? You like to watch her *dahhnsse*, Inspector?'

Quinn did not like Waechter's lascivious tone. It almost sounded as if Waechter was accusing him of some culpability in what had happened to Dolores.

'What happened to your eye?' Quinn realized this was a question he had wanted to ask for a long time – from the first moment he saw Waechter in fact.

'It . . . *kaputt* . . .' Waechter made a popping sound. 'Doctors take it out. Say it no good any more.'

'You *lost* an eye?' Perhaps it sounded as if Quinn believed this had been very careless of Waechter. But really the involuntary emphasis came from his excitement at learning the true nature of Waechter's impairment.

'Were you duelling with pistols or swords?'

Waechter looked at Quinn without speaking for some time. '*Ein kleiner . . . Splitter – ja*? Splitter?'

'Splinter?'

'*Ja, ein* splitter. Man shoot me. *Ja*? Shot – woo!' Waechter signalled the shot flying past his head. 'But *ein* splitter . . . *ein* splitter go in my eye.'

'Why did the man shoot you?'

Waechter shrugged.

'And what happened to him?'

'I shoot him. I not miss. The man . . . dead.'

'How long have you known Dolores Novak?'

'I use her in my films. One times. Two times.'

'Have you ever had intimate relations with her?'

'*Nein.*' It seemed to Quinn that Waechter gave a small private grin.

'What about you, Mr Porrick?'

'I never really knew the woman.'

'Are all your films about eyes, Mr Waechter?'

Waechter answered in German.

'I'm sorry, I don't understand.'

'*Philister.*'

'Is this another of your films?'

'My films are about many things. But always they are about . . .' Waechter pounded himself on the chest. 'Vot is in *der* human heart. I create poems, visual poems, that express what is in *der* heart. *Ja*?'

'I would like to see all of your films. In fact, it is necessary that I do.'

Porrick's eyes widened in an expression of surprise. He mouthed something quietly and nodded to himself, as if some inner thought had just received confirmation.

'You will arrange for copies of all your films to be sent to me, Detective Inspector Silas Quinn, Special Crimes Department, New Scotland Yard.'

'This vill take time. I do not have prints. I must speak to Herr Hartmann.'

'But it can be done?'

'*Ja.*'

'Good, now do either of you two gentlemen have information regarding the whereabouts of Mr Novak?'

'Do you think Novak did it?' Porrick leaned forward now. He seemed eager to push this hypothesis on Quinn.

'Why would you say that?'

'I don't know . . . you're looking for him.'

'We are naturally anxious to speak to him. If either of you hear from Mr Novak, you must urge him to contact the police, so that we may eliminate him from our enquiries. And in any event . . .' Quinn handed out business cards. 'Please let me know.' Quinn thought back to the scene he had witnessed outside the kinemato-graph theatre. 'How would you describe the relationship between Mr and Mrs Novak?'

'It was . . . unusual,' admitted Porrick. 'She was with Lord Dunwich at the party. They were getting pretty familiar. Novak didn't seem to mind at all.'

'He's a foreigner,' remarked Quinn.

'A Yank.'

'His name, though – Novak?'

'*Serbisch.*'

'Serbian?'

'*Ja.*'

'And you are Austrian? Not German?'

'I am citizen of *der* Republic of Art.'

'I understand you cannot go back to Austria. Or dare not. There are tensions, are there not, between Austria and the Serbians? The Serbians resent the Austrian yoke. Perhaps there is some bad blood between yourself and Mr Novak?'

'Bad blood? No. I don't care he is Serbian. I only care he acts.'

Quinn moved closer to Waechter's desk and looked down at the pages spread out around the typewriter. He saw that the typescript had been annotated by hand in green ink. 'I will need a sample of your handwriting.'

'Vy?'

'I am not at liberty to say.'

'Did the killer write a note?' wondered Porrick.

'You do not suspect me in this *maurtter*?' It was unclear whether Waechter's last word was *murder* or *matter*.

'It is to do with another aspect of the investigation.'

'Vot about *him*?'

'Yes, Mr Porrick too. If you could both use that pen, please. Mr Waechter's pen.'

'Vot do you vant me to write?'

'I would like you to write the name of the man who left with Dolores Novak.'

Waechter's single eye bulged with something between indignation and amazement as he regarded Quinn. 'Vot game is this?'

'It is not a game, Mr Waechter. I assure you I am deadly serious.'

THIRTY-SEVEN

Q uinn was shown into the same room in the Admiralty Extension as before. The blinds were again drawn on the day, and on any prying eyes outside. Lord Dunwich nodded to him without speaking, unlocked a drawer in his desk and took out a small package loosely wrapped in brown paper. 'Come with me.'

Lord Dunwich led him down into the basement of the building, and opened a door to a small, windowless room furnished with a round table and no chairs. The room was lit by a bare, flickering electric light bulb, like lightning in the night until the bulb gave out completely. With the door closed, they were plunged into darkness.

The darkness was filled with Lord Dunwich's tense, urgent whisper. 'I have the object we discussed last night.'

Quinn felt something pushed into his hands.

'You may take it away and examine it at the Yard.'

'Has anyone other than you handled the object?'

'No. Of course not.'

'That's good. I will have to ask you to come into the Yard at some point so that we may take your fingerprints, in order to eliminate them from our forensic examination.'

'Naturally.'

'Perhaps you would be able to do that on Monday?'

'If you wish.'

'Thank you. However, Lord Dunwich, it was not on account of this object that I have come to see you.'

'It is not?'

Quinn could not see Dunwich's face but he heard the nervous apprehension in his voice. 'There has been another attack. A young woman associated with Waechter's film – and therefore with your friend Hartmann – has had one of her eyes forcibly removed from her head. In this case, unfortunately, the injury resulted in her death. She was found this morning.'

'How terrible. But what has this to do with national security?'

'The victim was last seen leaving the party at Visionary

Productions in Cecil Court in your company, Lord Dunwich. The dead woman is Dolores Novak.'

Quinn heard the sharp inarticulate cry of shock. Followed by a softer murmuring of her name: '*Dolores-s-s-s!*' The final sibilant fragmented into uncontrollable sobs.

'Sir. What happened last night, after you left the party?'

It was some time before Dunwich could answer. 'We went to Dolores's . . . to their . . . to a room. Dolores and I . . . well, we are both adults . . . we both wanted the same thing. As far as I could tell, her husband took a . . . let's say a modern attitude to marital fidelity. I even got the impression he encouraged it. At any rate, the husband, Novak, came back and kicked up an awful fuss. I say, you don't think he . . .?'

'If you have any information about his whereabouts . . .'

'No. I left, naturally, soon after he turned up. You might try that Porrick fellow. He was with Novak.'

'Porrick? But I have already spoken to Mr Porrick. He said nothing about this.'

'I dare say he was trying to be discreet. Novak has a motive, doesn't he, Quinn?'

'How was he when you left him?'

'I wouldn't say he was in a jealous rage, if that's what you mean. I've been thinking about what happened. I think he knew that he would find me there. I think he came purposely. In order to blackmail me. He did not try actively to extort money from me, but he put me in a position where I naturally offered him money. Which he was happy to accept. I dare say that other fellow was there to get what he could out of it too. The only innocent party was Dolores. Quinn, what do you say to this? Dolores and Novak argued after I left. She wanted nothing to do with the blackmail affair and reproved him over his behaviour. It was this that enraged him. Influenced by the example of the film we had just seen, and by what happened to that poor girl in Cecil Court, he attacked her in the manner you have described.'

'It's more likely that she was in on it too. On the blackmail I mean. I observed them before the screening. They were working together.'

'No. I will not accept that. What Dolores and I had, though brief, was . . . genuine. Good God, man. I would have done anything for her. She had no need to get mixed up in a sordid blackmail business. She knew I would have taken care of her.'

'Would you have left your wife?'

'What conceivable necessity would there have been to do that?'

Quinn let the question go unanswered. 'Who saw you in her company?'

'I don't know. Everyone there, I suppose.'

'When news of her death comes out, your name . . .'

'My name will be kept out of it. Not on my behalf, you understand. But for the good of the country.'

'You were very indiscreet, Lord Dunwich. Are you aware that not only was there a newspaper journalist present, there was also a newspaper proprietor there?'

'Yes. Harry Lennox. Of course. I think we can trust Lennox to do the right thing.'

'Why do you say that?'

'Well, I know he's Irish, but we can count on his support in this, I think. Harry Lennox always acts in accordance with Harry Lennox's own best interests. And I think I can persuade him that his interests in this case are best served by keeping my name out of his newspaper.'

'But there may be others – your friend Hartmann, for example – who would wish to use the threat of exposure as a lever to ensure your cooperation in their own enterprises.'

'I really cannot accept that Hartmann is anything but . . . a friend to our country.'

'And I find it hard to understand your faith in him.'

'Let me just say that in the past, he has proved himself in this capacity.'

'He has supplied you with secrets regarding German military intentions or arrangements?'

'He has proved himself to be a friend.'

'Is that not an excellent way to earn your trust? Which he may hold in reserve until such time as he may employ it to the greatest effect?'

'Do you not have any other theories?'

'Theories that are not based on evidence are merely wild speculation. We know that you were sent an object that has the appearance of an eye. Subsequent to that, two women were attacked in a similar manner that seems related to the object you were sent. That is to say, their eyes were gouged out. One of those women is dead. The other has disappeared.'

'Is that so?'

'Yes, unfortunately. One of the victims can be linked to you. The other – well, I have not asked you about her, Lord Dunwich. Did you see the woman who was attacked in Cecil Court?'

'Yes, I saw her.'

'And . . . how may I put this? Have you ever had relations with her of a similar nature to those you had with Dolores Novak?'

There was a pause before Lord Dunwich answered: 'I had never seen her before last night.'

Quinn was unable to see Dunwich's face. Hard to know, from his voice alone, whether he was telling the truth.

'Where do we go from here, Quinn?'

'In the interests of public order, I would request that Waechter's film is withdrawn from exhibition.'

'That is a matter for the Home Office. You will have to apply to them. I dare say Sir Edward will arrange it for you. But, if I may say so, is that not rather a case of closing the stable door after the horse has bolted?'

'Two women have been attacked already. Both are connected with the film, one as a spectator, the other as an actress performing in it. If there is another attack, we *will* be criticized – and rightly so.'

'But do you really think it's possible that watching this film could prompt someone to carry out these attacks?'

'As yet we don't know what the attacker's motivation is. And so, we have to proceed with a general, widespread caution.'

'But if the attacker is the person who sent me this, and the attacks are related to this – then he formed the intention to carry out the attacks before he saw the film, unless . . .'

'Yes, Lord Dunwich.' Quinn completed the thought that Dunwich had balked from saying: 'Unless he is connected with the production of the film in some way. The most likely suspect at the moment is Konrad Waechter himself.'

'But why would Waechter initiate a series of attacks that might lead to the banning of his film?'

'Like all those of an artistic temperament, Waechter labours under the burden of an immense arrogance. This blinded him to the possibility that his acts might have a consequence that he could not control. At the same time, he is driven by an obsession that is rooted in his disordered psychology.'

'An obsession?'

'He is clearly obsessed by eyes. In particular, by the idea of removing them. It is possible that his actions have no logical wellspring. No motivation that you or I would understand. That he is mad, in other words. I intend to study his previous films to understand his psychology more fully.'

'Are you qualified to undertake such an operation?'

Now it was Quinn's turn to pause before replying: 'There are resources outside the department that I can draw upon. In the meantime, I will have my men keep a close eye on him.'

'Very well. If there is nothing more to discuss . . .'

Quinn felt Lord Dunwich's fingers probe his eye. 'I say! Have a care!'

'I do beg your pardon, Quinn. I'm trying to find the blasted door.'

It was up to Quinn to grope the pitch-black infinity behind him until he teased an opening out of it.

THIRTY-EIGHT

Mika Novak waited out the day in a cheap hotel near King's Cross station. He knew that they would be looking for him. Night was the best time to move. He had had the foresight to bring with him his case of theatrical make-up. The day had been spent experimenting with different facial hair styles and colours. He decided also to bulk out his body shape by strapping the shrunken musty pillow from the bed around his torso.

The disguise would serve a dual purpose. It would enable him to evade capture by the police. It would also mean that he could slip out of the hotel without the inconvenience of having to settle his bill.

There's nothing wrong with killing two birds with one stone, thought Novak.

So Dolores was dead. Or Gladys, to give her her real name. No doubt he ought to be more upset about it than he was. If anyone had been able to look into his heart, they might have been surprised to see how little feeling there was for her there. *Poor little bitch*, was about the extent of the regret he could summon up on her behalf.

He smiled as he thought of the sight that would greet this imaginary spy into his heart: blackness. Utter blackness. The image of a rotten, wizened lump of gristle came to mind. Of something charred and empty.

No doubt it was all very wrong and all that. But he couldn't make himself feel what he didn't feel. And all he had to go on were his feelings.

Like fear. The healthy fear that prompts self-preservation. That was why he had run from the room on Dean Street. A sensible enough move, taking everything into account.

Of course, the police would try to pin it on him. They always blamed the husband. That was a laugh, though. Him and Gladys had never got married. There'd never been any talk of it. Nothing could have been further from either of their minds.

Theirs had been entirely a business relationship. Though of course that hadn't stopped him sampling the merchandise from time to time. Just to make sure it was up to scratch. Quality control, you might call it.

And now, due to unforeseen circumstances, their business dealings had come to an abrupt end. Regrettable perhaps. But Novak had little use for regrets. Regrets were dangerous. You made a mistake, the thing was to move on.

No point crying over spilt milk. Wasn't that what they said?

And besides, what had happened to Gladys, that wasn't for him to regret, was it?

The police wouldn't see it that way, though. They'd try to pin it on him, for sure.

Still, they'd have to catch him first.

Novak pulled back the greasy curtain. The air was thick with smoke the colour of French mustard. He could taste the nearby station through the dirty panes, and the gasworks and the factories along Regent's Canal, the airborne scum of industry lining his teeth. The factory chimneys pierced and sanctified the murk like giant fingers pointing heavenward. From his third-storey room, Novak had a view over the rooftops of the closely packed houses in the surrounding streets. Or rather of their chimney pots, lying like ruined battlements over a smoking ground.

The settling dusk freighted the smoke with a ponderous gloom. Soon the darkness would be deep enough to encompass him.

He had the money that Dunwich had given him. It was enough to get him across London and out of the country. Once he was on the continent, he'd make his way to Serbia. Look up some distant cousins and put all this behind him.

He could see the future as if it had already happened. The past
. . . the past was nothing but a smear on the grimy, cracked window.
Keep moving, that was the thing. Always, ever, forwards.

He was glad to leave the hotel behind, though the darkness outside
was choking. Invisible particles clogged his throat. For a man of
his habits and lifestyle, Novak was in many ways a fastidious individual. Paradoxical as it might seem, it was even possible that this
was the driving impulse of his character. The need to leave it all
behind, the detritus and the waste. The dirty, peeling walls, the
flea-ridden bed, the palimpsest stains of previous occupancy. The filthy
air. The dead and discarded business partner.

He kept moving through the shrouded streets. But didn't hurry. It
was important to keep his step steady and consistent. No shrinking from
the beam of a passing vehicle. No cowering from doorway to doorway.
And if there was a street lamp ahead, his step wouldn't waver or deviate.

You see, it wasn't just a question of donning false whiskers, dying
his hair and stuffing a pillow up his shirt front. He had to become
the character. And for that he needed a new walk. He had experi-
mented with a stoop, and then a limp, but rejected them both as too
obvious. They would only draw attention, when what he wanted
was a walk that would render him invisible.

Novak looked upon it as an acting challenge, although his objective was exactly opposite to an actor's. An actor wanted to be noticed,
to steal the scene if possible. The audience couldn't love you if it
didn't see you.

And so it took some self-control to tone down his walk, to draw
it organically from the character he was seeking to create. To imagine
a man, and then imagine how he would move.

Of course, Novak congratulated himself on understanding all this.
There were few actors he knew who would be able to pull this off. They
were all such show-offs.

His first real test came at the end of Albion Street. A policeman,
held in a cone of yellow light from a street lamp, bobbing on the
balls of his feet (*Was that why the limeys called them bobbies?* he
wondered), flexing his wrists against interlocked fingers. Looking
for trouble, up and down the street, with one eye larger than the
other. They always had one eye larger than the other.

The thing was not to panic. Hold steady. Trust the whiskers. Trust
the padding. But most of all, trust the walk.

He passed the bobbing bobby without provoking anything more than a courteous nod of greeting. To which he responded with a more deliberate bow, in keeping with the character that his walk imposed on him. He was careful, at any account, to look the policeman squarely in the eye. The golden rule.

It was all a question of timing. Don't hold the gaze for too long. That would seem bold, provocative. As much a sign of guilt as shifty evasion. Keep it natural, that was the thing.

Oh, he was good. There was no point pretending otherwise. He didn't even allow himself a small smirk of triumph once he had left the bobby in his wake.

He heard the chug of trains and the screech of steam whistles. A moment later he saw the looming shadow of King's Cross station ahead of him.

As he stepped out of the churning smog into the flux and bustle of the station concourse, it occurred to him that perhaps he needn't be in such a hurry to leave the country. His experience with the policeman had given him confidence, and the beginnings of a new plan. As long as he had his theatrical make-up and his talent, he could go anywhere he pleased.

THIRTY-NINE

The house was in darkness when Quinn got home. He had remained at the department for as long as possible. Not because there was much that he could usefully do, more because of a reluctance to return home. This, he knew, was connected to the arrangement he had established with Mrs Ibbott concerning Miss Dillard's rent.

His mouth stretched into a private grimace as he closed the door behind him.

He was surprised to see Mrs Ibbott coming towards him with a candle in her hand. 'Oh, Mr Quinn. I'm afraid something has happened to the electricity supply. Mr Timberley and Mr Appleby are looking into it for us. They think it is something to do with a fuse.'

'I see. Thank you for telling me, Mrs Ibbott.'

'We never had this problem with gas, I have to say.'

'That's true. But there are other advantages to electricity, are there not? It is cleaner and safer, I think.'

'It's all very well when it works, Mr Quinn. Would you like a candle for your room?'

'I believe I have some candles, thank you, Mrs Ibbott.'

'Very well, Mr Quinn. I shall light your way upstairs for you.' Mrs Ibbott turned and then hesitated. 'Oh, Mr Quinn . . .' There was an ominous tone to her voice. Quinn recognized an old detective's technique, to begin the conversation with something inconsequential, before dropping in the main thing on your mind, as if as an after-thought. 'I'm a little worried about Miss Dillard.'

Quinn said nothing. He felt a weight of dread settle inside him. His feet dragged to a halt behind her.

Mrs Ibbott still had her back to him. 'I'm afraid she found out about your generous offer.'

'She found out? Mrs Ibbott, I asked you not to tell her!'

'I did not. I did, however, tell my daughter, who must have let it slip to the Misters Appleby and Timberley. I fear those two gentlemen may have conducted some indiscreet banter on the subject, which Miss Dillard somehow overheard.'

Quinn groaned.

Mrs Ibbott at last turned to face him. 'She has practically kept to her room since, although Betsy saw her coming out of the kitchen earlier. She seemed to be hiding something, according to Betsy. We wondered whether she had stolen something to eat. The silly woman, she knows she only has to ask. At any rate, no one saw her at dinner. I do not believe she has any gin left to consume, or money to buy more.'

'I truly wish you had not said anything to anyone about our arrangement.'

'I am sorry, Mr Quinn. I do regret my indiscretion.'

'What is to be done?'

'Perhaps we might . . . look in on her . . . together. You and I. As concerned friends.'

'Is it not rather late?'

'I do not think Miss Dillard has been keeping regular hours recently. I do feel that it would be better to have everything in the open, if we are to move to the arrangement you suggested. I feel Miss Dillard has a right to know who is paying her rent. And why.'

Quinn had to accept the justice of this remark. He nodded for Mrs Ibbott to lead on. 'Very well.'

They came to the first landing. Mrs Ibbott tapped on Miss Dillard's door. There was no reply. Mrs Ibbott pressed her ear against the door. Her eyes widened in alarm.

'What is it?'

Mrs Ibbott stood back, allowing Quinn to listen at the door. He braced himself for the sound of weeping. But that was not what met his ear. It sounded like someone was throwing furniture around. Or using the bed like a trampoline. If he had not known Miss Dillard better, he might have said she was entertaining a lover in a violent and energetic act of coitus. 'Good grief!'

'I don't like the sound of that,' cried Mrs Ibbott.

Quinn rapped on the door. 'Miss Dillard? Miss Dillard? Are you quite well?' The thumping inside the bedroom intensified in speed and volume. Quinn tried the door. It was locked. He turned to the landlady. 'Do you have a key?'

She produced a large fob from her apron. Her hand shook as she held out a key. 'I'm all fingers and thumbs.'

Quinn snatched the fob from her and began trying the keys in the lock. It seemed an age before he had the door open.

They were in the same room now as the thumping. It was like a heaving of the darkness. A giant hand pounding a box of springs. The bed: it was coming from the bed. It was the sound of the bed rattling and kicking against the boards. It was not quite rhythmic. There were pauses in it. Then it would come back with renewed force.

'Give me the light!'

Quinn held the candle out in front of him. Miss Dillard, wracked with convulsions, was throwing contorted forms of herself around on top of her bed. Her body would lie in a backward arch of tension and then spring upwards, clearing the mattress by an inch or so.

'What's the matter with her?' cried Mrs Ibbott.

'She appears to be having some kind of a fit,' said Quinn. 'Is she an epileptic, do you know?'

Mrs Ibbott could not answer. She too was shaking now, uncontrollably. She held her hand out to a small dark bottle on Miss Dillard's bedside table.

'What is it? What's in that bottle? Do you know? What has she taken?'

The answer came from Mrs Ibbott in a shriek: 'Strychnine!'

That raised any number of questions, which would have to wait for now. 'We must get her to a hospital!' Quinn tried to hand the candle back to Mrs Ibbott, who seemed incapable of doing anything other than making a small, helpless whimpering sound. She stared at the candle, as if he was offering her the extracted spleen of her daughter. Eventually he was able to thrust it into her hands.

Quinn then stooped over the convulsing woman, looking for a way to lift her. Her body shifted position constantly, arching and collapsing, closing down his opportunities to get a handhold.

Her eyes were open, more than open, bulging starkly from her head. The pupils were fully dilated; the wonderful, miraculous pewter grey of her irises shrunk almost to a fine circle. For all their dilation, it was clear that she saw nothing.

Her mouth was stretched back into a grimace of helpless agony. Flecks of foam appeared on her yellow and grey teeth, seeping out through the gaps between them. The flecks grew quickly to an abundant froth.

He knew that the longer he hesitated the worse it would be for Miss Dillard.

He touched her quivering frailty, and was repelled. This was a strange, unasked-for intimacy. The effect on Miss Dillard was catastrophic. Her convulsions redoubled in ferocity. It was as if she was trying to throw herself away from herself, to escape the misery of her existence by some final, doomed act of self-discarding.

Her body, her flesh was patently present to his touch, a blazing heat beneath the delicate nightdress. She was on fire, it seemed. His touch wracked her like raging flames. He pulled her to him in a firm embrace, clinging to the muscular writhing of her body. Her convulsions were transmitted to him. He became convulsed too.

At first he carried her like a groom bearing his bride across the threshold, but she was a bride who struggled every inch of the way. So much so that he was forced to swing her over his shoulder into a fireman's lift.

It shocked him to discover how little weight there was to her. She could have been made out of crumpled foil for all she weighed. No, it was not her weight that made her hard to carry; it was the tensioned kick of her body, every muscle wrought and spasming at once.

A small group of the other residents had been drawn by the commotion, including Messrs Timberley and Appleby. 'One of you run ahead!' shouted Quinn. 'Flag down a cab on the Brompton Road. We have to get her to the infirmary.'

But the two young men seemed incapable of movement, like the specimens they pinned at the Natural History Museum. 'What's the matter with her?' asked Mr Timberley, his face contorted with distaste.

'She's dying. She will die, unless we get her to St George's.'

'Dying?' Timberley regarded Miss Dillard with a scientist's interest, as if he had always wanted to see someone die and this presented a rare opportunity.

'For God's sake, will one of you not go for assistance?'

Timberley held a balled fist over his mouth and coughed. If the cough was forced, it soon turned into an uncontrollable hacking fit. He turned reluctantly from the interesting spectacle and began to make his way slowly downstairs, one hand on the wall to steady himself against the crashing waves of his coughing.

'Hurry, will you! This is a matter of life and death!'

Timberley waved a hand, an impatient gesture that seemed to convey that he was going as fast as he could. Quinn had to accept that he seemed like the wreckage of the man he had once been. He turned to Appleby and directed his gaze meaningfully towards the invalid.

Appleby seemed to take the hint. At any rate, there must have been something in Quinn's gaze that spurred him on. 'I say, Timberley, wait for me. I'll come with you.'

'I suggest you run ahead,' wheezed Timberley through his coughing. 'I cannot run. My doctor will not allow it. Mr Quinn will have two corpses on his hands if I am forced to run.' He was projecting this back over his shoulder. Clearly it was intended for Quinn's benefit. 'I am perfectly serious, you know. Perfectly.' He pressed himself to the wall and allowed his friend to thunder past.

By the time he got to Brompton Road, Quinn was staggering. Not under her weight. But under the certainty that he was too late. She was hammering against his shoulder, and her breath came in a rasping, strangulated whine. It was not the death rattle. It was something worse than the death rattle. It was the sound a body makes when it rebels against the action of breathing.

Appleby was in the middle of the road, shouting and waving both arms to stop the traffic. At last something of the urgency of the situation seemed to have struck him. Timberley stood at the roadside and hung his head disconsolately. He cast sly, fascinated glances towards the heaving burden over Quinn's shoulder.

At last Appleby persuaded a motor taxi to stop. He screamed the destination at the driver, who when he saw the intended passenger seemed about to refuse the fare.

'I am a police inspector,' said Quinn. 'If you don't take us to St George's I will kill you.' He had meant to say 'arrest you', but the stress of the moment had added a certain bluntness to his words.

'What's wrong wiv 'er, guv? She ain't gonna be sick in me cab?'

'You had better hope that she does not *die* in your cab.' Quinn was bandying death around like loose change, in the hope that it would get things moving.

It was a hard job getting her into the back of the taxi. Her arms were flailing everywhere, her feet kicking out. Quinn received a punch to the eye and a knee in the groin that fair took the wind out of him. The blows landed so expertly that if he hadn't known better he would have said she had aimed them. At one point, one of her legs locked itself in an acute angle around his thigh. Eventually, he and Appleby together managed to prise it loose. They put her in head first and laid her down on the back seat. Quinn went round the other side and eased himself under her now freakishly juddering length. He nestled her wracked and quivering head against his chest and tried to soothe away her spasms by stroking her hair. Her feet kicked rhythmically and violently against the door. The driver's anxious glances back weighed his concern for his taxi against his fear for his life. In the event, the latter won out. He said nothing.

'Hudge up!' said Appleby, squeezing himself in beside Quinn. It meant somehow rotating the angle of Miss Dillard's rigid body closer to the vertical. Timberley peered in with a forlorn expression, like a child deprived of a treat.

'Drive as quickly as you can, without occasioning undue shocks,' directed Quinn.

The taxi lurched off. It was soon apparent that the driver wanted them out of his cab as quickly as possible. Quinn's admonition for caution was largely ignored.

The strangulated sound at the back of Miss Dillard's throat tightened. Her hands became claws, clutching at their own pain. One somehow lodged on to Quinn's forearm and again he was astonished by the strength hidden away in this frail, ruined woman.

He clung on to her as tightly as she clung on to him. He was trying to close down her convulsions with the firm press of his embrace. But also, he was aware that he was trying to hang on to the life in her. That if he let go of her, he would lose her.

The high pointed tower of the St George's Union Infirmary, with its arched windows and weather vane, gave the building the appearance of a massively enlarged church. No doubt its vaguely religious architecture was meant to inspire hope. Now it was just a looming shape in the darkness. A shadow within a shadow.

Appleby sprang out and ran towards the great cathedral of medicine.

Quinn extricated himself more carefully. As he laid down her head, her body was wracked by its most violent convulsion yet. The foam at her mouth had blood in it now. There was every chance that she had bitten through her tongue.

In the dark, he could not see her eyes. He was unable even to imagine the beautiful shimmering grey of her irises. It was as if the blackness of her hugely dilated pupils had spread out and swamped everything. He felt a wrench at his heart at the thought that the beautiful pewter grey was lost forever. If only he could see her eyes, that grey, she would live. Everything depended on his being able to see her eyes. He wanted to call for a lamp, or a torch, to shine into her face. To dispel the blackness that had seeped into everything.

Her legs gave a final double kick against the inside of the cab, then stiffened. Her arms formed jagged shapes, and held them, as sharp and permanent as the branches of petrified trees. The strangulated gurgling in her throat was no more.

FORTY

The next day, inside the curtained house, he could not dispel the blackness from the corners of his vision. He looked for the gleaming pewter grey of her eyes everywhere. But the only grey was the dour cheerless grey of an empty English Sunday. A godless, lifeless grey.

There were murmured consolations, though why it was felt that he needed consoling more than anyone else he could not grasp.

The other lodgers wanted to discuss why she might have done it. They sat in the front parlour drinking tea. The question came to their lips as regularly as the bone china.

'But why, that's what I cannot understand?' *Clink.*

'Why would she do such a thing?' *Clink.*

'What on earth could have possessed her?' *Clink.*

And all the other variations of *why?* punctuated by the chinking of cup against saucer.

The question was never answered, except by a furtive, meaning look in Quinn's direction.

Were they placing her death on his conscience? But how could it be his fault? All he had done was offer to pay her rent until she was in a better position to pay it herself. How could that be the reason she had killed herself?

Mrs Ibbott distracted the attention from him somewhat by blaming herself, not without some justification, Quinn felt. But the focus of her self-recrimination was entirely on the means by which Miss Dillard killed herself, rather than her motivation. It seemed that the strychnine had been given to Mrs Ibbott years ago by a male cousin who was a gamekeeper on a Suffolk estate. At the time, there had been a problem with rats in the cellar. The bottle had remained at the back of the scullery cupboard ever since. How Miss Dillard had known about it, or whether she had simply gone looking for some suitable substance to achieve her goal, was a matter of speculation.

Betsy, the maid, was distraught. She was the last to have seen Miss Dillard alive, leaving the kitchen with something concealed in her hands. She had thought at the time that it was a crust of bread or an apple, perhaps. But it now seemed clear that it was the bottle of strychnine. '*If only I had said something . . . It's all my fault . . .*'

'No.' Quinn was watching Timberley and Appleby as he spoke. He noticed that for once they had little to say for themselves. Perhaps they sensed that their characteristic facetiousness would be out of place. Or perhaps it was a sense of guilt that inhibited them. Quinn continued: 'You were not to know. You said nothing out of kindness, because you feared it would embarrass her if she had taken something to eat. You mustn't blame yourself.' His words were meant for Betsy, but he continued looking at the two young men.

At last, Appleby looked up and caught his eye. Colour rushed to his cheeks.

'Mr Appleby, would you step outside the parlour and speak with me for a moment.' Quinn voiced it as a command, not a question.

In the hallway, he closed the door with quiet precision on Mr Timberley's anxious, inquisitive face.

'How may I be of service?' Appleby whispered.

'She overheard you. You and Timberley, speaking of a matter that related to me. What did you say?'

'I beg your pardon?'

'What did you and Timberley say to each other?' There was a quality to the sudden firmness of Quinn's voice that was consistent with the moment he had threatened to kill the cabbie last night.

Appleby must have sensed this. 'We . . . we may have talked about the fact that you had offered to pay her rent. Mary – Miss Ibbott – told us.'

'And she heard you? Miss Dillard heard you?'

'I don't know. How can we know? We were on the landing. Her door was ajar. And then it closed.'

'It closed. Can you remember exactly what had been said just before the door closed?'

'It wasn't anything. Not anything that could have precipitated . . . this.'

'What did you say? What were the exact words?'

'Exact words? I don't know. You can't expect me to remember the exact words. One of us might have said something about you taking pity on her.'

'*Pity?*'

'Yes. Well, isn't that what it was?'

Quinn narrowed his eyes but did not answer.

'At any rate, I cannot see the harm in that. How could that induce her to take her own life?' Appleby even had the effrontery to add: 'You mustn't blame yourself, old chap.'

But Quinn was thinking only of her eyes, trying to remember the exact quality of their metallic hue. It was there, in them, that Miss Dillard was beautiful.

'I say, it wasn't more than that, was it? It wasn't more than pity?'

Quinn wondered if he should try to explain it to Appleby. But first he would have to explain it to himself and he was not sure that he could. He did not know why he had offered to pay Miss Dillard's rent, but he did not think it was out of pity. It was rather because he had found the thought of never seeing her eyes again unbearable.

FORTY-ONE

Quinn got out of the Model T in Harley Street and looked up. His gaze deliberately sought out the sun. The effect was as he knew it would be. The white orb turned black. The blackness spread out from it, contaminating the milky sky.

An all-encompassing darkness descended.

He had brought this darkness on himself, because today he could not bear the sight of the world, the pitiless cruelty of its renewal.

In many ways Miss Dillard's death had come as a release from the intractable difficulties of her life. It was all very sad and unnecessary, but he should not reproach himself. He had done all he could for her. Of course, *all he could* was not enough to save her life. But that was not the same as to say that he was to blame for her death.

Her younger, married sisters had turned up yesterday. They filled the house with sniffles and whispers and husbands. These were tall, silent presences, who made no comment but held their heads at sympathetic angles.

The question – *why?* – was brought out again and aired, like a wound from which the dressing was removed, while those present peered at it with a mixture of curiosity and distaste. Quinn knew from his own experience that it was a question that the living would never tire of asking, but to which no adequate answer could ever be found. Because the only one who had the answer was dead.

The fog of his temporary blindness lifted partially, enough to allow him to make out the dark rectangle of Dr Casaubon's door. He perceived it as black, though whether that was its true colour, he could not remember. He pushed against the field of blackness, this time without ringing the bell first. It was within the hours of Dr Casaubon's surgery, and the doctor was expecting him.

Now the self-imposed darkness was absorbed into the drapery-imposed darkness of Dr Casaubon's surgery. The voice of that darkness had just asked him a question about his father's suicide.

'Once again, I did not come here to be psychoanalyzed by you.' But the question of why he had come to Dr Casaubon was only vaguely answered in Quinn's mind. He might justifiably say that it was to do with the investigation. But even he sensed that was a pretext rather than a reason. Was it possible that it was to do with Miss Dillard's suicide? If so, it was strange that Quinn was scrupulous in avoiding any mention of what had happened at the lodging house.

'And yet you have consented, once again, to lie down on my couch.'

'I did not want to. I did it to please you.'

'Are you often driven to do things to please others?'

'Far from it. Those who know me would find that rather amusing.'

'Do you feel the need to earn the approval of your father?'

'How can I? He's dead.'

'But that need may still be there. Especially as he died unexpectedly, when you were a young man. What will happen is that you will transfer these feelings on to other men, older men, father figures, we might call them. That is why you lay down to please me. There is someone in your life whom you would describe as a father figure? Your superior at your work, for example?'

'Sir Edward.'

'You work hard to please him. You sometimes go too far, in fact. That is why people die. It is all because you are trying to please Sir Edward, and through him your father.'

'But Sir Edward frequently disapproves of my methods, or so he says.'

'The eternal tension between father and son is played out. You seek his approval, which he perpetually withholds.'

Quinn shook his head impatiently. An invisible gesture in the darkness. 'I did not come here for this. Doctor, have you any experience in the psychology of murderers?'

'I have had the privilege to speak to a number of murderers in my career.'

'The privilege?'

'Murder is an act of wish-fulfilment. Wish-fulfilment is the cornerstone of Freudian dream analysis. Anyone who has lived out an impulse of wish-fulfilment to such an extent is naturally of interest to a doctor of the mind.'

'It is a strange word to use.'

'Do you not find yourself drawn to murderers? Could that not be why you have chosen this unusual profession? Is it not a privilege for you to be able to hunt them down and kill them?'

'I do not always kill them. That is certainly not my intention when I begin an investigation. Sometimes it is necessary to take steps to protect myself and the public. But I have not come here to justify myself to you.'

'You have so far told me several reasons why you did not come here today. You have yet to tell me why you did.'

'I have come to ask for your assistance in an investigation.'

'My assistance?'

'If you were to look at the work of a particular artist, would you be able to tell if that artist had a predisposition to murder?'

'A lot would depend on the nature of the work. Are these paintings?'

'Not paintings. Motion picture films. The subject is a film director.'

'You have piqued my interest, Inspector. However, I cannot promise any definite results, and it might be rash in any event to offer firm pronouncements, especially if there is a danger you might act upon them.'

'How do you mean?'

'I wouldn't want to be the reason you killed someone.'

'I would not act solely on the basis of your opinion. I would only make an arrest if there were also material evidence against the suspect. And as I said before, it is not my intention to kill anyone.'

'I confess, it is an intriguing proposal.'

'My sergeant is waiting outside in a car. Would it be possible for you to accompany me to the Yard now? We have the films there. And a projector with which to view them.'

'Very well. You have come at a good time. I have finished my appointments for the morning.' Dr Casaubon began to draw back the drapes. 'But tell me, Inspector, what is the name of this director? I am quite an aficionado of the kinema.'

'Konrad Waechter.'

There was a beat. 'Of course!'

'By that, do you mean that you think it is possible, after all?'

'Let us watch the films, Inspector. Then I will be able to offer a more informed opinion.'

A rectangle of light shimmered and fluctuated, as if trying to latch itself on to something solid in the darkness. Its edges sharpened and softened. Swirling flecks and particles swam across it, as it shrank and expanded, jerking itself into its ideal size.

Macadam positioned the projector to shine its beam on to the one vertical wall in the department, the wall that usually used held the photographs of victims, sketches of crime scenes, biographic details of suspects and other notes and documents relevant to the investigation. This was no ordinary wall, it was *the wall*.

That morning, Tuesday, after a day of prompting, Waechter's back catalogue of films had finally arrived from Visionary Productions. It was at that point, when he realized that he had no real idea what he was looking for, that Quinn decided to involve Dr Casaubon of Harley Street.

And so they were now about to cast upon *the wall* the product of a man's imagination. A man who had the power and the habit to give his dreams form and to make them move and dance across the dark.

They stared at the blank rectangle of light waiting for these dreams to form. As long as Quinn kept his focus on that luminescent area, he could keep whatever horrors the darkness contained at bay. The darkness held the memory of her trembling body, the constricted rasp in the back of her throat, her pupils dilated to the full.

'So, do you fancy him for Dolores Novak, guv?' asked Inchball.

Quinn felt a strange disconnectedness, almost a disembodiment. It felt like he was cast under a spell he was reluctant to break.

Macadam answered the question for him, as he made his final adjustments to the projecting lens. 'You know there is nothing to place him at the scene of her murder, sir.'

'Nuffin' to say he was there. Nuffin' to say he wasn't,' argued Inchball.

'The only men we know were there were her husband, Porrick and Lord Dunwich,' countered Macadam, laying the ground for a theory. He closed the shutter between the arc lamp and the projector, plunging them into near darkness. He worked the end of the film through and into place on the sprockets. It was an operation he had practised many times since the projector had arrived.

Quinn was generally content to let his sergeants argue it out. In the past their back and forth bickering had often led to new insights. But now he felt compelled to intervene, as much to prove to himself – as well as his men – that he was present in the semi-darkness. 'And who of them has a motive?' He felt his lips tremble in the aftermath of the question.

'Dunwich, if she was trying to blackmail him. Novak, if he was jealous of her with his lordship.' Macadam was keen to develop his theory. He adjusted the tension on the receiving spool. The first film was in place, ready to begin showing.

'What about Porrick?' said Quinn. It was as if his voice was coming from someone else in the darkness. And yet he was aware of an impulse to keep the voice going. There was safety, recourse, in speech. If he talked about the investigation, he did not have to think about Miss Dillard. 'When I spoke to him, he failed to mention that he had gone back with Novak. It is rather too convenient that he claims to remember nothing of what happened after he left the festivities in Cecil Court. He is a blank. And I am always suspicious of blanks.' Quinn acknowledged a sense of surprise at discovering his suspicion of blanks.

'Perhaps he's in on the blackmail racket with the Novaks.' Despite his natural inclination to oppose Macadam, Inchball was evidently warming to the idea that one of the three men they could link to the crime scene was the murderer. 'Perhaps they fell out over it. Maybe he done for them both. That's why Novak's disappeared, 'cos Porrick's stiffed him and dumped his body somewhere.'

'A lot to accomplish in one night.' And now it was Macadam arguing broadly against the position to which he had led them. 'And why is he doing this?'

'I dunno,' admitted Inchball. 'Maybe he offered to get rid of them for Lord Dunwich.' Inchball rubbed his thumb and forefinger together: *money.*

'We will have to have another chat with Mr Porrick.' Quinn wondered how his two sergeants would react if he had told them about Miss Dillard and had tried to explain to them how her suicide had affected him. He almost laughed at the absurdity of the idea. 'Also, we should talk to his associates. Find out more about his business affairs. He seems an affluent and successful fellow, but we know that he argued with Mrs Porrick at the party. What was that about? Perhaps he had had his own dalliance with Dolores Novak. Alternatively, if the business was running into trouble, that might provide a motive for him to join the Novaks in trying to extort money out of Lord Dunwich.'

'You don't need the business to be strugglin',' said Inchball with a grim, cynical sneer. '''Is type don' need any excuse. It's second nature, innit. If they see an opportunity for makin' some readies, they'll take it. It don't matter how.'

A fourth voice, tinged by a soft Edinburgh brogue, reminded Quinn of the presence of their guest. 'Fascinating. You gentlemen are, I would venture to say, veritable psychologists.'

'Are you ready to show the first film, Macadam?'

The answer was the click and pitter-patter of the projector, the forward rush of light, bearing shape and tone and movement in its blazing van.

The title came up in German.

'The Tailor's Dream,' translated Dr Casaubon. 'An eternal theme, that of a pact with the Devil.'

The title faded. The first scene showed Berenger, the same mournful-faced tragi-comedian who had played the jilted cavalry officer in Waechter's most recent film, sitting cross-legged on the floor of an artisan's workshop, stitching together a coat. An inter-title in German was again translated by Dr Casaubon. 'A simple tailor dreams of fame as a musician.'

The tailor seemed to prick his ears. He rose to his feet, as if in response to some auditory signal that they of course could not hear. He was shown looking out of the window of his workshop. The scene then switched to a band of troubadours parading through the streets of a medieval city, followed by an appreciative crowd. At the head of the musicians was a kindly looking old man in motley, playing the fiddle. 'Ah, yes,' continued Dr Casaubon. 'The fiddler there, you see. He is the Devil.'

The scene switched back to the tailor's workshop. He threw down the coat he was working on and rushed out.

'If I remember rightly, for it is some years since I saw the film, our tailor enters into a contract with the Devil, surrendering his soul in return for musical talent. The devil gives him a magical violin which he is able to play as a virtuoso. He becomes a famous concert violinist, performing to packed houses at the greatest concert halls in the world. Beautiful women fall at his feet. Inevitably, the time comes for the Devil to collect on his side of the deal. And just as inevitably, the tailor tries to escape. The Devil pursues him to a strange castle. The tailor finds himself in a room containing giant musical instruments, including an enormous violin. He hides in the case for this instrument, the inside of which is curiously cushioned, in a manner reminiscent of a coffin. The Devil, who up until this point had appeared as the mild old gentleman you see now, is suddenly a beast of colossal size. He lifts up the violin case with the tailor inside and carries it easily down to the dungeon of the castle, where the door to Hell is located.'

'Lumme, he's spoilt it now!' cried Inchball. 'We know what happens!'

'We are not watching the films for entertainment,' said Quinn. 'But in an effort to understand better the mind of the man who created them.'

'And what does this tell us about his mind?' wondered Macadam.

'Doctor?'

'The Faustian figure is one in which driving ambition overrides any moral considerations. The ambition may be said to be pathological. It is interesting that in Waechter's version of the story, his hero seeks fame as a creative artist – a musician – rather than as a scientist seeking knowledge, as in the original myth. There is perhaps something autobiographical about his choice of subject. It seems to suggest that Waechter is prepared to do anything in order to further his career as an artist.'

'And could doing anything include murder?'

'That's an interesting question, Inspector. This could be a coded message from a conflicted psyche. A kind of warning. Or it could, in fact, represent the exorcism of the drives that it portrays – which are by the very act of expression rendered safe. If he tells the story of Faust, he has no need to be Faust.'

The film was a one-reeler. It raced through the action Dr Casaubon had already described. They were now at the moment where the mild old gentleman presented himself at the successful musician's dressing room, after a triumphant performance. The Devil picked up the violin he had given the tailor and smiled. An inter-title appeared, which Dr Casaubon translated: 'Ah! The trusty Stradivarius! What would you be without it?'

The old man's expression became mysteriously threatening. It seemed to suggest that he could take the other man's talent away from him as easily as he had granted it. The tailor tried to wrestle the violin from the Devil's hands. In the process, the delicate instrument shattered. The tailor ran from his own dressing room. The old man threw back his head and laughed.

'Of course, an alternative interpretation,' continued Dr Casaubon, 'and one which had not occurred to me until now, is that Waechter in fact identifies himself with the Devil in this story. As a film director, he controls and directs the lives of his characters. He decides who lives and who dies. Perhaps . . . perhaps he has sought to exercise the same power in the real world.'

'Ain't that a lot of help!' Inchball gave a humourless chuckle. 'Either he's the poor feller who sells his soul to the Devil, or he's the Devil who buys it.'

'Your sergeant has made a very astute psychological observation, Inspector. In psychology, it is perfectly possible for opposing characteristics to exist in the same personality. A coin has two sides, does it not? As does the psyche. Waechter may well see himself as both the soul facing damnation and the Devil carrying the condemned soul off to Hell. He is both the tortured and the torturer.'

'But is he a killer?'

'On the evidence of this?' There was a shifting of shoulders in the darkness. 'He is a poet.'

'Funny kind of poet,' said Macadam, as the violin case containing the damned tailor was carried off to Hell. The film flapped and clattered out its last few feet.

There was a brief interlude during which Macadam rewound the film and set up the next.

It was another short. The title again appeared in German: *Totentanz*. Dr Casaubon translated: 'The Dance of Death. Or *Danse Macabre.*'

The film appeared to be a light comedy about madness and death. It concerned a man, again played by Berenger, who took pleasure in dressing up as Death in order to play pranks on his neighbours. He donned a black costume and hood, on to which a luminous white skeleton and skull had been painted.

The first neighbour he called on dropped down dead from a heart attack. The second victim was so frightened that he ran upstairs and threw himself out of a first-storey window. He broke his neck in the fall and died. When the prankster knocked on the third door, he was met by a figure dressed exactly the same as him, also carrying a scythe over his shoulder. The two Deaths confronted one another. The practical joker held his sides and mimed laughing, punching his counterpart on the shoulder, joshingly.

There was an inter-title in German, which Dr Casaubon was good enough to translate for them: 'I see you have had the same idea as me!'

The prankster then pulled off his mask, inviting the other Death to do the same with a merry laugh. But the neighbour refused. The practical joker made a grab for the supposed hood of the other figure. His fingers sank into the empty eye sockets of a real skull. A pile of bones collapsed on the floor, together with an empty cloak and discarded scythe. The practical joker's hilarity turned to terror. He began to scream.

The next scene showed him confined in a lunatic asylum, surrounded by other lunatics.

Quinn was aware of a sense of premonition. Perhaps he had seen something in the background of the scene that prepared him subconsciously for what was to come: the entrance of a man he recognized as the first Dr Casaubon, the very same man who had whisked away the wounded woman a few nights ago in Cecil Court. A moment later, he saw her too. She was there as one of the lunatics closing in on Berenger's character. In a final coup of trick photography, all the inmates and medical staff of the asylum peeled away the masks of their faces, revealing their death's head skulls beneath.

The prankster was not in an asylum. He had died and gone to Hell. The director of the asylum – the first Dr Casaubon – was the Devil.

FORTY-TWO

K onrad Waechter looked up at the vast concave entrance to the Islington Porrick's Palace, a kind of gigantic gilded conch shell set into the black, soot-grimed facade of Upper Street. He could not suppress a smile at the sheer visual splendour of it. It seemed to promise as much as it presented, leading kinema viewers into a grotto of fantasy and spectacle, away from the grim sordid reality of their lives. Indeed, it would make an attractive location for a scene in a motion picture. He closed his eye on the vision, as if overwhelmed by it. The darkness that overtook him was filled with the abstract, teeming shapes created by a film of living flesh drawn over a bright day. His mind began inventing scenarios.

Perhaps he had underestimated Porrick. He began to think this was a man he could go into partnership with, after all. And at least he had stopped trying to push that nasty little dog on him.

He heard Porrick's voice. 'At night we switch on the lights and the whole thing lights up like a beacon for kinema-goers.'

Waechter kept his eye closed, imagining rather than contemplating the countless electric bulbs that ran around the edge of the entrance. He always preferred his vision of a subject to the reality of it. '*Und* this is vere you intend to hold *der Waechterfest*?'

'It's actually the largest capacity of my theatres. Seats eight hundred. I am sure we will be able to fill it, given the . . . well, given the circumstances.'

'If the authorities allow you to go ahead.' Waechter recognized the voice of Kirkwood, Porrick's accountant. Kirkwood had come along to handle the financial side of the negotiations for Porrick. For his own part, he had brought Hartmann. It had been Hartmann's idea to have Eloise and Berenger there too. He knew how to impress a potential investor. The one other member of the party was Diaz, Waechter's trusted cameraman. In many ways, Diaz was Waechter's eyes, as well as his technical brain. Wherever he went, Waechter was always mulling over potential scenes and locations for future motion pictures. He liked to have Diaz there to advise.

'They'll allow it,' asserted Porrick. 'And we'll fill the place. Several times over. And even Mr Kirkwood will be happy.'

'I like it.' Waechter opened his eye and nodded decisively to his producer. 'We can make picture here.'

He gestured for Porrick to lead them inside. The kinema owner produced a large bunch of keys to unlock the several locks and padlocks securing the high ornate double doors.

The doors opened with a creak of protest on to a chill interior darkness. The kinema was evidently not open yet. But surely, Waechter thought, the matinee should have been underway by now? Their footsteps echoed cavernously as they progressed inside. The pungent whiff of charred air assailed his nostrils, mingled with the fresher smells of construction: sawn timbers, cement and plaster. There was the smell of something else too. Something organic. Not quite the smell of rotting. But possibly the smell of death. Certainly the smell of wet fur and piss. As if an animal had crawled in there to die. He expected to hear its whimpering. No doubt the workmen had put down poison for vermin. He imagined a doomed rodent twitching out its last in some dark forgotten corner of the building.

A thin silvering of feeble light seeped in from somewhere high up to leaven the gloom. It tinged the black figures moving through the treacly darkness.

'Can we have the lights on, Kirkwood?' demanded Porrick.

'Ah, well, no, Mr Porrick . . . actually we cannot. Not until we settle the outstanding account with the electrical company.'

'But that's absurd! Why hasn't it been paid? Pay it immediately!'

'We don't—'

But Porrick cut his accountant off. 'I don't want to hear any of your excuses. I know I authorized the payment. I consider it very remiss on your part not to have made it.'

Waechter heard his producer's voice in the darkness. 'Is it that the kinema is not in use at the moment, Porrick?'

'We have only just finished the refurbishments.'

'Haven't finished them, actually,' put in Kirkwood. 'In fact, we didn't get any further than restoring the entrance before we ran out of funds.'

Hartmann was not impressed. 'This does not bode well, Porrick. How can you expect to hold a festival here?'

'There are only one or two small jobs outstanding. I feel that if we are to go into partnership, Porrick's Palaces and Visionary Productions, perhaps the funds could be found from your side of the business?'

'But this is absurd! You have wasted our time. We came here to talk to you about your investing in Visionary Productions, in order to secure an exclusive distribution deal. You cannot expect us to put money into your failing business. Come, Waechter, we have seen enough here.'

'*Vait!*' Waechter knew how to command, even with a single word. 'It is better for my film that it is not . . . perfect. We can dress it, *ja*? I have an idea. I vill turn your kinema into a vision of Hell. *Ja*? You like?'

'I . . . I'm not . . . That sounds rather . . .'

'A young Fräulein . . .'

'Eloise?' wondered Porrick.

'*Off courssse!*' Waechter bowed steeply towards the silhouette of his leading lady. 'Your character, she loves the kinema. It is a drug to her. She comes every night. Spends all of her money. She must prostitute herself to pay for her habit.'

Eloise pretended to be scandalized. 'But what will my grand-mother say when she sees it!'

'*Der* golden entrance to your kinema, Herr Porrick, is a shining bright entrance to Hell. Inside, it is a dark palace. We have torches, burning torches, on the walls, *ja*? Mephistopheles is in the box office. Beautiful demon girls light the way for her to her seat. She sits and watches film. *Der* screen is filled with flames. *Der* flames come out of the screen and burn down the kinema. Everyone dies . . . *Und* goes to Hell. The manager of the kinema is *der Teufel*. *Ja*? The deffil. Berenger will play him.'

The darkness swirled exuberantly as Berenger doffed his bowler hat and executed a swooping bow in a gesture of gratitude.

Porrick was less appreciative. 'I . . . hmmm . . . I think we need to work on the scenario somewhat. Can it not be a little more cheerful? I'm not sure I like the idea of a fire in one of my Palaces.'

'It vill not be real fire. We create illusion, *ja*? Diaz, it can be done?'

The Chilean's response was obscure. Perhaps he nodded. Perhaps he shrugged. It seemed he sighed.

'There is problem?'

'No, Señor Waechter. Whatever you ask, I do. You know that.'

Waechter nodded tersely. That was all he needed to know. All he cared about. Any hint of pain or grief that he might have detected in the little man's hesitancy was no concern of his.

'But . . . uhm . . .' Porrick spoke in a whisper out of the corner of his mouth. 'You do know that there was a fire here, in which a man died? That's why we have been refurbishing the place.'

'I cannot help that.'

'I do not believe that the English motion picture viewing public will pay good money to see such a depressing subject enacted. Hartmann, what do you think?'

'Waechter is Waechter. His vision is his genius. If you want to make films with Waechter, you must surrender to his vision.'

'Look here, what if she is inspired by the films she sees to become a motion picture actress? She falls in love with her leading man . . . uhm . . . and is a great success. And they . . . they . . .'

'They all live happily ever after?' said Kirkwood sarcastically.

'Yes!'

'This is not a Waechter film,' pronounced Waechter. 'In a Waechter film she becomes prostitute and goes to Hell.'

'I don't see why it has to be like that.'

'If you do not wish to make Waechter film, you do not go into *eine Partnerschaft mit* Waechter!'

'Amen to that!' said Kirkwood.

'You vont Waechter films to save you from ruin?'

Porrick's voice receded as he turned away from Waechter and led the way further inside. 'You haven't seen the auditorium.'

There was a metallic clatter. In his haste, and anger, Porrick had walked into something: a metal pail or a tin box, by the sound of it. He gave a pained yelp of surprise as he sprawled headlong to the ground. 'What the devil!'

Waechter closed his eye and sniffed. He prided himself on his keen senses of taste and smell. The organic odour he had identified earlier had suddenly intensified, as if it had been released by Porrick's accident.

'Are you all right, Porrick, old chap?' It was Hartmann, fussing over the fallen businessman.

'I tripped over something. Kirkwood, are you sure we can't muster a light in here? I wouldn't want anyone else to come a cropper. Mademoiselle Eloise, for example.'

'There may be some candles in the box office. I shall investigate.' The scrape of phosphor against sandpaper gave a brief moment of match light as Kirkwood located the box office and headed off towards it. The match went out before he reached his destination. But before too long a second was struck, and in its brief flare, the candles were found.

Kirkwood came back holding two lighted candles, one of which he gave to Diaz, the other he waved vaguely towards Porrick, who was sitting on the floor groping blindly around him. 'I've lost the keys. They were in my hand and I dropped them.'

He gave a sudden cry of disgust. His hand had found something unpleasant, it seemed. 'Bring that candle down here, will you, Kirkwood.'

The accountant moved swiftly to obey. The candle flame flickered and left a swathe of light in its trail, demonstrating the principle of the persistence of vision upon which they all depended for their livelihoods.

And now they could all see what Porrick's hand had found. A tin box lay on its side, its lid splayed open, the contents tipped out. Waechter felt his mouth twitch up in a tight curl of satisfaction. The animal hadn't been dead long. Its little legs stuck out stiffly as if it had been frozen in mid bound. Its loathsome snout was stuck open as if it had choked on one last detestable yelp.

'Scudder!' cried Porrick.

They came back out blinking into the sorry light. All except for Waechter who kept his eye closed, savouring the darkness in which his imagination flourished. He had enough of a sense of direction to carry him on to the pavement without having to look where he was going. He knew that Porrick was clutching the black tin box. He knew that the dog was inside it. In his mind's eye, he could see both the outside of the box and its grim contents.

He was aware of a car pulling up at speed in front of them. He opened his eye to see the rear door fly open and the troublesome detective bound out.

'Konrad Waechter. You will come with us, please. We have some questions we wish to put to you.'

The car they had brought for him was as black as a hearse. He felt that if he accepted the detective's invitation he would be taken to some dark place from which he would never return. He imagined an oubliette in the basement of Scotland Yard.

Before he got into the car, he tried to catch Berenger's eye. But his leading man avoided meeting his own singular gaze, so studiously that he must have believed it cursed.

FORTY-THREE

Quinn had Inchball and Macadam escort Waechter to the Special Crimes Department, rather than an interview room. The projector and rheostat were still set up there. It was the most convenient place to show him *Totentanz*.

'Vy are you showing me this? I make this film. You think I haff not seen it before?'

'I would like you to watch the final scene carefully. You are familiar with the final scene?'

'*Off coursse*! I tell you, I make this film.'

Quinn walked over to the patch of glowing movement on the wall. At a prearranged moment, Macadam stopped the mechanism, so that a single frozen image was projected on the wall. Quinn pointed to the woman whom he had last seen being led away from Cecil Court as he held her eye in a handkerchief. 'You see this woman?'

'*Ja.*'

'She is the woman who was attacked last Friday.'

Waechter waited a beat before replying: 'She vos not attacked.'

'Her eye was not gouged out of its socket?'

'*Nein.*'

'I held it in my hand.'

'Zat is vot you *beleeff*. But it is not vot happened.'

'Who is she?'

'She is *eine* . . . actress. Her name is Lyudmila Lyudmova.'

'A Russian?'

'*Off coursse.*'

'I don't understand. I looked into the empty socket where her eye had been. I saw . . . I saw the black emptiness there.'

Waechter shrugged. 'She lost her eye when she vos a child. In

Totentanz she has glass eye. You can see. Her eyes do not alvays look . . . um . . . *too-gehtter*.'

'Well, blow me, she's boss-eyed!' exclaimed Inchball.

'*Ja*. Is so. There vos no attack. It vos . . . *ein Streich, ein* trick, *ein* gag, *ja*?'

Suddenly a detail from the night, which had troubled Quinn in his dreams, made sense. 'Her eye was the wrong colour.'

Waechter let out a rueful laugh. 'Is true?'

'Yes. The eye I retrieved was brown. But her eye, the eye on her face, was blue, I believe.'

'He would not think about that! We are too used to working in black and vite!'

'He? Are you saying that you are not responsible for this grotesque prank?'

'No. I knew nothing of it until the night. And then I keep silent because I knew that it had been done for the best of motives. A harmless prank. Maybe it would help to promote our film. But most, I *be-leeff*, it vos intended to make me *lahh-ff*.'

'Make you laugh?' Inchball's eyes bulged in disgust.

'I *be-leeff* so.'

Quinn turned away from the projected image and faced Waechter. He found his attention focused on the inky pool of blackness that was the Austrian's eye patch. 'Why would it make you laugh? Wouldn't it be more likely to cause you pain?'

Waechter's hand flew up to his eye patch. 'Because of this?' Waechter lifted the patch. Quinn felt his heart hammer. Once again he was going to stare into the potent darkness of an empty eye socket. But even in the chiaroscuro of the semi-darkened room, he could make out that what he expected to see was not there. There was not an absence of an eye, but an eye. The softly spreading beam of the projector revealed Waechter to be the possessor of a full complement of gleaming eyes. 'I do not lose my eye in a duel. I do not even lose my vision.'

'But when I asked you about your eye before, you told me that a splinter from a gunshot robbed you of it?'

Waechter shrugged. 'To me, it vos not any of your business.'

'So why do you wear the patch?'

'*Symbolisch*. I vear this to show how I am damaged.'

'It is a deception.'

'No. It is a confession.'

'So. Who? Who is he? The man who thought you would find this funny.'

'I do not know for sure. For that reason, I would rather not say. To make accusations *mit* no foundations, it is not *gut*.'

'Berenger? I noticed the way you looked at him when we came to arrest you.'

'Begging your pardon, sir,' said Macadam. 'May I start the film running again? I am nervous about holding it on one frame for too long in case it combusts.'

'By all means, Macadam. Run it to the other point we discussed.'

The action moved forward a few frames and juddered to a halt once more. Quinn pointed out the actor playing the director of the lunatic asylum. 'This is the man who escorted her away. Is he the one responsible?'

'Zat is Heinrich. Heinrich Klint. He is not responsible.'

Quinn nodded to Macadam to continue running the film. 'You must have known when you sent this film over that we would see them and recognize them.'

'It had gone on long enough. It started as an innocent prank.'

'Wasting police time! They are all three of them culpable. This woman, Lyudmila . . . Klint. Conspirators in an offence.'

'Vy offence? They perform *ein kleines Theaterstück*. A little play. That is all. They do not know that the police will come along. That you are at the premiere.'

'I was invited.'

'They do not know. I *be-leeff* they wanted to hoax your journal-ists. *Ja*?'

'And what about Dolores Novak? Is that a little play?'

'Berenger is nothing to do *mit* Dolores, *ja*? You understand that? He is a fool but no killer.'

'Nevertheless, we will have to bring him in and talk to him. Where will we find him?'

'You may find him at his hotel. He stays at the Savoy. *Off coursse*.'

'It is a far cry from the room in which Dolores Novak was found.'

'Berenger is *ein Stern*. A star – *ja*? Dolores vos . . .' Waechter spat out a German word that sounded remarkably similar to *whore*.

'I don't know what that means,' said Quinn. 'But it is no reason for her to be killed.'

'Berenger had nothing to do with it. I *svare* on my life that he is innocent.'

Macadam ran the film to the end, to the moment when the inmates and staff of the asylum removed their human masks and revealed the skulls beneath. The moment of Berenger's final surrender to madness and damnation.

'No man is entirely innocent,' said Quinn as the end of the film flapped around the spinning spool and the wall was lit up with a rectangle of blank light. 'Even if he did not kill Dolores Novak, there's a chance he put the idea in the killer's head. He showed the way. Her murder seems to have been modelled on his contemptible hoax, after all.'

Waechter returned the patch to its place over his perfectly sound right eye. His face possessed a stern, defiant dignity. He gave the impression of being a man convinced of the correctness of everything he did. Either he had lived a truly blameless life, or he was utterly devoid of a conscience.

FORTY-FOUR

The grainy twilight thickened overhead as Macadam turned the Model T off the Strand. An incandescent glow pooled out from the front of the great hotel, distracting Quinn momentarily from the purpose of their visit. They were not there to bathe in the glamour and glitz of the establishment. They were there for the darkness. The honk of a car horn brought him rudely back to earth. The car was coming directly at them, apparently on the wrong side of the road. But it was Macadam who swerved to avoid a head-on collision. 'I almost forgot, sir. This is the one street in the country where you drive on the right. God knows why.'

A flicker of darkness as they drove under the arch that spanned the short stub of a road, beneath the statue of an armed knight that surmounted it.

A liveried doorman held the door for them.

Somewhere a piano was playing, the pianist favouring the higher, more refined keys. Beneath a high ceiling dripping with chandeliers, the wealthy guests moved with what seemed like purpose but was actually entitlement. It was clear from the angle at which they held their heads that they had no intention of opening doors. And it was doubtful if they would be able to see the people who opened them on their behalf.

Quinn showed his warrant card at the reception. 'You have a guest here. Berenger is the name. Room number and key, if you please. Your bellboy may accompany me to save time.'

In the event, it was decided that the manager would go.

They rode the elevator to the second floor. It was frustrating to have to wait for the shuttering of the gate, for the lift to respond to the operator's touch, for the freighted shudder into motion and the gathering momentum as the cage ascended. And to wait for it all to unwind in reverse as they reached the floor.

Sensing the urgency of the situation, the manager hurried along the corridor to the door numbered 232. He stood back and allowed Inchball to pound his knuckles against the wood. 'Oi, you in there. Open up. Police.'

The door next to Berenger's opened. Eloise Dumont peered out. When she saw Quinn an expression of disappointment settled over her features.

'Ah, Miss Dumont, good evening. Do you remember me? I am Detective Inspector Quinn.'

'How could I forget? You were rude to me. Not many men are rude to Eloise.'

'I really don't have time for that now. Your . . . colleague – Mr Berenger – do you know if he is in his room?'

'I believe so. We came back from Islington together.'

Quinn nodded to the manager, who used his service key to unlock the door. The bedroom was in semi-darkness, the only light coming in from the street through the open windows, ruffling the lace curtains as it passed through them. There were signs of recent occupancy. A suit of clothes strewn across the floor. Shoes in flight from one another. The bed clothes in disarray.

A door leading off was ajar.

Quinn called out. 'Berenger?'

An echoing intermittent drip answered. But there was no sound of anyone stirring. A wet bathroom smell came through the gap.

He turned to Eloise, who had followed them into the room. 'Please, miss, I think it best if you go back to your own room now.'

'Be gentle with him. Whatever you think he has done. He is not a bad man. I know that. You only have to look into his eyes to know that.'

Quinn nodded acknowledgement of her admonition. That seemed to satisfy her. She slipped from the room, blown out on the same breeze that stirred the curtains. The darkness seemed to contract and harden at her passage.

The men allowed themselves one final look into each other's eyes before they burst into the bathroom.

Berenger was in the bath. He turned his doleful eyes towards them, registering no surprise at their intrusion. In fact, he seemed to welcome them with a small bow of the head. It was almost as if he were expecting them.

'Paul Berenger? We have to ask you some questions concerning your role in an incident that occurred in Cecil Court on the evening of April the seventeenth. Konrad Waechter has made a formal statement naming you as the perpetrator of a deliberate hoax designed to publicize a film in which you appeared. Do you have anything to say about that?'

There was a stir in the water. Berenger stood to his full height in the tub, his profuse black body hair plastered against his pallid white skin: he presented an image that was both imposing and disconsolate.

The water cascaded noisily off the end of his hanging penis. But Berenger was not in the least abashed. He faced them without embarrassment, and without any attempt at concealment. He was the image of a man with nothing to hide.

Quinn concentrated his attention on a crack in the marble fronting of the bath. 'Our main concern is to confirm that no actual attack took place and that the woman involved – one Lyudmila Lyudmova, I believe – is unharmed. We are naturally desirous to talk to her and the other individual implicated. I understand that this may have started as a harmless prank that got out of hand . . .'

Still Berenger did not speak. Quinn looked up to meet his eyes, which were full of regretful appeal. He held his hands out imploringly.

'Ah, yes. I understand. You wish to put on a robe, perhaps, or some clothes. We will wait for you in the bedroom. This need not take long. I imagine that the worst that will happen is a caution. With the appropriate contrition, and a generous contribution to the Police Benevolent Society, even that may prove unnecessary.'

Quinn noticed Inchball's frown, presumably at Quinn's

uncharacteristic promise of leniency. It suddenly occurred to him that he had not established whether Berenger spoke English. 'You do understand what I am saying?'

Berenger nodded.

'Very well. We will be in the bedroom.'

The first inkling Quinn had that something was wrong was when he heard the door to the bathroom locked from the other side. It seemed a redundant act, like closing the proverbial stable door after the horse has bolted. They had already intruded on his nudity, after all. And he had shown himself to be a man untroubled by physical modesty.

Quinn tried the handle, which was indeed now locked. He knocked on the door and pressed his ear against it. He could hear movement inside, a splash of water, as if Berenger had got back into the bath.

He allowed ten minutes or more to pass before turning to the manager. 'Can you open this?'

The manager shrugged. 'I am sure Herr Berenger will come out when he is ready.'

Quinn nodded to Inchball, who threw his shoulder against the door, but to no avail.

'Stand back!' commanded Quinn, drawing his revolver.

'No, no! Please!' cried the manager. 'There is no need for vandalism. I can get a key from downstairs.'

'A key ain't no use,' Inchball pointed out. ''E's already got his key in the other side, ain't he?'

'We are wasting time here!' cried Quinn. But it was the thought of Eloise next door that restrained him from firing. He could well imagine how the sound of gunfire might alarm her.

'With respect, sir,' said Macadam, 'he can't go anywhere. I did not see any window in the bathroom.'

'That's right,' confirmed the manager. 'There is no window.'

'He's mocking us.'

'I suggest we remain patient, sir,' said Macadam. 'He must come out eventually.'

But when ten more slow minutes had passed and Berenger had still not emerged, Quinn found his patience had run out. The gun was already in his hand. It was too bad if he frightened her. He had a job to do.

He discharged three deafening shots around the lock. Predictably enough, a scream came from the room next door.

Quinn paused only to inhale the satisfying odour of the blasted wood.

As he had suspected, Berenger was back in the bath. His head was slumped forward, as if gazing down in perplexity at the suddenly darkened water. A cut-throat razor lay open and bloodied on the side of the bath nearest them.

Macadam rushed forward and lifted one arm out of the water to feel for a pulse. But the darkness gathered at his wrist.

The sergeant's deep-felt groan confirmed the worst. He shook his head. 'Nothing.'

'Look at that, guv,' said Inchball, pointing at the mirror. 'Some kind of suicide note, by the looks of it.'

The words were smeared in the condensation on the glass.

'Do you speak German?' Quinn demanded of the manager.

The man appeared to be in shock. He stood with his mouth open, gaping at the dead man in the bath.

Quinn took out his notebook and hurriedly copied down the incomprehensible message before it disappeared: *Wenn ein Mann seine Kunst verrät, verrät er seine Seele.*

As he turned away from the mirror, he noticed Eloise standing in the doorway. She must have been drawn by the gunshot.

'What have you done?' Her eyes were fixed on Berenger.

'Please, you should not see this.' Quinn tried to usher her out. Her diminutive frame was surprisingly resistant to his pressure. 'We had no idea. We found him like this. We had just spoken to him. We were waiting to ask him some more questions. There was no indication . . .'

'What did you say to him?'

'Let us talk about this outside.'

'He is dead?'

'I am afraid so.'

'You never have anything nice to say to me.'

'I'm sorry. I cannot believe he has done this. There was no need for this.'

'Why did you want to talk to him?'

'Please . . .'

Eloise suddenly caught sight of the words on the mirror. She read them aloud fluently.

'Do you know what it means?' asked Quinn.

'When a man betrays his art, he betrays his soul.'

Quinn put his arm around Eloise's shoulder and gently, finally, turned her away from the spectacle of her dead friend. 'Come. Is there anyone . . .? You should not be alone.'

'You will not stay with me?'

'I?' It seemed an extraordinary, almost incomprehensible suggestion. 'Surely, there is someone better than me?' Quinn turned to the manager. 'Do you have the number for Mr Hartmann of Visionary Productions?'

The manager seemed to pull himself together, at least enough to nod in answer to Quinn's demand.

'Call Hartmann. Tell him that there has been an accident and Mademoiselle Eloise needs him. If I were you I wouldn't go into too much detail over the telephone. I will remain here to break the news to him about Mr Berenger.' Quinn looked at the words on the mirror and thought about their meaning. 'You might tell him to bring Konrad Waechter with him. I believe the two gentlemen will be together.' Quinn had released Waechter into Hartmann's care earlier. Now there were new questions to put to him. 'In the meantime, is there someone – a lady – who can sit with her until her friends arrive?'

The manager swallowed as if he was in danger of vomiting. But he managed to say, 'I will see to it.' With that he rushed out of the bathroom.

Quinn continued to steer Eloise away from the grim scene. And she continued to resist, looking over her shoulder at Berenger. She was plagued by the old question: 'Why? Why would he do this?'

'We may never know.'

'It must have been you . . . what you said to him.'

'I made clear that it was not a serious matter.' Quinn caught Inchball's recriminatory eye again. 'If anything, I made rather too light of the affair. It was to do with what happened in Cecil Court the other night. The business with the woman and . . . well, you remember the dog. Waechter claims that it was all a publicity stunt – and that Berenger was behind it all.'

'Paul?'

'That is what Waechter claims.'

Eloise shook her head slowly.

'Perhaps these words are a confession? By perpetrating the hoax, Berenger considered himself to have betrayed his art?' Quinn's tone was absent. He was voicing his thoughts aloud rather than addressing Eloise.

Her head-shaking denial became more emphatic. 'I do not believe Paul had anything to do with it.'

'Then who?'

'Waechter! Who else? He is the one who betrayed his art! Yes! Do you not see? He denied his responsibility for the act. It is as simple as that. And Paul . . . betrayed! The worst betrayal. Paul would not say anything against his friend. Would not contradict him. And so, this . . . Paul, dear Paul . . . he held Waechter in such esteem, such love . . . he could not recover from this betrayal.'

'But why would Waechter try to blame Berenger?'

'Because he is a coward. Even this trivial thing he does not want to be blamed for – after all the charges he faces in Austria. He does not want any more of the trouble. Not here. And, also, because he knew that Paul never would contradict him. He was relying on Paul's loyalty. He knew . . . he knew what Paul would do.'

'You cannot believe he foresaw this and still accused his friend?'

'You do not know Konrad Waechter.'

Quinn nodded. It was true. He did not know Konrad Waechter. But he felt that he was getting to know him a little better.

FORTY-FIVE

Quinn was pacing the corridor outside Eloise's room when Hartmann and Waechter arrived.

'Gentlemen.'

'What's going on, Inspector?' It was Hartmann who made the demand. He seemed both anxious and bullish.

'I'm afraid I have some very bad news for you. Paul Berenger took his own life earlier this evening.'

Quinn watched Waechter closely. Was the director surprised? It was difficult to say. Certainly a kind of energy seemed to enter his expression, an energy that could have been taken for surprise.

Perhaps Waechter had not known that Berenger would go this far. At the same time, Quinn sensed that Waechter drew strength from what he had just been told. As if the outcome had exceeded his expectations.

Yes, now that he thought about it, that energy in his face could just as easily be interpreted as exultation.

Hartmann at least had the decency to be shocked. He held a splayed hand over his face and muttered something dark and anguished in German. Then he asked Quinn: 'But why?'

'He left a note, of sorts. A message written in the condensation on his mirror. It has gone now. But I wrote it down.' Quinn showed them the words.

Hartmann shook his head in bemusement.

Quinn thought he detected a twitch play across Waechter's lips.

'Herr Waechter? Is something amusing you?' Quinn realized that he wanted to hurt Waechter. He wanted to make him feel responsible for Berenger's death. He wanted him to suffer pangs of guilt over it. As he had over Miss Dillard's.

Waechter's expression became duly solemn. He glared threateningly at Quinn. '*Off coursse* not.'

'How did he do it?' wondered Hartmann.

'He opened a wrist in the bath and bled out. We were waiting to talk to him about the allegation Herr Waechter made against him.'

'Allegation? What is this, Waechter?'

Waechter waved a hand dismissively. It was nothing, he suggested. A trifle.

Quinn needed to keep the pressure up on Waechter. 'Mademoiselle Eloise was able to translate the note for me. *A man who betrays his art betrays his soul.* Is that correct?'

Both men nodded confirmation.

'What do you think he meant by it? Herr Waechter?'

Waechter shrugged, as if he couldn't possibly imagine. 'Berenger *vanted* to be a great artist of the stage. He did not view the kinema as true art. It has to do with that perhaps?' He hardly sounded convinced by his own theory.

Hartmann was suddenly distraught on behalf of his female star – a delayed reaction, but one which hit him hard. 'But Eloise? My dear Eloise was there?'

'I'm afraid so. I couldn't prevent her. Perhaps you should both go and see her now. There is nothing to be gained from viewing the body. The living are more in need of your attention than the dead.'

And now Quinn felt his own lips twitch. He was playing his own game, out-manipulating the arch-manipulator. He knocked on Eloise's door.

Somehow Quinn managed to engineer it that Waechter went in first. It was not so difficult to arrange. The director appeared to be in a hurry to see her. Indeed, his eagerness was practically unseemly. Quinn's intervention, which came to him unprompted, was to push in front of Hartmann and close the door behind him, excluding the producer.

He wanted to see Eloise's reaction to Waechter alone.

She greeted him with a howl. It was a ferocious explosion of inarticulate recrimination.

Quinn's eye was on Waechter. Again he had the sense of an energy entering the man. He seemed to be absorbing the force of Eloise's uninhibited emotion. But instead of being chastened by it, he was himself enlivened. Enlarged. It seemed that this was what he lived for, for moments like this, moments of raw, violent, powerful emotion, viscerally expressed.

He basked in her outburst. He held his head at a provocative angle, inviting her slap. And when it came, he smiled appreciatively.

It occurred to Quinn that if the Austrian really was responsible for the incident in Cecil Court, everything he had done had been designed to lead to a moment such as this. He recognized in Waechter the same motivation as he had observed in certain homicidal maniacs, who commit their crimes in order to create and experience the emotional reverberations.

Perhaps Waechter's original crime was trivial. A theatrical deception. Arguably a victimless crime, unless one counted those who had been hoodwinked: Quinn himself, and the public who had fallen for the illusion through the accounts in the papers. But it had led to the death of one man. And had caused the suffering that streaked and tenderized Eloise's face.

Her pain brought to mind thoughts of Miss Dillard again. The feel of her taut convulsions as he had carried her over his shoulder had entered his muscles. It was more than a memory. It was part of him now.

He decided that there were a number of offences under which he could charge Waechter, including perverting the course of justice, conspiracy to effect a public nuisance and effecting a public nuisance. He could probably think of more. Someone had broken into a morgue and stolen a body part. He mustn't forget that.

He wondered if his own remorse – tears held back in an unacknow-ledged throb in his throat, a stinging hypersensitivity in his eyes – was influencing his decision to make Waechter pay for what he had done.

In the meantime, Hartmann was hammering at the door for admittance. The banging, together with Eloise's continued railing, was making it hard for Quinn to concentrate.

FORTY-SIX

With the Courts of Justice at one end and the dome of St Paul's overshadowing the other, Fleet Street seemed to exist as a thoroughfare between two opposing systems of morality. However, critics of the industry that dominated the street might argue that it served rather as a moral bypass, a place where the moral compass simply failed to function. It was perhaps appropriate that the presses were most often rolling at night, when both the church and the judiciary tactfully withdrew from sight.

The offices of the *Daily Clarion* occupied three floors of a grand five-storey building closer to the legal end of the street. An adver-tising agency and a magazine publishing company, both also owned by Harry Lennox, had the other floors.

The mighty printing presses themselves were on the ground floor, throwing their iron weight behind the flimsy ephemeral stories that their human collaborators spun upstairs. They were, in fact, visible from the street, as Lennox had had the idea to open up the front of the building and fit vast sheets of plate glass, which extended the full height of the first storey. He also kept the printing presses floodlit through the night. It was a stroke of marketing genius on his part, symbolizing the *Clarion*'s role as a Beacon of Truth that could never be extinguished. Lennox was inordinately proud of those plate-glass windows and insisted on their being cleaned twice a day. Every time he entered the building, he checked the glass to ensure that they matched the standards of cleanliness that he required. Not a speck or smear could be allowed to get in the way of this vision of industry and integrity.

The composing room and some commercial offices took the first floor, while the editorial offices were on the second. Content was sent down through the boards in vacuum-driven tubes by the sub-editors to be turned into copy by the compositors on the copy-desk. The constant clack and tap of the linotype machines sounded like the beaks of countless mechanical birds pecking the ground for grains of news.

The edition of Monday, 20 April 1914, had already gone to press when Bittlestone restored the telephone receiver to its stand. His hand was shaking, so it took him several attempts to jab it into the holder. As he leapt up from his desk, he was already shouting, 'Stop press!'

Finch was in his office with his feet on his desk, about to light his customary cigar to celebrate putting another edition successfully to bed. He viewed Bittlestone's intervention with sour suspicion, as if he believed the journalist was motivated merely by a desire to prevent him enjoying his smoke. 'What did you do to your eye?'

Bittlestone's hand went self-consciously up to his face. He had forgotten that he had taken off the dark spectacles, as they had made it difficult for him to work. The editorial offices were not as well illuminated at the printing presses on the ground floor.

'Nothing . . . I . . . Look, didn't you hear me? We have to stop the presses.'

'This had better be good, Bittlestone. No – it had better be better than good. It had better be *sensational.*'

'I've just had a call from a source of mine. A bell hop at the Savoy. Paul Berenger, the motion picture actor, has been found dead. It appears to be suicide. He climbed in the hot bath tub and opened his wrists. The place is in uproar.'

The editor was on his feet now. 'What are you waiting for? Get over there!'

Bittlestone took the stairs two at a time, rushing towards the thundering rumble of the presses. Finch's remark about his eye prompted him to feel for his dark glasses in his jacket pocket. He must have left them on his desk. No matter. The story was more important than his vanity, although there was perhaps a practical consideration. He knew from experience that the less obtrusive he made himself the more likely he was to get the story. His wound would only draw attention. He hesitated at the bottom of the stairs and was on the verge of going back for the glasses when the sight of the brilliantly illuminated, constantly turning rollers spurred him to go on.

The explosion happened as he walked across the foyer in front of the presses. There was no warning. No premonitory change in the air pressure. No sound of running footsteps. There was just a blinding flash, a boom so loud that it seemed to hollow out his ear drums, and a deep shooting pain burrowing into his eyes. He felt himself lifted by the blast. As if the sound of the explosion had formed a giant hand capable of taking hold of a man and throwing him off his feet. A rain of fine shards fell around him and into him. The strange thing was the unaccountable thing: there was no smoke.

The weight of the world came up to hit him on the back of the head as he landed. Then everything went black.

FORTY-SEVEN

Macadam kept the motor ticking over as he waited for a gap in the traffic. But the Strand was for the moment packed with vehicles, their headlights piercing the darkness with questing impatience, their horn blasts like the bleats of tethered animals.

Quinn felt the throb of the Model T's engine in every joint of his bones. He was thinking of his father. He peered out into the night, expecting at any moment to see Grant-Sissons. Lurking beneath a street light perhaps, or sinking back into a shop doorway. It was truer to say he was willing the man to appear.

Two suicides in three days. It was as if the universe was forcing him to confront his past. And Grant-Sissons was the nearest he had come in years to finding answers to the questions of the past.

'You let him go, guv?'

Quinn turned to face Inchball's question. 'For now, yes.'

'So he's to get off scot-free for making a bleedin' monkey of us all?'

'I would hardly describe the reception he received from Mademoiselle Eloise as scot-free.' But Quinn knew this was disingenuous. Eloise's rage was meat and drink to Waechter. He had lapped it up. 'At any rate, I need to confer with Sir Edward. He might wish for the whole Cecil Court affair to be swept under the carpet. We did not exactly cover ourselves in glory over that. Pressing a prosecution would only bring a dubious episode back into the public eye. In addition, it would serve to increase Waechter's notoriety.'

Inchball glumly pointed out a more serious obstacle. 'We can't touch him for it. Don't have no evidence, do we? Unless he confesses. Or we find that one-eyed bitch an' she tells us who put her up to it.'

There was a disapproving sound from Macadam in the front.

'Well, it's true, ain't it?'

'More serious is the question of the connection between Waechter's irresponsible prank and the murder of Dolores Novak.'

Macadam seemed to have given up trying to pull out into the Strand. 'Do you think Waechter could have killed the Novak woman, sir?' he asked.

'The murder of the victim and the removal of eyes suggests an escalation from the first attack. But if the first attack is not an attack at all – as it appears not to be – but simply a stupid stunt, well, then . . . what are we to make of that? It is not an escalation. It may actually be unconnected, except thematically. And the theme of vision – the fixation with eyes – that could have been taken independently from Waechter's film by a particularly disturbed spectator.'

'It could be anyone!' cried Inchball in dismay.

'Not anyone. Someone linked to the film. Possibly someone who was present at the party. That is the line I would encourage us to pursue.'

His sergeants nodded in unison.

And then they heard it. A distinct boom, followed by the tinkling of glass, a sound more refined than the piano in the Savoy.

'Good God!'

'Wha' the bleedin' 'ell?'

'It came from that direction,' said Macadam, pointing east. 'What shall I do, sir? Back to the Yard, or . . .'

'We should go and investigate. By the sounds of it, it was very close.'

'Fleet Street, I reckon,' said Inchball. 'We could leave it for the City of London Force. Technically speaking, it's none of our bleedin' business.'

'This is beyond police jurisdictions, Inchball. It could be the beginning of some kind of attack on our national interests. On our freedoms. An attempt to cow us before open hostilities are declared.'

Inchball nodded. A note of admiration seemed to have entered his voice. 'How very Bismarckian.'

The traffic on the Strand began to move. Macadam eased his way into it.

*   *   *

The sign above the devastated window read: H AIL C ARION.

Quinn struggled to make sense of the letters, until he at last made out the fire-blackened T, E, D, Y and L. And now he struggled to make sense of the coincidence.

The target of the bomb blast was the *Daily Clarion*. Quinn remembered the last time he had seen Harry Lennox: at the offices of Visionary Productions in Cecil Court, moments after the hoax attack, and shortly before the murder of Dolores Novak. What was the connection? *Was* there a connection? It didn't seem possible.

Lennox was now walking towards him, his shoes crunching on the fragments of glass that littered his foyer like brittle confetti. An expression of bewilderment and betrayal was directed at Quinn, almost as if Lennox blamed him for what had happened. But no – it was simple incomprehension.

Quinn could imagine well enough what he was thinking. *How could this have happened? To him, to Harry Lennox? Fortune's favourite.*

For Quinn, the more interesting question was *why.*

It was strange, he had to admit, how the confusion and destruction focused his mind. The air was filled with shouts. Men ran in every direction, with the purposeless energy of panic. But Quinn felt himself to be calm. The disarray of others clarified his thoughts.

Quinn recognized this as one of those moments that do not come often in a man's life, unless he happens to be a policeman. A moment when a man is tested and his true mettle revealed, by whether and how well he keeps his head. If Quinn had a talent, he believed it was to think clearly in these situations. To carry on thinking, even when he did not know he was doing it.

Lennox came up to the empty space where his window had been and held a hand out to it tentatively, as if he still expected it to be there.

The newspaperman's mouth dropped open. A faint, pathetic croak escaped, as if the explosion had blown away his faculty of speech.

Quinn looked past Lennox to a man lying on the floor, his face completely red and glistening. It was as if, instead of blacking up like a Negro minstrel, he had daubed bright-red stage make-up all over his face. The man was moaning quietly. Quinn could not help noting that Lennox had walked past the injured man to gawp at his missing window.

Quinn rushed in to kneel down beside the man on the floor. He saw now that it was the reporter, Bittlestone.

'You're going to be all right,' he told him. He could hear the sirens of the London Fire Brigade approaching. He trusted that an ambulance would come too.

'I can't see,' said Bittlestone. 'My eyes . . . There's something in my eyes . . . It's so . . . it's so bloody painful.'

Quinn could see that Bittlestone's eyes were as red as the rest of his face, which was covered in countless cuts, a palimpsest of crimson cross-hatching beneath the wash of blood.

'You're going to be fine.'

'There was no smoke!' cried Bittlestone, as if this was the most outrageous aspect of the attack.

Quinn looked up at Macadam, who had followed him into the ruined foyer. Inchball ran ahead, into the room beyond.

'A flash. And then *boom*! And then the glass blew out in the blast. Have I got glass in my eyes?' Bittlestone began to shake violently. He was in deep shock.

'There'll be an ambulance here soon. We'll have you sorted out in no time, Mr Bittlestone.'

'Who's that? I can't see you. Who is it?'

'It's DI Quinn. You remember me, don't you, sir?'

'Inspector Quinn? What are you doing here?'

'I was just passing, sir. Lucky for you, I was.'

They were joined by Lennox. 'You, Quinn, is it? This is an outrage, Quinn.'

Quinn rose to his feet and nodded to Macadam to stay with Bittlestone. He led Lennox off to one side. 'Yes, sir.'

'Who has done this?'

'We don't know yet, sir. We've only just got here. Can you think of any reason why your paper should have been targeted like this? Could it be because of a stance you have taken? On the Irish question, for example?'

'You think the Tories have done this? Would they stoop so low?'

'There has been talk of civil war, sir. What has your position on Germany been?'

'We have been for the dreadnought programme. We have urged war preparation. At the same time as encouraging dialogue.'

'You have wanted it both ways, sir.'

'But neither way merits this, surely?'

'Sir, what is your relationship to Oskar Hartmann?'

'Hartmann? Why do you ask about Hartmann?'

'You were at the premiere the other night. You seemed to be on good terms with Waechter and the other film people.'

'What has that got to do with this?'

'That's what I'm trying to discover, sir.'

'I don't understand. Hartmann . . . Hartmann is not a militarist. Neither is Waechter. They are only interested in making films. That's why they have chosen to live over here.'

'I understand that Mr Waechter cannot return to his native Austria because he is wanted by the authorities in connection with a serious offence. A man died, I believe.'

'You're clutching at straws, Quinn. It's because they're foreigners, isn't it? I know all about that. You bloody English. A bunch of damn xenophobes, that's what you are. I wouldn't be surprised if it turned out an Englishman was behind this.'

The Englishman who naturally came to Quinn's mind was the strangely ubiquitous Mr Grant-Sissons. But his grudge was against the film industry, not the newspaper industry. 'Do you have any business connections with Hartmann? Have you invested in Visionary Productions?'

'Yes . . . Why do you ask?'

Grant-Sissons was an inventor. Presumably he also knew how to construct a home-made explosive device.

'One last question, Mr Lennox. Have you received any packages recently upon which the address was written in green ink?'

Lennox stared at him as if he were a table illusionist who had just pulled off a particularly startling trick. 'Yes. Yes, I did. How on earth did you know?'

'And what did the package contain, may I ask?'

'A playing card.'

'A playing card? A single playing card?'

'Yes.'

Dunwich had been sent a billiard ball. What was the message behind these missives? That the sender was playing some kind of game? 'And was there anything unusual about this card?'

'It was the Jack of Hearts, I seem to remember. And, well, here's a thing . . . The eye . . .'

'The eye?'

'The eye had been poked out.'

'I see,' said Quinn.

'Well, I don't!' answered Lennox. 'I very much don't see.'

The angry clang of a fire engine alarm cut off any further discussion. Quinn turned as the open-topped vehicle screeched to a halt at an angle in the street, blocking half the road. The brass-helmeted firemen leapt down. Each man there had a purpose, which he set to with well-practised determination. One assessed the state of the building while others unwound the hose and others again extended and positioned the large ladder that was carried on the back of the truck.

Two men, wearing helmets with protective masks which covered their whole faces, marched into the wrecked building with their axes at the ready.

The energy seemed to go out of the whole crew when it became clear that there was no fire to put out. A second engine arrived. The disappointing news was passed on to the firemen who jumped down from that. The faces of all the firemen made it clear they felt cheated.

Quinn walked outside and showed his warrant card to the fireman whom he had seen making the initial assessment of the building. 'DI Quinn of Special Crimes.'

'Blimey, you fellers were quick on the scene.'

'We happened to be on the Strand when we heard the explosion.'

'Did you see anything?'

'No. But I spoke to one of the witnesses. That man on the floor there. A reporter by the name of Bittlestone. It appears that he has been blinded.'

'Poor fellow. He seems to have borne the brunt of it. Did he say anything to you about what he saw before the lights went out?'

'He remarked particularly on their being no smoke.'

'No smoke, you say?'

'That's what he said. Is it possible?'

'Oh, yes, if the explosive material used was guncotton.'

'I see.'

'It's very popular in mines, because of the lack of smoke, you see. If you're working in a confined space you don't want it filling with smoke.'

'Is there anything else you can tell me about the cause?'

'Judging by the damage, it was a relatively small device, designed to make a point rather than wreak widespread destruction. Enough to blow the glass in and scorch the frontage, but no structural damage that I can see. It doesn't look like the work of the Fenians. If they'd been behind it, there wouldn't be anything left of the building.'

'That's not likely.' Quinn pointed Lennox out. 'The owner is himself Irish. And a nationalist.'

The fireman nodded as if this was consistent with his own theories. 'The direction of the shatter – given that all the glass was blown inside the building – suggests the bomb was placed here in the street, in front of the window. We'll look for residue, of course. The guncotton must have been placed in something. Possibly a length of pipe or a tin box of some kind. Don't worry, guv. Whatever it was, we'll find it.'

'And you are . . .? In case I wish to speak to you again?'

'Captain Alexander Hotty, of the Cannon Street Fire Station.'

'Hotty?'

'Yes, that's right. Hotty. Two Ts and a Y.'

'I will remember that, I think.'

Captain Hotty frowned, as if he could not for the life of him understand why his name was worthy of comment.

There was an awkward moment. Quinn wondered about trying to explain the joke to him. Thankfully, one of the firemen who had gone into the building broke the tension by approaching his superior. His protective mask was pulled up to reveal his face. He was carrying a circular tin container of shallow depth and about a foot in diameter. He turned it over in his hand, revealing the outside to be battered and dusty, and the inside completely blackened.

'What do you have there, Stoker?'

'Looks like this here's your bomb,' said Stoker. 'Or one half of it. He must have packed it with explosive, rigged up some kind of fuse and left it outside the window. This half got blown inside. Reckon we'll find the other half in the street somewhere.'

Quinn held out his hand to take the flimsy tin. He held it to his face and inhaled the charred interior.

'It's one of them film cans, ain't it?' said Stoker. 'I once got called to a fire in a picture palace when I was stationed in Islington. Saw a lot of them about the place, we did.'

Whether it was the smell from the film can or the information he had just been told, Quinn felt his heart kick viciously as if his system had just been infiltrated by an intoxicating stimulant.

FORTY-EIGHT

Macadam drove them north to Clerkenwell. Quinn still had the card that Grant-Sissons had given him. He remembered the man's bandaged hand and the wince he had been unable to conceal.

'An old wound, that's what he had said.'

'What's that, guv?'

'Grant-Sissons.'

'This feller you fancy for the bomb outrage?'

'His hand was bandaged when I saw him at the hospital. He said it was an old wound. But what if it was fresh? What if he had sustained it while attacking Dolores Novak? It's perfectly possible that she would have tried to defend herself.'

'So you fancy him for that too?'

'Let us moot the hypothesis that he is waging some kind of vendetta against the film industry. He is a failed inventor who nurses a great grudge. He claims he invented the motion picture camera and believes that he has been robbed of his share of the profits of every film made.'

'But why attack that newspaper?'

'Harry Lennox, the proprietor of the *Clarion*, is an investor in Hartmann's production company.'

'There's more to it than that, sir,' put in Macadam from the front. 'You know that I am a subscriber to the *Kinematograph Enthusiast's Weekly*. The editorial address of that publication is the same as the *Daily Clarion*. It is printed on the same presses and is owned by Lennox too.'

'So he is not just an investor in the film industry; he is an active promoter of it,' concluded Quinn.

The Model T's headlamps picked out a crenellated arch suspended over the road: the grey nocturnal ghost of St John's Gate. The car slowed as it passed under, a shadow slipping through a shadow.

Macadam pulled up in St John's Square. All three policemen got out of the car.

'I think it's better if I speak to him alone,' said Quinn. 'He knows me.' Quinn was thinking of his own unfinished business with Grant-Sissons. He had no desire for his sergeants to hear whatever Grant-Sissons had to say about his father. Quinn felt his left breast, touching the hard metal where his pistol was holstered. 'You need not fear for my safety. I am armed.'

He sensed Macadam and Inchball exchange an uneasy look.

'With respect, sir . . .' Macadam did not press his point.

Inchball was less tactful: 'It ain't *your* safety we're worried about.'

'I understand perfectly. And it is precisely for that reason that I should go in alone. If he sees the three of us, he may well panic and therefore do something stupid, in the face of which I may be forced to take self-defensive action. Besides, we have no concrete evidence to place him at either scene. At the moment, we are acting on nothing other than conjecture.'

'Is there something you're not telling us, guv?'

'He knew my father. I hope to use that to our advantage. It will be easier to do so if I am alone. I want you two to position yourselves at either end of St John's Passage, in case he tries to make a run for it.'

'What if he's not there, guv?'

'Then I shall wait for him. If he returns, don't try to apprehend him. Leave him to me.'

Quinn turned abruptly from his sergeants, and from further discussion.

He entered a tight passageway with high brick walls on either side, a channel of night cut into the city. The stench of urine marked it as a stopping place for drunks. Quinn stood for a moment, allowing his eyes to adapt to the gloom. A spill of light from the square seeped along the walls, and there was a light in a window at the end of the passage. It was enough for Quinn to make out two doors set side by side into the wall. The second door was the one he was looking for.

He balled his fist and pounded the door. Somewhere, a dog barked in response.

A dark figure approached from the square. From the body shape, he guessed it was Inchball. The two men did not exchange a word as they squeezed past one another. Inchball's footsteps receded as he took up position at the far end of the passage.

For a moment, Quinn felt as though this bleak forgotten place was all that was left in the universe. He did not believe in the square beyond Macadam, or the workshop behind the door, or whatever now lay at Inchball's back. He felt as if all that was good and all that was evil in the world, all the hope and all the fear, was being channelled through that narrow alleyway with a policeman at either end and one in the middle. He knew from experience that things could go either way now. He might get what he wanted from Grant-Sissons, a confession, resolution of the crimes he was investigating, and perhaps of even more. The truth about his father. Another outcome was conceivable: that the night would end in death, either his own or Grant-Sissons's. Possibly both.

But it was too late to back out. That had never been an option.

He was about to resume his pounding, when a crack of light appeared at one side of the door. The crack widened to reveal the face of a man peering out. It was not the face of Grant-Sissons but there was something familiar about it, a resemblance to someone whom Quinn could not for the moment place. It was the face of a young man who must have been about the age Quinn was when his father died. Perhaps it was a strange way to frame the matter, but after all he had come to see a man who had promised to tell him about his father's death. And so, it was not so eccentric that his mind should run in this direction. He even wondered if the resemblance he detected was to himself as a younger man.

The other man said nothing, but stared at Quinn with a distracted hostility.

'I am looking for Grant-Sissons. I am Detective Inspector Quinn of the Special Crimes Department.'

'I am Grant-Sissons.'

'I was looking for an older man.'

'You want my father.'

'Is he here?'

'Yes. But he's resting.'

'It's very important.'

'Who did you say it was?'

'Quinn. Inspector Quinn. He will be expecting me, I'm sure.'

The door was shut in Quinn's face.

An enquiry came from Macadam's end of the passage. 'Is everything all right, sir?'

'He's here,' said Quinn.

The door began to open once more.

The workshop was lit by an oil lamp that hung from a hook in the ceiling. It cast a feeble yellow wash over what appeared to be a cave hollowed out inside a mountain of scrap metal and general refuse. Grant-Sissons lay on a camp bed, a coarse, grubby blanket pulled up to his chin, his hands hidden from view beneath it. His bed was like a raft floating on a sea filled with the least buoyant flotsam and jetsam imaginable: rusting cogs, the skeletons of obscure machines, industrial coils of copper wire and other electronic components, a detritus of useless parts and tools. The inventor's face had a sickly tinge to it that Quinn had not noticed before. He felt instinctively that he was in the presence of a dying man. Perhaps now at last that unusually persistent bitterness made sense.

With every step, Quinn's foot either came up against a new obstacle or came down on something that crunched or scraped or buckled under his weight.

'So.' Grant-Sissons's voice was weak and worn-out. 'You have come to find out the truth about your father.'

'I am more concerned, at this present moment, with a current investigation.'

'If this is about that girl, I've told you, Waechter is behind it . . .'

'It is likely that that attack was a hoax. However, another woman has been attacked and killed, and unless you know of a way to bring corpses back to life, I fear that this will not prove to be a hoax.'

'Why do you want to talk to me about this? I know nothing about it.'

'The victim was a film actress of sorts. She had been employed by Visionary Productions. You were seen in Leicester Square outside the theatre which was presenting a film in which she appeared. You were seen to behave in a manner that may be described as erratic and aggressive, as well as suspicious. The next time I saw you, you were outside the Middlesex Hospital where you had gone to make enquiries about the girl who had apparently been attacked. The incident had obviously made some impression on you. Perhaps it had inspired you to carry out your own attack, only you went further.'

'I told you, I was at the hospital on my own account. As you can see, I am not a well man.'

'Today a bomb was placed outside the office of the *Daily Clarion*. We are currently pursuing the theory that both the murder of the actress, Dolores Novak, and the bomb outrage were motivated by a desire to damage the interests of the film industry. The proprietor of the *Clarion* is an investor in Visionary Productions. He also publishes a weekly organ promoting film production and exhibition. The home-made bomb was placed inside a film canister. This seems consistent with our theory, as an embittered perpetrator with a grudge against film people might consider it ironic to use one of the tools of their trade against them. Do you not think?'

'It's an interesting theory.'

'It would require someone with a certain degree of technical and scientific proficiency to construct, prime and detonate an explosive device, do you not agree?'

'And you think that I am this person? But that is a conclusion of startling ineptitude and stupidity, Inspector. It is a travesty of logical deduction. Do you think I am the only man capable of constructing such a device?'

'Ah, but you are the only one who also has a viable motive, so far as I am aware.'

'And there the whole absurdity of your position is revealed, in that "so far as I am aware". Surely even you must be able to grasp the possibility that your perpetrator may simply be someone who is not yet known to you? Inspector Quinn, after I saw you outside the hospital, I came here and took to my bed. I have not stirred from it since, except to discharge the necessary functions of my body. My son has been here with me the whole time, tending to my needs.'

'Your son could well have placed the device on your behalf.'

'But he has been here the whole time, I tell you. By all means, ask him.'

'It's true, my father hasn't moved from his bed the whole time. And I haven't set foot outside this . . . place.'

From a legal standpoint, a father and son each providing the alibi for the other rather left something to be desired. However, there was something about the bitter, resentful despair in the son's voice that inclined Quinn to believe he was telling the truth. 'Someone else may have put it there for you.'

'I'm dying, Inspector Quinn. I have no wish to hurt anyone. My only remaining desire is for my part in the development of the motion picture camera to be acknowledged, and for my son to receive the financial rewards that should have been mine. The only weapons I have ever used in my fight are peaceful ones. I have stood up and spoken out. I have picketed. I have written letters. I have canvassed support. But always, I have been ignored. I am resigned now. I have no energy left to continue the fight. And I am not sure that Malcolm has the will to carry it on after my death. It will all have been for nothing.'

'What's wrong with you?'

'I have cancer.'

Quinn remembered the bandage he had seen on Grant-Sissons's hand. 'In your hand?'

'It started there, but it has spread. I was fortunate. I had some weeks of remission. I tried to use that time to make one last protest. And to see you, of course. But the disease is racing through me now. I have seen the end. The horrible end. There is no way to stop it. Do you really think a man in my position would run around planting bombs?'

'Why did you want to see me?'

'I have already told you, I knew your father.'

'How well did you know him?'

'We worked together as business associates. He came to me with an idea for an invention. He hoped to combine the techniques of photography with the properties of X-rays, thereby developing a machine that could capture images of the internal arrangements of the human body, which he believed could be used to facilitate diagnostic practice in medicine.'

'What happened?'

'We were forced to abandon our work.'

'Why?'

'My research assistant became ill. She – my assistant was a young woman – Louisa . . . Louisa Grant-Sissons. She was my wife. Louisa volunteered to be the subject. She was captivated by the magic of it. By the idea of having the inside of her hand made manifest. Of seeing the delicate interconnections of countless little bones. We took many hundreds – thousands even – of photographs of her right hand, exposing her to radiation over and over again. We now know the harmful effects of such rays, but at the time, no one . . . no one anywhere knew. We were not the only ignorant fools. Of course, I should never have permitted it. I should have insisted that I was used as the subject. But she was so charmed by the wonder of what we were doing, she begged us to conduct our experiments on her. And we were swayed, both I and your father, for we were both in love with her, you see, and neither of us had it in us to deny her what she wanted. She developed the cancer in the bones and tissues of her right hand, precisely as I have. Only in her case it took hold immediately. Whereas it has lain in wait for me, biding its time over the decades, waiting to find me at my weakest and most disappointed.' Grant-Sissons fell silent.

'She died? Your wife died, I presume?'

'Louisa had such pretty, delicate hands. The doctors tried to prevent the spread by amputation. First the hand was removed, but the cancer revealed itself in the radius bone. So then her forearm was amputated, all the way up to the elbow. But it was not a success. The cancer was found to have entered the humerus already. They next amputated at the shoulder, though by now without much hope. And so when I say that I have seen the end, I mean it literally. I have seen what fate awaits me. I have declined the proffered amputations.'

'Why has it affected you, if your experiments were conducted on your wife?'

'Your father and I both blamed ourselves for Louisa's death. His response, we know. There. You have the explanation of his suicide. Your mother thought that he had squandered the family fortune on gambling and God knows what other depravities, but in truth, he had used it to fund our experiments. And to kill Louisa. It was then that I realized how deeply he had been in love with her. I looked back at their dealings with each other, and it became clear to me that they had conducted an affair right under my nose. But I forgave him, because he had loved her. And I forgave her, because – well, had she not suffered enough? Had she not been punished far more severely than her crime warranted? And what crime had she committed, really? She had followed her heart, that was all. I never truly believed that I deserved her, you know. I always thought that our time together was temporary, fortuitous, provisional – and therefore all the more precious. That does not mean that I was ready to give her up. But even though she was unfaithful to me, I remain grateful to her for our time together. I have never loved anyone else. I still love her.'

Grant-Sissons's hands stirred under the blanket. The bandaged right hand emerged. 'And this . . . I inflicted this on her.' With his other hand, he worked away at the bandage and began to unwind.

'Father, no.'

But Grant-Sissons was deaf to his son's entreaties. 'To punish myself, for not loving her enough, for allowing her to take part in our work, I exposed my own hand to the same levels of radiation that she had received. It should have been me in the first place, after all.'

He continued to peel away the bandage, which was now discoloured with the seepages from his wounds. And now the bandage fell away together. A horrible discoloured dressing was revealed, clinging to his flesh. Grant-Sissons winced and teased the dressing away, discarding it on the floor.

He held up his hand as if it was a trophy, or a prize vegetable in the county fair. In the glimmering of the oil lamp, Quinn could see a glistening, misshapen mess of raw flesh. The skin was entirely missing. A number of angry, ugly tumours erupted from the surface, moist, suppurating yellowish clumps of mutated cells.

'Look at it! Look at it, Inspector! Do you really believe that I could do what you accuse me of with this hand?'

The hand in question dropped. Grant-Sissons fell back on to his camp bed and closed his eyes. But he was still conscious, and he had more to say to Quinn. 'If I were not determined to suffer everything that she suffered, I would ask you one remaining favour, Inspector.'

'What?'

'I would ask you to kill me. I know you have a reputation for being somewhat trigger-happy. I might have used your suspicions against me to provoke you to shoot me. But I have decided against that. It is a recourse that is not available to me. It would be an evasion on my part. A terrible act of cowardice and weakness. I must see this through to the end.'

'I would do it, if you wish.'

'I know you would. But I do not wish it. I do not deserve it. I do not deserve release. It would only serve to complicate your investigation, I fear. And I could not lay another death on your conscience. So I will ask you a different favour.'

'Yes?'

'After I am gone, will you look out for Malcolm? Keep an eye on him, for me. A brotherly eye, I might almost say.'

'What do you mean? What is he to me?'

But Grant-Sissons's face was twisted into a sharp grimace. He was lost in his pain. And nothing other than his pain reached him or had any meaning for him.

Quinn turned to regard the young man whose care Grant-Sissons had apparently entrusted to him. They both seemed aware of the complications of the relationship that existed between them. At the very least, if what Grant-Sissons had said was true, Quinn's father had been in love with the younger man's mother. But with that 'brotherly', Grant-Sissons seemed to be hinting at even more.

'If you have any compassion in you, you would kill him now, while he sleeps.'

'He asked me not to do it.'

'But what about me? He wasn't thinking of me. Of what I will have to go through, seeing him suffer the torments of a horrible death.'

'I cannot do it.'

'That's cruel, you know.'

'I'm sorry.'

'Do you believe what he said?'

'I'm not sure what he said.'

'That we are brothers. Half-brothers. I think his meaning was clear enough.'

'Has he said anything of this to you before?'

'He has hinted at it. In all honesty, he wasn't much of a father. But that was not because he didn't acknowledge me as his own. I even believed he loved me, in his own way. There was rather too much of duty in it. And he was always a little distracted, shall we say. But I believe he fought his battles on my behalf, to leave something for me. It all came to nothing, alas.'

'I had never thought of myself as having a brother.'

'That need not change. I don't require looking after. I'm not a child.'

'What will you do?'

'What do you mean?'

'When he's dead.'

'Carry on his work, of course. I have been working with him on a method of producing three-dimensional motion pictures. We have a patent pending.'

Quinn closed his eyes briefly, blocking out the chaos of the workshop. He imagined himself holding his gun to Grant-Sissons's temple and pulling the trigger. 'I wish you luck,' he said.

FORTY-NINE

Oskar Hartmann held the monocle up to his eye and squinted through it. He closed his other eye to hold it in place. The room flickered and darkened. The glass lens was coated with a layer of translucent grey tinting, as if it had been held in the smoke of a charcoal fire.

He took the monocle away from his eye and examined it. It was now that he noticed the hairline crack running through it.

Why would anyone send him such an object? A cracked monocle. It was possible that it had been damaged in transit. He examined the padded envelope it had been sent in. His name was written clearly in green ink. There was no note, or invoice enclosed. The sender's address was not given on the outside.

He looked through it again. The glass disk had no refractive effect on what was observed through it; that is to say, it was not a functioning lens, just plain glass, apart from the colour. So the purpose of it was presumably to protect a single sensitive eye from the effects of bright sunlight? Hartmann himself suffered from no such condition, and could say with certainty that he had not ordered the object on his own account.

And yet there was something satisfying about squinting at the world through it. The layer of colour softened the harshness of existence somewhat, provided a barrier between the observer and the observed. Today, of all days, he felt the need for such a boundary.

He wondered if it were something Waechter had ordered. Perhaps he was thinking of exchanging his eye patch for a shaded monocle? Was that a lesser or a greater affectation? Hartmann could not decide.

Hartmann did not object to Waechter using the Visionary Productions' office as a postal address, but the use of his name, without having first asked, caused him some mild annoyance. Did this now mean that Hartmann could expect a bill for the article in the next post?

Of course, he would overlook it, as he did all of Waechter's misdemeanours. One had to indulge a genius. The expense would not be great, and it was possible the object was intended as a prop in some future film. In which case, it was perfectly valid to order it through the company. But he would ask him about it when he next saw him. He had a duty to do that at least.

At any rate, with the flaw running across it, it was useless, whatever purpose Waechter had in mind for it. It would have to be returned.

But of course, Waechter had other things on his mind at the moment.

He had left his director at the Savoy last night. The scene with Eloise had been upsetting for them all. His priority, once that fool of a policeman had let him into the room, was to get the two of them apart. He had escorted Waechter to the bar, although it pained him to leave Eloise on her own. Fortunately, he had run into Diaz and his nephew, who had come to the Savoy in expectation of meeting Berenger. The actor had always demonstrated a commendable sympathy for the world's downtrodden. He no doubt discerned some quality of oppression in the Chileans' eyes and been drawn to them. In Hartmann's view, it made him something of a soft touch. Perhaps it had even contributed to his unfortunate demise.

At any rate, Diaz and his nephew's appearance was fortuitous. He could send them upstairs to be with Eloise until he had calmed Waechter down.

Of course, it was a terrible blow for them all, Berenger's death. They were a family. Hartmann had worked hard to foster that feeling, to keep them together. But Waechter might be expected to bear it more heavily than anyone. He and Berenger went back a long way. The actor had starred in all of Waechter's films, and had even worked with him as a mime in the theatre in Vienna. It was impossible to think of a Waechter film without Berenger in it.

And yet, he had to admit it, there had been something that unsettled him about Waechter's reaction. The gleam in Waechter's eye was not the dewy film of grief. But a self-absorbed, chilling excitement.

Hartmann held the monocle up to his eye once more. The world was dark enough without viewing it through a tinted lens, he decided.

FIFTY

Light filled the room. Quinn stood with his back to the window, as if he didn't have the courage to face it. But in truth it took more courage to confront the wall in front of him.

At the top left-hand corner he had pinned two enlargements of frames taken from Waechter's *Totentanz*, showing respectively Lyudmila Lyudmova and Heinrich Klint. Next to them was a police photograph of the partially chewed eye he had retrieved from Cecil Court.

A pathologist's report concerning the eye had just come in. In short, the medical opinion was that the eye had ceased to be a part of a living organism several days at least before Friday, 17 April. The pathologist even ventured to suggest the possibility that the eye had been removed from a cadaver. This was consistent with Waechter's version of events, namely that the incident was a hoax. Who was responsible for that hoax had yet to be decided. A photograph of Berenger slumped in a tub of dark liquid raised the possibility of his culpability. Quinn had to admit, Waechter was a far more likely culprit. Quinn's instinct was to bring him in and hold him. But Sir Edward had not yet reached a decision on what they should do with Herr Waechter.

And then there was the question of the eye itself. It seemed likely that it was the eye stolen from the body of Edna Corbett. Was it a coincidence that she was a victim in a case Quinn himself had investigated? Or had everything been designed from the outset to draw Quinn in? But into what?

If this was the case, was Waechter really behind it? Or was he merely the instrument of other, more sinister agents?

Quinn's eye was naturally drawn to a photograph which occupied the centre of the wall: of Dolores Novak's body on the bed in the rented room.

'Penny for 'em, guv?'

Quinn's brow rippled with annoyance at Inchball's invitation. To be asked to share one's thoughts was inevitably a disruption to thinking. However, it was often by talking through a case with his sergeants that he was able to make progress. 'When do we get the full medical examiner's report on Dolores Novak?'

'Should be this week sometime, I reckon.'

'I want it today.'

'I have a pal at the morgue, sir.' Macadam had a pal everywhere, it seemed. 'I shall see if anything can be done.'

'You think it can tell us anythin' we don' already know? She 'ad 'er throat cut and 'er eye plucked out. There's your cause of death, guv, with respec'.'

'It might tell us something about the weapon. Or weapons. Presumably a different implement was used to cut her from that which gouged out the eye. They found no eye at the scene of crime?'

'No, guv.'

Quinn looked at a photograph of Novak. 'And there has been no sighting of Novak?'

'Nothing as yet, sir.'

'I would like some scene of crime photographs from last night's bomb outrage. And can we not get our hands on a photograph of Lennox?'

'Do you think the bomb blast is connected to Dolores, sir?' asked Macadam.

'And what's it all got to do with bloody German spies?' Inchball shook his head dubiously.

'Possibly nothing,' said Quinn. 'It doesn't matter that we were looking for spies and found . . .' Quinn gestured to the wall. 'This. Last night Lennox told me he received an anonymous missive containing a damaged playing card. The eye of the Jack had been poked through. The address was written in green ink. If we are looking for connections, we have one here. Two men receive anonymous deliveries written in green ink. Both attend the party at Visionary Productions. Two disconnected violent acts occur as the sequels to these events. It was at the party that Lord Dunwich met and left with Dolores Novak. So if there is some link between Lord Dunwich receiving the billiard ball and the murder of Dolores Novak – if it is the same person behind both acts – then it is someone who was at that party and saw them together.' Quinn thought back to his own impressions of Dunwich's behaviour that night. 'There was something about the way he looked at her. A gleam in his eye that was more than desire. Almost, you might say – someone observing them might have concluded – that Lord Dunwich had fallen in love with her.' Quinn turned to Macadam. 'Have you finished your review of the names on the list Hartmann sent over?'

'Yes, sir.'

'And?'

'Nothing. No known criminals. I am just now cross-checking them with the companies in St Swithin's Lane.'

'Very well. Get on with it.'

'What do you want me to do, guv?'

Quinn looked uncertainly at the wall, avoiding Inchball's questioning gaze. He had no clear idea how to answer his sergeant. 'Connections, Inchball, connections. That's what we must find. The question we must ask ourselves is this: what links the death of Dolores Novak and the bombing of the *Daily Clarion*?'

'Sir?'

'What is it, Macadam?'

'I think I may have found something.'

Quinn turned from the wall and bent his head to avoid cracking it on the sloping ceiling.

'The London Nitrate Company. According to the Stock Exchange Yearbook, Lennox and Lord Dunwich are both board members. Hartmann is given as the chairman. The other directors are all foreigners too, judging by their names.'

'Nitrate?'

'It's used in the manufacture of explosives, sir. Guncotton. If a war is coming, the control of nitrate supplies could prove decisive. Perhaps Hartmann is trying to frighten his board of directors in some way, so that they withdraw from the company and control passes to him, or to other men of his choosing? That is to say, fellow German nationals, or other foreign types. He could effectively cut off this country's access to nitrate and channel it all to Germany.'

'So that's his plan!' cried Inchball. 'How very Bismarckian!'

But Quinn was not convinced. 'How do these attacks further that objective? Would it not be simpler just to kill Dunwich and Lennox?'

'We do not know what other pressure he might be bringing to bear on them. *You see what I have done to the woman you loved . . . You see what I can do to your business interests . . . Now, give me what I want.*'

'But why send them the strange packages? A billiard ball and a playing card?'

Macadam thought for a moment about that. 'The billiard ball painted like an eye seems to convey the message that the recipient is being watched. *I have my eye on you . . . you cannot escape.*'

'But in the playing card, the eye was poked out – does that not convey the opposite message?'

'I confess, sir, I do not have every detail worked out.' Macadam bowed his head, crestfallen.

'But it is indubitably a connection, Macadam. And precisely the kind of connection we were looking for. Please be so good as to bring the Ford round to the front of the building. I will meet you there. The time has come for another talk with Herr Hartmann, I feel.' He felt Macadam's eyes on him, suddenly expectant. 'And arm yourself. If what you say about Hartmann is true, he may prove to be a very dangerous individual.'

FIFTY-ONE

A circle of darkness fell from Hartmann's eye. It shattered into pieces on his desk.

'You appear to have broken your monocle,' Quinn observed as he stepped into the German's office.

Hartmann gave a shrug. 'It is no matter.' The German eyed him warily. No doubt it did not escape his notice that Quinn and Macadam held their hands in such a way to suggest they were preparing themselves to draw guns. Hartmann remained calm, nonetheless. If he was surprised by the abrupt entrance of two policemen, he gave little indication. 'How may I help you, gentlemen?'

'We wish to talk to you about the London Nitrate Company.'

'I see.'

'You are the chairman of that company, are you not?'

'Is that a crime?'

'Not in itself. Lord Dunwich and Harry Lennox also have an interest in that company, do they not?'

'Yes, of course. This is publicly available information. No doubt you discovered it by looking in the Stock Exchange Yearbook, though why you would wish to do so, I cannot imagine.'

'Last night there was a bomb outrage at the offices of the *Daily Clarion*. That may be construed as an attack on something very dear to Harry Lennox. The murder of Dolores Novak could be interpreted in a similar way. Lord Dunwich was in love with her.'

'Are you sure? I cannot help thinking that is a rather polite interpretation of the facts, Inspector. You saw them at the party. His feelings for her were purely carnal, I think.'

'At any rate, she was a woman in whom Lord Dunwich took an amorous interest.'

'You will have to ask his lordship about that.'

'But you see the connection?'

'I am afraid I struggle to.'

'Both men were on the board of the London Nitrate Company. Both men received strange anonymous packages addressed in green ink – such as you use here at Visionary Productions. Both men are connected to acts of violence. Acts that may be designed to cow them into submission in a ruthless battle for control of the company.'

'I am afraid I really don't understand what you are hinting at.'

'Nitrate. It is used in the manufacture of guncotton, is it not? Incidentally, it is highly likely that that was the explosive used in the attack on the *Daily Clarion*. But more to the point, control of the world's nitrate resources could play a pivotal role in any future war between our nations.'

'You are talking about celluloid nitrate. It is used to make many products. You could say, it is a very useful material. My own interest in it stems from the production of kinematographic film stock. Were it my ambition to control the world's stock of sodium nitrate – which it is not, I hasten to add – my sole motivation would be to place myself at an advantage over my competitors in the motion picture production industry. But I was interested in what you said about the packages Lennox and Lord Dunwich received. How did you describe them? Strange and anonymous? I myself received a strange and anonymous package, also addressed in green ink, this very morning.' Hartmann held out an envelope.

'It is the same hand,' observed Quinn. 'What was it that you were sent?'

'Why, this monocle that I broke as you came in. There was already a crack in the lens, so it was useless anyhow. I cannot conceive of a reason why anyone should send it to me. What were the objects sent to the others, may I ask?'

'A billiard ball painted to look like an eye. And a playing card. The Jack of Hearts. Curiously the eye had been poked through.'

'Curious indeed, Inspector.'

'Sir, may I have a word with you?'

Quinn noticed the brimming, barely contained excitement in Macadam's voice, the telltale tension in his face. He recognized the signs. Macadam was on to something. Evidently not wanting to divulge whatever it was in front of Hartmann, he beckoned Quinn over to one side and whispered his discovery urgently into his ear.

Quinn nodded and turned back to Hartmann. 'My sergeant tells me that both billiard balls and playing cards involve nitrate in their manufacture. Is this so?'

'Celluloid nitrate, yes. Though due to the explosive qualities of the material, its use in billiard ball manufacture is limited these days. There were one or two cases of billiard balls exploding against one another when struck particularly forcibly, I believe. Interestingly, celluloid nitrate may also have been used to create the layer of tint that has been put on the glass of this monocle lens.'

Quinn exchanged glances with Macadam. 'You received this today?'

'Yes.'

'How do we know you didn't send it to yourself?'

'Why would I do that?'

'Sir, there is a chance . . .'

'Yes, I know, Macadam. If someone wanted to hurt you, Mr

Hartmann, to damage or destroy the one thing or person that is dearest to you, what would they attack?'

'What an extraordinary question! If this is some kind of joke, Inspector . . .'

'I am perfectly serious.'

'I . . . well, I have no family here in England. I live mainly for my work. For the films, you understand. My colleagues are my family. The cast and crew that I work with. I suppose someone might attack Visionary Productions, or perhaps . . .'

'What is it, Mr Hartmann.'

'Eloise. Eloise Dumont – she is my star. Without her, I would not be able to go on.'

'Where is she now?'

'She is safe. She is still at the Savoy, as far as I know. She is being looked after by two of our people.'

'We could telephone the Savoy from here, sir,' suggested Macadam. 'To reassure ourselves. Then perhaps we could arrange for a police guard.'

Hartmann found the number for the Savoy and made the call. The German clamped the ear piece tightly in his right hand and held it to his ear, as if he was jealous of the crackle that emanated from it.

Quinn thought back to what Eloise had said to him last night: *You never have anything nice to say to me.* So she had remembered their conversation at the party. Of course. How could she forget the boorish policeman who insulted her art, her profession.

Quinn could not escape the feeling that this was all in some way happening in order to teach him a lesson. This was the way it had been going all along. From the very outset, from the arrival of the invitation to the premiere, everything had been designed to leave him with a very bad feeling about himself. To reveal him to himself in his true, despicable colours. He had not even meant the mean-spirited things he had said to her. What he had wanted to say was how powerful her presence on the screen was, how magical a transformation her image had wrought on his soul. And what was it he had said? He closed his eyes at the memory of his shame and embarrassment.

I've seen some horrible things, it's true. But the most horrible thing I've ever seen was that film I was forced to sit through tonight.

At last the news was imparted that Mademoiselle Dumont was not in her room.

As soon as Hartmann replaced the earpiece, the telephone rang again, its brittle chime like a tray of cutlery being dropped repeatedly in the next room.

'Hello? . . . One moment . . .' Hartmann held the earpiece out to Quinn. 'It is for you, Inspector. Someone by the name of Sergeant Inchball.'

Inchball's voice sounded like the buzzing of a wasp dancing on a snare drum. 'We've had the pathologist's report in on Dolores Novak, guv.'

'Go on.'

'Something very rum about that wound on her throat. The blade went in at a point an inch or so to the right of the jugular. Then curved round sharply to sever the carotid artery from behind. The angle of the wound is extremely acute, is what the medical examiner says.'

'Does he offer an explanation?'

'Some kind of curved blade, a hook, or one of them foreign knives. Looks like it's a foreigner what done it, guv, as we always suspected.'

'But an Englishman may purchase a weapon of foreign manufacture, Inchball.'

'There's something wrong with the line, guv. It sounded almost like you said an Englishman would use a foreign knife.'

'Thank you, Inchball.' Quinn returned the earpiece to Hartmann. He conveyed the burden of Inchball's message to Macadam.

'It's very true what you said, sir. A pal of mine has a collection of knives from all over the world. And some very interesting specimens there are in it too. I believe there are a number with curved blades.'

'Are you suggesting we arrest your pal?'

'No, sir. Just that an Englishman may indeed own a weapon of foreign manufacture. As you said, sir.'

Quinn turned to Hartmann. 'Who are the people to whom you have entrusted Eloise?'

'Diaz, our cameraman. And a young compatriot of his, who I believe is his nephew. Inti, the young man is called. Diaz has raised him as his own son.' Hartmann's face was suddenly drained of colour.

'What is the matter, sir?'

'Diaz and Inti are Chileans.'

'What of it?'

'Most of the world's nitrate is mined in an area of northern Chile called Tarapacá. That is where we . . . where the London Nitrate Company sources its nitrate.'

'Where will we find them? Are they staying in the Savoy?'

'No, we only put the stars and the director up at the Savoy. We found a place for Diaz and his nephew in Islington. We have it on a short let for them.'

'Do you have the address?'

'I can certainly find it for you.'

Hartmann looked through a box of index cards. Quinn felt that his fate depended on what card was pulled out.

He hoped to God that his burgeoning fears were misplaced. And that the theory that had given rise to them was mistaken. In short, that Eloise was still alive, and he still had the chance to tell her how sorry he was for what he had said.

FIFTY-TWO

'**A**re you all right?' Eloise asked in English. She sensed the boy's unease. It was cold in the darkened auditorium of the Islington Porrick's Palace, and Inti seemed to be shivering. She thought she could hear his teeth chattering. 'Do you want me to get your uncle?'

He shook his head energetically. An emphatic no.

They had climbed in through a broken window at the back. Diaz had even brought a towel to lay over the window frame so that Eloise would not cut herself on any fragments of glass. 'Is okay,' Diaz had reassured her. 'Mister Porrick no mind. Max say Mister Porrick no mind.'

'Who is Max?'

'He work for Mister Porrick. Mister Porrick no mind.'

'But what are we doing here, Diaz? I don't understand.'

'I show you my film. You said you wanted to see my film.'

'But there is no electricity here. You cannot show it.'

'I do not need electricity. There is limelight. And I can turn the projector by hand.'

And so Diaz had slipped away, leaving Inti to lead her into the auditorium.

A musty, abandoned smell surrounded them. Tinged with faintly uric wafts.

In the darkness, she sensed the boy's eyes on her, all the time. She had seen the suffering in his eyes, and could not get it out of her mind. Depths of unimagined suffering. At first she thought it was sorrow for Paul Berenger. But now she knew that it went deeper than that.

'Where is Diaz?'

It was better when Diaz was there. In Diaz's eyes there was sorrow, but something else too. A kindliness. A gentleness. The glimmer of human sympathy.

Last night they had come to her rescue, Diaz and Inti, a pair of diminutive guardian angels.

'Don't worry. We will look after you,' Diaz had said, his small, stubby hand clasping her forearm. His eyes poured out their understanding. They were eyes that had seen terrible things, tragedy and horror, but which had grown more human and compassionate as a result.

At the same time she had felt his nephew's eyes on her, watchful, cold, damaged. She could not bear to think what those eyes, so young and yet so empty, had seen.

'Why does your nephew live with you?' she had asked Diaz. 'What happened to his family?'

'You do not want to know. Not tonight. There has been too much sadness tonight.'

But as soon as he said that, she knew that she would have no peace until he told her. She would take that pain on too. She had not been able to help Paul. But perhaps there was something she could do for Diaz and his nephew.

And so Diaz had told her Inti's story, and now she understood the terrible emptiness in the boy's eyes.

'I am sorry,' said Diaz, looking solicitously into her face. 'I should not have told you.'

'How can the world allow such horror?'

'The world does not know,' said Diaz. 'One day I tell the world. I make film. I was there. The soldiers not see me. I film it all. One day, the world will see my film. The world will know the truth.'

She thought of Paul. Of his sad, lonely death. Paul had always seemed to have a connection with Diaz. Perhaps he had sensed the Chilean's suffering, and experienced a feeling of kinship. 'Has Berenger seen your film?'

Diaz nodded. 'It is not finish. But some parts of it I show him. He very sad. I hope not my film make him . . .'

'When did he see it?'

'Today. I show him today.'

And she had gasped to hear that. Had the film played a part in pushing Paul over the edge? 'I wish to see it,' she had said. She had to know.

She had not wanted to spend the night in the Savoy. No, not there, not in the room next to Paul's. So Diaz had taken her back to their digs in Islington, giving up his bed for her, while he topped and tailed with his nephew.

She lay in the strange bed, staring up through the strange darkness, lost, alone, adrift. She tried to imagine the scenes that Diaz had described to her, the film she had not yet seen, projected on the ceiling. But they were scenes beyond imagining. And they chased away any more comforting images. She tried to conjure an image of her mother. Her failure only served to remind her how far from home she was. How far from home she always would be.

And what was strangest, perhaps, was that it did not occur to her to be afraid.

FIFTY-THREE

Macadam took the intersection of Pentonville Road and Islington High Street at a reckless lick. The narrow Model T banked and tipped. For a moment, Quinn was convinced that two of the car's wheels left the road. He instinctively leaned his body against the tilt, as did the be-goggled Macadam in the front. The car righted itself with a bouncing thump. For no good reason, Macadam sounded the horn, as if another driver were to blame for the car's temporary imbalance.

Quinn looked out and saw the looming bulk of the Angel Hotel sweep by, blotting out the sun in its course. A great brown edifice of substance and mass, it was impossible to conceive of anything less seraphic. And yet it floated past, as if borne away from him on invisible wings of celestial energy.

Soon they were bumping along Upper Street. The conch-like entrance to the abandoned Porrick's Palace drew his attention. He watched its concavity rotate and vanish as they left it behind.

The address that Hartmann had given him was a rundown property in Almeida Street. Macadam stood in his driving goggles as they waited for the door to be opened, watching Quinn with an inscrutable gaze.

'What is it, Macadam?'

'I am concerned, sir.'

'You needn't be. Not on my account. If that's what you mean.'

'I seem to remember that one of the knives in my pal's collection was of Chilean origin. A rather vicious-looking hooked blade it had, somewhat like a crow's beak. If memory serves me right, the weapon is called a *corvo*.'

'I see.'

'Funny how these things come back to you.'

'I don't know what I would do without you, Macadam.'

'I do hope you will be careful, sir. In all respects.'

The door was finally answered by a mildly inebriated middle-aged woman who somehow reminded Quinn of Miss Dillard. He looked into her eyes in the hope of seeing something miraculous there. But they were a murky green colour and stared him down without compassion or intelligence.

Quinn informed her who they were and why they were there. The woman answered that she had seen 'the funny little foreigners' go out.

'Was there a woman with them?' Quinn asked urgently. 'You would have noticed her. She is the most extraordinarily beautiful woman you will ever have seen.'

Yes, now that she came to think about it, there had been someone with them, quite possibly a female. Though she couldn't say for certain that it had been the most extraordinarily beautiful woman she had ever seen.

So there was hope. They had gone out less than an hour ago. Eloise was still alive less than an hour ago. She could still be alive now.

'Where do you think they've taken her, sir?'

Everything depended on his being able to answer that question.

'Look like they were goin' on a picnic, if you arsk me,' said the woman.

'A picnic? Why do you say that?'

'Well, one of them was carrying this big pie. Leastways I think it was a pie. It was a big round tin. I don't know what else you would put in it if it warn't a pie!' A burst of gin-scented laughter erupted from a mouth of high gums and sparse teeth.

*   *   *

Macadam climbed into the driver's seat after cranking the engine.
'Where to now, sir?'

'That wasn't a pie, was it, Macadam?'

'I would say it was not, sir.'

'A reel of film perhaps?'

'My thoughts exactly, sir.'

'What might you have in mind if you are carrying a reel of film?'

'It could be that they intend to show the film?' suggested Macadam.

'And to show a film, you need . . .?'

'A projector?'

'Very good, Macadam.'

'And for a projector, you might be advised to go to . . .'

'A picture palace?'

'Quite so. But if you wanted to show the film somewhere quiet,
somewhere where you might not be disturbed? Let's say you had
other ideas in mind. Ideas of a criminal bent.'

Macadam didn't answer the question, except to nod his be-goggled
head decisively.

FIFTY-FOUR

'Should I get your uncle? Should I get Diaz?' There was a
desperate edge to her voice now, the necessity of fear at last
making itself felt.

But before Inti could answer, if indeed he had any intention of
answering, a beam of swirling light shot out from the back of the
auditorium.

She was compelled to watch. There was some simple physical
law at work. If you cast a luminous image into the darkness, people
near it will look towards it. They will feel their heart enlarged by
the potential for drama and escape that it promises. Until the horror
of what you are showing dawns.

The opening shot was of a sign: La Escuela Santa Maria de
Iquique. This cut to a wider shot, which showed the same sign in
the centre of a low, strung-out building. A stream of people were
converging on the school, and filing in through the main entrance.
The sequence continued for some time. The people kept arriving,

and disappearing inside the school. The men were all hatted. Some appeared dressed in their best clothes, as if for church. Though many, the majority in fact, were covered in little more than rags, some even bare-chested. Their wives and children were with them.

Now the camera was looking down from a higher viewpoint, presumably from the roof of the school, on to a huge, massing crowd packed densely into an enclosed square. Eloise could make out the hatted heads of men in the crowd, bobbing and stirring. There was an air of expectancy. Movement was limited and everyone seemed to be facing the same way, as if they were waiting to be addressed.

The film cut to a different camera angle. Diaz was down on the ground now, among the crowd. Faces looked resolutely into the camera. No one was smiling, but they were not dejected. There was a patient dignity to their stance, which even the children shared, for, yes, there were children there too. Some, the smallest, ran heedlessly between the adults' legs. But the older ones stared with the same calm defiance into the lens. She looked to see if she could recognize Inti among the crowd, but then remembered he would have been a lot younger. Diaz had told her last night that he was ten when the film was made.

A sequence of shots emphasized the vastness of the crowd. There must have been tens of thousands of people jammed into that school yard. They were penned in like cattle.

The camera angle changed back to the original high viewpoint. There was a stir of agitation in the crowd. The boaters on the heads of some of the men bobbed more rapidly. A flow of bodies began, away from the direction they had been looking, but had nowhere to go. The movement became frantic, and frustrated. It was like watching a pan come to the boil. The camera shifted slightly on its tripod, revealing the entry of a detachment of soldiers, led by an officer on horseback.

The soldiers were armed with machine guns. A cannon was wheeled in behind them.

The soldiers drew up in formation and raised their sinister black guns towards the crowd. A small ball of death was tipped into the barrel of the cannon.

If the crowd was meant to disperse at the sight of this threat, it was difficult to see how they could. Diaz's establishing shots had made it clear that there was nowhere to go. The soldiers were blocking the exit. The land they were on was enclosed by buildings on every side.

There was, of course, no sound with the film. But it was clear when the soldiers began firing. The people began to fall.

They fell, not one by one, but in groups, tens at a time. In a few short minutes, the field of people was devastated. Bodies lay everywhere on the ground. Those that had not fallen ran, in a blind, desperate panic. Some continued to fall. Whether because they had tripped over the bodies on the ground or because the soldiers were still firing, it was impossible to say. At any rate, they did not get up. Or move.

The film ran out. The empty beam continued to cut through the darkness.

Eloise struggled to breathe. The auditorium seemed suddenly to be devoid of air.

There were footsteps. Diaz was at her side, speaking. 'At this point, I could crank the camera no more. I packed it up and ran off before the soldiers saw me. It is impossible to know how many of the miners and their families were killed, because the authorities did not acknowledge their deaths, not a single one. Some say three thousand. It is a figure I can believe. The soldiers gathered up the bodies and threw them into a mass grave under cover of darkness. Among the dead were Inti's father – my brother – and the rest of his family, his mother, two younger brothers and a sister. Inti only survived because he pretended to be dead. He too was thrown into the pit with the dead. He lay there among the corpses and waited until the soldiers had gone before he climbed out. Our government ordered its own soldiers to fire on its people to protect the interests of a few foreign nitrate companies.'

'I am so sorry.'

'You are not responsible. But your friend, Herr Hartmann . . . he must bear some responsibility. And that is why . . . Inti . . .'

There was a stirring in the darkness. The sound of something being sloughed off. A sudden merciless glint curved up from the boy's hand.

'He saw what no child should ever have to see. He saw his family gunned down. Those dearest to him. The ones he loved. How can we imagine what this felt like for a child of ten? It is a wonder his eyes were not poisoned by the sight. He lost everything that day.'

'I will speak to Oskar. He will—'

'He cannot put things right, if that is what you were going to say. There is no way to put this right, my dear lady.'

'He will help you finish your film. The world will know about this. I know Oskar. He is a good man. He would not have wanted this. He would not have allowed it, if he had known. He will help you.'

'I am not a fool. People here are not interested in my film. They are not interested in the deaths of three thousand miners seven years ago in a far-off land. The film will not make them interested. War is coming. They will need nitrate for their bombs. They do not care about the men who toil under the baking sun to dig it out of the ground. They do not care that the men were paid in tokens, not money. That they can only use those tokens to buy expensive commodities from the company shops. That the companies refuse to pay for half the nitrate they dig up because they say it is substandard, but they still use it because all they have to do is refine it a little. People do not care about any of this. They will not watch my film. They will not take notice.'

'We must find a way to *make* them take notice,' urged Eloise.

'Oh, we have found a way, my dear. Inti has found a way. It is good that you have been able to see my film. We did not get a chance to show it to Dolores. She did not understand why we must do this. Why we must make the men responsible know what he has lost.'

Something snapped in the darkness, then snapped again. Eloise realized these were the sounds of gunshot.

She felt a hand clamped over her mouth, felt herself dragged from her seat and pulled towards something hard and hot. Felt the prick of something sharp and unrelenting touch the skin of her neck.

FIFTY-FIVE

'Let her go!' Quinn held out his revolver at arm's length. He peered along the sight. It was hard in this gloom to get a clear view of the one holding her, the boy. The danger was, of course, that he might fire and hit Eloise.

But he could see the viciously crooked knife at her throat. He had to do something.

'It's over. There's nowhere for you to go. Killing her won't save you. It will only make things worse.'

'She must die.' The boy's voice cracked with emotion. There was an almost pleading tone to his words, as if he was not sure that what he said was true and needed confirmation. He looked to his uncle, imploring him with his eyes. Quinn thought he could see the trails of tears, silvered by the fall of light from the projector's beam.

'No.' Quinn's authoritative negation drew Inti's gaze. The boy was just a child. He would do whatever he was told. 'Why do you say that, Inti? Why must she die?'

Inti again looked to his uncle.

It was Diaz who answered for him. 'She must die because of the massacre of the Escuela Santa Maria de Iquique. In 1907, thousands of striking nitrate miners and their families were slaughtered by soldiers of the Chilean state. Why was this done? It was done for men like Hartmann. My nephew's family was killed for Oskar Hartmann. Now he will know what it is to lose the most precious thing in his life. I am sorry, Eloise. It must be.'

Quinn addressed his words to Inti. 'You want to kill her to punish Hartmann. Because you think she is as dear to Hartmann as your family was to you. But the truth is Hartmann does not care about her at all. She is only a commodity to him. Hartmann is not the one who loves her . . . I am. All men are. We. You and I. Her public. We are the ones who love her. Not Hartmann. You will not be punishing Hartmann if you kill her. You will be punishing innocents. Whatever you think Hartmann has done, this will not hurt him.'

Inti looked again towards his uncle. Quinn sensed the imminent commanding nod that would seal Eloise's fate and the boy's too. He spun his gun round to take aim at the uncle. He did not issue a warning. He fired. Diaz fell into the blackness that pooled at their feet.

Quinn knew immediately it was a miscalculation. Inti howled like an animal stripped raw. And thrust the knife into Eloise. The glinting blade darkened. Eloise gave a piercing scream.

The boy let her fall. Almost threw her away from him, as if he could not bear to hold on to her any more. And now there was nothing to shield him from Quinn's aim.

'No, sir,' whispered Macadam's voice gently. 'That's enough.' Quinn glanced round and was surprised to see that his sergeant's gun was pointing straight at him.

FIFTY-SIX

She was propped up in bed, her throat bandaged. The starched hospital sheets gleamed in the expansive spring light.

She seemed surprised to see him. The daisies he held out

to her were evidently completely baffling to her. She took them from him with a frown, did not pause to inhale their passing scent.

'I have come to apologize. I once said some things about your . . . about what you do. I did not mean it. I don't know why I said it.'

She waved an insouciant hand. 'I don't remember.'

He let it go. 'I trust you are well looked after?'

'Oh, it is just a scratch. The poor boy did not know how to handle that horrible knife.'

'I am not so sure. We believe he has killed before. Dolores Novak. A hooked knife was used in her murder. He has not confessed as yet. But we are confident that he will.' Quinn avoided looking at Eloise, knowing that he would have to face her disapproval. 'I understand that it was necessary for your wound to be sutured?'

'I do not know why they felt it necessary.'

'You are very brave.'

He risked a glance in her direction, in time to see her look away. The hint of a blush was on her cheeks. 'I have just lied to you, Inspector. I do remember what you said. Your words hurt me at the time, and for a long time after.'

'I am sorry.'

'I am not hurt now,' she said bluntly. 'Now, I do not care what you think.'

It was as if suddenly his internal organs had turned to stone.

She glared fiercely at him. 'You did not need to kill Diaz. You should not have killed him.'

'He . . . he was going to tell the boy to kill you.'

'You do not know that. You cannot know that. And even if he had, I do not believe Inti would have killed me.'

'The boy would do whatever his uncle told him.'

'And so, you think that you saved my life?'

'You do not?'

'Perhaps he would have told him to put the knife down. After your little speech . . .'

'It wasn't true, what I said about Hartmann, you know. He cares about you very much.'

'He looks after his investment.'

'I think it is more than that.'

Eloise nodded. 'He has asked me to marry him.'

'Congratulations.'

'Is that all you have to say?'

It seemed it was. On the subject of matrimony, at least. He remembered her spectacular rage against Waechter. 'I thought you might be interested to know, we have detained Konrad Waechter. He is not being charged in relation to the incident in Cecil Court. However, we are awaiting the arrival of a police officer from Vienna who will escort him back to his homeland to face justice there. A more serious offence than any we can charge him with is outstanding against him. Your friend – beg pardon, your fiancé – Herr Hartmann assisted us in tracking down the Russian woman, Lyudmila Lyudmova, as well as the actor who pretended to be a doctor. They confirmed that it was Waechter who put them up to it.'

'You had to spoil it.'

'I beg your pardon?'

'Your speech. I heard you say that you are the man who loves me. But then you had to spoil it. You had to say that there is nothing special about this love of yours. That it is just the same as the love of every man who sees me on the screen. That is why I do not care what you think any more.'

'I see.'

'No, Inspector. You do not see at all. You are a very stupid man.'

'I hope you will be very happy with Herr Hartmann. I trust that you will be.'

'I did not say that I've accepted his proposal.'

Quinn frowned. He was not sure what he was meant to make of this information. Was it presumptuous to believe that she hoped it would be of interest to him? Did he have a right to be interested in her marital intentions?

He breathed in the ward's antiseptic aroma, overlaid with the more unruly, organic odour of the flowers. 'I hope that you will be happy, whatever decision you make.'

'A very stupid man.'

'You're quite right.'

As he turned to leave, he heard a groan of impatience from her bed. Then an agitated rustle and a muted whipping sound, as if something soft had been hurled against a hard surface. Glancing back, he saw the flowers he had just given her scattered on the floor.

He could only assume that she did not like daisies.